SOMEONE ELSE'S SKYE

MEN OF BRAHM HILL, BOOK ONE

CHRISTINE WENRICK

SOMEONE ELSE'S SKYE is a work of fiction. Any resemblance to persons, living or dead, is purely coincidental. No part of this book may be reproduced or transmitted in any form or by any means, electronic of mechanical, including photocopying, recording, or by an information storage and retrieval system— except by a reviewer, who may quote brief passages in a review to be printed in a magazine, newspaper, or on the Worldwide Web —without permission in writing from the publisher—Red Tree House Publishing—or the publisher's representative.

PRINT - ISBN 13: 978–0-9882069–7--7

E-BOOK - ISBN 13: 978–0-9882069–6--0

For information, e-mail Red Tree House Publishing, Seattle, WA at:
christinewenrick@redtreehouse-publishing.com

Cover design by Whitney Maass, Mill Creek, WA
Contact e-mail: Whitneymaass@gmail.com

Editorial/interior design by OPA Author Services, Scottsdale, AZ
Contact e-mail: Info@OPAAuthorServices.com

Printed in Unites States of America – Oct of 2013

"I'm in charge, darlin'," Kane announced confidently, with an extra little twinkle to his eye thrown in there just to impress her.

The tiny blond then blew out a noisy breath that might possibly have been a snort. "Oh, I just bet you are," she replied, clearly challenging his authority.

Kane couldn't help the sudden lift of his brows. He was intrigued. This little snow angel was a spitfire. His smile only got wider as he took another step forward. "OK," he started slowly, "what would you like to bet? I have a suggestion or two."

"Did you really just say that?" she blinked back. "Surely that line doesn't work for you."

Kane just stared back at her as if he didn't understand the language she just spoke.

***

Was this guy for real?! The instant Skye laid eyes on the dark-headed Romeo she could see he was gorgeous and obviously well aware of how to use that fact to his advantage. I mean, the man was wearing sweatpants . . . SWEATPANTS . . . and he was sexier than, well, *everybody!*

There was no mistaking that this man was all male. As in that delicious, stop traffic, testosterone-dripping—*Hello!*—deserves a loud whistle of appreciation kind of *all male.* But she certainly couldn't let him know that, because he was also *all* ego. At least she told herself that because she really needed him to have a flaw.

"It's not a line," Kane defended. "I genuinely had a suggestion or two. And they were good ones, trust me. That is merely a statement of fact."

Skye couldn't imagine how blank her expression must have been to that response. "So you're in charge, but you would rather stand here and lay wagers with me than ask what I'm doing here?"

"Well, no, I need to do that too. But I'm a multi-tasker, so we're good." He kept talking, but Skye didn't hear a word. She was too dumbfounded. Then she found herself distracted by the very lips that were speaking to her. Wide and full, they were perfect for displaying that amused quirk he'd already displayed a couple times—the quirk that seemed to sit so effortlessly at the corner of his mouth.

Everything about this man screamed 'do-not-touch-unless-you-want-your-heart-crushed-like-a-grape!' So what woman in her right mind would be silly enough to try her luck against such a blaring caution flag? *Not her.*

"I said is there a problem?" he apparently asked for the second time.

Yes, there was a problem! She was acting like an idiot!

Also by Christine Wenrick

Book One: The Charmed
Book Two: The Charmed Souls
Book Three: The Charmed Fates

DEDICATION

For Tracy, who, one night,
over a glass of wine,
shared with me
a wonderfully romantic story
that became the roots for this book.

PROLOGUE

Three Weeks Earlier
On Brahm Hill, just east of Athabasca River, Alberta, Canada

Under a night sky cast with a supernatural blue moon, Kane shuddered in disbelief as he watched a dagger's blade being plunged deep into Lucas Rayner's chest.

This couldn't be happening!

"That's it, boy," came the evil rasp of the vampire holding the other end of the blade, twisting it, embedding it deeper into Lucas's heart while showcasing his thirsty fangs just over the major artery in the dying man's throat. "Just let it come for you."

'It' meant death, and in that moment Kane felt as if his own chest was being split in half at watching his friend, one of the strongest humans he had ever known, gasping from the pain and looking as though he were about to crumble to his knees had it not been for the vampire holding him upright by the blade. The whole scene was wrong. Since when did vampires use a dagger to kill their human prey, anyway?

"*Goddamnit!*" Kane cursed under his breath while racing across the field, hurdling over lifeless body after body along the forested ground. On this night, a bloody war was being waged, a battle between good and evil, supernatural and human. Kane knew what to expect when they had traveled up here. He knew it every time they confronted the bloodthirsty vampires that were hell-bent on sucking their way through the human population. But he never gave a moment's consideration to the possibility of one of his own team going down. It just wasn't supposed to happen.

"You son of a bitch," Kane warned in a low, animal-like growl as he lunged toward the vampire, driving him back from

Lucas's body, which had fallen heavy to the ground, unmoving. Without effort, the vampire leapt back to his feet. Kane noticed that the vampire's eyes were not the shocking electric blue common to most vampires in their battling form, but a thick coal black that told everyone how recently he had been turned. "Come on, shifter. Wanna play?"

"Any time, Reese." In fact, Kane was ready to wipe the vampire's immortal ass from his supernatural existence. It didn't matter that this vampire had only months ago been very human—and their leader. His betrayal of all of them had been as sharp as the dagger that now stopped Lucas's heart. Kane recognized that he could somehow feel the life leaving his friend's body at the very moment he reached for his revenge. But before he could exact justice for Lucas, Alec Lambert, his current leader, raced past him, roaring loudly, and stole the moment by driving a silver-tipped arrow straight into the vampire's chest. The Nightwalker, alive but frozen by the paralyzing silver lodged in his heart, hit the ground hard as a board, his petrified expression filled with a mix of shock and betrayal. Kane could see in Alec's furious gaze that he wanted to be the one to finish the vampire off but seemed to pause at the realization of what he was about to do—kill the vampire who was once his uncle.

That spilt second of hesitation was all it took for fate to snatch the decision from Alec's hands. A piercing howl rang out from the trees ahead of them just a half-second before a Lycan, a ravenous, wolf-like creature, slashed through the trees and grasped the vampire's still body in his sharp claws. The Lycan lifted him effortlessly, and retreated into the cover of the trees and darkness before either Kane or Alec had a chance to react. Both men flinched at hearing the cracking of bone happening just beyond the trees, then they exchanged the same '*holy shit*' expression. There was no time for either of them to reconcile what had just happened. Not even a moment to mourn the loss of their friend. There was only time to turn toward the chaos of the dozens still locked in battle and see their fourth team member, Phin Daniels, as a Lycan's jaws snapped into his shoulder. Phin's face twisted in agony as the much larger creature gnashed through his dark flesh and started dragging him toward the tree line.

"Phinneas!" a woman's terrified voice cried. The voice of the woman Phin loved, Maya Brunetti. The slender brunette drew her lance high and plunged it deep into the back of the retreating Lycan. Even at a distance, Kane could hear the damage as the blade tore into the creature's flesh. With a colossal roar, the Lycan twisted its upper body and reached to pull the offending lance from its back, dropping Phin from his jaws before turning on Maya in fury.

"Shit," Kane cursed, reacting quickly, accelerating into a full sprint and, without breaking stride, hooking the arm of a fallen vampire and lifting the inert body over his head. As the Lycan reached for Maya, Kane hurled the injured vampire—like an offering—at the Lycan's feet. Immediately, the Lycan became fixated like a dog with a bone, his eyes appearing to bulge and water in thirst as he snatched up his new victim and scurried off to the temporary security of the trees.

"Keep her back," Kane shouted to Alec while dropping to one knee beside Phin. Phin choked and sputtered from the poison that was currently surging through his veins. Kane held him to the ground with one hand and dug through his pockets with the other until he found a small vial. "Hold on, buddy. You're going to be just fine."

That was a lie, and they both knew it. The Lycan's bite was often fatal for a vampire. So it was certainly fatal for Dhampirs, human—vampire hybrids like Phin and Maya. Phin merely responded with a hard jerk of his chin at Maya. "Get her out of here. I don't want her to see this."

Kane glanced back over his shoulder. The nearly hysterical brunette was fighting to get free of Alec's grip so she could be at Phin's side, but Alec was managing to hold her back. He wasn't doing it to be cruel, but rather for *her* safety. They all knew that Phin had little time before the effects of the poison would take over and would cause him to lash out at anything in his path, including the woman he loved more than his own life. "Drink this!" Kane ordered, shoving the vial to his friend's lips.

Phin shook his head away. "It's too late," he said, growling with a fierceness that implored Kane to accept reason.

"Take it!"

Phin choked back the contents but continued to stare up at Kane with a silent plea. Kane understood what his friend was asking, and in that moment he hated him for it—for giving up. "Do it!" Phin snapped, grabbing a fistful of Kane's shirt. "Don't doom me to this life!"

"No!" Maya screamed, her hands reaching past Alec. "Don't you dare, Kane! Don't you dare kill him!"

Kane felt frozen in the moment, wanting to do the right thing, but he knew he couldn't kill his friend, even if by doing so it was a more merciful action. "I can't."

Phin's defeated gaze then slid to Alec and rested there. The pain of the Lycan's bite couldn't possibly compare with the agony in Phin's eyes at that moment—the look of a man tortured. Alec simply nodded once in reply. "I'll take care of her."

Kane's throat went dry, understanding what was happening as he watched Phin give Maya one last, longing look and then push to his feet and stumble toward the tree line, where the Lycans waited for him.

"Nooo!" Maya screamed in anguish as she continued to fight against Alec. "Come back. Please, Phinneas, come back!"

After a few stunned moments, Alec indicated that Kane should take Maya from him. "Get her out of here," he ordered, then darted away, back across the field to the heart of the battle, which was now slowing down as a result of the enormous losses on both sides.

Kane pulled Maya to his chest and took one last glance to where Lucas's body lay on the ground. It was finally sinking in that they had lost him—and Phin, too. Nothing would ever be the same from that moment on, and the pain of that realization was ripping at Kane as he rose to his feet with Maya firmly held within his arms. Then he saw something so strange that his mind simply could not process it. A young woman—*a beautiful woman with short golden hair and dressed like an angel in flowing white*—emerged from the nearby trees and walked calmly toward the place where Lucas lay. Caringly, she knelt before him and stroked her palm over his dirty cheek, appearing to whisper some final words to him in death. She then raised her gaze and looked straight at Kane. Her face radiated sadness, as though apologizing to Kane for his loss.

Kane decided he must have hit his head at some point and been knocked delirious, because what he was seeing didn't make any sense. This woman should be floating on a cloud, not walking from the trees to where a bunch of bloodthirsty Lycans lay in wait, ready to pick her off like a bug.

Her expression changed then, in a very strange way—as if she was surprised he was staring back at her. She blinked, and he suddenly became aware of those eyes—the greenest he had ever seen, the color of emeralds in the sun—and he could see them with amazing clarity, even at a distance. No, he thought, it wasn't about seeing, it was about *knowing*. He knew those eyes!

Every fiercely protective instinct he possessed came charging to the surface as he accepted that he needed to get this woman to safety before she got herself killed. He pulled Maya to his side and marched them both toward the woman, who had just released her hand from Lucas's and was rising to her feet. With a hoarse voice, he called out, "Hey, you there! Stop!"

But before he could get to her, she vanished.

CHAPTER ONE

"Umm . . . Do you think we should be doing this . . . here?"

A deep, male groan rumbled through the breath-heavy air around them as Kane drew his lips from the honey-haired beauty who had just managed to interrupt the paradise he'd found in her arms. Perfectly curved, perfectly lovely, and perfectly willing, this woman had all the assets required to make a man's blood boil with lust. Then again, most women could make Kane's blood boil, given the right setting. And this small, dark and absurdly archaic phone booth they were crammed into was, in his opinion, the perfect setting for stirring a man's blood.

But *damned* if he didn't just draw a blank on her name. *Was it Laurie? No. Lucy?*

Oh, screw it, he thought. That was the problem with being a full-time playboy, seducer, rake, philanderer, or whatever label might fit a man who lived and breathed almost solely for finding pleasure from women's bodies . . . forgetting their names. In this case, though, he was pretty sure there was an 'L' in there somewhere. *Linda?*

Kane's fingers dug into her wonderfully soft, fleshy thighs, drawing them snug around his hips as the thought struck him that he should just call her Lemon, because her skin smelled of the temptingly tart citrus, mixed maybe with a little lavender. Lemon, he decided, was a perfectly nice scent that reminded him either of lounging with lemonade on a hot summer's day, or—unfortunately—the smell of the cleanest kitchen.

Frowning inwardly, Kane decided he had the sudden, inexplicable need to sneeze, causing him to wonder if, on some level, he might be allergic to lemons. He hadn't considered that until now. But they had never seemed to bother him before.

"I mean, maybe . . . ," she continued, the pink blush to her cheeks and the shy quality of her voice really quite charming, " . . . we could go back to your room, where we could have some privacy and talk. Someone might catch us in here, and . . . I kind of wanted this to be more special."

Kane couldn't prevent his shoulders from visibly slumping just a bit. There was almost nothing he wouldn't do to accommodate such a lovely creature for the privilege of sinking himself deep within the lush warmth of her body. But this playboy had two rules (actually he had, like, ten, but the other eight were generally enforced more on an as-needed basis).

One: never, *ever*, have sex without a condom.

And two: never, *ever*, in a bed.

Admittedly, the second one could be inconvenient, to say the least, but sex in a bed was just *way* too personal. It gave the woman the wrong idea right off the bat, and he always tried to be clear up front about what he wanted—and it wasn't a commitment. Hell, it wasn't even a relationship. He always liked to think of it more like a vacation. Some he regarded as overnight fly-overs, while others might stretch into a long weekend getaway . . . but still minus the bed. The bed was *his* space, his domain, whether his own or a borrowed one. It was the one place where he could relax and sleep without worrying about anything other than just that—sleeping.

Was he a selfish bastard? Of course. But he was also a fitful sleeper, so he needed the least possible amount of disruption in order to even hope for a few good hours of shut-eye. And that meant separating the place where he slept from the places where he had sex.

Instead, Kane preferred his sexual adventures a little more public—of course, without being, well, *too* public. He decided it must be the '*chance*' of being caught that charged his blood so. For example, a lusty midnight tryst on one of the dining hall's serving tables, a setting in which anyone suffering from their own bout of sleeplessness could walk in on them, would be an exhilarating way to start the day. What dish could possibly be displayed as perfectly as a woman's curved body stretched over starched, white linen?

He contemplated the decadence of it all while palming Lemon's lush hips under her skirt, the heat of their mingled breathing hovering in the darkness around them as their bodies contorted into all sorts of deliciously bendy positions within the tight, wall-to-wall-carpeted booth.

God, was there anything better?

Perhaps one thing, he thought wickedly. He loved the sensual rawness of taking a woman from behind. As in the stretched-over-her-back-stroking-into-her-warm-body-to-the-rhythm-of-her-own-moans-in-front-of-floor-to-ceiling-mirrors kind of behind. Just the thought of it had his fingers kneading impatiently into Lemon's thighs, imagining what she would look like at the very moment she hit the highest point of her pleasure. *Beautiful,* he thought.

Luckily, he had a lot of floor-to-ceiling mirrors available to him to enjoy just such a rendezvous. There were several in the on-site training rooms at the century-old former hotel he called home—The Oracle.

The Oracle had been converted to a sort of dorm-styled home for Kane and the other members of the secretive group he belonged, an organization known simply as The Brethren. The Brethren owned and operated twelve such properties around the world. They were places for the hybrid offspring of humans and supernatural beings—such as vampires, shape-shifters, witches and warlocks—to live year-round, to train for combat, and to work to protect humans from the supernatural world that unknowingly surrounded them.

The North American Oracle site, with its mountainous Chalet feel, magnificent high gables, and wooden bargeboards, was nestled between a pristine glacial lake and the base of the Canadian Rockies in the south western corner of Alberta, Canada. Simply put, it was spectacular, and had truly felt like a home to Kane for well over a decade.

Kane had no illusions that The Brethren's motives as a whole were entirely pure. When you take in the hybrid offspring of those you are fighting against, innocent or not, lines tend to get blurred, to say the least. And after two centuries of war with some of the darkest denizens of the supernatural world, The Brethren had managed to amass more resources, power and wealth than any one organization should rightfully have. But Kane was happy here. He'd found a home after feeling like he didn't belong anywhere for most of his thirty-four years. He had friends he would give his life for, innocents he genuinely wanted to save . . . and he *loved* the fringe benefits, such as sneaking into a curtain-fronted phone booth with one of the scorchingly hot women he cohabitated with.

How did a man get this lucky?

As Kane stared back at the aforementioned Lemon, his lids drew lower and he licked his bottom lip, savoring the orange taste she had left there before offering her his sexiest smile. "I think this is the perfect place," he drawled before capturing her mouth once again in a playful kiss, nibbling at the corners with the practiced skill of a man who could make a woman forget her own name . . . just as he had forgotten hers. "We're comfortable," he added between kisses, "and you are simply too irresistible in this short skirt." His long fingers, already exploring under said skirt, twined around her bikini strings. "Very irresistible," he added.

Soon, Lemon was melting once again beneath his kisses, her breath hot and heavy as she pressed herself against him, having already forgotten any notion of stepping one foot from this delightful little phone booth. "No one's gonna find—"

"Kane?" The sound of a familiar male voice calling his name at that exact moment had to be some kind of karmic joke. *Had the planets all aligned just then?* His pretty Lemon screeched and squiggled out from under him as she straightened from the bench seat he'd had her firmly pressed into. She frantically adjusted her clothes, re-hooking the lacy yellow confection he had just managed to get open.

No. No. No! This was all wrong.

"What?" Kane growled as he drew the velvet drape back over his shoulder just enough to poke his head through to the other side. There stood his long-time friend, Aiden Rowan, his facial expression pulled into an easy smirk. Aiden knew damn well what Kane had been up to. It was obvious just from the fact Kane was looking up at the six-foot-six mountain of a man from his knees.

"Am I interrupting?" Aiden asked, his brows lifting curiously while his chin stretched in an effort to peek through the curtain.

Kane didn't even get a chance to answer him because Lemon suddenly burst through the curtain as though her skirt was on fire. A startled gasp escaped her the moment she ran smack into the wall in front of her that was, unfortunately, Aiden's chest. She probably would have bounced right from it if it weren't for the fact he caught her in his long arms. Their eyes met with equal disbelief. His ambered-browns seeming to collide with her golden-green orbs that had grown to the size of saucers after realizing who it was that held her in his grip.

"Lily," Aiden said with a thick swallow.

Lily . . . That was it! Thank God! Kane knew there was an 'L' in there somewhere!

"I'm sorry," Aiden continued, "I—I didn't know it was you. "

Kane noticed that his friend appeared truly and thoroughly flustered by the whole event, a behavior completely unlike him. Aiden was always very careful about what he let show on the outside, always had been. But right now he looked as transparent as a glass pane. Just what the hell did he have to be flustered about? He wasn't the one still ridiculously on his knees with a raging hard-on in his pants. "This had better be good, buddy," Kane grumbled when he finally rose to his feet, straightening his shirt over his jeans to cover the evidence of just exactly how *un*flustered he was.

"Excuse me," Lily said, quietly, dropping her head and running off like someone was chasing her . . . who, at the moment, wasn't Kane.

"Well, hell. Look at that," Kane said, staring after her. "You scared her off."

Aiden swung back on him with a fierce scowl. "Perhaps she's a bit embarrassed at getting caught in a phone booth with the hotel gigolo after being here only three weeks."

Kane's gaze narrowed on his friend carefully. *Had he missed something here?* A signal that Aiden was interested in the lovely Lemon? It wouldn't be hard, since Aiden kept his feelings regarding the fairer sex close to his chest, especially lately—which in itself was a good clue. But Aiden knew him well enough to know that if a man had staked a claim on a woman, Kane would back off—no questions asked. He would never poach on his friend's woman. There were simply too many other fish in the sea to risk ruining a good man's friendship. "That's a bit harsh," Kane declared. "If I didn't know any better, I'd say you had a thing for the fair Lem—,"—he quickly cleared his throat—"I mean, *Lily*, yourself."

When Aiden just continued to scowl at him without a reply, Kane went on. "No? Of course not. That would be ridiculous. You're far too tall for her. What's the rule? Never date someone who's less than half your height plus seven inches? . . . Or maybe that's never date someone younger than half your age plus seven years. Either way, you've got a good foot on her, buddy. It won't work. You'd need to be an even six feet, like me. Not too tall or too short."

"You're an ass hole," Aiden replied flatly as he turned and started down the hall. Then he looked back over his shoulder and said, "Come on. Alec wants to see us."

Kane hitched his hands at his hips and shook his head with a silent groan. Alec Lambert was an Elder, the highest position within The Brethren, and he was also a direct human descendant of one of the original twelve men who founded the movement more than two centuries ago. Each Elder was responsible for a Brethren site around the world, and The Oracle was Alec's baby. "Shit," he murmured under his breath. "What've I done now?"

Minutes later, Kane and Aiden followed Alec's security detail into his private suites on the top floor. For Kane, it was always a 'trip' to visit the Elder's office because it was an utterly pretentious and overblown space. Not that any of that was Alec's doing. He didn't give a damn about pleated drapes, nail head trim, or tufted leathers. This was the office he inherited from his uncle, Reese Lambert, who had it decorated a few years ago to fit *his* personal taste, which evidently resembled an old English library that someone had vomited jacquard print all over. It was in complete contrast to the dark, wood-paneled wainscoting and simple, clean, old-European feel of the rest of the floor. And considering that Alec couldn't even stand to be reminded of his deceased uncle these days, it was a wonder he could work in these offices at all.

Not surprisingly, Alec was standing at a large, gabled window that overlooked the incredible property before him—a wide, grassy plateau that rolled into a lake a couple of hundred yards out. He appeared to be considering something quite intensely—but then, Alec always appeared to be considering something. At only thirty-two, it seemed he had more responsibility than God, but he bore it well. It had come with some adjustments, though, such as trading in the comfortable jeans and tee shirts everyone had seen him in since he was a boy for Italian, wool-lined slacks, silk shirts, and even more expensive leather shoes.

Kane had no idea whether Alec liked his new clothes or not, but he wore them well, as though he was comfortable with the man underneath the clothing. And Kane figured that's what was really important.

The Elder's hands were tucked into his pockets until he removed one to rake stiffly through his short, spiky, blond hair, almost as if he were trying to excise some tension that wasn't outwardly on display. But Kane knew Alec too well. They were friends . . . though it hadn't initially started out that way. They had been Guardians first, men brought in and trained by The Brethren to watch over and protect humans that were in danger from the supernatural world. Alec himself was human, which meant he had to work ten times harder than almost everyone else around him. His accomplishments as a former Guardian, team leader, and eventual Elder were all the more impressive, considering he was at such a disadvantage speed- and strength-wise when compared with a Shifter like Kane. It took time, but he and Alec eventually forged a bond that on the best days could be as close as any friends, and on the worst could be like chest-thumping boys.

By Alec's current serious expression, today looked liked it was leaning toward a worse (or worst) day. "That's all, gentlemen. Thank you," Alec said, dismissing his guards but never moving his eyes from Kane. Deciding he needed to get comfortable because he was in for a long lecture, Kane settled into one of the tufted leather arm chairs in front of Alec's desk, a position that by now he was very familiar with. In the three weeks since the bloody battle of Brahm Hill, where they had lost two of their team to their vampire and Lycan enemies, the lectures seemed particularly insufferable. Kane had tried to allow the Elder some slack, knowing that the outcome of the battle had been particularly difficult on the leader, but it was getting harder and harder; Alec's moods were becoming increasingly sharp.

Alec's former uncle, Reese Lambert, had killed Lucas Rayner, a man who had been like a brother to Alec. They all missed Lucas, but for Alec it was more than that. He and Lucas had grown up together at The Oracle since they were boys—trained together. They shared everything. And to his credit, Lucas had never once been jealous or resentful of the leader Alec was destined to become. Instead, he embraced the idea, always standing beside Alec, protecting him from those who would try to hurt him, even from his own family in his very last breath.

Lucas's death truly seemed to stun Alec, because he never imagined ruling without his best friend beside him. The realization of that over the past three weeks had changed Alec. Kane could see it, though Alec tried hard not let it show. But the betrayal the Elder must have felt over his uncle turning to the immortal dark side and then taking the life of his best friend would leave scars. Lucas's life had been the last thing Reese had taken from Alec before Reese himself was killed by a Lycan.

Unfortunately, it was also the biggest.

"So . . . ," Alec began slowly, the large dimple in his chin stretching a bit as he observed Kane dangling his legs casually over the arm of the ridiculously expensive leather chair. "I'll get right to the point. It appears that our head kitchen mistress no longer wants to serve you in the dining hall."

Unfortunately, Alec hadn't directed that statement at Aiden, who was standing at respectful attention beside him with his hands clasped behind his back. The man was a kiss-ass, Kane decided, as he rolled his eyes—but he smiled inwardly. No one would ever hear a bad word said about Aiden from him, and vice versa (other than their common affinity for referring to

each other as some type of 'ass'—kiss-ass, smart-ass, asshole—
you name it). Aiden was, quite simply, his closest friend. "Does
she plan on bringing my meals directly to my room?" Kane
replied easily.

"No," Alec said slowly, obviously trying to keep those sharp
edges in check. "If she had her way, she wouldn't feed you at
all. Two of her top servers mysteriously can't seem to get along
anymore. In fact, they are engaging in cat fights, not only with
each other but also with the rest of the staff." Alec took a deep
breath and thinned his lips as he slowly leaned forward. "Any
guesses why?"

"Competing recipes?" Kane quipped with an innocence that
impressed even him. But beside him, Aiden—the traitorous
bastard—snorted with laughter. That certainly didn't help the
situation. Still, Kane worried when his flip response only
managed to elicit a gleam in the Elder's light brown eyes, as
though he had just watched a mouse walk into a trap full of
cheese. Kane understood he was the mouse, and he was
officially concerned.

"No, not recipes," Alec continued, now speaking more
slowly. "Mrs. Stippich proceeded to explain to me"—he
stopped and lifted a sharp finger—"in much more detail than I
cared to know, mind you, how one of these women walked in
on a certain man and the other woman in—shall we say—a
compromising position on top of Mrs. Stippich's butcher
block."

Aiden stifled another snort, and Kane very much wanted to
reach out and smack him upside the head just then. He was *not*
helping!

As Alec waited for him to respond, Kane thought back to
the particular incident. It had been well before sunrise and he
hadn't been able to sleep a wink. So he'd been wandering the
halls when he came across the slightly plain but wonderfully
curved Serena in the kitchen. A little while later, admittedly,
things hadn't ended as he planned when Candy had walked in
on them at *exactly* the wrong moment. I mean, who knew the
breakfast shift started so early, anyway?

Fortunately, he had just come so hard his brain had been in
the midst of a sexual freeze, so he had been fairly out of it when

the shouting had begun. Instead, he gathered himself and concentrated on disposing of the condom. He'd been unable to avoid the messy scene altogether, though, once the nails had come out . . . literally.

Kane remained relaxed in his chair even though he felt like squirming, because he absolutely refused to let Alec see him flinch. But he couldn't be sure that a bead of sweat wasn't about to break over his brow.

"Well, I told Mrs. Stippich," Alec continued as he walked around his large mahogany desk and leaned back against it with his arms crossed, "that I couldn't believe any of my Guardians—men trained and trusted with other people's protection—would ever do something so irresponsible."

Kane wanted to roll his eyes at that. Alec might be an Elder and have more responsibility than God, but he was young, good-looking, fit, and most definitely sexual in nature. He loved his indiscretions just as much as the next guy. In fact, rumor was that Alec had a special fondness for female Dhampirs drinking from him. Kane could go along with that, he supposed, if the woman initiated it, but it wasn't his thing —a little *too* much pain for his taste. Now, granted, this was an unsubstantiated rumor because Alec had the good fortune of an entire floor of a hotel to provide discretion. *So unfair.*

"Nonetheless," Alec continued, seeming to read his next thought, "I promised her that I would give it my fullest attention." The Elder then smiled and Kane finally fidgeted perceptibly in his chair. Alec was starting to enjoy himself way too much over this whole, tiny, misunderstanding. "Her request was that I ban you from the dining hall altogether while either of the two women in question is on duty. But since their schedules have now been separated and at least one of them is there from sun-up to sundown—that would be a bit inconvenient for you as far as eating's concerned."

"You think?" Kane grumbled as Aiden bust into full-fledged laughter behind his hands, unable to retain what little control he had maintained so far.

Alec simply clasped his hands behind his back and began to walk the room. "No worries. I would never be so cruel as to deny you basic food . . . although you may deserve it."

"That's good to—"

"But I do think it's good for you to stay *out* of the dining hall and *out* of Mrs. Stippich's sight for a while. So I have a better solution in mind. One that keeps you fed and occupied so I don't have to waste my time dealing with any more crap like this any time soon."

"I don't suppose I'm going to like this idea," Kane said dully.

Alec gave him the knowing smile of someone who just watched the mouse go for the cheese. "You're leaving for The Trek outpost—"

"The Northwest Territories?" Kane blurted before Alec could finish. "It's nearly winter up there now. It'll be like five degrees and about five hours of daylight this time of year."

"You exaggerate," Alec countered. "It's October. You've got some time before winter fully hits. And I'm afraid this can't wait. It appears we have an Unidentified roaming around up there."

Unidentified, was the term for 'unknown supernatural being'. They didn't get those very often, since they were aware of just about every type of being and where they were located these days. But a new 'being' had to be evaluated as to whether it posed a threat to humans. Not every supernatural being was a threat, but many were, and that got onto Alec's radar every time.

"Lucky and his team have spotted him as close as the south east corner of Wood Buffalo National Park."

Aiden raised a brow. "Near the Lycan Dead Zone . . . That's a quick way to become extinct. Why not just let the Lycans take care of the problem . . . because they will."

The Lycan Dead Zone was to be avoided at all costs unless you had a really good plan. When gathered in large groups, the Lycans collectively emitted a scent that warned off all other creatures. From the smallest squirrel to the largest grizzly, everything within a five-mile radius was gone, creating a dead zone powerful enough to render even a Dhampir's gifted senses practically useless. And for humans, there's no warning at all until it's far, far too late. "Lucky's telling me this thing's too fast for the Dhampirs to catch."

"What?" Aiden blurted. "That's impossible—unless this thing's faster than a vampire."

Alec leaned back against the front edge of his desk, while Kane remained quiet in his chair. "I agree," he said. "But when the Dhampirs try to get close enough to see what we're dealing with here, it apparently vanishes into thin air."

"Vanishes?" Kane questioned. "To where?"

Alec seemed to light up at Kane's interest, as if he'd been waiting for it. "That's one of the questions I need you to answer for me."

Kane snorted. "So you're saying we have a Lycan-stalking phantom causing a ruckus up north—the very same Lycans *we* are also trying to take out. And you want me to go up there and do what, exactly? Make sure he *only* takes out Lycans? For Pete's sake, Alec, you could send anyone up there to babysit this thing."

Alec inhaled slowly, looking completely at ease with the power he knew he held over Kane at that moment, but he never used that power lightly. Alec had learned the lessons of his uncle's mistakes. He never abused his power with either deception or an iron fist. "Not true. If we're going to be able to identify this thing we need to be able to find it first. That sounds like a job for my best tracker, does it not?" When Kane didn't look convinced, Alec sighed and added, "I need your jaguar's gift of smell on this."

There it was. He needed Kane's shape-shifting abilities. And considering he was one of only about a handful of Natural Shape-Shifters left in the world, of course Alec would send him. As a natural born Shifter, the jaguar was Kane's inner animal, the token form with which he was most comfortable and shifted into regularly. He could also shift into other living, breathing forms, as long as they were somewhat similar in size or could be projected larger, but it was much more painful to shift into forms his body was not readily familiar with.

"And it's a bonus," Alec continued. "I'm killing two birds with one stone. I get the information I need on our mysterious phantom while also satisfying Mrs. Stippich's request that you stay off of her butcher block."

"I wasn't the one on her—"

Alec waved his hand dismissively. "Never mind, I don't need details. I just need to hear you say you'll do this for me."

"Do I have a choice?" Alec didn't even bother with a reply, his eyes saying, *'not at all.'* "Fine, I'll do it," Kane sighed. "As long as I know that when I get back there'll be no ban from the dining hall."

"Elder's honor," Alec replied with a smile.

Aiden just continued to chuckle under his breath. "Dude . . . babysitting duty in a subarctic climate? That'll teach you to be a little more discrete."

Before Kane could hiss out a blistering reply, Alec added, "I'm glad you're so amused by this, Aiden. Because you're going with him."

CHAPTER TWO

Aiden's jaw dropped. "*Me?* What the hell did I do?" he asked over Kane's blooming smirk. "Unlike *some* around here, I keep my nightly fun under wraps."

"Nightly," Kane replied. "That's your problem, buddy. You're depriving yourself of heaven for *half the entire day.*"

In that moment it was pretty clear. Aiden was about to tell Kane exactly where to shove his advice. Fortunately, Alec's disapproving glare at Kane took care of that for him, *and then some*, before he returned his attention to Aiden. "This isn't a punishment, Aiden. You know you're one of my best men."

Aiden's lips thinned as he breathed out hard. "You mean, I *was* one of your best—"

"No. I mean *are*." Alec straightened from his desk. "Look, I know it's been a rough year, but I've spoken with Dr. Li and he agrees you're ready for this. Your treatments have been going well and you've showed no signs of problems with your testing. Or is there something you're not telling me?"

Aiden shook off the answer as if it was unimportant, but Kane and Alec knew better. To say that Aiden had endured a rough year was like saying the sinking of the Titanic was a rough night. It simply didn't cover it. "I haven't had any problems." But when Alec and Kane just continued to stare at him, he added, "Look, if you want to hear me say that I'm ready to get back out there then the answer is definitely yes—without hesitation." Aiden then cracked one of his endearing scowls—endearing because it was almost as much a smile as a scowl, and it made his face appear younger while still managing to convey his wholehearted disapproval. "But ask me if I'm excited about freezing my nuts off following *his* ass north . . . yeah, not so much. He's not exactly the easiest to follow, you know. He doesn't travel the highways."

Kane's chest puffed out with pride at that. Aiden loved to take shots at him about being a Shifter. Kane would just dismiss it, often responding that Aiden was just jealous because Kane was so special and rare, which usually elicited a simple grunt in reply.

"You'll ride together," Alec suggested. "Over the last fifty miles or so, Kane can shift and see what he picks up." He then paused for a moment as he seemed to consider something. "I would appreciate it, however, if you would keep him in line on his other stuff. The last thing I need is another public incident because he can't keep it in his pants."

Aiden blinked, and although Kane would have loved to think it was a blink of indignation on his behalf, he knew better. Aiden hated being relegated to any kind of babysitting duty. "Exactly how is he going to get himself in trouble in a subarctic climate? It's not like there's a bevy of single women prancing around up there in G-strings this time of year."

"Oh, I don't know," Alec responded, without enthusiasm. "How did he manage to get locked in a hotel pantry with the niece of the Governor of Illinois?"

Aiden's disapproving scowl looked more like an admission of defeat, as if he were silently confessing that he had no defense for that. Then he shrugged his shoulders. "At least he's consistent in his fondness for commercial kitchens."

Kane rolled his eyes. He just wanted to start this day over again. Or at least go back to the fun part in the closet with Lemon. "You know I'm sitting right here, people!" he growled as he clutched the arms of his chair and launched himself to his feet to concentrate on something very important out the window, though he hadn't the faintest clue as to what.

Alec turned to Aiden, his expression grim, and nodded once toward the door. Aiden understood perfectly that Alec was asking to speak with Kane alone, so he walked over to his friend and clapped him reassuringly over the shoulder. "I'll meet you downstairs?"

Kane nodded his silent acknowledgement but never moved his gaze from the window.

In the long silence that followed Aiden's exit, Kane wondered if Alec would ever admit what was really bothering him. He was pretty sure it had nothing to do with a woman on some butcher block. Alec had not been the same since that night at Brahm Hill when Lucas stepped in front of the blade meant for him. Kane had seen the look many times on The Elder's face since then—a*nguish.* That was the only word to describe it. On some days, Kane could still see that pain in his Elder's eyes, but Alec never spoke of it. To Kane, his leader's behavior announced to the world that he would give anything to be able to go back and take the blade himself. Lucas would never have allowed that to happen, though. As Elder, Alec's survival was paramount to The Brethren and they all understood that.

"You know," Kane began, staring across the enormous mountains to the north. "For a man who's so big on the truth, you certainly are doing a good job of lying to yourself about what this is really about."

Alec moved to stand quietly beside him, staring out the window as if fixed on the same point somewhere in the distance. "And what is this really about, Kane?" he began calmly. "Other than your obvious obsession with fucking yourself numb inside every room of The Oracle?"

Kane turned his head and fixed Alec with a neutral expression. "I see the adult part of this conversation is over."

Kane was definitely irked at this. Alec had always believed in the power of truth. He would always choose to face the ugliness of a situation rather than a partial truth. It was why everyone at The Oracle respected him so much. When his uncle had betrayed those under his charge with his lies and abuse of power, Alec had stood against him. Never once did he hide from it. He faced it, accepted it, and moved on, barely acknowledging the scars it left behind. But the loss of Lucas and Phin at Brahm Hill had been a different story. He wasn't facing it. He wasn't moving on. And where Lucas was concerned, he just seemed to be growing angrier by the day, fueled by a hatred of his uncle, who was responsible for taking him.

"I know you miss him," Kane said quietly, trying to remain focused. "Both of them . . . we all do. But there's a chance Phin's still alive. And as long as there is, we need to do something about it. You know I can infiltrate the Lycan Dead Zone and find him. Isn't that more important than surveillance on some imaginary phantom who hasn't actually done anything wrong yet?"

Kane believed that Phin had survived the Lycan's toxic bite and was out there somewhere. For Dhampirs, the Lycan's bite was usually a death sentence; it worked through the blood stream and burned so hot that they eventually blistered into ash. But there were a few vampires who had been known to survive it. Something in their DNA, in their makeup, was different from other vampires. No one knew why, but Kane thought of little else as he forced every drop of the vampire blood he had down Phin's throat in an effort to strengthen the Dhampir's vampire half. He had no way of knowing if it worked, but there was a chance. And as long as there was, he wouldn't give up.

"You and I both know," Alec began carefully, "that *if*—and that's a big if—Phin's still alive, he will be more beast than man —a Lycan. It's not worth your life just to confirm it."

"You're wrong." Kane replied flatly. "It *is* worth it. It's worth it to me. It's worth it to Maya. Or have you forgotten about her?"

Alec swung on him sharply, his brows pinched in fierce anger. "You will not mention a single word of this to her. She's been through enough. I won't have you filling her head with ideas and getting her hopes up like that."

"And you think she's not sitting in that damn room of hers, shut off from the rest of the world, thinking the exact same thing? She's lost her gift to *feel*, for Christ's sake. She needs some kind of hope. We *all* need hope."

"Not . . . One . . . Word," Alec repeated emphatically. "I promised him I would take care of her. The best way I can do that is to help her move on—"

"Is that what you've done, Alec? Moved on?"

For a long moment, Alec remained silent. Then he surprised Kane by not giving him the scathing rebuke he probably deserved for challenging his leader so disrespectfully. Instead, the Elder exhaled a deep sigh—the lengthy sigh of a man who was tired of fighting. "I need you to go to Yellowknife. I need your focus there. I can't explain it, but I don't have a good feeling about this. Call it a gut instinct."

Another long silence followed as both men continued to gaze out the window, but this was a comfortable silence—which made little sense, considering they had just been sniping at one another. But that's how it had always been between them. They debated, disagreed and bickered regularly. And now it was sort of expected. They were two men who believed they were very different from one another, when in reality they were very similar in many ways. But both men understood they had each other's back when it counted, and that was what mattered.

"And I do still value the truth," Alec finally added. "Enough to know that we *all* have to let them go."

Kane turned from the window and walked toward the exit, willing his body to display a calm he didn't really feel inside. "We'll leave within the hour."

✷✷✷

About thirty-six hours later and with only one stop for a few hours of sleep, Aiden parked the black Hummer just outside The Trek, The Northwest Territories outpost for The Oracle. Heaving a long sigh, he rolled his shoulders and sat back, taking in the view of the plain brick building in front of him. Not exactly a sweeping mountainous Chalet under picture-perfect mountains, like what he was used to at The Oracle. This was more like a large 1960s rambler with a decent front porch, closer in size to a single family home than a hotel. The positive point for Aiden was, it was unassuming and remote, so there was no reason for anyone to be looking too closely or asking any questions.

On the other hand, the property surrounding The Trek was spectacular. The rolling terrain went on for miles in all directions. Yellowknife was known as the Land of the Midnight Sun, the place where one could gaze upward at night to see some of the most spectacular views of the Northern Lights, or look out in daylight across the endless tundra punctuated with trees and bristly pine. It could be beautiful and rugged and dangerous, often in the same moment.

And it was most definitely cold.

Damn cold. Which was why, he and Kane needed to figure out what this Unidentified was up to and then get the heck out of Dodge before the snow began to stick and they found themselves in the middle of a bad episode of Ice Road Truckers.

Aiden opened his door and reached back for the duffle bag from the passenger seat before coming around to the back of the SUV. Sitting off in the distance, looking almost bored, was the sleek, powerful form of an enormous black jaguar. Aiden chuckled to himself as he watched the cat lift from its haunches and slowly stalk toward him, the gray, late-afternoon light catching the intricate rosette pattern all along its coat. He was always amazed at how easy it was to see Kane within his jaguar form. The deliberate and confident stalk of the apex predator was a form quite parallel to who Kane was as a man. He embodied a fearlessness that allowed him to shape-shift and blend into any foreign situation with the ease of someone who had existed in those surroundings for an entire lifetime.

It was all about the body language . . . and Kane had that—in spades.

If he decided to apply that confidence to a beautiful woman he wanted to bed, then she was a ball of yarn trapped between a cat's paws, a rattling toy he wanted to chase. And how he loved the chase! She was something to play with, to tease, something worthy of his full attention. But just as the cat would eventually grow tired of the ball of yarn, so Kane would the woman—every single time.

Six-and-a-half feet in length and easily three hundred pounds, the jaguar halted just steps from him, then ducked its head as a deep throated growl rumbled from its chest. The thickly muscled body began to tremble, and Aiden watched the jaguar shift from powerful predator to a powerful human— right in front of his eyes. It still amazed Aiden, no matter how many times he'd seen it. Kane always managed to make the transformation look easy, but Aiden knew it wasn't. Even in the animal form he was most comfortable in, the change could be draining and painful, sometimes both, depending on how much energy he had to expend while the shift occurred. Kane kept himself in peak physical condition to endure the demands on his body. He was well muscled but not overly bulky—perhaps better described as powerful and lean. And in cold weather like today, his jaguar coat could keep him warm. But in his naked, human form . . . he wasn't so lucky.

"Here," Aiden offered, tossing him the duffle bag. "Get something on before you freeze to death. And how the hell do you always manage to keep up with me when I'm driving the vehicle?"

"I take the direct route," Kane smiled, shuffling quickly into a loose pair of sweats and boots.

Aiden just rolled his eyes as Kane quickly scanned the cold terrain around them. "There's little snow. I'd say we're damn lucky."

Nodding in agreement, Aiden asked, "Did you pick up anything? Any scents?"

Kane snorted, pulling a thick fleece shirt over his head. "Not an easy thing to do when you don't know what exactly you're trying to identify. But no, I didn't pick up anything, other than the lingering stench of some Lycans about twenty miles back."

"They're probably trying to track down our boy. Lycans aren't stupid. They know when they're being watched."

"No doubt. And . . ."

Kane didn't get a chance to finish his sentence because the entry doors to The Trek blew open in front of them and a tall, slender, red-headed man appeared with several others following him, a wide grin splitting his freckled face. "Well, if it ain't trouble on four legs!" Lucky Molloy bellowed, obviously referencing Kane's jaguar half. "You must be in Alec's shitbox again for him to banish you all the way up here."

✹✹✹

Kane stepped forward to greet Lucky with a firm handshake. "Maybe I volunteered," he offered, flashing a mischievous smile.

"Ah, bollocks," Lucky replied. "*You*—volunteer to leave all those fine Dhampirs you fellas have stashed away down there? I don't buy it."

"Took you long enough to notice we were here," Aiden laughed quietly.

Lucky tossed out a dismissive hand. "Nah. The fellas heard you pulling up about a half mile back. They were just taking care of a small problem inside."

From the first day Kane had met Lucky Molloy, he'd referred to his team of four Dhampirs as 'the fellas' and would brag to anyone who would listen that he was one hundred percent Irish, as pure as the lush central plains of his homeland. And though about fifteen years older than Kane and very human, what he lacked in physical strength and speed he more than made up for in his knowledge of the supernatural world. He had a quick mind, and his instincts were, in his words, *'luckier than a leprechaun'*. That's why Alec trusted him to run his own team.

"Small problem?" Kane questioned.

Lucky smiled, his Irish blue eyes seeming to twinkle with a bit of mischief. "Aye, but the fellas have it handled now." The smile then faded as he scratched his messy red hair and clicked his jaw. "I'm glad you're 'ere, though. I sent word to Alec a couple of weeks ago that I thought we had a mess on our hands up 'ere."

"What's been going on?" Aiden asked.

"'Bout a month ago the fellas started finding naked human remains on the edges of Lycan territory. Manky sight, I tell ya. Spine severed . . . guts ripped out. Their yellow eyes told us they'd been Lycan before they met their maker."

A visible shiver seemed to work its way through Lucky just then. "Someone really had a problem with these bloody bastards . . . a lot of them. So far, we've found just over a dozen."

"A dozen?" Aiden echoed with surprise. "It's hard to kill one Lycan—let alone a dozen."

"That's definitely a problem," Kane noted with a grim expression. "How did you connect these killings to this Unidentified?"

"You mean our Wraith?"

Kane's brow rose curiously at that.

"That's what we call 'em around 'ere. It fits with how 'e disappears right in front of a fella. One minute you see 'im . . . and the next you're questioning whether 'e was really ever there. The whole thing makes about as much sense as a cig lighter on a Harley." Lucky then added, with a shake of his head, "Plain truth of it is, these problems started when this thing showed up. Not sure what else to think. We've found black hair with the bodies. Only one of our corpses had black hair, so we're assuming it's from our Wraith."

"Human hair?" Kane questioned.

Lucky shrugged. "I doubt it. The thing moves too damn fast for it to be human. But I tell ya, if it is human, there's a demon inside the bloody thing the way 'e tears up these bodies. It's like it's not enough for them to die, they have to suffer."

The more Kane learned, the less he liked what he was hearing. Lycans were powerful, bloodthirsty creatures who didn't care how many they killed to sate their hunger. Normally he wouldn't have a problem with someone wanting to decrease their numbers, but the sheer quantity and brutality of these killings, not to mention the ease with which they seemed to be being killed, sent a warning chill up his spine. Whoever was doing this was announcing itself as a powerful killer, and until The Brethren identified what they were dealing with, it posed a very real threat to the human world.

As much as Kane hated to admit it, Alec had been right to send him.

"I swear, I ain't never seen anything this bloody fast," Lucky continued. "It's faster than any of the fellas. It literally blows in and out so quick all you feel the force of the air as it hits you on the arse. There's no time to react. Not one of us can even give you a single physical description. 'E doesn't stop long enough, and so far we haven't able to track him. Can't pick up a scent. . That's crazy, right?"

"Nothing surprises me any more," Kane said, lifting his palm to the light snow that just started falling around them, snow that they would probably have them stuck until spring if they didn't figure out this problem quickly and get their '*arses*' back south.

"Has it only targeted Lycans?"

"Aye, so far as we can tell," Lucky said as he turned and nodded toward one of his men, who quickly disappeared inside, "but 'e's tried to capture a human."

"Tried?" Kane questioned. "If this thing's so damn fast, how did it fail?"

"That's the strangest part. We have no—"

"—Look, I'm really not going to ask you again," a distinctly feminine voice cut in from just inside the doorway of The Trek.

Kane's and Aiden's brows lifted in unison as they both swung toward The Trek's doors to see a petite blonde dressed in white being escorted toward them—e*ntirely in white.* She wore white boots with faux fur trim, white jeans that hugged her very small curves to mouthwatering perfection, and a white sweater with matching turtleneck that tucked right under her jutting little chin. She wasn't trying to pull her arm away from the man holding her. Rather, she appeared to be allowing him to lead her. That was probably a good thing, because Kane guessed she was just over a buck ten with sandbags in her pants. Harboring this thought, Kane was completely unprepared to see her smile smoothly at all the men in the group and then swing her knee up with lightning quickness to crush the large man dead center in his balls.

"Son of a bitch!" the man gasped, releasing her arm as he, a man easily twice her size, folded inward in pain.

Several male hisses of empathy sliced through the group while Kane watched a decidedly feminine smirk curl the edges of her pretty pink lips. "I warned you nicely, didn't I?" she giggled, *actually giggled,* before innocently brushing back a wispy fringe of golden blonde hair that had fallen into her eyes.

"I take it this was your *small* problem?" Kane smiled, savoring the irony

Lucky laughed, full and loud, from his belly. "Yep. She's a fine lookin' lass, for sure. But I can't decide if she's an angel or a devil."

Kane knew. This little snow angel with the flirty haircut, pink cheeks, and even pinker lips, had his mind and body already at complete attention.

But what the hell was she doing all the way up here?

She raised her hand to cover an exaggerated yawn. "I'm really tired of all these questions, boys. So if you would just be so kind as to tell me who's in charge around here, I'll point out a couple of simple facts and be on my way."

"That depends, lass," Lucky answered. "Are you goin' to kick 'em in the bollocks, too?"

Her responding expression was priceless—simultaneously innocent and wicked. The men laughed uneasily, while a slow, wide grin came over Kane's lips at the fortunate turn of events this day had brought him. *Was it Christmas morning already?* Perhaps he wouldn't mind being stuck in this winter pit of despair for a few days, after all. He stalked toward the golden beauty, the exact same stalk of his jaguar half, slow, deliberate . . . sensual. But there was no mistaking he was now a man on a mission as he stared into the prettiest eyes he'd ever seen. "I'm in charge, darlin'," he announced confidently, with an extra little twinkle to his eye thrown in there just to impress her.

The tiny blond then blew out a noisy breath that might possibly have been a snort. "Oh, I just bet you are," she replied, clearly challenging his authority.

Kane couldn't help the sudden lift of his brows. He was intrigued. This little snow angel was a spitfire. His smile only got wider as he took another step forward. "OK," he started slowly, "what would you like to bet? I have a suggestion or two."

"Did you really just say that?" she blinked back. "Surely that line doesn't work for you."

Kane just stared back at her as if he didn't understand the language she just spoke.

"Unbelievable," Aiden muttered under his breath. "Don't tell me there's a G-string under there."

CHAPTER THREE

Was this guy for real?! The instant Skye laid eyes on the dark-headed Romeo she could see he was gorgeous and obviously well aware of how to use that fact to his advantage. I mean, the man was wearing sweatpants . . . SWEATPANTS . . . and he was sexier than, well, *everybody!*

There was no mistaking that this man was all male. As in that delicious, stop traffic, testosterone-dripping—*Hello!*—deserves a loud whistle of appreciation kind of *all male*. But she certainly couldn't let him know that, because he was also *all* ego. At least she told herself that because she really needed him to have a flaw.

What had caught her off guard even more was that she immediately recognized him. She had seen him the night of the great battle between the humans, vampires and Lycans. He was there, fighting with such strength, such determination to save his friends. Even in the middle of all that chaos it had been impossible not to notice him. Certainly, he was good looking, but it was more than that. He was just one of those people who commands your attention. When he stood tall, like he did now, with his hands planted at his hips, he oozed strength, almost arrogance, really, but she had to admit it worked for him.

Ridiculous.

Yet from the first moment her eyes made contact with his on that field, the breath felt sucked from her lungs, a little bit like it did right now. The jolt of it was like a moment of recognition, a physical touch across the distance. She knew this man, but she didn't know how.

Of course, he wasn't showing any sign that she had affected him in the same way. In fact, he wasn't showing any sign that he remembered her from that night at all! Perhaps he hadn't really seen her. Maybe she only thought he had. That would probably be for the best because then she could stop diddling-on about some man she didn't even know and get focused back on her assignment. But . . . there was an awful lot to diddle about.

"It's not a line," he defended. "I genuinely had a suggestion or two. And they were good ones, trust me. That is merely a statement of fact."

Skye couldn't imagine how blank her expression must have been to that response. "So you're in charge, but you would rather stand here and lay wagers with me than asks what I'm doing here?"

"Well, no, I need to do that too. But I'm a multi-tasker, so we're good."

He kept talking, but Skye didn't hear a word. She was too dumbfounded. Then she found herself distracted by the very lips that were speaking to her. Wide and full, they were perfect for displaying that amused quirk he'd already displayed a couple times. And that hair . . . wow! Wonderfully dark, the richest color of black-brown she'd ever seen. Not a blue-black. No, it had more depth than that, a flinty carbon color and it curled carelessly in different directions at his nape. But the messiness of it seemed to only add to this 'naughty boy' mystique about him, and there was no mistaking that he was definitely naughty. Though it was Skye who felt naughty as she imagined herself for a second wrapped around him.

What the hell was wrong with her?

Everything about this man screamed 'do-not-touch-unless-you-want-your-heart-crushed-like-a-grape!' So what woman in her right mind would be silly enough to try her luck against such a blaring caution flag?

Not her.

Skye had commitments and too many people counting on her *not* to get sidetracked by a teenage-type crush. She blinked up at him as she realized he was still talking to her, but for the life of her she had no idea what he had just said because she got stuck on his eyes. They were like sunny pools of the most unusual silver color, so light they just popped from his face. Yep. Totally 'movie star yummy' . . . and he knew it. It was obvious just in how he stood there looking at her as if he knew every wicked thought in her head. There was no way she could afford to let this man know what she was thinking or how he was successfully managing to divert all her thoughts to him.

"I said—is there a problem?" he apparently asked for the second time.

Yes, there was a problem! She was acting like an idiot!

She inhaled slowly, deliberately scanning the land around her, hoping she was coming off as having nothing better to do than take note of the chilly winter air. But what she really was trying to do was regain some kind of logical thought, or even conjure up several words that might form an intelligent sentence. Her gaze returned to him just as the corner of his lips curled into an even fuller smile. It had to be obvious to everyone around them now that he was affecting her. *"Arrogant jerk,"* she thought. For him it was probably a common occurrence, watching a woman forget her next sentence.

"Are you all right?" he asked while working his thumb and forefinger over the second-day scruff on his chin.

Skye swallowed convulsively and she was pretty sure she could feel her palms were beginning to sweat (because, really, her palms had never sweated a moment in her life, so why *not* pick then to start). The moment then stretched into one giant and awkward span of time where he was suddenly watching her way too closely. His pupils dilated as he focused in on her. A quick flash—nearly so quick she had missed it—ran through his eyes, telling Skye that he just figured out he'd met her before.

Thankfully, the moment was interrupted by the sound of her sister Lake's flirtatious giggle coming through The Trek doors behind her. "Oh, Ollie," she cooed, "you're so funny, and such a good story teller. Tell us another one."

Ollie?

Skye just rolled her eyes. That was Lake—flirty, incorrigible and, at sixteen, completely infatuated with the concept of love. How could Skye ever crush her sister's hopes by telling her that love was little more than a mass of swirling emotions, certainly not as powerful as everyone fussed about, an illusion that left one feeling confused by the male sex in general? Kind of like the mass confusion she felt now. But that wasn't love, just general confusion.

"Another story?" her other sister, Autumn, sighed as she followed Lake from the building. At twenty-two, Autumn was four years younger than Skye but six years older than Lake, and —*thank God*—much more practical about men. She didn't get caught up in the romantic fantasy of it all. Lake, on the other hand . . .

"Well, Ollie can't help it if he has such a gift for story telling?" Lake replied, gently laying a hand on Ollie's forearm. She then fixed her gaze on him—batted eyelashes and all.

"No, don't touch him!" Skye unsuccessfully tried to blast a message into her sister's head. It did absolutely no good, as Ollie (or Oliver as his given name turned out to be) was already puffing out his chest in clear pride at having the young woman shower him with attention in front of the masses. This caused Skye to roll her eyes a second time. She loved her sister dearly, but they didn't have time for this!

"Are we having a party, fellas?" asked the *very* tall man standing next to Mr. Stops Traffic. *Good Lord,* if he spread his arms wide and sprouted leaves, one would think you were suppose to climb him. He was that tall.

"Not exactly," Lucky responded. "The fellas were just questioning Miss Matthews"—he cleared his throat and gestured to her—"Skye, and her sisters, Lake, and Autumn." Lucky then nodded to the tall man and added, "This is Aiden, and he's Kane."

Kane was his name. It fit. It definitely fit.

"Oliver and the others had been out tracking our Wraith when they spotted 'em going after Miss Matthews 'ere."

"What happened, Oliver," Kane asked, his tone suddenly much more quiet—and actually a bit serious. Skye had to admit, when Kane said he was in charge before, she thought that had been for show. He seemed way too relaxed to be someone in charge. But the way he was acting now, focused, to the point, his mind visibly turning, she realized he'd been telling the truth. His control faculty had literally flipped on like a switch.

"When we came over the hill we were a good distance away and saw him coming at her in the lower ravine like a tornado. You couldn't even get a glimpse of him, he was moving so fast. And even at our best Dhampir speed we knew we wouldn't make it down to her in time. That's when he came over her like a hurricane—and we thought . . ." Oliver didn't finish his sentence and seemed to try to shake off his own thoughts. "Well, I don't know what we thought, but he was just gone. And she was there, crouched against the ground. None of us are quite sure how she managed to escape."

"They checked her for injury and brought her back 'ere for questioning," Lucky added.

Skye decided she needed to do something to change the whole direction of this conversation or she and her sisters would never be getting out of here. "Boys, now tell the truth," she began, instantly drawing all of their attention. "You've been questioning me all morning, and I've answered you as best I can. I told you it really wasn't a big deal. I think that blustery thing was just lost . . . or mistook me for something else. He didn't hurt me. Actually, I felt rather sorry—"

"*Sorry?*" Kane repeated with obvious surprise, taking several steps closer toward her, 'til he was standing practically over her. That was particularly unfortunate because the incredibly distracting scent of wood—cedar, if she wasn't mistaken—and something spicy, like pepper, hit her nose as soundly as sunflowers on the breeze, and suddenly she didn't want to move. That smell, *his smell,* matched him perfectly, even if his currently sour expression was ruining the effect a bit. "Let me get this straight. You're saying you just happened to cross paths with a . . . blustery thing . . . ?"

"A supernatural being," she clarified for him, matter-of-factly.

"You know about supernatural beings?"

She nodded. "Yes. They're not exactly a secret blowing around like that, out in the open."

Kane's brows lifted in surprise at that. "All right, so you crossed paths with a supernatural being who has left at least a dozen mutilated Lycans in its path—n*ear* Lycan territory, mind you." Kane looked to Oliver, expectantly, for confirmation, which he got with a single nod of confirmation. "But you felt *sorry* for it?"

Skye blinked at the same moment one of her sisters gasped behind her (she wasn't sure which one). They had *not* known about that rather large detail. "Well, perhaps I misspoke . . . my sisters and I are—"

"Were you injured?" he questioned sharply.

Thrown off by the quick change of subject and the very real concern in his voice, Skye just shook her head at him dumbly.

"Skye," Lucky broke the uncomfortable silence that followed. "Kane and Aiden are both with—" Kane swung around toward Lucky, cutting off his next words with a sharp gaze.

Before Kane had a chance to reprimand Lucky, Skye confessed, "We are aware of The Brethren and the supernatural world."

Kane turned his attention back from Lucky to Skye and now watched her much more carefully. "Yes, I suppose you would be." Skye realized that any response she could give would likely make no sense to all the people standing around them, but it would make perfect sense to Kane if he had remembered seeing her that night on the battlefield three weeks ago.

"Kane . . . ?" Lake dangled, emphasizing with an expectant lift to her voice and a young twinkle in her eyes that she was asking him to add a surname.

"It's just . . . Kane," he replied.

Lake came forward and placed her hand gently on his arm. She smiled up at him, but after a few moments her breath caught and she blinked, replying, "One name? That's so . . ."

Skye stiffened. *Was her baby sister trying to hit on Kane?* He had to be at least fifteen years her senior—and way too experienced—too experienced for any of them, actually. "Lake!"

Determined to cool her sister's jets before she caused a world of trouble, Skye wedged herself between them. She wasn't exactly graceful about it, and there certainly wasn't a lot of room. And now the one thing she knew for sure as she pressed up against Kane . . . was that the man was fit. She cleared her throat and glanced up to see him staring down at her with that magnificent silver gaze. As she swallowed awkwardly he asked, "Problem?"

"N—no."

Kane's gaze then moved passed her to the blue-eyed, honey-haired Lake, and then over to the brown-eyed, red-headed Autumn. Skye wondered what he was thinking. She was well aware that she and her sisters didn't look a thing alike, but that didn't change the fact that they were, indeed, sisters. The real question was, why did she care what he was thinking at all?

"Well, it's been fun," Skye announced without warning as she tried to un-wedged herself and take her sister with her. "But as I said, I wanted to point out a couple of important facts and then be on our way. One, we've done our part to answer your questions. And two, if you don't let us leave, this will feel suspiciously like kidnapping. And that would just cause a whole lot of trouble for you if a woman like me should complain to the local law enforcement, don't you think?"

Next thing Skye knew, Kane had one hand firmly gripped around her upper arm and was marching her right back up the steps of The Trek. She was starting to wonder if he had actually heard her last sentence. If he had, he didn't seem to be concerned by her threat in the least. "You know," she said, with some authority to her voice, "I'm really getting tired of being manhandled around here."

Kane's murmured response was right at her ear. "Deal with it, Skye. I have a lot more questions, and you're staying right here until I get some answers." His words instantly sent a shiver through her spine. But it wasn't a shiver of fear, it was a shiver of excitement—and that pissed her off. She shouldn't be responding to him in this way. She shouldn't even be giving him a second thought.

He proceeded to pull her through The Trek's entry doors and into the main room. The space was much larger inside than it appeared from its simple exterior. The cathedral ceilings soared over one great room that encompassed an open kitchen, a good size dining area set with several smaller tables, and a soft seating area in front of a stone fireplace that appeared large enough to heat the entire building during a brutally cold winter. Everything was modern enough, but the finishes and décor were about as exciting as milk toast. *"Only men could live here,"* she thought.

Skye found herself plopped firmly on one of the chairs in front of the fireplace, while Kane dropped the dining chair he had grabbed in his other hand on his way in before her. She had to admit, the warmth from the fire felt much better than the wet chill outside.

"You say you know of The Brethren and the supernatural world?" he began. "Then what the hell were you doing wandering alone near known Lycan territory? If you'd been attacked, it would've been all over with in about two seconds."

"You don't know that! You don't even know me."

"Lady, I can sense you're human, and guessing from your size, you wouldn't even be able to lift a sword to defend yourself. You're lucky I gave you two seconds in my estimation."

"Are you really this arrogant?"

"I'm really a lot of things. Now, what were you doing near Lycan lands?"

A frown built between her brows. How exactly should she answer that?

❈❈❈

Wow. The moment Kane looked into Skye's eyes, *the greenest damned eyes he'd ever seen . . .* he knew. *Holy shit,* he knew those eyes! The most beautiful eyes. The color of emeralds in the sun

Suddenly and completely involuntarily, Kane had an insatiable need to run his tongue over his teeth. It was as though the jaguar inside him was screaming to be set free. He wanted to protect. Why in the world had this small woman, dressed like some floaty little snow angel, been wandering in the middle of nowhere with an unidentified Wraith and probably several Lycans hot on her 'arse', as Lucky would say? And what? She wanted to leave here as if nothing had happened?

Not on her life!

The idea was enough to drive a perfectly normal man insane. There was no way Kane would have that on his conscience.

"I obviously wasn't alone," she finally answered. "My sisters were nearby."

"Well, of course they were," Kane replied dryly. "And if the Lycans had shown up, the three of you could've pulled out your pom-poms and scared the furry beasts away."

Skye inhaled sharply and shot to her feet, only to have him shove her right back down into her chair—but she wasn't done yet. "Of all the insulting and . . ."—Kane was impressed at how fast her face was becoming flushed with anger, considering how she had been trying to play things off as no big deal since her first words—" . . . arrogant things to say! I'll have you know, I'm perfectly capable of handling myself against a Lycan."

Lake's effervescent giggle sounded behind them, reminding both of them that they were not alone. "That's not exactly true, sis," she said, twirling a ringlet of her hair around her finger.

"Lake! Shut up," Autumn warned.

"Hey, I'm just sayin'."

Lucky added a single approving nod, as if he were glad to finally hear someone saying something that made sense to him.

Kane forced himself to contain his smile. He was very much starting to like Lake Matthews. She was obviously the youngest of the bunch, and so she was probably the easiest one to wriggle some answers from. Unlike the stubborn woman in front of him—who refused to see any kind of reason. "Lake, is it?" Kane began with a deep edge to his voice, deciding to use to his advantage the teenage crush she so obviously seemed to have on him.

Lake blinked back at him with a wide-eyed innocence that would have most men disgusted with themselves for taking advantage of one so young, but right now he needed answers. "I'd like to think you and your sisters just accidentally crossed paths with this Wraith in the basin—because no one here would want to see any of you hurt. But my gut's telling me this was no accident. Would that be correct?"

Lake nodded her head soundlessly as Skye started to blurt out her objection, but Kane stopped her by whipping his hand over her mouth, leaving her mumbling into his palm. That's when the feisty little blonde clamped her hands over his arm and tried to yank it down, which was pretty much a waste of time. As a Shifter, Kane was much stronger than a human. Maybe not vampire strong, but it worked in a pinch.

When her first few attempts to pry his arm away were unsuccessful, Skye tried another tactic—darting her tongue out to lick over his palm. He nearly groaned out loud as his mind was suddenly flooded with images of what else he'd like her to do with that sweet tongue. Kane swung around on her. "If that's supposed to disgust me so I'll pull my hand back—it's not working."

Skye's brows lifted in surprise before stilling said tongue behind his hand.

"*Good*," he thought. That'll keep her quiet for a minute.

He then turned his attention back to Lake. "How do you and your sisters know about this Wraith? We've only become aware of him the past few weeks."

"Wraith?" Lake smiled. "That's a good name for him." Then she shrugged her shoulders negligibly. "Papa told us. He knows about all of the creatures in the supernatural world."

"Your father?" Kane was taken aback as Skye continued to mumble something incoherent into his palm. "Why would your father let you come here if he knows how dangerous it is?"

"He wanted us to help Skye with her assignment."

Lucky sighed. "That's about all we could get out of the lass, as well. That they're 'ere on some sort of assignment for their father."

"Assignment?" Aiden snorted. "This isn't high school. These are bloodthirsty demons they're dealing with here."

Kane ignored Skye's more urgent mumblings and looked up at Autumn. "What assignment are you supposed to do for him?"

"Not us . . . Skye. And that's between her and Father. Just as our assignments"—she nodded toward Lake—"will be ours."

"This is crazy!" Kane sputtered, raking his free hand through his hair as his other remained fixed over Skye's mouth. How could any father send his daughters to face a supernatural being without protection? It was unconscionable.

"Who's your father?" Aiden asked the young girl.

Lake looked as if she was about to clam up, so Kane had to think fast. "You can tell us, Lake, or we can keep you and your sisters here until you do."

Skye was now trying to yell right through Kane's palm, but it didn't do much good. Lake glanced at Skye, who was trying to shake her head, but Kane managed to keep her jaw locked in his hand. "It's all right to tell him," Lake replied to a squirming Skye, just before she answered, "Argus Matthews."

Kane stopped to consider that. He'd never heard the name before and yet somehow it was familiar. Right now he had three women who, despite what they said, had no business challenging a Lycan or this mysterious Wraith. So the first order of business was to get them home safely. Well . . . maybe two of them home safely. The other was going to help him get the answers he needed about this Wraith, because she obviously knew more about the creature than she was telling. It would also help him get things wrapped up as quickly as possible so he could get his ass back down to warmer temperatures.

His palm was getting warm over Skye's mouth, and he worried he wasn't giving her much room to breathe, so he released her. "You've no right to detain us!" she blurted the instant his hand pulled free. Her mouth had reddened noticeably around her lips.

Kane didn't respond and instead turned to Lucky. "Can you spare two of your men to escort Lake and Autumn safely home to their family? Then I want them to bring Argus Matthews here, in person, to get Skye."

"Er . . . OK," Lucky replied, casting a sideways glance to Aiden.

"We're going to meet the man who would let his own daughters face a Lycan like some sort of bait."

"We're not bait!" Skye nearly squealed. "And I'm twenty-six years old. I don't need to be picked up by my father."

"Well, obviously, you're old enough to still be taking assignments or missions or whatever the hell you want to call them. So he can just come here and explain the situation to me before I let you go."

"Are you insane?" Skye blinked back at him, suddenly not looking so calm about everything. "Keeping me here against my will is called *kidnapping*."

Kane rose to his feet, then leaned down, surrounding Skye with his threatening presence as he braced his arms on each side of her chair and lowering his head so far toward hers that he could feel her startled breath on his own lips. He could see in those amazing eyes of hers that she was going to put up a fight, and he was looking forward to every single second of it. "You're dealing with the supernatural world now, darlin'. I prefer to look at it as *guarding*."

"We don't exactly live close by," Autumn offered as perhaps an explanation of Skye's wordless stutter. "And Father may not be there when we return. He . . . travels around a lot. We all do."

"That's all right. Our team can drive you to . . . ?"

"Ontario."

Kane scrubbed his hands tiredly over his face as he mentally calculated how long it would take to get them practically to the other side of Canada. That was when he noticed that Skye's scent was held in his skin. It was a beautiful, soft scent, mixed with some type of exotic flower essence lingering underneath. He found himself wanting to place his nose right behind her ear so he could linger there and decipher each note. "Fine," he said instead, trying to shake the need from his brain. "Lucky, have your men take Lake and Autumn to . . . Ontario . . . then wait for her father to return and bring him back here to me."

Aiden cleared his throat and whispered, "Kane, this wasn't exactly what Alec had in mind. Are you sure this is—?"

"Oh, yes. Alec sent us here to learn about our mysterious Wraith. Well, it seems we've stumbled onto someone who knows more than we do, so she's going to keep us company until we know everything she does."

"I don't think so," Skye replied stubbornly.

Before Kane could respond, he found himself being yanked across the room toward the kitchen. "Have you gone mad?" Aiden scolded him in a low voice. "She's right. This is kidnapping!"

"Which is exactly why we're driving them," Kane answered simply, as if the reason why he was not returning the sisters to Ontario via public transportation somehow explained everything.

Aiden just stared at the man in complete befuddlement. "What? Alec's going to skin you alive when he finds out you're holding a human woman against her will."

Kane just calmly slid his gaze to Aiden's hand, which was currently gripping his arm tightly. Aiden often forgot that his strength was now ten times that of what it used to be and was growing stronger every day. Realizing that his grip might be painful, he opened his hand quickly.

"We don't know for sure that she's only human," Kane defended. "I was sort of rolling with it on that one."

"Look, while you were busy hauling her in here like some sort of conquering caveman, I asked the Dhampirs." Kane's brow arched at the description. "You're right. They don't sense she's hybrid. And you would be able to smell if she was just about anything else."

"True . . . And there's no doubt I would like to keep smelling her."

Aiden didn't seem to catch his comment as he glanced back across the room at Skye, who was jutting her chin defiantly and informing Lucky and the others that she would be leaving with her sisters immediately. When he returned Kane's gaze, he gave him a look that silently said 'she's going to be trouble'.

Of that, Kane had no doubt.

"This is all a game to you, isn't it?"

Kane sighed, his expression turning more serious. "I assure you, it's not."

"No bullshit, man. What's really going on? You're the ranking member here, but it's not like you've ever given a damn about that before. What is it about this woman that has you acting so rash?" Aiden then clapped his hand to his forehead and shook his head as if silently admitting that he had just asked a stupid question. "Well, I mean, aside from the obvious fact that she's beautiful and you, no doubt, want to fuck her."

"This isn't about that," Kane growled, acting offended by the mere suggestion, but even *he* was laughing at the ridiculousness of that thought. There was no doubt he wanted to fuck her, and he planned to just as soon as he got ten minutes alone with her. "Well, not totally that," Kane clarified. "Look, Skye was there."

"Skye was where?"

"Brahm Hill."

Aiden did a double take at that. "She wasn't there."

"Yes, she was. I saw her . . . and she wasn't afraid. She walked onto the middle of that battlefield like she was on some sort of sightseeing trip. Explain that to me."

Aiden was definitely looking at him like he was one can short of a six-pack, but Kane just continued to stare at him expectantly. "I can't. Unless her father—"

"Unless her father has her and her sisters believing they are somehow immune to the dangers of the supernatural world. It's completely irresponsible of him. He should have his ass thrown in front of a few Lycans to give him some proper perspective."

"So what's the plan, then? Force him to come here for Skye, pump him for what he knows, and then throw him in front of a few Lycans?"

"Exactly!"

Aiden blinked back. "Well, that's a bad plan."

Kane frowned. "You're just pissed you didn't think of it first."

"*No,* I'm not. And I'll tell you something else . . . Alec's not only going to skin you—he's going to skin you in front of Mrs. Stippich, just for the hell of it."

"*No,* he's not," Kane said, mimicking Aiden's exaggerated tone. "Because we're not telling him. At least not yet."

And there was Aiden's perfectly timed scowl.

"We need more information before we bring this back to him. He'd never admit it, but he hasn't been the same since Brahm Hill. Lucas and Phin weigh too heavily on him. I'm not going to drudge up that night until I at least know what we have."

"I suppose you're right," Aiden replied quietly. "But we could use some help here. We're going at this a little blind."

"Agreed, and I know just the person. I'll make a call tonight."

Aiden nodded as he looked back at the sisters, who were now talking animatedly. "And just exactly how do you plan to get Skye to trust you? As pissed off as she is right now she isn't going to let you anywhere near her, and you know she'll try to take off the minute we take our eyes off of her."

Kane clapped his hand over Aiden shoulder and gave him a quick wink. "I need a favor, buddy."

"Great," Aiden said with defeat. "This is going to end badly for me, isn't it?"

CHAPTER FOUR

"They can't be serious," Skye blinked in astonishment. Lake and Autumn were bustling around on Oliver's order, preparing to leave as if they didn't have a care in the world. *What the heck was wrong with them?* Weren't they the least bit concerned about their sister who was being forced to stay behind against her will?

Skye thought for sure that once Kane had a couple of hours to reflect on the ridiculousness of this situation he would change his mind. For the most part, he seemed reasonable (albeit a woman's worst nightmare from the standpoint that she couldn't take her eyes off of him), but this was insane! He was actually planning on holding her against her will. Were they back in the dark ages here, when men ran around with swords and merely grunted when they wanted something?

She decided if Kane was serious about this, then she was left with only two options.

One: she could gain the men's trust with a few smiles and some batted eyelashes until such time she could find a way to pull the rug right out from under them and escape. That would require her to continue concealing all the current emotions rolling around in her head: frustration, disbelief, and just the general need to stomp on Kane's foot. That would be difficult.

Two: she could simply be an obnoxious pain in the ass so they would practically be begging her to leave. That could actually be fun.

She found herself staring at Kane across the room with a narrowed gaze, tapping her index finger over her jaw as she contemplated both scenarios. "Ah, which should it be?" she murmured, when suddenly she covered a yawn that had caught her by surprise. She realized the problem with both plans was that they required her to outsmart Kane. Normally, that wouldn't be a problem, but today she was nearly too tired to think. Skye hadn't slept well at all the past few nights while trying to complete an assignment that was proving to be much more difficult than she had originally anticipated.

Of course, she wanted to blame Kane for this, but she had just met the man a few hours ago, so there was some logic missing from that. If she was honest with herself, it was more a fear of failing her assignment that kept her up at night. Each of the sisters' assignments was very important to the supernatural world. "*Failure is not an option*," her father would always say. "*The result must hold to what is destined.*"

There had been a time when that hadn't made much sense to Skye. If a course was destined, how could they fail? But she had come to learn that it most certainly could. No course in life was guaranteed. That's why it was good that Skye had never failed an assignment her father had given her. Argus Matthews could always count on her for that, even if she had failed him in other ways.

Then a horrid thought struck her. *What if this assignment was her first failure?* She couldn't let that happen! That thought looped in her tired brain as she watched Lake cross the room to where Kane was standing, once again with his shoulders back, his weight on his right leg, and his hands planted casually on his hips. The man really needed some self-esteem issues.

Lake smiled up at him and then sensuously slid her palm down his forearm.

Just what the hell was her sister up to now?

Kane appeared to be wondering the same thing as he followed her hand, showing just a slight pinch over his brow. But that pinch, of course, smoothed into an expression that Skye recognized as interest, and it infuriated her. Lake was playing with fire this time, and Skye was going to make sure she knew it. She marched across the room with more purpose than she could remember having felt in quite a while. As she approached, she overheard Kane promising Lake that no harm would come to Skye while she was a guest here.

A guest? Skye snorted at his choice of words to describe her terrifying captivity. Well . . . maybe not terrifying, exactly. Perhaps it was more inconvenient. But definitely bothersome!

Skye knew Kane would never hurt her. Even though on the night of Brahm Hill she had seen how fiercely he would fight for his brothers and his cause, he was clearly more a lover than a brute. That was the problem.

Lake laughed and squeezed Kane's arm lightly, her expression so bright and innocent it completely reflected her youthful age. "I know you'd never hurt her."

"You're so sure of that?" he asked curiously.

"Call it intuition," she winked.

Skye cleared her throat loudly as she came to a stiff halt directly in front of them and yanked Lake's arm off Kane's arm. That move brought a wide smile to Kane's lips and Skye swore she was two seconds away from kneeing him in the nuts—just because he deserved it (although he looked as if he might be prepared for it). "Excuse me, Mr. . . . Kane . . ."

"Yes, Miss Skye? What can I do for you?"

"You can wipe that smug smile off your face," was what she wanted to say, but she thought better of it. He was obviously making fun of her for using his first name to address him, but what else was she supposed to call him? He had no last name. The man was infuriating. "I've decided it will be acceptable for me to stay here for a day or two until my father arrives. My sister's will attest that I can be very accommodating that way."

Lake and Autumn chose to remain silent at that moment.

"But mostly it's because I can't wait to see what my father's going to do to you once he gets his hands on you."

"How generous of you," Kane smiled dryly.

She nodded once in agreement with her chin held high. "But,"—she raised her index finger for extra effect—"I have a few requests . . ."

It was to be plan number two, then—a giant pain in his ass.

Lake's giggle beside her was perfectly timed, a confirmation that he should prepare himself for the very worst. At the moment, though, he didn't appear to be overly concerned. He just crossed his arms comfortably over his broad chest and stood there with an almost bored expression. "Yes?" he replied.

"Well, aside from the basics that I expect . . . to be treated as a *guest,* did you call it? I have a few specific diet requirements that I will need to go over with your cook. Nothing too terrible, mind you. No allergies or anything; well, except maybe one—to corn."

She laughed at herself for that one because she knew corn was in half the food products on the planet. "Everything must be prepared fresh and must use only natural, organic ingredients."

Skye had to give Kane credit. He didn't even flinch. In fact, one corner of his lip curled upward as those silver eyes practically sparked at her in response to the challenge. There was no mistaking that he had heard her loud and clear, both in what she said and in what she didn't say. The game was on, and he apparently believed he was going to win. *"Arrogant. . . . man!"* she blurted in her own head, frustratingly stuck for anything worse to call him.

Kane seemed to read her thoughts as he broke into a full-blown smile. Skye's heart went tha—thump inside her chest, and for a moment she felt an uneasy itch at the tip of her nose. When she looked back up at him he was staring at her as if he knew exactly how he wanted to shut her up.

Lake giggled again, giving her sister a quick hug before kissing her on the cheek and leaving a visible trace of cherry flavored lip balm behind. "We'll see you in a few days. Now try to behave, and keep yourself out of trouble."

Skye was taken aback. Lake was talking to her as if *she* were the baby sister. Just when had Skye lost her big sister advantage? "Lake?" Skye sputtered. But after exchanging a hug with Autumn, she watched them both follow Oliver out the door. She was stunned. They had acted as though this was going to be some sort of slumber party. They seemed to have no problem with her being practically kidnapped and held against her will by a handful of men.

"Ooohh!" Skye huffed, then swung around to stomp away but was suddenly halted by a firm grip on her shoulder. It wasn't painful—just firm—but it definitely said she wasn't going anywhere at the moment.

"Not so fast, darlin," Kane drawled.

For a man who didn't have a trace of a Southern accent, he sure did seem to love their endearments. "We need to discuss what you know of our friendly neighborhood Wraith."

"No," she said simply, determined to make herself as insufferable as possible. "We need to discuss my accommodations."

Back to plan number two.

"I would like something large, private, preferably with a decent sized window for fresh air. Clean silk sheets—cotton and flannel make me itchy." She threw up her finger again as if she'd remembered something significant. "Oh, and a firm mattress. I like them really hard. I can't take it if it's too soft. I'll roll around all night long and—"

"I'll take care of that one personally. And I promise it won't be soft," Kane said, with a surprisingly straight face, causing her to choke out her next words. He had managed to stop her in mid-sentence once she realized the sexual wordplay she had just walked right into.

Now completely flustered, she glanced down and saw the pink flush that had bloomed all over her skin. There was absolutely no way she could stop it. God, how did he do that so easily? "I . . . I—I," Skye stuttered, completely at a loss for words.

Kane simply un-tucked one hand from his crossed arms and pointed a finger down the long central hallway that led to the other rooms. "Your room is the last door on the right. I believe you will find everything to your satisfaction. If not . . . as I said . . . I'll come and take care of it personally."

In other words, if there were no silk sheets, don't bother complaining unless she wanted to deal with him for the rest of the night. Ordinarily, she would have kept this little battle of wills going, but tonight sleep sounded like a much better idea, so that won out.

Skye began walking toward her room, muttering almost aloud her disappointment at not having managed to best him with her ridiculous demands, when suddenly she remembered she had no pajamas. She swung around. "I don't suppose one of you would be so kind as to let me borrow a clean tee shirt." She looked directly at every single one of the men—except Kane.

The other four men appeared dumbstruck for the moment before simultaneously looking to Kane, who effortlessly drawled, "So, you prefer clothes then when you sleep. I would've thought with your unfortunate allergy to cotton and flannel that you would prefer to sleep bare as the day you were born. In fact, I can just picture—"

"Never mind! I'll find something," she snapped, then turned back toward the bedroom.

"Miss Skye?" Kane called with an amused lift to his voice. She paused, her spine stiff and refusing to look back at him. "Sleep well."

How was it possible that he almost purred that statement?

OK, that was it! She couldn't just slip quietly back to her room. She had to get the upper hand back. There was no way this womanizing, sex-on-the-brain ape would best her. She turned slowly, controlling the need to stride back and smack that smirk from his face. "I assume you're going to have someone watch me this evening."

"You assume correctly."

Skye scanned each man and gave each one her sweetest smile, then looked at Kane—and the smile died on her lips. "I won't be able to sleep if I think someone's watching me, so they'll need to stay outside my room."

"That's not going to work for me," he shot back.

Skye blinked. "There's no debating this. I won't have a strange man staying in my room."

Kane just stood there, smiling wickedly, as if he was already ten moves ahead of her. She was quite sure she didn't want to know what he was thinking. There were probably two or three thoughts rolling around in there that most likely bordered on perverse.

He walked straight over to her then, and—with some sort of supercharged will power—she stood stock still. With each step he took toward her, the difference in their height became clear. He was just so *broad* . . . in his shoulders, that is. She straightened and lifted her chin, trying to give herself that crucial extra inch just before he leaned into her, his face only inches from hers, and whispered, "You don't want to play this game with me, darlin'; I assure you, you won't win."

Skye held her breath much longer than she should have. When he was this close he just seemed to fluster her, but she wasn't about to let him know that. "We'll see about that," she exhaled, displaying a confidence she didn't quite feel at that moment. She then proceeded to her bedroom and slammed the door behind her with a loud thwack. Once inside and feeling safely concealed, she sunk back against the door and fanned herself with her own hand.

How had she gotten herself into this mess?

When she opened her eyes, Skye was pleasantly surprised by the tidy room in front of her. It was a bit spare and a touch masculine, but clean and bright, with a roomy, queen-size bed and several extra blankets to protect against the cold, northern nights.

Of course, there weren't any silk sheets, but she hadn't expected any. Still, she was pleased to see something she hadn't requested—an attached bathroom. It was small, with only a walk-in shower, but just the thought of standing beneath a hot stream of cascading water for about twenty minutes sounded like heaven. And about twenty minutes later, a hot plume of steam followed a towel-wrapped Skye from the bathroom. She was now so warm and relaxed that she wondered if she would last two minutes before she completely conked out.

Then she noticed a man's black tee shirt laid out for her at the end of the bed. Well worn and soft, the black tee fell to just above her knees. She supposed she should be uncomfortable with the idea that someone just walked in while she was in the shower. After all, she could have been wandering around naked for all they knew. But she assumed that one of the Dhampirs had taken pity on her after Kane had embarrassed her. They would have been able to sense exactly where she was in the room.

That all changed as soon as she inhaled the scent embedded in the shirt: cedar wood and something spicy. This was *his* shirt—Kane's shirt. She knew it! It was *his* scent. *Not* that she cared, she told herself. She would sleep in it just fine, and she quickly proved it by pulling it over her head. Pushing the bed covers back, she was about to crawl inside the crisp cotton sheets (she'd actually never slept on real silk before) when she suddenly froze and turned to the wall behind her. She had been so excited by the shower that she hadn't bothered to notice the large exterior window that looked as if it opened from the inside.

A wide grin pulled at her cheeks. *"Suckers."*

Tonight she would get five or six hours of sleep—frankly, because she had to have it—and then would make her escape with the help of that very window.

Simple.

With a happy sigh, she had just managed to snuggle under the covers when a knock sounded at her door. "I knew it," she muttered, rolling onto her back and flipping her hand against the pillow. Kane was up to something. Well, she would be ready for him. Crawling back out of bed, she walked to the door and yanked it open, expecting to see Kane standing on the other side. "Don't even think—" she started but was cut off by her own screech as she bounded backwards on her heels and then onto the bed in a rather odd bounce.

Aiden was standing there, accompanied by an enormous black cat—a jaguar, if she wasn't mistaken. She had never even seen a jaguar live before, but she was pretty damn sure they weren't suppose to be that big. Or have that many teeth! "I'm sorry," he offered, but there was a slight ironic twitch to his lips that said he had expected her reaction—the reaction any sane person would have if confronted by a giant jaguar! "This is . . ."—he paused for a long moment—"Bogart." Looking as if he wasn't entirely comfortable, he rapidly continued, "He's a trained pet—of sorts."

The jaguar growled low, a sound that implied it had taken issue with something Aiden said, but Aiden just ignored it and continued on. "Kane wants him to stay with you tonight."

"What?" Skye blurted in an odd sounding croak as she watched Bogart pad a few steps closer toward the bed she was currently huddled on, then settle on his large haunches. Her mouth went dry as she scooted to the farthest corner, shaking her head. "That *thing* is not staying in here with me. It'll eat me in my sleep."

Aiden laughed, stepping forward to pet the animal between his ears. "Bogart won't hurt you. And Kane said it was either him or the jaguar guarding you. Personally, I would choose Bogart. He's slightly less flirty."

"I don't need anyone guarding me!"

"Really? So the thought hasn't crossed your mind to try and leave out that window?"

Skye glanced at the window, swallowed, and then stared back at him dumbly. "Of course not," she lied. "I . . . I . . ."

"Mind you, it's a bad idea," Aiden continued, "since it'll be below freezing tonight. Much too cold for a woman to be outside on her own in a tee shirt."

Skye wasn't exactly planning on escaping in just a tee shirt, but it was true that she didn't have any of her warm clothes she would need for such an escape at night. She needed the suitcase inside her vehicle, which she and her sisters had parked outside, near the ravine. She would have to hold her escape until tomorrow, after she retrieved her things. Besides, there was no way she was leaving tonight with a cat the size of a refrigerator purring nearby.

Damn! She had been outsmarted by Kane—again!

"I have to say, I'm a bit surprised," Aiden added. "Given your confidence this afternoon at defending yourself against a Lycan, a jaguar should be a walk in the park by comparison."

"Th—that's different," Skye said quietly. "They can't see me."

Aiden brows lifted. "What was that?"

By the upward tilt to his lips there was little doubt that he had heard her just fine and understood the significance of it. This whole situation was starting to become a nightmare. She hadn't planned on being here long enough for them to know anything about her or her family. "Never mind," she sighed, realizing she might be staying here a little longer than a few hours. "I'm going to need to get my things from my truck tomorrow. You know, so I'll have something warmer to sleep in."

"Of course. I can send a man to get them in the morning."

"No!" she blurted. "I mean . . . I need to get them. They're my things."

Aiden expression quirked. "I assure you, the men have no need of a woman's personal belongings."

She knew that, but it wasn't her personal belongings she was worried about. She had something that the Wraith wanted, and she wasn't about to let it fall into the wrong hands while she was stuck here. "Look . . . I'm asking nicely. *I* need to get my things tomorrow. You tell Kane. If he wants me to cooperate he'll accommodate this request."

Another deep-throated growl rumbled behind her, and she prayed that the obscenely large cat wasn't about to pounce on her. "You can't be serious about leaving me in here with that thing!?"

Aiden didn't answer her question. He simply said, "If Kane agrees to let you retrieve your things, there's no way you'll be going alone. So I would get used to that idea. In the meantime, get some rest . . . unless, of course, you need something?"

Skye shook her head and turned away, and soon she heard the click of the latch.

Bogart was still just sitting there, his head tilted curiously to one side, ears lifted to attention. Keeping her eyes carefully fixed on the cat, Skye slowly eased off the other side of the bed and curled into a hard wood chair at the farthest corner of the room. Feeling utterly exhausted, she rubbed her hands over her face and then glanced back at the enormous feline. Even just calmly sitting there, the jaguar seemed to crowd the entire room. She curled her stockinged feet onto the edge of the chair, stretching the tee shirt over her knees to her ankles and then wrapping her arms around her legs. She wasn't at all comfortable and doubted she would be for the rest of the night.

"Let's get something straight," she began with a pointed finger, not quite sure why she was talking to an alpha predator as if it could understand her. "You stay on that side of the room, and I'll stay on this side."

Bogart merely sniffed the air as if he caught a whiff of something that interested him, then padded closer toward her. "No," she screeched again. "Over there! Over there!"

Before she could move, she found herself practically nose-to-nose with him. She swallowed hard. "*Oh God*, please don't eat me."

✹✹✹

Kane watched Skye as she slept, knowing if she woke to see him sitting there naked as the day *he* was born she would probably think he was some kind of pervert. But Kane was very comfortable with his nudity. He had to be, as often as he found himself in situations where clothing was not in easy reach after a shift. He tried to be prepared, and his Brethren brothers helped him out as much as they could. Like the small pack Aiden had slipped into Skye's room when she had been terrified the jaguar was going to eat her.

As if? That would be cannibalism.

He kept the basics in there—a cell phone, minimal first aid supplies, some warm clothing, energy bars, and condoms. He always had condoms handy. It was rule number one, after all. And rule number two . . . the no sleeping with a woman in a bed rule? Well, he was very close to breaking that just by sitting on this bed. Granted, he was the only one on the bed, while she was crammed awkwardly into a chair, but it was very much along the same idea. It was strange, though, how he didn't seem to mind all that much. He liked watching her sleep.

Skye was mumbling something incoherent when she turned stiffly in the wood chair, her small, contorted frame teetering over the edge as if she were about to plummet off at any second. She was a restless sleeper, just like him. He smiled inwardly, deciding this odd woman with her emerald eyes, her fearless bravado, and her often jutted chin intrigued him. He couldn't help it. She wasn't quite like any other woman he had ever met.

She had finally managed to doze off after engaging in a lethal stare-down with him . . . or *Bogart*, he should say (Aiden was going to pay for that one!). The woman had been tired. Any moron could see that. Kane wondered what her story was. How long had she been roaming around up here in the middle of nowhere? Hunted? Unprotected? The thought of that made him want to claw at something.

Neither he nor Aiden missed the moment when she dropped that little bomb about the Lycans being unable to see her. He had no idea who Skye Matthews was, but being invisible to the Lycans would explain a lot, including why she had been unafraid that night at Brahm Hill in the middle of a battlefield full of them, as well as why she was so confident at being able to protect herself (which was still a ridiculous notion in his opinion), and maybe even why the Wraith was unable to take her.

What Kane needed to understand was if this ability of hers was something she was able to turn on at will or something else entirely.

He also didn't miss her desperation at wanting to go for her things tomorrow. She was a woman of many secrets, and he was man enough to admit she had his complete attention. But it was more than that. About five seconds after meeting her today he felt the need to pull her close and kiss those deliciously pouty lips until her knees gave out from under her and she was too dazed to do anything except give in to it. The excitement of that thought pumped through his veins even now. His body, whether in human or animal form, was at complete attention whenever Skye Matthews was near him. It was the damndest thing.

He inhaled slowly, trying to clear the thoughts that were only serving to stir his body further. He had to focus. One of this woman's secrets was among those items she was hell bent on retrieving tomorrow, he was sure of it. He rose to his feet above her and smiled. He had a plan to outwit the lovely Skye Matthews. And if she fought him even half as much as she had today, then he was definitely going to enjoy tomorrow.

CHAPTER FIVE

"I don't understand," Skye said as Kane drove them eastward, toward the newly-risen sun and in the direction of Mastiff Ridge, the wooded bluff where she and her sisters had left their truck, "why are *you* driving me out here?"

Kane had one hand loosely on the steering wheel and the other on his thigh. He was pretending to feign interest in the road ahead while trying to resist the shit-eating grin that wanted to erupt from deep inside him. He had been waiting for her to express what had so obviously been rolling around in that pretty head of hers since the moment he announced they would be driving to retrieve her bags this morning. While he gave her credit for making it about ten miles before pressing the issue, and even though he acknowledged that it was wrong for him to be having so much fun at her expense, he just couldn't help himself. She simply brought out the beast in him . . . literally, as well as figuratively.

"I mean, I appreciate you being reasonable about getting my things," she paused, then continued, " . . . but why waste your time? Don't you have people to order around or something?"

Kane laughed aloud at that, even though it wasn't exactly what had piqued his humor. He normally ordered very few people around. He saw his role within The Brethren as more of an independent contractor. Not that he wasn't devoted, or that he wouldn't give a hundred-and-ten percent to something he committed to. He was confident in his ability to handle almost any given situation. He just wasn't into the importance of rank. Kane preferred the unstructured chaos of waking every morning responsible for only himself, versus someone like Alec, who was responsible for hundreds, if not tens of thousands once you considered all of The Brethren locations around the world that he and the other eleven Elders commanded. Kane preferred not knowing what the day would bring. In part, it explained why he found such amusement in his regular trips to Alec's office.

He threw a casual glance over his shoulder to Skye. *Damn,* but those green eyes of hers were beautiful, even when shimmering at him with disapproval. Just making contact with them reignited a need in his gut to kiss her, and kiss her hard. Yes, he decided that was what she needed—a long, hot kiss, something that would leave her breathless and dizzy. "Perhaps you've captured my attention," he offered lightly, while wicked thoughts still floated in his head.

She rolled her eyes. "Yeah, like that's hard to do. I have breasts," she announced, straightening slightly in her seat and drawing his attention with her hands circling over the two small mounds. He had already noted that her breasts were on the smaller side, but he estimated there was just enough there to fill his palms. He could definitely work with that. "Two, in fact," she continued. "I believe that qualifies?"

His grin got wider. *Oh, he could do this all day with her.* "Yes, those do work for me quite nicely," he confirmed, his tone effortless, as if he didn't have a care in the world. She was about to throw him a gasp of indignation when he added, "So, did you sleep well last night? Everything was to your satisfaction, I hope." Kane already knew the answer, since he had watched her toss and turn most of the night, doubting that she got more than a couple good hours of restful sleep. He was just curious what she would admit to.

"It was fine," she said crisply, lifting her nose before redirecting her stare out the window. He could see that she was trying to figure how she had awoken tucked comfortably under her covers rather than stiffly in the hard wood chair. It had been a beautiful sight to carry her sleeping form to the bed dressed in his shirt, a pair of lacy, pink boyshorts (though she was obviously freezing in them), and oversized white athletic socks to keep her feet warm. Once he had tucked her in, she had slept better, her breathing coming more evenly and greatly relaxed as she sank into her pillow. She was like a little angel, and if tucking her in helped her to sleep better then he would happily do it for the next few nights, at least while she stayed here with him.

"*With him?*" That was a curious thought.

"I'm sure you thought your little surprise with the jaguar would have me in hysterics, but you were wrong. Bogart turned out to be well behaved and much less troublesome than some *people* I know."

Ha! That was a good one. When she first woke that morning she had carefully inched her way to the small bathroom, slamming the door when she believed she had reached a minimal safe distance. Actually, that had annoyed him because he would have preferred to be watching her from *inside* the room as she took her shower.

"You find me troublesome?" Kane asked curiously. "Now we're getting somewhere interesting."

"Whatever," she sighed, pointing off in the distance. "Take a right up there. It's about a half mile up the road."

As he drove along the bumpy dirt road that would take him to the campsite where the truck was parked, Kane surveyed the terrain around him. It was beautiful here. There was no doubt about that. The air was crisp and clean, and there was an abundance of pine and birch trees mixed with smaller brush that blanketed the land in green. Yet, this last one-mile stretch seemed isolated, devoid of any scents or sound. It was eerie and, unfortunately, all too familiar to him. "You were camping here?" he questioned. "This is practically on Lycan territory."

"Don't be ridiculous," she said, smoothing her jeans at her knees. "Do I look like a camper to you?" Kane did a double-take at that, amazed at how she had completely missed his point. But when he caught her knowing blink as she slid her eyes away, he knew she hadn't missed a thing. "We stayed at a hotel in town and then drove out here."

"Then we should be getting your things from the hotel?"

She turned her gaze to him, nervously licking her pink lips, and he swore if she didn't stop doing shit like that he was going to have to pull the car over and kiss her right there. "We had checked out of the hotel. My things are in the truck."

"Then you'd planned to leave town that day the Wraith attacked you?"

"I s'pose."

"Ah, so forthcoming with information. I don't *s'pose* you'll tell me where?"

She stared back at him dully. He hadn't exactly thought it was a dumb question, but she was looking at him as if it had been. "Why are you so secretive, Skye? It seems a simple enough question."

"Maybe I'm not being secretive. Maybe it's just not any of your business."

He didn't even consider that for a second. "Sorry, darlin'. Anyone connected to this Wraith is my business."

"Says who?"

"Says me," he answered then tapped on the communications link at his ear. "Aiden, Lucky, take a right on Farsgrove, we'll be a half mile up—"

"They're following us?" Skye squawked. "How many of you does it take to grab some suitcases from a truck?"

Kane scowled at her. "You do remember it was just two days ago that you were wandering around—?"

"I wasn't wandering. And I told you, I'm more than capable of handling myself."

"Yes, Aiden mentioned something about that this morning," he began as he pulled the vehicle to a stop beside the full-sized red Chevy truck with an extended cab. He had to laugh. The thing was completely oversized for her. He bet she had the seat scooted all the way forward so she could reach the pedals. "He said the Lycans can't see you?"

She swallowed hard, obviously realizing that she hadn't gotten away with that little slip. Her lips thinned for just a moment, then puckered into a perfect pink bow, as if she were contemplating something very important. In response, the muscles in his stomach tightened and his hands gripped the wheel until his knuckles were white. Man, he wanted her. The woman simply had no idea how much restraint it took on his part to keep himself on his side of the vehicle.

"Aiden. Lucky," he nearly growled into his comm. "Flank out wide to each side of us and stay out of sight. Hold there for two minutes. Then pull in slow. I want to make sure we have no surprise guests following us in. It's a dead end up here."

"Aye, you got it," Lucky answered, followed by Aiden's confirmation.

Skye watched him with a rather flummoxed expression and then reached for the door handle beside her. "Don't!" Kane ordered sharply. "Just stay right there." He was out the door and over to her side of the vehicle within seconds. She was, of course, stubbornly disregarding what he had said, pushing the heavy passenger door open wide and swinging her legs over the edge of the seat when he leapt in front of her, blocking her escape with his body. Skye stared up at him with bewilderment, but before she could utter a single syllable, he curled his hands under her knees and hoisted her legs around his hips until she found herself wrapped around him.

"What're you—?"

That was all she got out before Kane's mouth came crashing down on hers.

❋❋❋

Skye froze, literally stunned for a moment beneath the most tempting and obviously experienced lips she had ever known, and then hating her traitorous body for responding to them. Actually, not just responding, but melting into the pleasure, into him.

Of course the man could kiss. In truth, he should be writing a 'how to' book on getting a woman from point A to silly in seconds. His lips were soft but confident, insistent, making no attempt whatsoever to hold back or hide how much he wanted her. *Just* how was a woman supposed to fight something like that? His fingers dug into her thighs and he groaned into her mouth as he wrapped her legs so tight around him that she felt overwhelmed by him—by that wonderful scent of cedar and pepper. He licked at the seam of her lips almost playfully before easing his tongue inside her mouth and wrapped it with hers until she swore she was dizzy. The taste of him seemed to explode over her senses, filling her with excitement and warmth to the point her only thought was yanking him into the SUV with her and closing off the rest of the world. Her head was screaming— *"What the hell are you doing?"*—but her body couldn't pull away from him at that moment if her life depended on it.

Her last coherent thought was, *two minutes.* He had ordered his men to hold for two minutes. This was why. *He had planned this!*

Then she could barely remember her own name as his breathing deepened and he put a sensual assault on her lips that had her reduced to a puddle of goo beneath him. Skye grabbed hold of his shoulders to keep herself steady so she didn't fall back against the console, but really it was just a convenient excuse to hold his body against hers. And he knew exactly why she was doing it, smiling against her lips as the last of her resistance (if she ever really had any) became non-existent.

Just when she became aware that her arms and legs were curled around him like a pretzel, he pulled away, dragging his lips downward over her chin and throat, leaving her gasping in the air above him. He nearly growled into the curve of her neck, "We'll finish this later." Next thing she knew, she had been released from his tight embrace so quickly she nearly did hit the console. He saved her at the last second, pulling her out of the vehicle and trying to steady her onto her very unsteady feet. "Are you good?" he whispered thickly into her ear, his strong arms bracing her.

She nodded at his shoulder, unable to tell which direction the sky was at that particular moment. After a last-second tug on her earlobe with his teeth, he pulled back with a wide grin and stepped away, just as the other two SUV's pulled up, flanking them simultaneously on each side per Kane's instructions.

When Skye finally was able to catch up to the moment, absolutely disgusted with herself that she had offered zero protest of his stolen kiss, she threw him a hard scowl that he merely brushed off with a playful wink, then ran a thumb over his bottom lip. It took her a moment to realize he was giving her a signal to straighten herself up. Because she probably looked like she had just been tossed in the front seat of a frickin' SUV!

With little grace, she whirled around, combing through her hair with her fingers and wiping the smeared gloss from around her lips before facing everyone as if absolutely nothing had happened only moments before, even though her insides were still fluttering like the wings of a hummingbird. Kane, in the meantime, went to greet the men exiting the other vehicles. There was an extra lift to his step that just made her want to go over there and kick him in the shin!

"Everything all right?" Aiden asked.

"Just fine," Kane replied with a slight rasp to his voice.

"We picked something up a little ways back," Aiden continued, casting a quick glance at her over Kane's shoulder, then back to Kane. It was a very discreet signal between the two men that showed how long they had been working together. "I think we should check it out."

Kane gave a single nod in reply, obviously getting whatever message was being conveyed.

Being left out of the loop didn't really work for Skye. She cleared her throat. "I'd like to go—"

"Not on your life, Skye," Kane cut in. "You're staying right here with me where I can keep an eye on you."

Skye's stomach did a little flip. The way he had said that sounded almost possessive, and she couldn't decide if she was irritated or turned on by it.

She went with irritated. "Well, if this affects me, then I have a right—"

Kane was already shaking his head at her. "Nope. As detainer to your *detainee*, I just revoked it."

"You mean *kidnapper* to my *hostage*," she snapped.

"Whatever," he smiled, obviously deciding that for the moment their little disagreement had concluded.

He was so wrong.

❋❋❋

Kane, Lucky, and Aiden were huddled in conversation when suddenly a loud 'thwack' broke their attention. They all turned in unison to see Skye clapping off her hands after just throwing one of her bags roughly into the back of the SUV. Hell! That might have just left a dent in the sidewall of his vehicle.

She was shaking her head and muttering something to herself as she marched back to the truck, and Kane acknowledged it might have something to do with his heavy-handed approach to her just then, but he wanted to believe it had more to do with that kiss. He had to believe it, because *that kiss* had his own blood still boiling in his veins. *Damn*, he'd wanted more. She was just lucky that the others had interrupted them, because if they hadn't, he would have kept going until she was breathless and begging him not to stop.

He couldn't help cracking a sly smile. Kane was pretty damn sure being practically tumbled by a kiss wasn't something she had let happen very often. There had been an initial timidity in her kisses that told him she had been selective about who could or could not touch her. Yet, as she warmed and heated beneath him, he could feel her come alive in his arms—and he loved that!

Shaking his head, he wonder why he was acting like a man starved. It wasn't like he hadn't just sated his lust with a woman before he had left The Oracle, but you sure wouldn't know it now by how his hands were itching to touch her again. He hadn't even considered asking Skye for that kiss, he took— pouncing on her like the apex predator that he was. He realized now that was something he wanted: he wanted her to *ask* for his kiss. There was no doubt she had responded to him, but he wanted her to ask him for the next one, which, in his mind, assured that there *would* be a next one.

"Aye, you need some help there, lass?" Lucky asked, showing a bit of concern.

She raised her head and tossed them a plastered-on smile just before she slammed the next bag into the SUV. "I've got it."

Kane was still watching her with an amused smile when Aiden suddenly socked him in the shoulder. "What the hell did you do?"

"*Me?* I didn't do anything." Kane wasn't even sure how he said that with a straight face.

Aiden scowled at the obvious lie as the two men parted ways. It was so like Aiden to jump to conclusions where he was concerned. Of course, most of the time he was right. Kane's history with women was no secret at The Brethren. He never had much of a relationship with any one woman beyond a few clandestine meetings in a room of his choice. Women weren't with him because they wanted a boyfriend. They knew better. They were with him because they wanted what he could offer them—great sex. And he loved giving it to them. As he saw it, they both got something out of the deal. Maybe he was arrogant. No, he definitely was. But he knew what he wanted. Usually it only took seconds upon meeting a woman for him to form a plan on how to seduce her. Skye had been no exception to that. The first time he saw her straighten her spine, jut out that little chin and stare him down as if she could shrink his balls with a mere thought, he wanted her.

Badly.

What had been different was how powerful his reaction had been to her in every moment since. How aware he was of her every movement—of her every breath. He was constantly reaching for her scent, his body responding to it as if it was out of his control. She didn't stir just him, she stirred the predator inside him. *That* had never happened before.

Kane walked back toward the truck and watched her for a moment as she lifted a hard-sided suitcase from the back. *Good Lord,* this one was big enough, and hard enough, to cause serious damage. In two steps he was there, pulling it from her small hands. She blinked at him in surprise just before the crease returned between her brows. "I can get it," she said, reaching back for it. Kane smoothly ignored her, swinging on his heels to take the case to the SUV. Even with his back turned to her he could hear her thinking. She really didn't like him carrying this suitcase. He was willing to bet whatever had driven her to come out here today and get these bags had little to do with just wanting more clothes and a lot to do with this suitcase.

She watched him as he loaded it into the back with extra gentle care, demonstrating how not to take it out on his poor vehicle. But her emerald stare never moved from that bag. "You need something?" he asked, feeling only a twinge of guilt for toying with her like this when she so obviously seemed distressed over that case.

"No," she murmured with a shake of her head.

"Kane?" Aiden called just then into his comm. link.

"Yeah, go ahead."

"We've got another body about a quarter mile south east of you."

"How the hell did you get there so fast?"

"Look, I got here, all right," he said in a tone that let Kane know he didn't want to discuss the subject further. "But you need to get your ass here to see this."

Kane turned back to Skye. She didn't show any signs that she had heard Aiden through the comm. link as she turned back to the truck to go for another bag. *Just how many bags did the woman have?* He was grateful for that, though, as he didn't want to frighten her unnecessarily. "I'll be right there. Lucky, can you send a couple of your men back to me?"

"The fellas are already on their way."

A few minutes later Kane was standing under a grouping of pine trees, viewing the barely recognizable remains of some unlucky bastard who had obviously been in the fight of their life. "Bloody hell," Lucky cursed under his breath. "Will you look at that."

The body was bloated and stunk with an acrid smell that was god-awful, especially for someone like Kane, who was so sensitive to smell. The victim's spine had been severed like the others, only not by a sword. It looked as though he had been literally ripped in half by bare hands. His internal organs were splayed all over the cold ground in front of him, every piece of viscera covered with maggots.

"Yellow corneas," Aiden noted. "He was Lycan."

"This Wraith didn't kill for self-defense. This was rage," Kane said.

"Yeah, and it would have to be awfully powerful to do this to a Lycan," Aiden added uneasily. "What are we dealing with here, Sasquatch on steroids?"

"I don't know," Kane murmured, thinking it odd that animals had not already scavenged the body, but then again, there were no animals around. He would be able to smell them. "It looks like he's been here a couple of days. That puts his death around the time Skye was attacked here. I don't like it. She's right in the middle of this thing."

"Actually, this might be good news," Aiden offered. "Skye may have been attacked because she accidently interrupted a fight between the Wraith and this Lycan? That would suggest the Wraith wasn't targeting her specifically."

Kane worked his thumb and forefinger over his chin. "Accidently, my ass. I've got a bad feeling that she and her sisters were here looking for either our Wraith or a Lycan."

Lucky snorted at that. "No defenseless lass in her right mind would be lookin' for either?"

Kane nodded and turned to him. "Well then, we've just established that she may be crazy. Either way, she's way too curious about what we've found and I don't want her to see this. Can you stay behind and burn the body?"

"Aye."

Aiden followed a quiet Kane as he turned and headed back toward the direction of the vehicles at a brisk pace. "You're worried about her."

"Of course I'm worried. I'd be worried for any defenseless human caught in the middle of something like this."

"You would . . . but I think it's more than that where she's concerned." Kane just shot him a quick scowl. "Besides, according to her, she's not defenseless. She's invisible to them. How else do you explain how she got away from him?"

"You believe she's invisible just about as much as I do."

"We've seen stranger things. Is that what you really think, or is that what you're telling yourself? Because you're definitely not acting normal."

"Fuck off, I'm acting fine." Kane didn't say another word but began walking faster. He couldn't explain it, but he would just feel better when he saw her again.

A few minutes later they cleared the trees and saw Skye standing by the truck about thirty yards ahead. She was speaking to one of Lucky's men, who looked inordinately confused as her hands gestured wildly at him in wondrous description of something.

Kane exhaled deeply. He refused to try and explain it to himself, but he just needed to see her.

She glanced back at him as he continued to walk toward her. God help him, she was beautiful. It seemed to take the very breath out of him sometimes. Maybe it was the way that flirty golden hair of hers always threatened to fall into her eyes. It made her appear like she had a secret, and he would give anything to discover it. When he had kissed her, she tasted of the maple syrup she drowned her pancakes in that morning before they left. The woman had a hearty appetite for such a little thing, and she definitely loved pancakes.

Somehow everything in that moment seemed right, and it was taking all of his will power not to go straight to her and kiss her again in front of everyone. He didn't care who saw.

But then the moment changed.

There was a sharp pop that came from somewhere in the trees, and then a whooshing sound that broke like the howl of the wind through a canyon.

"Shit!" Kane cursed under his breath as both men took off toward Skye.

Skye had heard the sound, as well, and tried to react, but not before all hell broke loose. Kane literally held his breath in the middle of a dead run as he watched her turn toward a second even louder pop and then dive for the ground to try and roll under the truck for cover. But the instant force of air that was being created by the supernatural fury coming at them pulled her just short of the truck. She fought and clawed just to grab on to the truck's hitch step, and when she did Kane could already see the blood on her forearm where it had scraped against the gravel. That's when Kane saw something he could only describe as a mini tornado blow through the tree line and into the campsite, blasting straight for Skye. *Straight for her!*

She wasn't invisible to this thing! What the hell had she been thinking? What had *he* been thinking bringing her out here?

The Wraith caused such a disturbance in the atmosphere it felt like the whole sky was opening up above them as he bulldozed through there without even stopping. The chaotic airstream suddenly shifted directions and whirled the Dhampirs clean off their feet, like falling dominoes, then shoved Skye forward under the truck as though she were nothing more than an empty plastic bag.

Kane was sure he saw more blood as she disappeared under the vehicle.

"Skye!"

CHAPTER SIX

Kane's blood pressure went from perfectly calm to sky-high in two seconds.

Everything had happened so fast. One moment things were fine, and next there was a blast of air so powerful he and Aiden could feel the edges of it thirty yards away. The Wraith literally blew through and then disappeared like a puff of smoke, with Kane and Aiden too far away to do anything but witness the whole event. That made Kane crazy!

An angry growl erupted from his chest as he dropped to his knees beside the truck. Skye had been blown under it when the left side of the wide-bed was tipped up in the air, its wheels lifting a full three feet off the ground. *God*, it had scared him half to death to see the vehicle slam back down and bounce a few times against the ground, concealing Skye under there somewhere. He was going to kill her for scaring him like this! And for giving him that bullshit story that she would be invisible to the Lycans. He *assumed* that would also apply to their supernatural Wraith, but that obviously was not the case. "Skye?" he called, just before spotting her lying motionless between the ground and the underside of the truck. Her hands and arms were scraped up and blood was seeping from what looked like a deep gash on her forehead that she'd obviously gotten from hitting her head against either the ground or the underside of the cab. "Skye, can you hear me?" Kane felt like his throat was stripped raw with his words. "Come on, darlin', say something."

Kane looked to Aiden, who was crouched on the other side of the vehicle. "She's losing blood fast. We need to get pressure on that cut."

"I can reach her from this side," Aiden assured him.

Of course Aiden could reach her. At his height, nearly six-and-a-half feet, the giant of a man had the arm span of an NBA player, but reaching her wasn't the problem at the moment. "No!" Kane replied quickly. Don't move her. She might have injured her neck. We need to examine her before we move her —but first we need to get this damn truck out of the way."

"Not a problem," Aiden responded, motioning quickly to one of Lucky's men to jump behind the wheel while he moved around to the front of the truck. "Put the gearshift into neutral and keep the wheel straight," he instructed as he began to push the vehicle back. Kane eagerly bent over Skye the moment the moving truck cleared her body. Cursing fiercely under his breath, he checked the bleeding head wound and found it a little too out of control for his liking. A scarlet pool had seeped into her hair and her skin had become several shades paler than normal. He checked her carefully, noting that no bones seemed to be broken, but she appeared so child-like and fragile at that moment that he wanted to break something with his bare hands for all the anger surging through him.

"How is she?" Aiden asked in a harsh voice that was nothing like his own. He tossed Kane a small first-aid kit and backed up a step as the fresh scent of Skye's blood seemed to hit him squarely. His normally dark eyes suddenly sparked with a lighter, gray-blue color and his nostrils flared as his breathing grew deeper.

Kane turned back to Skye, his face grimacing as he refocused on her wound. "I'd feel better if she could open her eyes and tell us herself. But there don't seem to be any broken bones." He tore through the first-aid kit until he found some clean gauze he could use to put pressure on the cut, which he did, then glanced back at Aiden. "Are *you* all right?"

"I'm fine," Aiden growled, but Kane could tell immediately that wasn't true.

"You're not fine. You're responding to the scent of her blood. Step back!"

Aiden blinked at him in surprise, then looked down at his hands. They were shaking as he brought them closer to his face. He quickly pulled them down and formed tight fists at his sides before glancing at the unconscious Skye, then took several more steps back. "I won't hurt her."

"I know," Kane replied with a calmness that was completely sincere. Though he would speak to Aiden later about trying to hide the side-effects he was obviously experiencing, right now his priority was Skye.

"I think Lucky's got a bunch of supplies in his truck," Aiden offered. "Let me see if there's something we can use to make a stretcher."

"Good thinking. Let's move fast!" The worry in Kane's voice was clear to everyone as he kept pressure on her cut. She just looked so pale, lying there motionless. What had he been thinking, bringing her back out here? The anger he felt toward himself showed as he barked orders left and right the entire time they loaded her into the truck and drove back to The Trek. Two Dhampirs carried a now somewhat conscious but completely confused Skye inside on a makeshift stretcher of two backpack frames, a compact camping mattress, and some rope. She had come awake not long after they had gotten under way, but she hadn't been happy at all with the fuss everyone was making over her.

Kane didn't care. He told her to stay down and be still until a doctor could take a look at her. "Get her to her room," he barked. "Lucky, where's the damn doctor?"

"'E's about two minutes out," Lucky called back, the phone glued to his ear. Lucky had convinced Kane that since The Trek was halfway between their location and the closest hospital in Yellowknife, they would save time by taking Skye back to the outpost and have the doctor meet them there. Apparently, the local M.D. had saved their hides on more than one occasion where discretion was of the utmost importance. He did his job and didn't ask a lot of questions

Aiden had fully backed Lucky's plan, reminding Kane that he was basically holding Skye against her will and that perhaps taking her to a public hospital was not the smartest idea. Kane just grumbled and dismissed that concern flatly.

Lucky's men set her down easy on the bed she was borrowing, but she lay there stiffly, her eyes blinking slowly, as if she could fall unconscious again any second. Kane was examining her cut for what had to be the fifth time, then took a closer look at the scrapes on her arms. Despite her bravado since she woke, he could see that she had been caught totally off guard by what had happened, and it was ripping at his gut. And yet, somehow, this entire scene seemed familiar to him—*she* seemed familiar—but he had no clue as to why. He had never laid eyes on Skye Matthews before he saw her at the Brahm Hill battle site, but he kept having a feeling of déjà vu when he was around her. "Come on, darlin'," he murmured, gently stroking her cheek. "Keep those pretty green eyes open for me."

Just then a short, stocky man pushed his way into the room, blurting out commands in French that Kane didn't feel very obliged to interpret at the moment. He had other things to worry about. Lucky followed right on the man's heels, and Kane soon realized the rude Frenchmen was the doctor Lucky had sent for and that he wanted Kane to move out of the way. . . . But Kane wasn't moving.

"English, doc," Lucky told him. "Not everyone here speaks French."

Dr. Nigel Goode scowled back at Kane and then said, "Out of the way." Kane didn't like the sound of that any better in English than it had been in French. "I can hardly examine her from behind you, can I?"

Kane stood and stepped aside, slowly, deliberately, his gaze glued to the man in silent warning that said he had better do his job well.

"Come on, Kane," Aiden began. "Let's wait outside and give the doctor some room to work." Kane had no intention of leaving the room until Aiden added, "I know you want to stay and make sure she's all right, but Gideon's here. He wants to speak with you. And we'll be just outside."

Kane's brow rose sharply in surprise. "Gideon's here?"

Aiden nodded. "Just arrived. I assumed he's the person you contacted to help?"

"Yeah—by phone . . . to call me back," he said, as if the point should have been blatantly obvious. "Not to drive his ass all the way up here!"

"His *ass . . .* ," Gideon repeated in his very mannered accent from just outside the hall, "was already in Edmonton and decided that, given the tone of your message, you needed some help up here."

Kane took one last glance back to make sure Skye was getting all of the medical attention she needed, then stepped out into the hallway with Aiden, all the while thinking that he was going to have some quick explaining to do to avoid having Alec charging up here once he heard Kane had been holding a human woman against her will.

Although Kane liked to think it wasn't really against her will.

Gideon Janes was standing there with an odd quirk to his expression. The man was the textbook definition of a scholarly bookworm . . . and he dressed the part in a truly drab sweater vest and slacks. A damn brilliant human being, but he had the social sophistication of a toad. But then, Kane didn't need him to be social, he needed him to find answers, and answers were something Gideon was very good at getting. He was a Guide for The Brethren, a man known for translating whole libraries of history on the supernatural world since the beginnings of the written word. His job was to give input and provide guidance for effective strategizing based on events of past supernatural history. And right now they could use a little input.

"From all the commotion around here," Gideon noted as he glanced around, "I see little reason why you should object to the help."

"We're just dealing with a little situation here," Kane replied. "Nothing that will unhinge the stability of the supernatural world or anything."

Gideon's brows rose sharply at that comment, not quite sure what to make of it.

"Does Alec know you're here?" Aiden asked Gideon as he stepped forward to nudge Kane in the side as a reminder to tone his frustration down.

"Actually, he insisted that I come once I mentioned that Kane had rung me."

Kane rolled his eyes. "I'm sure he did." Kane should have known better. Gideon was faithfully loyal to Alec and The

Brethren. And right now his Brethren Elder was impatient for answers and way too damn perceptive, even while he was still grieving.

"You hadn't checked in, Kane. You shouldn't be surprised that he wants an update on what you've discovered so far. He's really quite concerned—"

"Yes, I know," Kane grumbled. "We've got a couple of balls we're juggling here. Our resident Wraith is at least as dangerous as Alec suspected. He's fast, faster that any vampire —and killing Lycans as if he's determined to extinguish the entire species."

"Wraith?" Gideon questioned.

"It's sort of a nick-name," Aiden clarified. "He has a habit of disappearing right in front of you, like a ghost."

"Really . . . ? Fascinating."

"No, not fascinating—dangerous." Kane turned toward the room where Skye was being checked by the doctor. He really should be in there. "The woman you just saw us bring in? Our Wraith wants her very badly. We're not sure why yet."

"Why don't you just ask her?" Gideon proposed dumbly.

Kane scrubbed his hands over his face, in a gesture that revealed his fatigue, while Aiden cleared his throat beside him. "Miss Matthews is very short on answers . . . intentionally. Kane has tried to question her, but so far we know very little."

"Well, perhaps *you* should question her then," Gideon said pointedly to Aiden. "Maybe she'll respond better to you."

The sound of Aiden's sharp inhalation of breath was lost in the explosion of anger and insult that Kane felt at Gideon's remark. "She *responds* to me just fine!"

Gideon turned to Kane, obviously caught off guard by his sharp response. This often brilliant but sometimes clueless Englishmen had a knack for missing the little stuff . . . or in this case, not so little . . . like a man taking offense to a woman not responding to him. But Gideon knew it was not like Kane to be moved to such a reaction. Things usually just rolled right off him quite easily. The Englishmen cleared his throat and tried again. "Perhaps it would be best then to stay focused on the Wraith for now. I'll do some checking, but I don't recall anything in the text of a supernatural being with the characteristics you're describing."

"There has to be," Kane countered. "Because he exists."

"That's rather my point," Gideon said as he cleaned the lenses of his small, wire framed glasses on his shirt. "We could be dealing with a *new* being or hybrid here."

"Well, I need to know what, then—and fast. I can't protect her from this thing if I don't know what I'm dealing with."

"Protect who?"

"*Skye*," Kane clarified, befuddled as to why the man couldn't keep up. "She's in the middle of this whole thing."

"Have I missed something?" Gideon asked, obviously confused. "Middle of what thing?"

"Skye was there that night at Brahm Hill. Remember the angel Olivia mentioned seeing? She was talking about Skye. I saw her there too."

Gideon's eyes widened with surprise. "You never mentioned that you'd seen her, as well. That was rather an important bit of information to leave out, don't you think?"

"Well it didn't seem important at the time," Kane pointed out. "We had just lost Lucas and Phin. Olivia was possibly dying, and Maya was falling apart over Phin. There were other more important things to be worried about then."

Gideon's expression dimmed. "You're quite right. I apologize."

Kane rubbed the back of his neck to try to ease the tension that had been building there since he'd seen Skye blown under that truck. "She had walked onto that battlefield that night in front of a bunch of vampires and Lycans as if she were venturing to a shopping mall. She wasn't afraid—*at all*. Now she shows up here and has been attacked by this Wraith twice. I'm telling you we need to figure out who she is, because they're connected."

"That does seem logical," Gideon offered as he looked toward the room where Skye was being attended. "So why've you not reported any of this to Alec?"

"I *will* tell him," he said, raising his hand out slowly from his side in a "hold on" gesture. "I just don't want to bring back that night for him until I know it's worth it."

Gideon, who had been vigorously rubbing his glasses on his short for all this time, finally returned them to the bridge of his nose. "By not telling him, you're implying that he can't handle the information? You know better."

"What I know is . . . that Alec hasn't been himself since that night."

"I would venture that few of us have. It's been difficult for him," Gideon acknowledged as he stared pointedly at Kane. "But not just for him."

Kane heard the message, loud and clear, that he was also in denial about how much he struggled with the loss of their team. But he just didn't see it that way. He didn't keep himself secluded in his office (not that he had an office), and he certainly hadn't been somber, reflective or hesitant with his decision making as of late, like Alec had.

"It's very human, Kane, to deal with loss differently than the man standing next to you. While one man's emotions may be right there at the surface, another may mask his in those things most comfortable and familiar to him."

Kane's gaze narrowed shrewdly. "Don't psycho-analyze me, Gideon. I'm not in the mood."

Aiden, who had been standing there listening quietly, finally stepped in to aid Gideon. The poor Englishmen had no idea that a five-foot-four blond bundle of trouble was turning Kane more inside-out by the hour. "At first we thought Skye was human," he began as way of explanation.

"She *is* human," Kane growled. "I was an idiot for even considering that cockamamie story she came up with about being invisible to them."

"Invisible to whom?" Gideon questioned.

Kane tossed his hand through the air dismissively. "Lycans, Wraiths . . . Take your pick."

"Interesting," Gideon responded.

"No," Kane scowled, "not interesting. It's suicide!"

Gideon paused as if giving thorough consideration to everything Kane had just said. "Perhaps she was telling the truth. Maybe there were some parameters today . . . some factor we're not aware of—that made her gift fail her. Because if you consider the possibility that it's true, it certainly would go a long way toward explaining why she was not afraid at Brahm Hill. A situation in which she clearly should have been."

Kane snorted. "Well, I'm certainly not sticking her in front of another Lycan to test that theory."

"No, that probably wouldn't be a good idea," Gideon agreed. "What else do you know about her?"

"She has sisters," Aiden offered. "Two of them were nearby at the first attack."

"Yeah, and their *ass* of a father puts them in the line of fire like that regularly. He calls them '*assignments*'." Kane accentuated with quote marks in the air. "He's just damn lucky he hasn't gotten one of them killed already."

"Kane?" Lucky called as he stuck his head out into the hallway. "We've got a wee bit of a problem. The little lass is all stitched up . . ." Lucky's expression then died on his face. "And her temper could freeze the balls off a brass monkey."

Kane took a relieved breath. He liked hearing that she had some fight back in her. "I'll be right there," he answered before turning back to Gideon and Aiden. "I need some answers, Gideon. There's got to be something in the text about this Wraith—or something like it. Find it."

After Kane left the room, Gideon turned to Aiden, appearing to be momentarily speechless. "Kane," he began carefully, "appears to be very attached to this woman. That is . . . most unusual."

Aiden snorted. "*That is* an understatement. He's holding her here until Oliver brings back her father. Kane wants to have '*words*' with him. I've never seen him like this."

Gideon sighed. "If she's human, Alec will be rather upset about him keeping her here against her will. What's that expression you Americans love so much . . . he'll hit a brick?"

Aiden laughed quietly. "Something like that. I think Kane's right, though—about her somehow being connected to this Wraith. My guess is her father knows something. Why send her here in the first place if he didn't?"

"True. But what would her father have to gain by sending his daughter against a supernatural being?"

"Make that nine daughters. And according to Skye's sister Autumn, they all have these assignments. It sounds like a damn cult, if you ask me."

Gideon's eyes suddenly opened wider as Aiden spoke.

Aiden knew he had hit on something important.

"Nine daughters?" Gideon questioned curiously. "What's her father's name?"

"Argus Matthews," Aiden replied, watching Gideon carefully. "Do you recognize the name?"

Gideon shook his head. "Not the name . . . Let me look into it."

"Man, I hate it when you hold out on us like that. Check quickly. Because my guess is, it won't take long for this Wraith to track Skye here. And if that happens, Kane just might shift into a saber-tooth instead of a jaguar."

CHAPTER SEVEN

The doctor had just finished the last of Skye's stitches and placed, in her opinion, a perfectly awful looking bandage on her forehead when Kane burst through the door with the finesse of a bulldozer, completely oblivious as to whether it appeared strange for him to do so.

He sank onto the mattress beside her hip and she was caught off guard at how that one, simple gesture comforted her. She just seemed to feel better with him being near—and that was a big problem. One she needed to remedy.

"How is she?" Kane asked the doctor, not her.

"I'm fine," she interjected before the doctor could answer him. "I don't need all this fuss."

Kane's shrewd gaze looked her over from head to toe before turning back to the doctor, his glance asking wordlessly if the medical man agreed with that assessment. "She'll be fine, with some rest," Dr. Goode replied, "and she'll feel pretty relaxed from the local I gave her before stitching her up."

Kane glanced back at her. "She doesn't look relaxed."

"He wasn't asking for your opinion," Skye replied sourly.

The doctor's lips twitched slightly in amusement. "She has a minor concussion, which will need to be watched carefully, but it should clear up on its own. Call me if she shows any signs of continued dizziness, nausea, headaches, or blurred vision. Otherwise, I'll be by day after tomorrow to check on her."

"Thank you for your help, doctor. Lucky will take care of your payment and show you out." Kane said, abruptly excusing the man. The doctor picked up his things without saying another word, while Kane glowered at Skye as though he'd already decided upon the few choice words he would have with her once the doctor left the room.

Skye was definitely feeling a bit unbalanced, dizzy even; but it had nothing to do with her concussion or the local anesthetic the doctor had given her. She'd felt this way ever since the Casanova had kissed her on the front seat of his SUV.

In truth, that kiss had shaken her to the core. Even as she was bleeding and a strange doctor hovered over her with one of the longest needles she had ever seen, all she could think was, *where's Kane?* Why wasn't he there with her? It pissed her off, actually. She considered herself fairly immune to the perceived charms of an overconfident playboy. After all, she had an assignment to do—an assignment that so far she was failing at. Instead, she was spending her time thinking of him—and not in the right way, like how to escape. Had she even once thought about how to *escape* from him or this place today?

No.

She was letting those beautiful silver eyes of his distract her to the point of mind-numbing incompetence. She needed to toughen her shell, her resolve . . . right now. It needed to be so steely that Kane's presence would barely register in her mind. *Right, right, now.*

With a hard jut of her chin, an easy 'tell', she knew she displayed often when trying to stiffen her resolve, and one that Kane was obviously aware of because before she even said a word he scowled at her as if he understood exactly what she was doing.

"I told you I'm fine."

"Oh, right—because you're so used to getting flattened by a Tasmanian devil to the point where you're unconscious and bleeding under a truck."

She stiffened at that. "I told you I could take care of myself."

"No, you lied to me. You said he wouldn't see you. But you were nothing more to him than the red center of a damn bull's eye!"

Her delicate brows scrunched with confusion. "Who wouldn't see me?"

Kane fisted his hands and then released them as if trying to release the tension from his shoulders at the same time. "The Wraith!"

"I never said—"

"Yes you did."

"No—"

But before Skye could utter another syllable, Kane came forward until his lips were on hers, subjecting her to another spine-tingling kiss that left her lips numb, her toes tingling, and her brain questioning what the hell was happening. *Where was her steel resolve?*

Kane's hand curled around the back of her neck, pulling her toward him in slow, careful inches. His kisses were gentle this time, his lips soft, as if he were worried he might hurt her, but he was definitely well schooled on how to kiss a woman, his thumb stroking her cheek as his tongue coaxed her to open deeper for him. She was sinking into him faster than a stone into water, her head spinning with warmth. Or was that just the dizziness from her concussion? A few more seconds of this and she would be completely lost, and she couldn't allow that to happen. "Stop," she said quietly. "I don't want this."

Kane released a heavy breath, pulling back from her enough to look into her eyes. "That's not what your kisses are saying."

Was she going to lay it out there and tell him the truth— that nothing could happen between them—ever? "It's just that my head's woozy and I'm tired."

No. She was going to chicken out, because blaming her reaction to him on a concussion was much easier than admitting that no one had ever made he feel like he did when he kissed her.

Kane watched her for a long moment, studying her, looking as if he were about to ask her something but then was thinking better of it. He stood up, stiffly, then walked slowly toward the door, every muscle in his body appearing to be held in tight control. He almost acted as if he were upset. That couldn't be right. Kane wasn't the type of man to get upset about a woman rejecting him—at least she thought he wasn't. "I never said the Wraith wouldn't see me," she said softly to his retreating form; she wasn't sure why. "I said the Lycans wouldn't see me."

Kane kept his back to her, refusing to turn around. "If you knew the Wraith wanted you, that he could hurt you, then why did you let me take you back there? Why did you willingly put yourself in danger like that?"

"I have an assignment to do, Kane. You may not respect that, but it's important to me. It's important to a lot of people."

"What assignment? This isn't school, Skye. These are dangerous supernatural creatures"

She shook her head, her voice fading now as she spoke, "That's not what I meant."

He finally turned to look at her, his face a careful mask. "Then tell me. My team and I know a lot about this world you're dealing with. You say you know of The Brethren—then you know we're trained to deal with it. Trust us—trust me—to understand and help you with it instead of trying to handle everything yourself."

She blinked, startled that this man who appeared so transparent at first was surprisingly, remarkably . . . complicated. "I . . . I can't."

A grim line of disappointment contorted his expression. "This assignment—this mission from your father—is going to get you fucking killed! Have you thought about that?" The intensity of his words caught her off guard, and he didn't give her a chance to respond before adding, "I have. And I'll tell you right now I'm going to do everything in my power to stop you from doing something stupid."

"Why does it even matter to you?"

His eyes seemed to fix on one point, as if he were in search of the answer to that question himself. There was a long, uneasy silence in the room, like an electric current, that seemed to make the space between them impassable as they simply stared at one another. When Kane finally broke the stare and turned back to the door, his hand reaching for the knob, he added, "You wanted that kiss as much as I did. I felt it in how you responded to me. It's in your every touch. Why won't you let yourself have what you want?"

"Why?" she asked with a crack to her voice that she hated. It made her feel so vulnerable. "So I can begin to feel something for you just as you decide you're bored with me? Are you going to tell me that's not what you've done with every other woman in your life up to this point?"

"You don't know me, Skye."

But Skye was sure it had to be the truth. Of course it was. He was too damned good looking, too sexy, too charming for it to be anything else. "Maybe not . . . But that's what your touch says, Kane—that you know how to please a woman without apology. And how to leave her before anything gets too complicated."

"What's so wrong with uncomplicated? What's wrong with just giving into the pleasure for a little while? No one has to get hurt. Why do you women as a gender always make it about something more?"

Skye sighed. "I think the better question is, why don't you want it to be about *more?*"

✹✹✹

Later that night, *Bogart* decided to make a re-appearance in Skye's room. It had taken most of the day for Kane to cool down after he felt as though Skye had hit him with a direct missile. The woman was stubborn, with a spine (and often jutted chin) stronger than steel, despite the angelic innocence that radiated from her like warm sunshine.

And he couldn't stop thinking about her.

He once again watched her as she slept, the sound of her soft breathing seeping into every trace of frustration he had felt earlier—and relaxing him.

Kane had never been ashamed of what or who he was. He liked being a Shifter. The ability to adapt and change on the outside felt natural to the core of who he was as a man on the inside. He enjoyed the pleasures of life. More specifically, he enjoyed pleasing women, which in turn pleased him. There was no more beautiful sound in the world to him than hearing a woman at the moment he gave her release. Whether it was a full-blown scream, a broken cry, or a soft, happy sigh, he loved them all, and loved how each one was specific to that woman. But when Skye Matthews had challenged him to ask why he didn't ever want there to be more, Kane, for the first time in his life, felt unworthy of someone he wanted . . . and that just didn't sit well with him.

He was a confident bastard, through and through. That was the reason why he could infiltrate any given situation as a

Shifter with such ease. He also liked to think he was smart, but if that were truly the case, he would have sent Skye Matthews on her way the first moment he realized she was starting to get under his skin. But he didn't. He couldn't. *Why?* Because he didn't want her to get herself killed, which was exactly what was going to happen if he took his eyes off her for one second.

Just then, Skye stirred in her sleep again, kicking her legs several times under the covers. She was such a restless sleeper. He reached out with his fingertips and brushed back the hair that was about to fall into her eyes, careful not to wake her or she would once again be in for a very naked surprise. After a couple of minutes, she seemed to relax. He continued gently stroking her temple, realizing that his fingertips were warming from the contact with her skin. Actually, it sent heat shooting down his spine then straight through his cock. *Unbelievable.* One touch and he was hard for her again, painfully so. He feared if he didn't get away from her soon he might never get his body to calm down.

He sighed and moved away from the bed, feeling the chill the moment he left her side, but also realizing he was spending too much time with this woman on a bed. He had his own assignment to carry out: finding out about this Wraith, and what Skye's connection to him was. Kane went to the closet and silently pulled out the hard-sided suitcase she had so vehemently *not* wanted to let go of earlier that day. When he opened it up there was nothing in it. She had already hidden whatever had been inside.

But when had she had the time to do that? In between stitches?

Nothing in the room smelled unusual, unless you counted her scent, which tonight held an even softer complexity with notes of floral and cherries. So intoxicating that he stayed hard, just as he damned well had been the night before—all night long. *Man,* he was going to have to take a long, long, cold shower.

Quietly, he made his way outside her door and down the long hallway, knowing he needed to get some distance before he felt compelled to kiss her in her sleep. That wouldn't go over so well, mostly because of the fact he was still naked. But it did make it an ideal time to check the grounds around the building. Even if Skye woke and tried to leave, which would be doubtful given the local the doctor had given her, he would be able to catch the scent of her on the grounds. Yet, somehow he knew she wouldn't try to leave, despite the threat in her eyes to do just that the moment she got a chance. He simply felt in his bones that she was as drawn to him as he was to her.

Kane stepped outside and closed the main doors behind him before turning to see a very introspective Aiden standing there on the porch and staring off into the night. Of course, Aiden always looked introspective. He was a quiet man of few words, but when he did speak, people tended to listen because they could see he had a sharp intelligence about him. After a moment his somber, thoughtful expression opened into an amused and quirky little smile. He didn't even try to conceal his awareness of Kane's nakedness. Aiden didn't care. He'd seen Kane naked hundreds of times—not usually with a hard on this bad, but what was a man to do? Being naked was just a general condition his friends had to accept, since he was always shifting. Although, in retrospect, it probably hadn't been necessary for him to walk birthday-bare through The Trek at three in the morning, either. He just spent so much time without clothes, he didn't really think of that stuff too much.

"Problem?" Aiden asked, noting his friends obviously *strained* condition.

"Fuck off," Kane growled back.

"Actually," he laughed as he looked away, "it seems I should be giving that advice to you."

"Yeah, whatever. Still can't sleep?"

Aiden shrugged off his answer. "It comes and goes."

Kane could have questioned his friend further, but he could tell Aiden didn't want to talk about it so he decided to let it go for now. Barefooted, he hopped down to the ground and began running along the icy cold snow that had accumulated through the day. As his legs stretched forward, the muscles in his limbs warmed him against the cold, signaling the change happening within him. The energy it took for a shift was immense, and it was never easy, even if he was shifting to the form he was most comfortable in—the jaguar. But he had become used to the stresses on his body long ago.

The more the animal within him clawed to take over, the more imperative it became for him to stretch forward and extend both his hands and feet. By the time his hands hit the ground they were already transformed into giant paws with long claws, perfectly adapted to move over this uneven terrain. His eyes then adjusted to the night, becoming ever sharper, until he could see as well as he could during the day. In this form, nothing now would escape his notice, escape his hearing, or deceive his powerful sense of smell. He was free to race over the land, expend all the energy in his body, and take in every scent, smell and odor around him. Some were good, some not so good, but very little was unfamiliar to him. His brain had become a catalogue of scents, each one pushing forward on cue like some sort of electronic rolodex as a familiar sensation resurfaced.

It was nearly an hour later when he returned, his body exhilarated from his all out run across the grounds. He felt good, but he thought he would feel better—more relaxed or tired enough to at least to sleep for a few hours—but he didn't. Aiden was still outside when he returned, his amused mood from earlier seeming more serious now as Kane padded to a stop and began the process of shifting back to human form.

"Anything out of the ordinary?" Aiden asked while handing him a pair of sweats and a coat.

"No," he said as his extremely gravelly voice settled back into his own. "Are you ready to talk about what happened today?"

Aiden's lips thinned. "I didn't hurt her."

"That's not what I mean. I could see how much responding to her blood scent bothered you. You should talk with someone about it."

"I'm fine. I'm dealing with it. You don't need to worry about me. I'm fine."

But Kane did worry about him. He considered Aiden his closest friend, one he'd nearly lost when he, along with everyone else at The Oracle, learned that a dozen of the human Guardians had secretly agreed to be transfused with vampire blood in an effort to increase their strength. Basically, they were being used as guinea pigs by Alec's Uncle Reese, who was obsessed with creating a genetically engineered super-solider, a human/vampire hybrid that was to be the blueprint for an entire army. Reese didn't give a damn about the effects on those he was testing, like Aiden, and it pissed Kane off to no end.

The night of Brahm Hill, when he saw Reese dragged into the trees and mutilated by a Lycan, Kane thought immediately that it was too merciful an end for the former ruler. Reese would not live to see the eventual effect on those men's lives he ruined with his tests.

After the first test subjects appeared to have been successfully transfused, Reese had ordered more to be tested, and Aiden was one of them. But over the course of a few weeks, those who were first transfused began exhibiting severe side effects. Sleeplessness, black outs, violent seizures, and uncontrolled rage were now just *some* of the things Aiden was still trying to deal with as one of only two men left who had survived the tests. Within months, the other ten had died or had been killed because they forced the issue with their violent actions.

Aiden seemed to be just as surprised that he and fellow Guardian Zane Merrick had survived, and sometimes he even appeared to feel guilty about it, which Kane couldn't understand. He was damned grateful Aiden had survived. If Alec's uncle weren't already dead, Kane would have killed the man himself. "That's a lot of '*fines*'," Kane pointed out. "Look man, I'm your friend. You don't need to hide any of this shit from me. It's not like I'm going to tell Dr. Li so he can yank your ass back to The Oracle."

"What the hell am I supposed to say, Kane? I agreed to the tests."

"You're supposed to say what's happening so I can help you, not playing some stupid bullshit game of '*oh, I did this to myself so I'm going to live with it*' crap."

After a moment, Aiden's scowling expression gave way to the tiniest smirk. "I'll try to remember that."

"Well, good, because I know you're smarter than this. You don't deserve this."

Aiden then nodded toward The Trek doors. "If you're done scolding me now, I thought you might want to know she's still inside sleeping. She hasn't tried to run."

Kane pulled his shirt down over his shoulders. "I know."

"So have you decided to tell her who you are?"

"She doesn't want to know who I am. In fact, she's made it quite clear with that jutted little chin of hers that she doesn't want me to touch her."

Aiden's brows shot up; he was clearly surprised. "Don't tell me you're so far gone for this woman that you don't see what's she's doing?"

"I'm not 'far gone' for any woman, smart ass? But since you're so smart, why don't *you* tell *me* what she's doing."

Aiden shoved his hands in his pockets. "Well, I guess that answers that question." He shook his head with a sigh and took a couple of steps toward him. "She seems like a nice woman . . . a good woman. If your obvious interest in her was strictly from wounded pride at her not wanting to fall into bed with you, then I'd tell you to stop being a prick and to leave her alone."

"Nice," Kane muttered.

"My point being . . . ," he continued, "I don't think that's what this is about. I think that for the first time in your life you're genuinely attracted to a woman for more than her shell. A good friend would tell you there's hope to survive the 'whipped' path you're headed down because you've only known her for forty-eight hours." Aiden then burst out in laughter as he rolled back. "But not me. I'm having way too much fun just watching this whole thing."

"You really are an ass!" Kane moved around him and plopped himself on The Trek's front steps, shoving the shoes Aiden had brought for him onto his bare feet. He rested his elbows on his knees and rubbed his hands over his face and through his currently unruly hair. "And I probably deserve it," he added in defeated tone.

"Hey, look on the bright side. At least Alec isn't here to see this. He'd be rolling on his back by now."

"What did I just say about being an ass?"

Aiden's laughter died down, followed by a long silence that seemed appropriate for the dark, quiet snowfall developing around them as they sat next to each other on the steps.

"She seems scared to me," Aiden finally broke into the silence. "As much as you don't understand this attraction you have toward her, I think it scares her more. I see it when I catch her watching you. And—trust me—she *is* watching you. She seems confused by all of this."

"Well, that makes two of us," Kane muttered. "But this isn't just attraction. I've felt attraction before. I feel attraction on almost a daily basis. This is more like a giant magnetic pull. It's fucked up, man."

Aiden just stared at him with a quizzical expression clearly indicating that he already knew the answer but was just waiting for Kane to come to the same conclusion.

"Don't look at me like that. This is just for fun. Two people crossing paths and taking advantage of a short time together while in the same place. Nothing more."

Kane absolutely believed that. And he knew that once he had experienced the pleasure of sinking himself inside her sweet body, this crazy distraction (no, more like obsession with having her), would ease. He would want to move on to finding the next woman he wanted to sink his body into, and he couldn't wait for that moment because even just thinking about her now had his dick so hard he'd be able to drive nails with it. He couldn't understand it. He had just run himself into total exhaustion, something his inner jaguar was not inherently fond of, and yet this need for her refused to die down. He supposed, though, that he ought to consider himself lucky that, this time at least, he had clothes on to cover the enormous bulge in his pants.

Aiden just shook his head as if he were privy to some information the rest of the world wasn't. "Man, you really don't see what's happening, do you?" Kane just stared back at his friend, not in the mood for games. "Fine. Here's my advice. Just because she's pushing you away doesn't mean she's not interested."

Kane rolled his eyes. "I know that. I have picked up more than my fair share of women."

"No, you've fucked more than your fair share of women. *This* is new territory for you."

"Just what are you implying? I just finished telling you this is for fun only."

Aiden blinked back at him. "Do you want this woman? Because 'for fun' is not going to get you anywhere with her. You need to back down a bit. You can be a little . . ."—he did the whole scary hands over the head thing and snapped his jaw against his teeth—"overwhelming when you're all in predator mode."

"You look completely ridiculous doing that."

Aiden lowered his arms. "Well, you get what I mean."

"Yeah, but she's not lunch." He suddenly paused as a wicked thought seemed to occur to him, causing a sly smile across his lips. "Although . . . I guess she could be."

Aiden rolled his eyes. "You so are *not* paying attention," he mumbled more to himself. "What I mean is, you seduce women like prey. You can't help it. It's in your DNA." Kane nodded, not entirely sure he agreed with that assessment, but willing to concede it was a possibility. "It's important to Skye to be seen as capable. It's why she keeps reminding us that she can handle herself with the Wraith and the Lycans."

"Which, as we've already seen, she can't," Kane grumbled irritably. Honestly, if he had to replay that moment when she lay unconscious under that truck one more time in his head, he felt sure his jaw would crack from his teeth grinding against it so hard.

"And if she thinks you really believe that, asshole . . . then you don't have a shot!"

Kane blinked back at him with genuine surprise. "How does that make me an asshole? I just don't want to see her get hurt."

"Just trust me on this. Let her have the control. Let her make the next move."

Kane's expression fell into a sulk. "I could be old and grey before that happens."

"I'm not saying you shouldn't set up the opportunity . . . just that once you do, you go at her pace."

Kane seemed to consider that for a moment before a mischievous smile came to his lips, as if announcing that the light bulb had just gone off in his head. "Not bad advice," he began. "So since you're handing out such sage wisdom, does this mean you're going to admit you have a thing for the fair Lily Abbott?"

Aiden scowled; a quick defense for a quick change of subject. "No. I don't even know her. She's only been at The Oracle for a few weeks."

Kane's smile widened. He didn't believe Aiden for a second. "Makes no difference. Look at what Skye's managed to do to me in forty-eight hours."

"Yeah, but you deserve it."

"True. Still, I think there's something special about the fair Lemon—"—Kane cleared his throat—"I mean Lily. I can tell these things."

"Are you speaking of her with your other brain?" Aiden asked as he narrowed his gaze on his friend. " . . . 'Cause if you are, I may have to kick your ass."

Kane laughed. "Man, you hated catching me with her, didn't you?"

Aiden moved straight to his feet and made a beeline for The Trek doors without another word.

"Hey," Kane called with sincerity in his voice. Aiden stopped and turned to him. "What I'm trying to say is, I'm sorry. If I had known you cared for the lovely Lemon you never would have found me there with her."

"Why do you keep calling her Lemon?"

The smile came back to Kane's face and he knew he was simply incapable of leaving it at that. "Never mind, it's not important. But if you don't make a move on her soon then I have to tell you, you're just as big of a dumbass as me."

Aiden snorted inwardly. "That's certainly not something to strive for."

"So you've forgiven me . . . you'll help me, then?"

His friend's gaze narrowed. "Help you? With what?"

Kane came to his feet and walked forward 'til he was right beside him, planting a firm clap on his shoulder. "Plan B."

CHAPTER EIGHT

The next morning, Skye awoke slowly to the same darkness she had fallen asleep in, but now, fluffy-white snowflakes were falling by the bedroom window, each one illuminated into tiny, reflective sparklers by the lights around the outpost.

Seeing the snow brought a smile to her lips, though, she wondered if the lights were a way of trying to diminish the fact that it was always dark in this place. The darkness, like the cold, seemed to be a constant force, and it was only October.

Resting comfortably on her side and feeling toasty-warm under the covers, she noticed that her head felt much better. The pain and dizziness from the night before was now gone, seeming to have been replaced by a general feeling of soreness in her muscles. As much as she would have liked to set a plan in motion to leave here last night, there simply was no way that would happen after she was knocked silly by that Wraith. Admittedly, she should have been better prepared for that. Kane was right. She had known exactly how dangerous it would be when he drove her out there. But she still had an assignment to complete, and she was running short on time and options now that Kane was stubbornly trying to keep her here.

Skye decided that today would be the day she'd get her act together and avoid Kane while coming up with a plan to leave The Trek. Just as the thought flashed through her mind she noticed the feeling of heat against her back. It was a warmth so powerful it had more than likely been responsible for keeping her resting comfortably through the night as the temperature outside continued to plummet. In fact, at one point during the night she remembered having felt cold, the same bone-chilling cold she had felt many times since she'd arrived in Yellowknife. But then the warmth had returned and she had welcomed it, snuggling further into it before falling safely back into her dreamland. That's when it dawned on her that she was in bed and there shouldn't be a warm furnace snuggled behind her.

With a gasp, she pushed away quickly to the very edge of the bed (which was only about six inches, since the body beside her took up most of it) and turned to see who was there with her. Bogart raised his head from his paws where he had been quietly sleeping and gave her a huge yawn, displaying his *many* sharp teeth. "*Oh God,* you're going to eat me now, aren't you?"

The jaguar simply tilted his head as if in his animal voice he was questioning her sanity. It was remarkable how the expressions on his face, in his eyes, were so readable. She tried to pull the covers up to her chin in some silly effort to protect herself, but they wouldn't budge because they were trapped under the cat's huge body, and it was obvious that he wasn't planning to move any time soon. But neither was he being aggressive or threatening toward her. In fact, he looked rather confused as to why his sleep had been disturbed in the first place.

She stared widely at the animal. "You really aren't going to hurt me, are you?"

Bogart just tilted his head the other direction as if she had asked another silly question.

"That really doesn't make you a very good guard cat, does it? Not that anyone would challenge that notion." Skye turned back to the window. "Or would you stop me if I—?"

A low sound, somewhere between a growl and a snarl rolled in the giant cat's throat as he purposely showed her his teeth this time. Skye's brows lifted sharply in reply. "I guess so . . ."

Bogart's fierce expression smoothed as he extended his head over hers, forcing her farther back into the pillow, and immediately his very textured tongue licked over her cheek—or more accurately, most of her face. She scrunched up, put on a disgusted expression, and ducked her head away. But then, inexplicably, she giggled! "Gross! Good thing I haven't taken a shower yet."

Once she stopped laughing, she eyed the animal cautiously and stretched her hand over his back, waiting to see if he would give her permission to pet him. When the jaguar remained perfectly still, she let her fingertips thread into his thick coat, her knuckles curling into the silky softness as she followed the long line of his spine. All the wonderful rosettes covering his body created an intricate pattern that seemed almost too perfect to be left to nature.

"You really are a beautiful animal," she murmured. "But Bogart? I assume that's for Humphrey. You don't look like a Bogart to me. You should have a much more exotic name. Something proud, strong . . . like Mufasa." She smiled at him. "You know . . . from The Lion King?" Skye's whole face seemed to light up then as she continued. "I loved that movie. My father took all of us to the theatre to see it when we were kids. It was one of the few times we were all together as a family. We didn't have a television around my house so it was a pretty big deal. Yes, definitely more like a Mufasa."

"Why," she sighed, "am I talking to a jaguar?"

As she stroked him his low threaded growl from earlier turned into a full-blown purr. She blinked up at him in surprise, seeing her own reflection in his large silver eyes. "You're purring."

Skye rolled onto her side to face him. "Your eyes kind of remind me of Kane's. The color, I mean. Stupid, huh? I just woke and I'm already thinking about him. Maybe you could give me some advice on how to deal with him today?"

Without hesitation, Bogart licked her face again, causing Skye to giggle, even more joyously and loudly, her effervescent laugh seeming to bounce off the walls of the room. "What? You want me to lick him? That's definitely a bad idea." But the jaguar just continued to lick her neck, his rough-textured tongue tickling her so much that she backed away and clumsily stumbled out from under the bed covers. Immediately, Skye curled her arms around her to brace herself against the cold now that she wasn't resting against the jaguar's warm body. "I need to get away from here," she murmured, turning toward the wonderful, white landscape that had accumulated during the night. "From him . . . ," she continued. "Having him kiss me . . . feeling something for someone who's a virtual stranger to me . . . that wasn't part of the plan."

She turned back around, her petite form shivering in her pink, thermal leggings and the thick, white socks at her ankles .

. . and, of course, Kane's black tee shirt. She had other shirts, but she chose to wear his again. She just liked the way it smelled. Like him. "I wish I could take you with me. I think you would come in handy as a guard cat," she smiled. "And the scary things out there in this world don't know that you're just a big ole pussycat."

Bogart jumped down from the bed and walked around to stand in front of her. In animal form he was so big that his head nearly came level with her breast, which he seemed to focus on much as a man would. "*Good Lord, it must be the male species in general,*" she thought. They all had one track minds.

The huge cat then lowered his head and nuzzled against the hand at her side until she lifted it to pet him again. "Wow. Such an attention monger, aren't you." Skye scratched her fingers under his lifted chin a few more times before heading to the shower. The big cat followed as if he was fully intending to shower with her. But she turned him back at the door with a knowing look in her eye. "Uh-uh. Sorry big fella. You have to stay here. There's not enough room in there for both of us."

Bogart's eyes were amazingly expressive as he stared back at her. For a passing moment, she thought, they almost looked *disappointed* as she shut the door on him.

About an hour later, fully dressed and with her wispy hair going all over the place and her face freshened with minimal make up—the way she preferred—Skye re-entered the bedroom and was surprised to find Bogart gone and the door to the room cracked open several inches, allowing the delicious smell of fresh bacon and eggs to waft through. She could also hear now the chatter of several male voices in the distance. Opening the door fully, Skye followed the sounds and smells into the main area, where the rising sun was just starting to stream through the windows. "Aye, good day, lass," Lucky greeted with a smile as he flipped another pancake on the griddle. "You must be hungry this mornin' after eating only breakfast yesterday. We've plenty of food 'ere, so help yourself."

For a moment, Skye stared out the front windows at the winter wonderland that now blanketed the rough land around them. Soon it would be so cold and frozen here that her assignment would become much more difficult. She needed to refocus her energies and come up with a plan—fast. "It all looks and smells wonderful," she said, turning back to him. "I'm just not hungry yet."

"Are you feeling all right this morning?" Aiden asked from somewhere behind her, startling Skye a bit. She hadn't even noticed him seated in the corner. As she turned he came smoothly to his feet—especially considering his incredible size and height. Immediately, she scanned the room for Kane, but somehow she knew he would not be there. Unlike Aiden, who had such a quiet way about him, Kane entered a room with something like a soundless blast of trumpets announcing his arrival. It was irritating but annoyingly fitting for a man with such an enigmatic presence. "Any dizziness, headaches . . . ?"

"No. I feel much better this morning," she said, allowing herself a smile in Aiden's direction. I'm sure my appetite will catch up in no time." She scanned the room again. "So where's Bogart?" A loud snicker at her question caused her to turn again, rapidly in this case, in the direction of one of the Dhampirs, who, once she spotted him, quickly straightened out his expression and returned silently to his food.

"We let him roam during the day," Aiden answered. "He'll be back tonight."

Turning to address Aiden, she managed to say, "You let that big cat just roam the grounds? Is that a good idea?" but as if by magic, there was Aiden, right in front of her. The man made no sound as he seemed to move around the room.

"He's on the grounds but contained," was his answer, then he leaned in quietly, his mouth now hovering close to her right ear as he whispered, "Kane asked to meet with you after breakfast. That is, if you are up to it. And since you're not hungry quite yet . . ."

Skye felt her body go instantly tense. She hadn't prepared herself for meeting with him at all, much less first thing in the morning. Actually, her plan was to avoid him all together today. "I'm sure he just wants to hound me for answers that I'm not going to give him. So I see little point."

Aiden smiled politely. "He does want answers. It's his job to get them. But he's genuinely concerned about how you are doing after what happened yesterday."

Skye frowned at that. Of course he wanted to see her to ask questions. He wanted to *bombard* her with questions about what she knew. He warned as much when he announced to everyone that he was forcing her to stay here. "Can it at least wait until after lunch?" She was thinking maybe she could come up with a workable plan before she'd actually had to attempt an escape.

Aiden just smiled politely once again. "Knowing Kane as I do, my guess is that he will just come and find you if you don't come with me now. He can be very insistent about these kinds of things."

"Yes, I see that," she sighed. "Fine. Let's get this over with."

Skye followed Aiden down the hall to—wait a minute—*her room*. The door was shut, which was strange because she remembered leaving it opened when she left the room only a few minutes before. She narrowed her gaze on Aiden as he drew the door open and gestured for her to enter. When she did, she made it only a few steps into the room before she was stopped dead in her tracks by simultaneously hearing the door close behind her and seeing Kane, who was sitting on the bed—fully clothed, thankfully—his long legs crossed casually at his ankles while his arms were splayed high to each side of the backboard, tied to the bedpost by his wrists. By all appearances he was supposed to be the sacrificial lamb, but the lazy smile on his face said he was anything but. "Good mornin', darlin'. Sleep well?"

For the longest time Skye just stared at him, completely at a loss for words. What was he up to now? He had obviously gone insane, though he looked good doing it, she supposed. Clothed in faded, low-rise jeans that cut across his hips just right, black socks, leather hiking boots set neatly on the floor beside the bed, and topped with a soft, cotton pull-over in a charcoal gray that seemed to make those silver eyes of his pop. "*He's quite a sight*," she thought, able to admit her admiration even in the face of her distrust.

Skye should have insisted on having breakfast. Stuffing her face right now would be a much better idea than to having to face this *force* of sarcasm and sex appeal. "What do you think you're doing?" she finally questioned, displaying more confidence than she inwardly felt. "If someone comes in here and sees you . . ."

"Well, see, now I've just learned something new about you. You're not into audiences," he teased with a lightness that made no attempt to camouflage the sexual undertones. It was definitely time to for her to go. Her empty, fluttering stomach couldn't handle this right now.

"No, I'm not," she replied smoothly as she headed back toward the door, trying to not look affected in the least by the fact she had a gorgeous man—that she hated admitting she wanted to kiss again—tied to her bedpost.

"Why are you running from me, Skye?"

That halted her in her tracks. "I'm not running. It's pretty clear I'm walking away. I don't have the energy for your games today."

"Are you feeling all right?" he asked in a deep voice filled with not sarcasm, but concern. "Are your stitches bothering you?"

She pivoted on her feet to fully face him again, but her hand remained on the door handle as a reminder that she *was* leaving. "The only thing bothering me about my stitches—bothering me, at all, besides you—is this ridiculous band-aid in the middle of my forehead."

"So then you are running."

"No."

"Well, seeing as your hand is on the door knob and you look like you're about to bolt through it at any second . . . I would definitely say you're running." She pulled her hand from the door knob—and for the life of her couldn't figure out why. She had nothing to prove to this man. "Come on, Skye," he cajoled, "I'm completely at your mercy here. I can't touch you. I'm merely offering myself up for you to reach out to in whatever way you want." He then stretched his hands out against the tight ropes as if to prove his point.

"I'm going to pass." Skye was thrilled at how she said those words with so much conviction on the outside. But inside, she felt weak, so weak that she didn't seem to have the strength even to open the door of the bedroom, which was ridiculous. The only thing that could've made the situation more tempting was if the man had been smart enough to spread chocolate frosting all over his chest. There would have been no way then she could have refused the temptation to lick it away.

"You keep pushing me away, but I know you feel whatever this is between us, too. You're not immune to it."

"There isn't anything between us. There can't be."

He tipped his head to her with a smug smile. "Hate to break it to you, but it's already there. And it bothers you how much you want to kiss me again, doesn't it?"

Skye stared at him and didn't even realize she had taken two steps closer to the bed. "I'm not bothered! And I have no intention of ever kissing you again," she cried, louder than she meant to, realizing too late that Aiden and the others possible could have overheard. So she lowered her voice to a near whisper. "Don't look at me like that! Of course I know I *could* kiss you, but I'm choosing *not* to kiss you."

When Skye realized that statement didn't sound nearly as convincing out loud as it had in her head, she quickly added, "Because I don't *want* to kiss you—*at all!*"

Kane just seemed to settle more comfortably into the pillows, looking completely at ease in his bound state and with what she had just declared to him . . . which really wasn't the reaction she was going for. "Yep. Definitely bothered. I'm flattered, really."

"Oooohh," Skye steamed as she closed the remaining distance between them without a single thought about whether this was a wise course of action. "You're so arrogant! You don't bother me and I have no desire to kiss you again. Absolutely zero, *zilch*, none! In fact I'm pretty sure right now I would have more of a reaction to kissing a toad."

His smile widened. "Prove it."

Ugh, she was an idiot. She had walked right in to that. Skye was about to declaratively say '*No!*' when she realized she had practically dared him herself. If she backed out now, he would see it as a victory.

That couldn't happen.

Her finger came out in a sharp point. "Fine, I will. But when I do this and prove to you that I am right, you have to promise me that there will be no more kissing. No more suggestive comments. No more surprise kissing attacks. No more lip to lip. Got it?"

"Surprise kissing attacks? Oh, that does sound awful."

"You know what I mean." Skye was so flustered by this point she feared her skin was breaking out into a bright flush underneath her clothes. Meanwhile, Kane was just staring at her almost as if he already knew exactly what she would look like flushed and out of her clothes. That was her first clue that *this* was *not* a good idea.

But Skye Matthews wasn't a coward.

She swallowed hard, feeling her mouth go instantly dry. It struck her then that kissing the man to prove she didn't want to kiss him was not exactly how her day of avoiding Kane was supposed to start.

"Now," he continued as if he were simply negotiating a business arrangement between them, "let's discuss what *I* get when you melt in my arms like butter, darlin'." Skye was about to object but he didn't give her a chance. "I know! When you respond to my kiss, I will have the right to kiss you at least once a day for every day that you're here."

"*What?*" she said blankly. "Absolutely not!"

She did look outraged, even when in reality there was a slight (all right, more than slight) tingling happening low in her belly.

"What's the matter? Your father will be here soon to answer for his abominable behavior. We're probably talking a day or two, tops. And if you win, I'll leave you alone—Scout's honor."

"You couldn't have possibly been a Boy Scout. You're too conniving."

"No . . . but I was a *boy* who went camping a couple of times, so it applies by default?"

"No it . . ." Skye sighed with frustration. While it was certainly true that she wouldn't be there much longer, especially since she was planning to escape that very day, she questioned the wisdom of feeling she needed to prove anything. She knew herself well enough to know she could resist one kiss. She had resisted a lot of men's kisses in the past . . . or at least a few . . . or maybe just one. *Oh, who was she kidding? Kissing was just the best part.*

This had disaster written all over it.

Simply, she was going to have to focus on something really, really disgusting while kissing him—something like raw eggs, cheese mold, or chew wads. Yeah, that's it! She could imagine him with a giant ball of chew in his mouth while he was locked lip to lip with her. She found the habit utterly revolting. That would surely be enough to turn off any amount of her libido that might be tempted. "All right," she smiled, deciding she had a plan and that this was going to solve her immediate problem of needing him to back off. "I accept. If I win, you're not to kiss me again—"

"Hold on," he stopped her. "Let's just clarify. I won't kiss you again *unless* you ask me to."

Skye snorted in rather unladylike fashion. "Fine. I won't be asking you for a kiss, either, so it doesn't really matter. And if you win, you can have one kiss a day for as long as I'm here."

"At least one kiss," he clarified again. "I mean, when you beg me for more I'll be helpless to say no to you at that point."

Skye fisted her hands at her sides as she glared at him. Oh, she could definitely do this. Her plan was simple. Just lean over and kiss him—with her feet still firmly rooted on the floor. It would be efficient, to the point, and over in two seconds. But he was tied directly center of the tall, queen-sized bed. Reaching him from the edge presented a logistical problem.

Kane lifted his brows, expectantly, as if he'd figured out her very train of thought, and then he almost leered at her, looking way too pleased with her predicament and sure of what her solution might be.

The man was impossible.

Slowly, Skye eased herself onto her knees on the mattress, crawling over to him as his silver eyes following her the whole way. When she was in front of him she kept herself lifted on her knees, very purposefully keeping a wide distance between them until she was ready.

"You're going to have to get a lot closer than that," he commented.

"You are such a—"

"Ah! No foul language before a kiss. It can ruin the mood."

"Good!" she shouted as she plunked down to her heels over his legs. He grunted and laughed softly as she faced him and froze. *What on earth had she been thinking?* She was a good eighteen inches away from his lips and she could already smell his scent, cedar and something spicy—and clean! "You just showered."

"Yes," he smiled. "It's customary in the mornings, but I'm glad you noticed. Smell something you like?"

"No," she lied.

He then leaned forward as far as the ropes would allow and sniffed at her, his nose catching in the air, as if catching a whiff of something he didn't like. "Is that Bogart I smell on you?"

Skye inhaled sharply and started for the edge of the bed. She just didn't need this.

"Oh, so you forfeit then?" Kane asked her with glee. "Well, in that case, I want my victory kiss right now."

She swung around on him, squeezing her eyes closed tight and mumbling under her breath before crawling back over his legs. "You have not won by default!" Once she was reseated on his thighs she placed her hands at each one of his stretched shoulders. She exhaled a deep breath and could feel the muscles of his shoulders flex under her hands as she prepared herself to kiss him. *Chew wads,* that what she needed to focus on. She had the image in her head, the nasty smell in her nose, and was ready to go.

. . . And then he spoke.

"Hey?" His voice was gentle, his expression utterly sincere which caught her more than a little off guard. "I was teasing you. You smell way better than Bogart." He stretched himself forward, pulling him tight against his ropes, far enough so he could nuzzled into her neck. "In fact," he whispered, "I've thought of little else but your scent all night and all morning."

He sealed that thought with a single light kiss on her throat that made her breath halt. Just one, soft brush of his lips began a string of warm tingles under her skin. *Oh,* the man knew what he was doing. "It's like that perfect glass of red wine . . . layered and complex. And once you expose it to the air, let it breathe, there are a dozen more subtle scents you discover."

He was cheating! He had to know he was cheating!

But to her own disappointment, Skye wasn't about to do anything to stop him. Just feeling his slow breath on her skin had her sinking into him like she would a warm breeze. The feeling was just so comfortable and right. "There's cherries— dark cherries. And vanilla," he continued, placing several more kisses in a not-so-straight line over her jaw as he headed toward her lips. "Definitely vanilla, mixed with a little sunshine. When I smell you, Skye, I smell sunshine . . . which is nice, here where it's so dark and cold."

Skye was breathing a little slower as she tucked her head to his cheek, her hands coming up to his shoulders. She couldn't believe that she hadn't even initiated a kiss with him yet and he already had her leaning into him as if he were her life support. Had she *no* self control?

And now she was drawing a complete blank on the disgusting thing she was supposed to be thinking about so she wouldn't be thinking about him. All she could think about was his scent, which seemed to become a part of her as she moved closer to him. He took the lobe of her ear between his lips and began to play with it, to suck it, then to hold it tight between his teeth as he hissed in a breath. Completely involuntarily, Skye heard—and felt—a tiny little sound come out of her mouth—sounding suspiciously like a moan—a moan she very much did not want to admit to. Her hands slid from his shoulders to his chest, where they seemed to warm as she detected his strong heartbeat.

" . . . And an exotic flower." He inhaled a deep breath, as though he was trying to commit the scent to memory.

"Frangipani," she murmured. " . . . it's the Frangipani flower."

"I love that scent. It's my favorite on you. It warms itself on your skin, and I can imagine a day at a secluded beach somewhere with the sound of the ocean waves nearby . . . just you and me. No one else around. Nothing for you to worry about. Nothing for you to fear. Can you see that?"

"Y—yes," she answered breathily as she felt his lips wisp over her cheek.

"Then kiss me, Skye. Kiss me as you would if we were sitting there on that beach right now. How you would if you knew no one would find us."

Skye's heart was racing at a rate that would launch it right out of her chest. Her lips felt her way along his freshly shaved but rougher skin until she made contact with his mouth. He had been waiting for her. And once her lips skimmed over his, at first petal-soft, then deeper, he groaned and took the kiss further until they were fused together and she felt sure the world would spin out of control beneath her. She had to clutch at his arms to keep herself from flailing backward, then sank against his body for support as his kiss drew her in, bringing her forward with him until her body was draped over him like a blanket.

Oh, God, she was lost, lipped-locked to one of the most dangerous kissers on the planet, she had decided, and relishing every second. She could feel the sensation all the way down to her toes and up into the ends of her hair. The warmth of it relaxed her, sank into her skin like a long, hot, bubble bath. The taste of his kiss was unlike anything she had ever known, a taste that was all his: masculine, confident, with just a hint of coffee. "That's it, Skye. Touch me. I love when you touch me."

She loved touching him, too! Her hands tightened around his neck and then slid down over the muscled wall of his chest as she kissed him deeper. *She* was kissing *him!* Strong heartbeats were bursting through his skin, too, against her palms, and she knew he was just as excited as she was. There was no way she could deny herself any of this. She wasn't strong enough.

But she didn't have to be.

He pulled back from her with sparking silver eyes, a hard burst of warm breath, and a sincerely happy smile. She swore at that moment the beauty of him was positively devastating to her senses. "I think I'd like my kisses first thing in the morning," he murmured. "Tasting you is the perfect way to start a day."

Skye blinked and then blinked again as she realized what she'd just done. Not only had she lost their bet, but she never even went down swinging. He'd had her from the moment his warm breath tingled across her skin. That thought made her acutely aware of how vulnerable she was becoming where he was concerned. How *this,* whatever this was, was already way out of control. She brought her fingers to her lips in a sort of stunned admission. "I'm sorr—"

"Don't," he cut in. "Don't be sorry. Don't regret this. I know I can't be the only one who feels this."

She was shaking her head, but it was to agree with him.

"Hey." His head ducked lower to try and meet her now hidden expression. "Then what's the problem? There's nothing that says we can't enjoy being with one another until you leave."

"I—I can't be with you."

Kane paused, as if considering what he wanted to say next. "Look, I hadn't considered this before now . . . but if you're scared because this might be your first time, then let me reassure you. I know exactly what to do."

"That's not it. "I've already . . . *God,* this is so ridiculous."

Kane's expression smoothed to a mischievous smile. "Are you trying to tell me, sweet Skye, that you're not a virgin? Because that isn't going to change one bit how much I want you. In fact, in full disclosure, I feel compelled to confess that I'm not a virgin, either."

Skye raised her head, her eyes glistening on the edge of tears, and she could see in his face that her response had not been what he had expected. For just a moment, she wished he wasn't tied up so he could wrap those long arms of his around her. But it didn't matter anymore. Skye had been kidding herself. She honestly believed her frequent thoughts of him were just some sort of female fantasy, but that kiss, those many kisses, all added up to something that was becoming very real for her . . . *and she had no right to it!*

"I can't be with you, Kane, because I belong to someone else."

CHAPTER NINE

Kane hated that she just used the word '*belonged*'.

He felt a strong, visceral reaction to the word because in this moment he believed Skye Matthews belonged to no one but him; *no one else could have her*—and this was not like him at all.

Normally, a woman telling him she was in a relationship or married (although she wasn't wearing a ring; he'd taken note of that) would be no big deal. He would brush it off and say, "OK," and be on to the next lovely fish in the sea. But that was not what he was feeling right now—not even close. There was this gnawing in his gut that seemed to be building by the second at just the thought of her belonging to another man, at the idea that another man had been with her, had been with her first.

What the devil was wrong with him? She was twenty-six, a mature and beautiful woman. She had probably not been a virgin for some time, and here he was, like some clumsy jack-ass, making jokes about it. But in his mind he could think of nothing he wanted more in that moment than to be her first—to lie her down and slide into her silken body until she begged him, *begged him* for more. The thought was completely caveman and ridiculous, but he felt to his core that something had been stolen from him.

The asshole better have been gentle, because right now the unsure look in those vivid green eyes was tugging at his heart. "Will you please say something," she said, not realizing how tightly her fingers dug into his shirt.

"Untie my hands," he said.

He could see the hesitation in her eyes, but she reached for one of his hands. It took her a little while to loosen the tight cords, and when she finally got his hand free her fingers rubbed gently over the red marks left on his wrist. Until then she would've had no idea how much her touch had him straining against those ropes. For a moment, there, he thought he might break the headboard in half. "The other one," he said, nodding toward the other post.

Once both hands were free, she began to scoot off his legs. He reached for her and pulled her back against his chest as he relaxed against the headboard. His arm curled low around her back, while the other cradled her head against his shoulder. She was breathing quietly, completely comfortable, and the moment felt so unbelievably right and sincere to him.

What was happening? He was holding this woman in his arms while on a bed—*her* bed—totally disregarding rule number two. In fact, he'd slept with her in this very bed the night before . . . though, that was OK, because nothing had happened between them and he was in his jaguar form. There was no specific clarification to his rule number two that said he couldn't sleep with a woman on a bed in *shifted* form. He nodded to himself once, confident, feeling much better that he had justification for it.

"I wish I had met you first," she spoke quietly.

"It doesn't matter," he replied. She blinked up at him, obviously taking his comment as somehow a slight to her. She tried to pull away, but he squeezed his arms tight around her to hold her still. "Don't misunderstand me," he spoke quietly in her ear. "I still want you, Skye. More than you can possibly know. But you were right about me." He tilted her head back and held it gently between his hands. "I always leave. *Always.* I don't want to hurt you like that."

His stare was so fixed on her that he knew she could see the truth in his eyes. He needed her to understand that he didn't do relationships, he didn't commit, ever. He was all about the mindless pleasure of the moment, always had been, and he wouldn't try to pretend he was something different. Those few hours spent in a woman's arms, buried deep within her soft body, was a heaven unlike anything else. It was something he needed, an experience he wanted with the bouquet of different women available to him.

Ever since he was old enough to understand the pleasure a woman could give him, Kane had always carried that little devil on his shoulder, the devil that pushed him to find the next woman. There was never a moment's peace—and he was never satisfied. It was the part of himself that he knew was an ass, and yet he felt helpless to change it. He accepted who he was, as Skye had said, '*without apology*'.

"I need to go," she murmured as she tried once again to pull away, but Kane just couldn't let her go. She stared back at him as her big, green eyes filled with such vulnerability it was tearing at him from the inside. "Please, Kane. Let me go."

Kane didn't budge.

Skye jutted her chin slightly forward, as if she were trying to unearth some hidden strength. "I'm sorry. I should have told you before we made this silly bet. I just didn't think I would . . . well, it doesn't matter now. I just thought you should know there's really no point to holding to our bet."

Kane arched a brow high. "Oh, I still get my kisses, Miss Matthews. A bet's a bet."

Skye stared back at him in disbelief. "I just told you I am with another man—promised to him, in fact."

Kane reached for her left hand and raised it until her fingers were between them, rubbing his thumb over the back of her bare second one as he grinned. "And in the immortal words of Beyoncé, 'he should'a put a ring on it'."

She gasped. "You're quoting Beyoncé to justify hitting on another man's woman?"

"Skye, darlin', there's so much you have yet to learn about me. I'm a complicated man."

"Actually, you seem rather simple," she said dryly, even though he doubted very much that she really believed that. "I'm tied to him, Kane. I will always be tied to him."

"Then why did you kiss me."

That was a very good question, one that had her face flushing hotly in response because she didn't have a good answer—or even a decent answer. "I didn't . . . you kissed me! I mean . . . yes, I kissed you—but it was so you wouldn't kiss me." Then after she seemed to realize that made no sense she added weakly, " . . . anymore."

He couldn't stop smiling at her.

"I have to go," Skye said, trying to squirm out of his arms and off his legs.

Kane was about to inform her that she wasn't going anywhere when the loud slam of The Trek's front door was followed by Lucky's bellowed voice calling out his name. They both swung toward the closed door of her room. "Stay here," he said, placing a quick kiss on her brow, just beneath her stitches, before setting her down and pushing from the bed. He darted into the main room and practically collided with Lucky, Gideon and Aiden. "What's going on?"

Lucky threw a piece of torn and blood-soaked fabric onto the table in front of them. "Our resident Lycan hunter is getting closer. We found another body within a few miles of the property."

"Damn," Kane said under his breath. "He knows she's here."

"I would say that's a definite yes."

"He's sending a message," Gideon offered. "A warning."

Kane swung on the Brethren Guide. "You think?" he bit out, but kept his voice low so Skye wouldn't hear any more of their conversation. "What've you been able to find out?"

"Indeed, there are many questions that need to be answered here. I've not had a chance to finish going through all the text." Kane just rolled his hand through the air at him, indicating he wanted Gideon to get to the important part. "Regrettably, it's not much. However, I do find the fact he's here most interesting."

"Why?"

"This Wraith's movements are not logical. In fact, they seem rather scattered. It's as if he has no plan, he simply responds. That would imply his decisions are emotion based."

"Emotion is a human trait," Aiden offered.

Gideon considered that for a moment. "Perhaps there's a part of our Wraith that *is* human, or at least remembers *having been* human. That part of him would be connected to what's driving him . . . which, right now, appears to be Miss Matthews."

"This is personal for him?" Kane asked.

"I believe so, yes."

"Well, he's not going to get the chance." Kane turned to Lucky while picking up the torn piece of fabric. "Before we arrived, had the Dhampirs tracked anything unusual around here in the last few weeks? Any scents?"

"No. Nothin'."

"And you didn't pick up anything during your run on the property this morning," Aiden pointed out to Kane.

Kane handed the fabric to Aiden. "No, I didn't, which means our Wraith just got here, or this *thing* isn't leaving a scent. I can smell the Lycan he killed, but that's all. I also remember noticing that same lack of scent on the day he attacked Skye. At the time, I was focused on her injuries, but I remember clearly that there was no scent near the truck, even though he had just blown through."

Lucky grabbed the fabric from Aiden, who appeared not to notice because his attention was focused somewhere else. "How is it possible for something not to leave a scent?"

"Kane," Aiden said, slowly and calmly, but Kane recognized the warning in his friend's voice.

Kane froze, and followed Aiden's eyes toward the closed bedroom door he had left only minutes earlier. "Skye."

***

Kane had left the bed so quickly that Skye had practically bounced from his arms. She had wanted to go with him to hear first-hand what was going on, especially since it probably affected her, but right now she had other plans in mind as she scurried about the room.

In part, she hoped that if she kept herself busy enough, she wouldn't have time to think about the sweetness of the kiss she had shared with Kane. The time in his arms, the way he held her, spoke to her, had been incredibly intimate—they might as well have known each other for a lifetime instead of for only a couple of days. It was hard to reconcile the man she had enjoyed kissing with the 'player' she believed him to be, and the feeling of intimate familiarity was her only explanation for why she had mentioned Andrew—though not by name.

Kane had wanted her. She recognized the desire in his eyes and understood the restraint that had caused the rope marks to imprint themselves on his wrist, but he pulled back. And if she were honest with herself, she would have to admit she wanted him to. It was incredibly hypocritical on her part; she knew she couldn't have him. She knew that. She had already given herself, her body, everything she had, to the man she was destined to be with. That's why the feelings she had for Kane were so unsettling. Like, why did she literally *shiver* every time Kane touched her? It was wrong. So wrong! "It's not what's destined," she murmured to herself, shaking her head, as though that feeble gesture would be enough to get the man out of her mind. "I have to stay focused on what needs to be done."

She went back to the bed and slid her hand beneath the pillow, feeling just a twinge of guilt as she retrieved the small cell phone she had managed to ease from the pocket of Kane's jeans during their kiss. Of course, she had enjoyed the kiss. She certainly sank into it fast enough and seemed to forget where she was. But ultimately, she had agreed to his little dare because it provided a nice distraction for him while she lifted his cell phone. Skye congratulated herself for having pilfered the phone early, before he had kissed her senseless and *she* had forgotten what she was trying to do in the first place. All she needed was to make one short phone call. She was sure that once she slipped it back into his coat pocket he would never even realize it had been gone.

She slid out of the bed and punched the number in quickly as she paced the room and waited anxiously for someone to answer. "Hello?" came her sister Star's soft voice. It was wonderful just to hear her, since they had not spoken in over three months. Star's last assignment had taken her to another continent, while Skye had been traveling between Seattle, Alberta, and now the Northwest Territories. Communication between the sisters was kept to a minimum during assignments, anyway; it helped them stay focused so they could finish and return home to family all the sooner.

"Star, it's me," Skye whispered as quietly as she could.

"Skye? Oh, my God, where are you?"

Skye had to put her hand over the phone to muffle her sister's concerned but very loud voice. Star was the 'love the earth' beauty of the family, a free-spirited gypsy and the fourth daughter, almost exactly a year younger than Skye. Since they were closest in age, they had formed an especially close bond, something Skye really missed right now, given that her confusion about Kane was twisting her into knots. "Keep your voice down," she said as she made her way into the bathroom and closed the door, turning on the shower for extra effect. "There are Dhampir's here."

"Oh, sorry. Dad's in the living room right now yelling at two Dhampirs who told him you're being detained up in Yellowknife. Are you all right?"

"Yes, I'm fine. I had to make an unexpected side trip. But listen, I don't have long to talk. Can you get dad on the phone without letting the men know it's me?"

"I'm not sure. Dad's blowing a gasket at the moment—demanding to know why they're holding you. Not exactly the best time to mention he has a phone call, you know."

Skye stared nervously at the bathroom door. She couldn't hear the conversation happening in the living room, though every once in a while she thought she could hear Kane's tense curse. "Please try, Star."

"OK, hold on."

Skye could hear as her sister moved into the other room, where the men were yelling, and she decided that she, too, would find a more private place, so she entered the bathroom, locked the door, and turned on the shower. Listening more intently now, she recognized that by far, her father's voice was the loudest one emerging from the argument going on at the other end of the line. He really was about to blow a gasket. Kane had no idea who he was dealing with when he made the decision to have her father carted back to Yellowknife on his order. Argus Matthews let no man control him, and she doubted he would make an exception for Kane.

"Dad?" Star called. "Aunt Mary's on the phone and needs to speak with you. She says it's important." *Clever girl.* They didn't have an aunt, or an uncle for that matter. It would be a clear message to her father that he needed to speak with whoever was on the line.

Argus grabbed the phone. "Mary?" his gruff voice answered.

"Dad, it's me," she whispered as softly as she could.

"What's happened? How is he?" Argus asked; the voices in the background were fading fast. Skye knew he might be able to get farther away from the Dhampirs, but he wouldn't be out of their earshot, which meant he was going to have to speak in code.

"I'm fine. They've taken good care of me."

"Tell me where he is right now."

"I'm at The Brethren outpost just outside of Yellowknife. It's called The Trek. Don't worry, I was able to get my things . . . *all of them*," she emphasized. "But I haven't been able to complete my assignment."

"Lake!" Argus called back. "Show these men out to their vehicle. I'll be leaving with them after I grab a few things. You and your sisters are staying at your uncle's tonight. He's had an accident."

"Yes, Papa," she replied, without giving any hint that what he was saying didn't make any sense because they didn't have an uncle.

Her father undoubtedly had a plan up his sleeve. It was the only thing that explained the fact he was actually coming all the way up here. That wasn't like him. He knew she and her sisters could handle themselves. So did that mean he didn't trust that she would finish her assignment on her own?

Skye heard a door close in the background, followed by her father's more urgent whisper. "Tell me who's holding you." Skye inhaled and momentarily froze. She wasn't sure why. This was her father. She knew he loved her and only wanted her safe, but she also knew the storm he would bring down on Kane when he finally got here. Even though Kane had brought this on himself by technically kidnapping her in the first place, she didn't want him to face her father's wrath. "His name, Skye!"

"His name is Kane," she finally said. "He's a Guardian for The Brethren. But he just doesn't understand—"

"Listen to me very carefully," Argus began in a barely audible whisper. "I need you to get out of there as soon as you can. Do you understand me?" His voice rose. "I need you to get away from him. I don't care what it takes." Now at full volume and then some, he almost shouted, "Get the hell out of there!"

Skye was startled. She had rarely heard her father curse before. Her and her sisters were much worse about that sort of thing than he was. "But father, he hasn't—"

"Now, Skye . . . *now!* Do you understand?"

"Yes," she replied quietly. "But there are too many men watching me. I'll have to come up with a plan."

"You know what to do. Once you're gone, follow the Lycans home. Do you know where to meet me?"

"Yes."

"I'll play along with this farce and let them bring me there, but you are to be long gone by the time I arrive. Once I've made it clear they're never to bother you again, I'll meet you."

"I understand," Skye said, distracted by the sound of footsteps thundering down the hall and into the bedroom. "I have to go." She slammed the phone closed, ending the call just as the bathroom doorknob rattled.

"Skye, open the door!" Kane barked from just on the other side of the closed and locked door. His voice was tense, but she could hear the worry underneath. Suddenly, she felt bad that she was about to lie to him.

"Just a minute," she called back innocently, turning off the shower. "I'm just finishing up here."

"Don't lie to me, Skye. You already took a shower this morning. You were on the cell phone." After a bit of rumbling around she then heard his murmured curse. "*My* cell phone!" he growled, and Skye grimaced. She had totally been busted.

"Now open this door before I break it down!"

***

Kane was in the mood to break something. He had just held this woman in his arms, kissing her until she couldn't even remember her own name—or at least he thought she couldn't remember her own name—but instead, he finds she had outsmarted him! He had completely forgotten about the phone in his pocket while her hands clutched at him during their kiss. Worse yet, he knew she had just been on the phone with *him.* The man she was committed to. The man who had the woman *he* wanted . . . at least for one night, maybe two.

Had that been her plan all along? To distract him with kisses that stirred his blood all in a plot to get his phone? *Was he really that stupid?* He had opened himself up by telling her he could feel something between them, been honest when he said that he would eventually leave and that he didn't want to hurt her that way, and she'd made a fool out of him.

The lock on the door clicked and Skye came into view. She was fully dressed in blue jeans that hugged her body to mouth-watering perfection, paired with a long-sleeved white shirt, confirming that the shower had just been a ruse. With messy tendrils of hair falling into her eyes, those pouty little lips and the prettiest eyes looking up at him with an innocence that astounded him she handed him his phone. She said nothing. No apology, no nothing. That irked Kane even more as he jerked the phone from her hand and touched the screen to re-dial the last number. It just rang over and over. "Is he on his way, Skye?"

"Yes," she answered honestly.

"Good," he replied, though inside he was trying to decide how best to deal with both her father and the man she was promised to showing up. Perhaps he would give the boyfriend a good stiff punch to the jaw. Sure it wouldn't solve anything, but it would make him feel better.

When Kane said nothing else in reply, Skye jutted her chin forward and pushed her way past him, landing directly in front Gideon. "Miss Matthews," Gideon began, with that proper accent of his. "My name is Gideon Janes. I would like to speak with you if you have a moment."

She glanced back at Kane with a satisfied smile. "Lead the way," she said as she marched away from Kane with a sweet little 'extra' sway to her hips. She thought if she was speaking to Gideon then she wouldn't have to deal with him.

Boy, was she wrong.

Kane could feel the animalistic rumble inside his chest. His female guest-slash-prisoner-slash-detainee was driving him insane. She had to have been talking escape with her boyfriend on the other line, and it gnawed at him. That meant she'd be trying to escape from him. No woman ever wanted to escape from *him*. And it certainly wasn't going to happen before he could steal a few more of those lovely kisses from her.

Just then, Aiden's cell phone rang inside his jeans pocket.

"I need to speak with her first," Kane growled at Gideon.

"Kane?" Aiden called as he handed him his phone. "It's Alec, for you." Aiden then cupped his free hand over the phone and whispered, "He's not in the mood to be told you're busy."

OK, so speaking to Skye first might have to wait.

Kane released a long, hard sigh as he hitched his hands at his hips. *Could the man's timing be any worse?* "This isn't finished," he warned Skye before grabbing the phone from Aiden. "Alec," he spoke cheerfully, "what's happening down there where it's a decent temperature?"

"Miss Matthews . . . It's a bit chilly out," he heard Gideon say with one ear as the other was being chewed out from the other end of the phone connection, "but perhaps you would like to go for a walk outside. It can't be much fun being confined in here all day."

"That would be nice," she said, her eyes glancing pointedly at Kane one last time before she headed for the door.

Mercy, but the woman was driving him insane. Then he realized that Alec had just asked him a question—and he hadn't a clue what it was. "Uh, what was that?"

"Have you even heard a word I've said?"

"Of course. It's just noisy here." But he offered no more than that, purposely being vague as to not give away the fact he was already completely lost in their conversation.

Then Alec literally growled, "Tell me what the hell's going on up there!"

Kane's brows lifted sharply. This was most unusual for the Elder. Alec was known for keeping a cool head in even the tensest of situations. It was one of the characteristics that made him such a good leader—though, again, Kane would never admit that to the Elder. "I plan to give you a full update with all my 'I's dotted and all my 'T's crossed, oh, Elder One—but now's not really a good time. I don't have a lot of information for you yet."

"Really," Alec responded, and Kane could tell by his exaggerated tone he wasn't buying his load of crap for a second. "So you don't think it's important to tell me that the mysterious woman Olivia saw at Brahm Hill is there with you now?"

"Gideon!" Kane cursed under his breath. He thought he had done a good job of convincing The Brethren Guide why he

didn't want Alec to know just yet. Evidently, he was wrong. He shouldn't have been surprised. Gideon had always been fiercely loyal to Alec, especially after he had lost his father—and again last year, when his Uncle Reese had betrayed all of them and turned to the dark side. "Yes, she's here . . . but I don't have a lot yet. She's been a little short on answers."

"Then bring her back here. I'll question her. I need to know what she knows about that night."

Kane had expected that from the moment Alec knew who Skye was he would want her brought back to The Oracle for questioning. The answers she had were too personal for Alec. But everything in Kane's gut told him that was a bad idea, that she would clam up on them even more. She was protecting something, perhaps someone. Why, he wasn't sure, but he was willing to bet a part of her was scared. How could a human woman being chased by a supernatural creature not be, on some level? "I thought you wanted me focused on this Wraith?"

"I do."

"Well, she's somehow connected to him. And since the Wraith's here—not back at The Oracle—keeping her here is how we're going to get those answers."

"Wraith?" Alec questioned. "Is that what Gideon's determined he is? I've never heard of a Wraith."

"Not exactly," Kane sighed. "It's just a nickname we've given it. This thing's fast, disappears before you can blink. And it's single-handedly trying to take out the Lycan population on his own." Alec was silent for a long while and Kane could tell the man was debating the notion to have her brought back there anyway. As much as Kane would like answers himself as to what the hell Reese Lambert had been up to that night at Brahm Hill, he refused to let Skye be the sounding board for Alec's anger over being the one who had survived instead of Lucas. "She doesn't have the answers you're looking for, Alec. She can't tell you why Reese killed Lucas, or what his plan was for you."

Alec said nothing, which—thankfully—meant Kane had success-fully convinced him.

"Have Aiden bring her here to me in the morning while you keep tracking the Wraith. I need to hear that for myself!"

CHAPTER TEN

Skye felt the icy chill in the morning air as she and Gideon walked around the grounds near the house.

It was a partially clear day, the large clouds frustrating the sun's attempt to melt the snow that had fallen the previous night. '*Lord help me, I'm going to have to find some warmer clothes if I'm stuck here much longer*'. That thought was paramount as she gazed up at the British man she had latched onto in an effort to escape a stern grilling from Kane over one tiny phone call.

At the moment, however, Gideon Janes seemed to be contemplating something . . . which was probably not a good thing for her. This man might be a bit geeky, but he was definitely smart; one could tell that almost immediately. Yet, there was absolutely nothing intimidating about him. He seemed more like that sweet, quiet uncle who would listen rather than inundate you with his opinions. "I appreciate the walk, Gideon. It's nice to get outside for a bit. But I'm sure you didn't bring me out here just to walk."

"True . . . ," he began in his soft, mannered accent, seeming to consider what he wanted to say next. "My memory can be a little sketchy nowadays. A side effect of getting older, I'm afraid."

"You are human, then?" she asked, catching a glance of the two Dhampirs trailing them in the shadow of the trees. Their presence wasn't surprising. She knew this walk with Gideon wouldn't lead to an opportunity for escape. That would have been much too easy. But she had hoped it would afford her a chance to get the lay of the land she needed to escape from, which it definitely did. She assessed the terrain around her, location of the main road in relation to The Trek, and the suspicious absence of any other buildings within view.

Escape, she then frowned inwardly as her thoughts ticked back. Had she ever really felt like a prisoner?

"Yes, quite," Gideon answered, bringing her attention back to him. "I'm afraid my skills for The Brethren are with my mind rather than anything supernatural."

Skye smiled at him. No doubt that was true.

"I try to make the most of it," he continued. "As you can imagine, working for The Brethren means surrounding yourself with people who have truly wonderful and powerful gifts—especially the females."

"Why is that, do you think?"

"Well, I believe the truly remarkable gifts require wholehearted acceptance to realize their full potential. In my experience, we men as a gender, tend to question, to defend and fight for what we want and hold most dear. These are not bad traits and they lead us to a different kind of success, but women are the inherent nurturers. That gives them an advantage—a capacity to wholly accept and grow within their truly powerful gifts."

"So you believe that accepting your gifts—who you are—is key in the supernatural world?"

"I think trusting those gifts, trusting yourself, is important. How else can one find the courage to face the creatures that are physically more powerful than they are? Like a Lycan, for example," he seemed to say with a wink. Skye knew he was referring to the night of Brahm Hill; how she appeared unafraid among the Lycans. She simply nodded in agreement but still felt like she had just revealed something she had no intention of revealing.

"In fact," he continued, "that brings me back to what I wanted to ask. There is a friend of ours, Olivia Greyson Wolfe . . ." His dark eyes seemed to light up as he spoke, and it was obvious he held great affection for her. "A truly wonderful woman—a Dhampir. Her strength is mild by most hybrid standards, but her gifts are some of the most remarkable I've ever seen. She has the power to draw in supernatural beings with just her presence and touch. They're quite helpless to prevent it, actually." He paused for a moment as if considering something, and then added, "She rather reminds me of you."

Skye slowed her pace until she stopped, then turned to him. "Why? You barely know me and I do not claim to have any gifts."

"You don't believe being invisible to the Lycans qualifies as a gift?" Skye wisely didn't respond, and Gideon waved a hand dismissively. "No matter. My point is that she happened to mention to me that a woman came to see her at the blood clinic she manages in Seattle. Her encounter with that woman was short, but she remembered her because it struck her, intuitively, that she had another purpose for being there other than to donate blood."

"And what was her purpose?"

"We still don't know. Olivia claims to have seen the woman again on the night of Brahm Hill. Actually, she described her as an angel when she was close to death. Seeing this woman, according to Olivia, had saved her life, reminding her of what she wanted to fight for most—a life with her true love, Caleb."

Distractedly, Skye started walking forward again. "That's an interesting story, Gideon, but I'm not sure why you're telling me this."

Gideon paused, as if to give her a chance to reconsider that statement before saying, "I believe you were the woman who visited Olivia in Seattle."

Skye let out a small sound that resembled a decidedly feminine snort. She *had* gone to see Olivia, of course. And normally she wouldn't have worried about admitting such a simple fact. People often didn't put small facts together. But *people* did not include Gideon Janes. All this man *did* was put small facts together. "There are literally millions of woman who could have visited that day. Why on earth would you assume it was me?"

Gideon's lips lifted into a smile. "Because yesterday, when Kane told me he had also seen you the night of Brahm Hill, he used the exact same word to describe you—angel."

Skye licked her lips. Until now, neither she nor Kane had even mentioned that they recognized each other from that night, but he had obviously spoken about it with Gideon—and probably Aiden, as well. She needed to be careful here. Perhaps the wiser choice would have been to stay and deal with Kane's anger over her having lifted his cell phone.

"I'm standing right in front of you," Skye replied. "Clearly, I'm not an angel."

"Yes, but it's an interesting choice of description, don't you think?"

Skye shrugged her shoulders. "Perhaps."

Gideon gave her a passing smile. "And perhaps—if you had been the one to visit Olivia in Seattle—you did so because she was also an assignment? It would make sense, after all. She's very important to the supernatural world—a world you seem to be very well versed in."

Skye was versed on this world. Her father made sure of it. Ever since she became old enough to speak her first words he had been teaching her about the world that surrounded them but went unnoticed by all but a select few humans. He taught her to be observant of her surroundings, how to notice the physical clues and to trust her instincts. The same principals you would teach any woman to protect herself from a dangerous situation . . . except that the enemy could be a hundred times more destructive than any human attacker. "And the timing of when you show up seems to fit a pattern."

"Really? And what pattern is that?"

"When people are facing death."

There was a long, quiet moment between them while Skye contemplated what she should say and what she shouldn't Rubbing her hands over her arms for warmth, she turned back to see that they had already walked quite a distance from The Trek. "It's a bit colder out here than I realized. I think we should head back in."

Gideon nodded and gestured back toward the direction they came. "You won't satisfy my curiosity, then?"

"Death is a mystery to all of us. I don't have any answers for you."

Every step closer to The Trek doors seemed to tick off in her head, like a clock, as she continued to try to sidestep Gideon's questions.

"What about Kane, then?"

"What about him?"

"It's just that I've known him for a long time . . . and he doesn't appear to be quite himself. I'm wondering if your current assignment involves him"

"I'm not sure what you're trying to ask me, Gideon, but I'm not here for Kane. And I'm not . . . I'm not like your friend Olivia."

"I'm not sure that's true. While you may be different from her, I definitely believe you have a gift. That would be the only explanation for why your father would even consider sending you alone to face Lycans and vampires on that battlefield. Unless, of course, he didn't care."

Skye came to a sudden stop at the foot of the entry stairs to The Trek. "My father loves us," she replied. "He loves us so much he's prepared us our entire lives—" She stopped herself in one short breath. What had she almost said? She really needed to get away from this place, *tonight,* before she said too much—or worse—really started to care for these people.

Skye ran up the steps to the entry doors, leaving Gideon standing in the slowly melting snow.

"I don't doubt that, Miss Matthews," she heard Gideon speak quietly behind her. "I don't doubt that at all."

✻✻✻

Standing at the kitchen island Kane was raking his hand through his hair, still staring with unwavering concentration at the phone he had tossed onto the counter minutes earlier. What the hell was he going to do now? Alec had just thrown him a major curveball. Kane had underestimated the Elder's need for answers regarding that night at Brahm Hill.

"What did he say?"Aiden asked as he entered the room.

Kane could feel the snarl distorting his lips and exposing his teeth. "He wants you to bring Skye back to The Oracle while I continue to hunt down our Wraith."

Aiden's brows lifted. "I would guess that's not something you're open to."

"*Hell, no,* I'm not open to it! But he hung up on me before I could tell him where to shove it."

"You're lucky he did. You know you can't tell an Elder where to shove it. All you'll do is manage to get yourself permanently banned from the dining hall."

"The hell I can't! I used to do it on a daily basis when we were on the same team."

Aiden gave him a disapproving scowl. "You know Alec wasn't an Elder then. The only reason he puts up with half of your bullshit now is because he feels loyal to you . . . to the bond the four of you had as a team."

Kane swung around to the refrigerator. "Not with me. I was assigned by Reese after Ryan was killed. To them, I was just a replacement."

"That's bullshit, and you know it! I saw the way you all fought for each other at Brahm Hill. You can try to fool yourself all you want, but they trusted you with their lives—"

"Yeah, and look where that got two of them," Kane bit out before chugging almost a full glass of orange juice. Aiden didn't respond and gave Kane a moment to collect himself, which Kane appreciated. He hated discussing the night they lost Lucas and Phin. *Hated it!* "So, do you plan on telling me how you heard Skye on the cell phone . . . at the end of the hallway . . . in the bedroom?" Kane asked, taking a slower sip and finishing off his juice from before adding, "No, make that—in the bathroom—in the bedroom . . . with the shower running?"

Aiden shrugged his shoulders. "My hearing has been getting sharper for awhile."

"Mmm. And is anyone else aware of this new *little* development? You know as well as I do that the transfusions you had were meant to increase your strength. But you seemed to be picking up all sorts of *other* fun little gifts."

Aiden tensed. "I'm tired of being poked and prodded and tested, Kane. You don't know what it feels like to be treated like some sort of unnatural freak."

Kane arched a brow. "I don't? Oh, that's right, I know exactly what it feels like to run down the street and play with all my little jaguar-shifting friends."

Aiden at least had the decency to look duly put in his place.

"Dr. Li can't help you if you're not honest with him about what's happening." Kane then poked a hard finger at his chest. "You may not give a damn, but I do!"

"It's not that I don't care. I'm saying, I'm learning to live with the changes as they come."

"And I'm saying, you don't have to deal with them alone. I'm your friend. Talk to me."

"Oh. OK. So you'd rather stand here and discuss this than what Skye was saying to her father on your phone?"

Kane scowled at him. "Smart-ass. You know I want to know. But don't think for a second that this conversation—" Kane suddenly cut himself off. "Wait. Did you just say *her father?*"

"Yeah," Aiden replied slowly. "Who were you expecting it to be?"

He had thought it was the man who was supposedly *so* devoted to her, but now he was developing a definite suspicion that he was being duped. If that was the case, then when his little snow angel returned he was going to let her have it. Naturally, that would involve a few more kisses just to torture her. Then he'd figure out what was really going on.

"Argus ordered her to get away from here as fast as possible. I expect she'll try something tonight." Aiden frowned as he anchored his hands on his hips. "He sure as hell doesn't like you. I didn't realize you knew him."

Kane snorted. "Never met the man. But when I do I'm going to have a hard time stopping myself from breaking his jaw."

"Can't say I blame you there. His intention is to let the team bring him here, even after she's gone. My guess is he has a few choice words he'd like to say to you about detaining his daughter."

Kane grinned broadly. "I'm sure he does."

"He plans on meeting up with her afterward at another location. Neither of them let it slip where that was."

Kane roughly slammed his empty juice glass down on the counter. "So we have no idea where she's going or what she intends to do?"

"I wouldn't necessarily say that."

Kane stared at his friend with piqued interest. "Really? And why is that?"

"He said to finish her assignment she needed to 'follow the Lycans home'. My guess would be she intends to go back to the Lycan Dead Zone in northern Alberta. It's where they live in the largest numbers."

"Son of a bitch," Kane growled under his breath. "What? Is he going to have her confront a whole army of them? The man is scum."

"Yeah, well, that's only the beginning of our problems. Throw in the fact that our Wraith seems obsessed with following her and—"

"And you have a fucking hot mess," Kane finished for him, raking his hand through his hair like he intended to pull it all up by the roots. He was beginning to realize that he had no good options here. Skye was determined to escape so she could confront a legion of murdering Lycans with an insane Wraith hot on her tail. Alec was demanding that Aiden be on his way to The Oracle in the morning with Skye in tow. And her father was on his way here to confront him—a confrontation he was actually looking forward to.

Could things be any more crazy?

"She'll be all right," Aiden reassured him. "We'll stop her from leaving. We'll think of something."

"Yes, we will!" Kane replied emphatically, then allowed his thoughts to settle.

"What is it?" Aiden asked.

"Probably nothing," Kane murmured as Aiden stood there looking at him expectantly. "I just don't like the idea of this Wraith returning to the Lycan Dead Zone. He's going through Lycans as if they were tissues. Normally I wouldn't care, but . . ." He took an exaggerated pause as he seemed to consider what he was trying to say. "What if Phin's in there somewhere?"

Aiden sighed, reached for Kane's shoulder, and rested his hand there. "I think we have to tackle one problem at a time, starting with the immediate one. How we're going to make sure Skye doesn't escape from here tonight."

Kane's hand rose to cover his friend's, and his gaze swept up to Aiden's face, the silver of Kane's eyes seeming to light them up like a light bulb as a sly smile slid across his lips. "Actually, I think that's exactly what we should let her do."

CHAPTER ELEVEN

Skye came bursting through The Trek's doors and instantly came face to face with Kane and Aiden as they stood close together at the kitchen island.

Her loud entrance jarred them from their rather private conversation and now their attention was fully on her—exactly what she didn't want. She needed to figure out how she was going to get the heck out of this place before she ended up giving the cliff notes version of her entire existence. But even as escape was foremost in her mind, Skye found herself unable to look directly at Kane. Parts of her were still tingling from the kiss he'd given her that morning—or rather, many kisses—and she feared that the feeling would only get stronger if she stared into those beautiful eyes.

Although she was obviously intent on marching straight to her room, it really didn't surprise her when Kane stepped into her path, blocking her from proceeding any further. He had a knack for making things difficult. His furrowed brows stared down at her with clear concern, however, which was actually rather sweet, considering the undeniable fact that she had stolen his phone this morning. "What's wrong, darlin'? Did Gideon upset you?"

Skye didn't want to talk about Gideon or his questions, so she decided to focus on something she had been meaning to ask for two days. "Why do you keep calling me 'darlin'? By your lack of accent you obviously aren't from the South, so what's with the southern endearments?"

Kane's lips twitched in amusement. "Ah, so you want details—personal history details. That's a good sign that we've moved beyond merely detainer and detainee, don't you think?"

She blinked at him in utter amazement. The man was impossibly arrogant. She tried a few incoherent efforts at speech but soon realized there were no words in her vocabulary up to the tasks of silencing him for any length of time. So she decided instead to just move around him without so much as another syllable and continue to her room, slamming the door behind her.

✲✲✲

Satisfactorily amused at the speed and proficiency with which he'd been able to ruffle Skye's feathers (because it was so much fun ruffling her feathers), Kane turned back to see Gideon entering the hall, looking as if he had no clue that Skye was upset. But that was typical. The man was a damn genius, but more often than not he'd be completely clueless as to when he had pushed too many buttons. "Looks like you've upset the little woman."

"Me?" Gideon questioned, projecting a genuine sincerity that Kane almost had to laugh at. "Actually, Miss Matthews and I had a very lovely conversation—one which has given me great insight into possible clues about her true identity."

Kane waited for what seemed like an endless minute (but in actuality it was probably about two seconds) before throwing up an impatient hand and asking, "And . . . ?"

"Oh, well . . . ," Gideon stumbled, "I need to check on a few things before I can speak of something with any certainty." He was still mumbling something as he made his way to the private office door just past the fireplace, closing it behind him.

Kane's whole expression blanked as he tossed his hands up in the air and slapped them back against his sides. "What the fuck? Does he think I've got weeks to solve this mess?"

Aiden laughed with quiet amusement. "Don't you know him by now? That constipated look on his face means he's close to figuring something out."

"Well, he'd better be. I'm working a little blind here."

Kane walked back to Aiden at the kitchen counter and spoke very quietly, so no one else would hear. "Look, we need to get our plan in place. I'm going to go calm her down—keep her distracted—while you get one of the SUVs packed and ready to go. Make sure there's enough food, clothing and blankets. Oh, and some cash. Pack some weapons underneath."

"Why can't I be the one to calm her down?" Aiden replied, a mocking twist showing up on his lips. "That sounds like a lot more fun."

Kane's gaze narrowed on his friend. "I'm going to pretend I didn't hear that."

"All right, fine. I just can't believe you intend to go through with this cockamamie plan of yours."

"What? By *letting* her escape to head toward Alberta we're accomplishing several things at once here. One," he began, raising his index finger for emphasis, "she'll think she's escaped." He lifted his hands out in front of him and raised his brows as if to emphasize the obviousness of that point. "But it'll be on our terms, so we can keep an eye on her. And we'll make sure she stays far enough away from that damned Dead Zone."

Aiden nodded in simple agreement.

"Two . . . I'm buying myself more time before I end up having to kick her father's ass." That was an important one because rule number nine in the Kane list of seduction secrets was 'never punch out the father in front of the woman'. It was a sexual mood killer. "And three, she's technically heading back toward The Oracle, so I'm *technically* not lying to Alec."

Aiden snorted at that reasoning. It was a stretch too far, even for Kane. "Fucking semantics. You're not going to get away with that one."

"Of course I am," Kane announced in a tone that said he couldn't believe Aiden doubted it.

"Whatever . . . What about the fact the Wraith will still be hunting her?"

Kane smiled, confidence now radiating from him. "Getting her away from here will help solve that problem. And besides, I'm not taking my eyes off her for a second."

"You mean *Bogart* won't be."

Kane, who still had his index finger extended, a leftover from reason one, pointed it at his friend. "When this mission's done, if you ever call me Bogart again, I'm going to kick your ass."

"Please . . . You've been threatening to kick my ass for years over far less."

Well, this time I mean it."

"Duly warned," Aiden replied dryly, not looking overly concerned by the unveiled threat. "I suppose after you've left you want me to stay here and wait for her father. I mean, someone's got to clean up the mess you've created."

With a wicked, wicked quirk to one corner of his lip, Kane replied, "It's no more a mess than usual."

"True. Very true."

❉❉❉

Skye just couldn't seem to stop pacing. She was afraid to look down for fear she had burned a permanent trail into the wood floor. There was no easy way to escape with so much sensitive Dhampir hearing around. It would be difficult at best for her to leave The Trek on foot. And with temperatures below freezing at night and no buildings or homes nearby that she could spot on her walk of the grounds with Gideon, it would be some time before she could get access to a vehicle to drive. But she had to try. The longer she stayed here, the more inept she began to feel. She had a job to do. A simple job.

She knew what she would have to do to escape, but the problem was, she didn't want to hurt anyone—and that included Kane. As much as she didn't want to admit it, given the short time they'd been together, she cared for him. It was a ridiculous notion. The man was a bigger flirt than all the rest of the male species combined, but he wasn't a deceptive flirt. He always put himself out there honestly, even if it didn't show him in the best light—like when he was holding her in his arms after she told him she belonged to another man—and admitted that he would always leave.

Ironically, Kane was the biggest reason why *she* had to leave. He was a major distraction from what she needed to do. *Major!* She could try to blame it on those penetrating silver eyes of his, or perhaps on the distracting way he walked into a room. He had such a lazy, confident *stalk* about him, as if he had all the time in the world to enjoy life, love . . . and women. *God,* who was she kidding? It was his kiss! The man cold kiss a nun into offering her virginity at will. *She had to get out of here!*

Before she knew what she was doing, she dashed right back out of the bedroom and to the kitchen, where Kane was now standing alone. He was fixing himself a turkey sandwich and holding an adorably perplexed expression between his brows. Seriously, was the man not gorgeous enough already that even his contorted facial expressions caused endless fascination? "Where is everyone?" she asked him, a bit grumpily.

He never raised his eyes as he reached into the cupboard for a small plate, then cut his sandwich in half and slid the untouched portion in front of her. "I don't think you've had a chance to eat anything yet today."

"I . . . I haven't." *He was sharing his sandwich?* Now *that* threw her completely off balance. What was she supposed to do with this contemplative and considerate side of Kane? She decided not to over-think it, so instead of standing there perplexed, she headed for the fridge. "You like orange juice, right?" She reached around him for his empty glass, pulling a second clean one from the cupboard.

With a leisurely smile, he leaned his weight back against the counter, forcing her to shoulder past him on route to the fridge. "Ah, darlin', I love that you know me so well already."

"Don't get carried away. I can smell the orange. Actually, I know almost nothing about you, other than you're a Guardian for The Brethren."

"I suppose that's true," he offered, then seemed to consider something for a moment before he crossed his arms in front of him easily. "All right, what do you want to know?"

She should resist . . . but . . ."OK. How old were you when you went to The Brethren?" She returned his glass full of juice and his hand touched hers as he reached for it. Her breath caught with the contact, and that surprised her. You weren't supposed to feel anything when a man—who wasn't your current boyfriend—simply brushed your hand with his. That was just the stuff of chick-flicks and romance novels, and she had no time for either one of those.

She pulled her hand back a touch faster than she had intended. There was no need for him to see how he was affecting her, but she obviously didn't do a very good job at hiding it, as was evident when he chuckled softly with amusement before answering, "Eighteen."

Skye could see he was in a playful mood as he reached for his sandwich and tore into it with an enthusiastic bite, wagging his brows at her. "So, right after high school then?"

"I didn't really have a normal childhood—didn't attend any public schools."

"Were you home-schooled, then?" she heard herself ask—and wondered why she was so eager to know the answer. What the heck happened to the part about *not* getting close to this man? Before he had a chance to answer her question, she almost compulsively felt the need to share information about her own childhood, which she was never supposed to do. "My father home-schooled us. It was fine and all, but I think it would've been nice to meet more people at school. When my sisters and I were fighting it would become a pretty small house . . . you know?"

Kane remained contentedly quiet as he watched her top off his glass with more juice and then slide it beside his hip. She had moved in extra close, and in doing so she made it possible for him to get a good whiff of the bath oil he seemed to be so fond of, and it surprised her. She had no idea why she did it. She supposed that at the moment she just felt a little closer to him, like perhaps they might have something in common.

His easy grin told her he picked up the scent just fine, and that pleased her more than she ever wanted to admit, as evidenced by the wild butterflies currently fluttering through her stomach. "I think I've changed my mind about you," he drawled, leaning in until his breath was just a breeze over her neck. "You're no angel, darlin'."

Skye's heart was pounding like a speaker on volume ten. She quickly straightened from the counter, then scurried over to the other side, using the island as a barrier between them—which was what she should've done from the moment he'd handed her the damn sandwich. She cleared her throat in an effort to start this conversation over again on a more formal level. "You didn't answer my question."

He leaned forward onto his elbows and in one movement erased most of the distance she had just gained. "Yes, I was homeschooled. I also lived with a large family—an adoptive family of sorts." He waggled his brows for a second time. "All sisters. They took care of me after my parents died."

"I'm sorry to hear about your parents. How did they die?"

He paused. "It's a long story. One maybe better for another day."

Skye felt something sink inside her just then. She rather liked that he was sharing something of his past, something personal. '*A strange sentiment*', she thought, considering she was making plans to escape. A long silence followed, but it was a natural silence, not at all uncomfortable.

"And before you ask me your next question," he eventually continued, "the answer's yes. I loved growing up in a house full of women who showered me with attention and affection." He then leaned in closer (as if that was possible). "And yes, it probably has made me the irresistible man that I am today."

She laughed, a surprisingly unbidden and delighted chortle. That hadn't been her next question at all, but she believed he already knew that "Actually, when I said you didn't answer my question, I meant about where everyone was."

"Ah. Well, Lucky and the fellas can't spend all their time chasing down this Wraith. Alec has them up here for a reason. There's a nasty little clan of warlocks that have made a home up here. Every once in a while they like to cause all sorts of trouble. It's Lucky's job to keep tabs on them."

His stare was unflinching as he wolfed down another bite of his sandwich and capped it off with the rest of his juice. He certainly did love juice. She rather doubted he even took enough time to taste it as he swallowed. "And Aiden and Gideon?"

His tongue flicked out to wipe his bottom lip—and she hated that she noticed. "Gideon probably has his head buried in a bunch of text books, and Aiden's packing up one of the SUVs."

She took a much smaller bite of her sandwich and had to admit Kane was a darn good sandwich maker. He even had fresh avocado slices in there, which were her favorite. "Packing?"

Kane waved a dismissive hand through the air. "Oh, yeah. He and I are going hunting for our Wraith tomorrow. Could be a long day, so he's making sure we have everything we need for a *good . . . long . . .* day of tracking."

"Yes, you mentioned that."

But strangely, Kane seemed to want to go on. "You know, just the basics . . . food, water, blankets . . . some cash."

Skye finished another bite of her sandwich. "So you're going to be gone all day?"

The smile on his handsome face broadened and Skye detected a hint of mischief creeping into it. Honestly, the man had the ability to seduce . . . well, anything.

He pushed back from the counter and walked around to her side of the island. As he approached, she swallowed thickly, literally feeling the heat of him at her back. Calmly, she set her sandwich down and took another sip of her juice. "Gonna miss me?" he asked, presumptively, and without waiting for her response he drawled, "Aw, that's sweet. But don't be getting any bright ideas. Lucky's going to be watching over you carefully."

She couldn't be sure, but he said that almost as if he was daring her.

The next thing she knew, she was being swung around on her stool, his arms bracketing her on each side of the countertop, a position she was oddly comfortable with. He was so close, if she just lifted her chin the slightest degree she would make contact with his lips. And she wanted to, just like the first time he kissed her senseless in the front seat of that SUV. *How did he keep doing this?* How did he manage to make her feel as if she could just stay still with him in the moment . . . forever?

"We need to discuss this bad-girl behavior of yours," he said in a teasing voice. Skye simply blinked up at him, not quite sure what he was going to say next. "You had me so mindlessly distracted earlier with those beautiful lips of yours, I didn't feel you lifting my phone. That's impressive." Her breath came in a sharp rush as his hands slid down to her hips. "I consider myself very sensitive to that sort of thing."

"I . . . I just needed to borrow it for one tiny phone call," she measured between her fingertips. "I was going to return it."

He leaned further into her, crowding her, overwhelming her, and for a moment it felt good not to breathe. "If you'd asked me, Skye, I would've given you the phone. If you remember, I offered it to you and your sisters that first day."

"Well . . . I didn't need it that first day. I needed it today."

He laughed, but it sounded more like a growl, or maybe a purr. She swore the man could purr. "So who did you need to call? Mr. Fantastic? The guy who is just head-over-heels gone for you?"

"I never said he was head-over—"

That was all she got out because he interrupted her with a kiss—a sweet kiss, actually. Just an innocent brush, making her question if it had really been his lips she'd felt or merely the heat of his breath. But that question didn't last for long as those same soft lips met the skin of her throat and traced downward, his teeth scraping lightly until he reached the fleshy part of her shoulder and nipped playfully. *Mercy,* but he was good at the kissing thing, and she had no doubt he was good at a lot of other things, as well. "It was kind of implied with the whole '*I belong to him*' part."

"Kane," she responded with all breath, "someone could walk in."

"Yes, they could," he whispered, just before he captured her lips in a full-on kiss that captured her breath and instantly seemed to fuse her to him. She wished she could say she was fighting the stolen kiss, but instead she softened underneath it. Kane's shoulders curled into her as his fingers began to dig into her hips, the weight of him against her feeling like the perfect pressure as his kisses deepened and she tasted the orange on his tongue. *God,* he was delicious! And the moment was so incredibly powerful, possessive, intimate—whatever word that best describes bliss—that she began to shiver in his arms. She had never felt this way, this tingly helplessness. Like she knew she had no choice but to surrender to what he wanted.

"Kane?" This time his name was just a whisper on her breath as he released her from the kiss, but the heat in his eyes held her frozen. He stared at her as if he could see so much more than anyone else had before him—and it amazed her, amazed her as much as it excited her. Kane obviously felt it, too, because he seemed to come to a decision at that moment. His hands wrapped her legs around his hips, and next thing she knew he had lifted her off the stool and pulled her against his chest. She breathed heavily over his shoulder as he carried her down the hall as though she weighed next to nothing.

She should stop this. She *really* should stop this! Skye issued this warning to herself even as she felt her back sink into the mattress and the heat of his skin seep through her clothes. He followed her down, his body covering her, continuing to press against her until she felt sure she couldn't breathe. It was all too much. "Damn, Skye," he murmured in her ear, "I feel the heat in your hands when you touch me. Just don't stop touching me."

"We can't do this," she breathed, even as her hands continued to do exactly that—touch him. "I can't."

"Does *he* make you feel this way?" Kane growled, a raw roughness in his voice now. "Does he let you know how much he needs you to touch him?"

She didn't answer. She couldn't. The answer was too painful to face—because she knew it was *no*. And she was ashamed that in this moment she could barely remember what Andrew Darrington III looked like, but Kane sure didn't need to know that. "Y—Yes . . ."

"You're lying. I can tell you're lying. And if you reach into my pocket right now for that damn phone, I swear I will take you right here against this bed. I don't care who walks in on us."

Phone? The thought hadn't even occurred to her, but now the image of him taking her, making her completely his, wouldn't leave her head. Andrew would be furious if he knew she was betraying him beneath another man's kisses, fantasizing what it would feel like to have another man inside of her, but she still couldn't seem to stop herself.

Kane kissed her deeper and her whole body began to shiver. His kisses just had a way of making her feel truly desired, and that was something that had been missing between her and Andrew for a while. Still, Skye would have to put a stop to this little hot-n-heavy session, but part of her—the devilish part— wanted to continue experiencing this feeling of utter joy for just a little while longer.

She sighed as Kane sank against her body, the hard proof of his need pressing against her inner thigh as he continued to drown her in kisses. They were both still fully dressed, but Skye felt as though they were already stripped bare in front of each other. He smiled against her lips, the sweet taste of oranges exploding inside her head. "I need you, sweet Skye."

Her open palm lay against his cheek as she showed him a concerned smile. "It doesn't matter what you or I need. We can't do this," she told him. "I should've never let things get this far."

Kane just stared at her for the longest time, refusing to move from their very intimate position on the bed. "Just one thing," he finally asked. "If you were not with *him*, would you be stopping me now?"

"It doesn't matter, because I *am* with him."

"It matters," he answered soundly. "It matters to me."

Skye closed her eyes, trying to determine if she could fully admit to him the truth of her feelings. Somehow it just seemed easier to decide if she wasn't looking right at him.

'*I need you, too!*' Those were the words on the tip of her tongue just before she opened her eyes to see him begin to draw back, his breath now struggling as a lost glaze began to roll into his eyes. Both her hands now went to his flushed cheeks and held him gently in place before the powerful weight of him became heavier against her much smaller body. He tried to shake his head, but it didn't seem to clear any of the bleariness. "Damn it," he cursed under his breath. "What did you do, Skye?"

She stared up at him and could feel the heat stinging her eyes, the tear that had slipped from the corner and rolled into her hair. Kane had no strength left in his limbs as his body fell completely slack against her.

"I'm sorry," she whispered.

CHAPTER TWELVE

Kane thought he was going to have to pry open his eyelids with a crow bar, and the mere idea of it only seemed to aggravate the hammering going on in his brain.

He was trying to remember where the hell he was. Except for the obvious fact that he was sprawled face down and freely drooling onto a bed sheet, he wasn't able to deduce much of anything else. Rolling slowly onto on his side with a stiff groan, he said, "Son of a bitch," and it scraped against his throat.

A large hand then settled on his shoulder.

"Take it easy," Gideon spoke above him. "You've been dosed with a hypnotic. Chloral-hydrate, I would guess."

Kane had to blink back his amazement, but for a moment he feared his eyes had rolled back into his head. *Damn!* This was the hangover from hell. "What the fuck happened? I can't remember anything."

Gideon assisted him to a seated position at the edge of the bed. "No. No you probably won't. It appears that was Miss Matthews's intent."

"Skye?" Kane blinked with disbelief.

The sympathetic look in the older man's eyes confirmed that was the right answer, but Kane refused to believe it. "Do you remember her offering you any food or drink?"

"I'm telling you, I don't remember a damned thing." Kane had to admit, his ego was pricked. He didn't want to believe—couldn't believe—his sweet, defiant Skye, with her jutted little chin, had slipped him a Mickey. Had she wanted to escape here, escape *him,* that badly? If his muscles weren't so lazy from the drug, he swore he would be itching for a fight because of the betrayal he felt inside.

"I'm afraid that after leaving you here she made quick work of Aiden and Lucky with an offering of freshly squeezed lemonade. Lucky had just returned, ahead of his team, and she was probably very fortunate it was just him. Judging by how quickly Aiden recovered from the drug's effects, I don't believe it would've had much effect on the Dhampirs."

"Where is she now?" he asked with a thick tongue and some very nasty breath. "I need to give her a piece of my mind."

But before Gideon could answer, both men watched in stunned silence as the next events unfolded in what seemed like super slow motion, making the moment that much more surreal. A tall figure with a bright cap of red hair stumbled just beyond the frame of the door and into the room, then nosedived straight into the wood floor, his arms flailing as he emitted a single, guttural grunt, the likes of which Kane doubted even he could match. It was an embarrassingly clumsy display of a man hitting the floor if there ever was one. One would think it was the first time Lucky had ever tried to walk.

"Jaysus!" the Irish-laced curse boomed. Evidently, Lucky was having just as hard a time getting his feet firmly beneath him as Kane was, but at least Kane had the good sense to know not to move until the world stopped spinning. "I got it. I got it," Lucky announced with several hard thwacks against the wall as he literally crawled up it until he was standing on his feet again.

Sort of.

"Right now I feel as useful as tits on a bull," he declared in a voice that sounded as if it was speaking his first words in the morning.

Kane shook his head with an empathetic grimace. "Man, how much lemonade did you drink?"

Lucky removed a hand from the wall and pointed a sharp finger at Kane, but that simple action looked as if it might cause him to tip right back over. "I told you that little chit was the devil hiding under the face of an angel."

Kane then suddenly grabbed Gideon's arm. It wasn't a firm grip by any means, but it was enough to get his urgency across. "Where is she?"

"I'm afraid she's gone. She left with one of the SUVs."

"Where's Aiden?"

"I'm here," Aiden said as he pushed past Lucky, who currently looked as if he was trying to get the taste of dog shit off his tongue. The contrast between the two men was striking. Aiden was sharp, reactive, and most importantly standing just fine, while Lucky was . . . not.

"Did she take the right SUV?"

"Oh yeah," Aiden replied with clear sarcasm. "She fell for that part of the plan—hook, line and sinker."

Gideon's brows lifted curiously. "Plan? Miss Matthews escaping was a plan?"

"Yeesss," Kane answered, rubbing his hands over his face.

"Well, it wasn't a very good one," Gideon pointed out, always having a knack for the obvious.

"Not the part where she knocks us out with a psychotropic drug, no," Aiden added with an exaggerated sigh. "I overheard her on the phone, earlier, making plans with her father to escape. So we came up with a plan—granted, a rather stupid plan, looking back on it now—to provide her with a safe way of doing it. Then we could follow her. Kane was distracting her while I loaded the vehicle."

Aiden then turned to Kane with a sly smile. "By the way . . . you were doing a damned fine job of distraction."

Surprisingly, that raised Kane's hackles. He was worried about Skye being out there alone, but another, more practical, part of him was actually angry that he couldn't remember the time he'd spent with her before she left. Even if it was nothing more than simple kisses, he wanted the memory. He wanted all his memories with her. It was completely unlike him—but somehow important.

"I think it's clear," Gideon announced to everyone, "that we've all underestimated Miss Matthews."

"No shit," Kane snapped back. "And just how is it that you managed to escape the lemonade from hell?"

Gideon's head bobbed back slightly at the question before straightening his glasses on the bridge of his nose. "I was working in the office. Evidently, Miss Matthews did not consider me a threat to her plans for escape."

Kane rolled his eyes as he finally stood on somewhat shaky legs and mockingly replied, "Nooo. You—not a threat? Imagine that."

While Gideon seemed to give that comment some considerable thought, Kane's increasingly cranky mood turned on Aiden. "And how is it that you remember all the details before we were juiced and I don't?"

Aiden shrugged his shoulders. "Different reaction to the drug."

Kane glared at his friend. "Right."

He knew he should be grateful that one of them could remember something more than his name. The information would help them find Skye sooner. But to him it was only more evidence that Aiden's chemical make-up was changing faster than any of them could keep up with. "Tell me we've got a tracking device on her."

Aiden nodded. "Inside that suitcase she was so determined to leave here with. We also have the GPS tag on the vehicle. Looks like she's still moving south, as we expected . . . but . . . she's got a nine-hour head start on us."

Kane blinked. "Nine hours! I've been out for nine hours?"

"Yes, that *is* rather unfortunate," Gideon rather unhelpfully pointed out. "But on the better side of things, I'm making progress on getting you your answers regarding Miss Matthews's identity."

Kane threw his hands up in a sort of bewildered stutter. "And it's taken you this long to say something? What've you got?"

"I'm waiting for some information from Yannis to confirm some things."

"Yannis?" Kane questioned.

Gideon nodded. "Yannis Boros. He's a Guide for The Nave location—the Brethren in Munich. Fascinating man, actually . . . His insight into—"

"Gideon," Kane growled. "My head can't handle this right now." Skye was on her way toward the Lycan Dead Zone, *alone*, with a nine-hour head start and a Wraith possibly hot on her tail. The ongoing ramblings about some man's accomplishments could wait. "I need to know what you know. Now!"

Gideon placed a firm hand on Kane's shoulder, his eyes sincere. "I understand how important this is to you. But I don't want to give you misinformation. It's too important. Assuming the wrong thing could put her in even more danger."

"She already *is* in danger!"

"I will tell you," Gideon continued calmly, "that I believe she and her family are, in fact, part of the supernatural world, and that she possesses gifts that will help her protect herself."

"Gideon!" Kane began with emphasis, trying to keep his temper intact. "I've watched that Wraith nearly run her into the ground like a bulldozer. How can you possibly stand here and tell me she can protect herself?"

"Because there must be something specific about this Wraith we're missing. And as soon as we solve that riddle we will understand a much bigger part of the puzzle." He stood from his sitting position on the bed and patted his hand on Kane's shoulder once more. "I promise I'll have some answers for you soon."

"Call me when you do," he said with a raised voice to his retreating form. "I'll be on the road in twenty."

"I'm coming with you," Aiden announced, but Kane shook his head in return.

"I need you here to deal with her father when he arrives. Do whatever you have to do to stall him. Make him believe she's had to change her plans. It may force him to show his hand a little." He tapped at his forehead with his fingers, and was thankful his brain didn't start ringing. "And call Oliver. Tell him to make sure that Argus doesn't make any phone calls. That's the only way we'll keep the one small advantage that we have at the moment."

"And you?" Aiden questioned.

Kane, still under the influence of orange juice, was just trying to walk a straight line out of the room without looking like a complete idiot. That title could forever belong to Lucky after that eight-point-five dismount he displayed down the hallway. "When I find her," he mumbled, more to himself, "I'm going to take her over my knee and give her the spanking she soooo deserves."

CHAPTER THIRTEEN

Nearly twenty-eight hours later, after enduring winter driving conditions for much of the way and very little sleep, Kane was still mentally cursing Skye's name as he pulled into the sleepy little town of Hunter's Landing.

The village itself was set along the northern shore of the Peace River, at the edge of Wood Buffalo National Park, not more than a couple of hours from the Lycan Dead Zone. This was where his ballsy little escape artist had dumped her SUV before continuing east, but not before leaving a well-worded note of apology on the front dash for stealing the vehicle in the first place—and providing an address for its safe return. She even went so far as to re-fill the gas tank before abandoning it.

Unbelievable.

The lilac-colored paper she used still held a trace of her scent as he read the postscript. "Kane, I'm sorry."

Kane wanted to smile at that, but then he remembered that she'd drugged him and taken off without any regard for her own safety. And if she thought Kane would just shrug his shoulders and say 'Oh, well, have a nice trip', she was in for a rude awakening.

He had to admit, though, his behavior regarding a woman who couldn't seem to run away from him fast enough was a bit perplexing. If he scanned his memory banks he was sure he could think of another similar incident where he had detained a beautiful woman and then chased her ass all over Canada just to make sure she kept herself alive . . . especially if he wanted to bed her.

Thinking. Thinking. Thinking . . .

Well, maybe not a situation in which he traipsed all over Canada, or Alberta, or even The Oracle grounds, but he was quite sure he had to chase Astrid around the kitchen a couple of times . . . and it was a large kitchen.

As he continued driving east, keeping one eye on the device monitoring the tracker hidden in her suitcase, his mind conjured up all the trouble she could have gotten herself into in the many hours since he'd last seen her, especially considering she was back near Brahm Hill. Just the thought of her there alone made his hands tense over the steering wheel. He had a bad feeling that the Wraith was heading the exact same direction.

God, she was quite possibly insane.

But he still wanted to kiss her again. Almost desperately.

Those silky-soft lips of hers were more tempting than an ice-cold beer in sunshine or an afternoon catnap in a summer breeze. He would do anything to feel her lips on his again, or on any other part of his body that she wanted to kiss, for that matter. That's why, when he found himself standing outside the small cabin door he'd tracked her to in the middle of nowhere, the last thing he needed to hear was her raised voice arguing with someone inside.

The other voice was a man's voice.

❊❊❊

"I told you, you don't need to worry, I'm fine," Skye reiterated for the third time since Andrew Darrington III had surprised her at the door to her family's cabin. And '*surprised*' was the perfect word to describe it because she had not told him where she was—had not spoken to him since before her whole ordeal with Kane began. *That* had been intentional.

There was no doubt she had her father to thank for this little drop-in visit. Argus Matthews could be nosier than a hedgehog on pine, especially when he knew a man was "*the one*" for one of his daughters. She had let his unwelcomed interference slide in the past because she knew he only wanted to see her happy, and for the most part, Andrew was a good man. He was confident and handsome—in that socially polished sort of way —and he showed a sharp mind for numbers and business. If she didn't marry him (which was completely out of the question where her father was concerned), then there would no doubt be a line-up of available women waiting to take her place.

That was when Skye mentally checked herself, realizing what she had just thought: '*if she didn't marry him*'. She hadn't really considered that before now. Andrew had practically grown up with her and her family. He had been a good friend, her best friend maybe—besides her sisters, of course. If Skye wanted a counseling opinion, a sympathetic ear, or even a stick of gum, he was right there to offer it. It was just understood that he was the one she was meant to be with. There had never been any reason to doubt it.

Until now . . .

Now she did doubt it, and she was afraid to examine the 'why' too closely because she feared it had something to do with the most beautiful silver eyes she'd ever seen and kisses that melted her into a puddle on contact—kisses that even now she shouldn't be thinking about. But she was thinking about them as Skye poured two small glasses of orange juice, even though Andrew hadn't asked for a drink and he had never been a 'juice' kind of guy. He was strictly coffee in the morning and wine in the evening, but right now she felt comforted by the action of pouring juice. "My father shouldn't have sent you here. He knows I'm finishing an assignment."

"Damn it, Skye!" Andrew cursed with tempered frustration. "He's been worried sick about you—we've all been worried about you, and you left before we even had a chance to talk about what happened."

Skye downed her juice in one long gulp and then set the glass down on the counter, unable to evade the small burp that followed. "Maybe I didn't think there was anything left to say."

After a quick, hard blink, Andrew just stared at her. One would have thought she had just announced she could fly. "Nothing left to say?" he repeated back to her, setting his own untouched glass of juice down roughly and then sliding it away from her grasp when she reached for it. That action had surprised Skye. She just thought someone might as well drink the juice if he wasn't going to. "How about the fact we love each other? That we've been together our entire lives. I know

you better than anyone, and I respect you. Christ, I waited for
years until you said you were finally ready to sleep with me."

That was certainly true enough.

Andrew had been no less than a saint while Skye hemmed
and hawed about whether or not she was ready to give her
virginity to him. It was silly, really. She knew she was meant to
be with him, but still there was this tiny little part of her that
always questioned if she was ready, and so she waited. Then,
one day, after thinking about it long enough, she decided she
didn't want to be a virgin anymore. So she wasn't.

Their first time together hadn't been spectacular, but it was
nice. I mean, let's face it, Skye had been so wrapped up in
whether or not she should that she hadn't considered how
clueless she was in the whole '*lighting a man's world on fire*'
part. Andrew had been patient with her, though—definitely
patient—because she seemed to be a little slow in the heating
up department. He assured her it was just because she let
herself get too nervous and that things would get better as she
learned to relax and let go. That had been true enough, she
supposed, as she learned how to please him. Skye had now
shared a bed with Andrew for a couple of years, and she had
believed they had found a comfortable place with each other.
But still, after two whole years, her response was something
she had to work at, and she couldn't help wondering if she was
just less responsive than other women. And that bothered her
because generally she was a very secure person.

Kissing, she was fine. That was another story entirely. Skye
loved to kiss and felt as if she gave a hundred and ten percent of
herself in her kisses. She simply saw it as the best part of being
with a man, snuggling and kissing. And Andrew was a good
kisser, but Kane . . . well, he was something else—entirely.

"Sweet pea," Andrew broke into her thoughts, "we just need
some time together to work this out—to work through our
problems." Skye wanted to groan. She hated the endearment
'sweet pea'. She wasn't a vegetable, for *pea's* sake. "But
instead . . . ," he continued, his sandy hair having fallen forward
over his eyebrows, "you go running off to Seattle—then Alberta
—then the Northwest Territories. How am I supposed to keep
up? Are you wanting me to chase you? Because it's working."

"No, I don't want you to chase me. And I wasn't running," she defended. "I told you I had an assignment."

He stared at her as if he didn't believe her, but she really did have an assignment. "You were running and you know it." Skye studied him carefully just then, taking note of the patrician way he lifted his shoulders high and slightly back, the proud set of his jaw. Andrew was a man who had few self-confidence issues, a trait Skye was beginning to realize she was drawn to in men. Andrew Darrington III was like an immoveable object when he got a point stuck in his head . . . just like her father.

"I'll admit, the timing was convenient," she allowed. "I needed to think. It isn't every day you learn the man who supposedly loves you betrays you with another woman."

Oh, yeah, that part hadn't done much to bolster her confidence in her own lovemaking skills, either. She couldn't remember ever feeling such shame in her life as the night he had confessed to her the encounter he had with a co-worker. For just a moment she wondered if she should cut him some slack because he had come to her about it honestly. Andrew had recognized the problem and sincerely wanted to fix it. But she couldn't cut him any slack. She felt too betrayed.

It wasn't supposed to be like this.

"I told you I was sorry at least a dozen times," he said, exhaling an exasperated breath. "I came to you and was honest about everything because I was ready to commit to whatever it would take to make things right between us again. I've been practically on my knees begging for your forgiveness, and still you refuse to even talk about this so we can get past it."

Skye blinked. "Get past this? I don't want to '*get past this*'. I want to remember what it feels like to be betrayed by the man who's supposed to love you for all eternity. Maybe it'll prevent me from making the mistake of trusting you in the future."

"Oh Christ, now you're just being dramatic. It only happened one time, and I've promised you it won't happen again. What more do you want?"

She didn't know how to answer that question. Skye no longer knew if she loved this man, if she belonged to him without question, as she was supposed to. "Maybe this was a sign, Andrew," she murmured sadly. "A sign that we're no longer right for each other."

"I don't believe this," he said, slapping his hands against his leg. "You're going to use this as an excuse to come between us."

"It's not an excuse! Your affair has come between us."

Andrew rubbed his hand over his face, which now clearly showed the weight of his exhaustion. "Look . . . it's not like we are the only couple to have to work their way through some stuff."

Skye felt her blood beginning to boil at his words. "*Stuff?* This particular *stuff,* as you call it, was not something *we* did. *You* did this! You didn't love me enough to stay faithful to me. That's not good enough!"

And her father would back her a hundred and ten percent on this—if he had any idea. Skye had told him they had just been working through some things because she wanted to spare Andrew her father's full temper. Argus Matthews would be the first to kick the man out the door with a hard foot to his ass if he knew. That was one thing he would never tolerate from a man dating his daughter—cheating. And even though telling her father would give her an ally instead of the current force she was having to work against, there was no way she would tell him the truth.

Skye didn't want to admit to anyone that she was the only one of her sisters to ever be cheated on by a soul mate. What did that say about her? Was she not worthy of being loved faithfully?

"I made a mistake . . . a big mistake," Andrew said in a calmer voice. "I know I was wrong. But you're always gone on some assignment, and it just seems like this life your father has carved out for you is more important than everything else— even more than us!"

"My father didn't 'carve' this life for me. It's my calling. What we do matters to a lot of good people. And, quite frankly, I'm surprised you don't get that."

"I do get it," he groaned. "I mean, as much as I can with the limited information you're giving me. Why can't you trust me enough to tell me everything?"

That was a very good question, one she just couldn't answer. She should have been able to trust him with the whole truth years ago, but again . . . she didn't.

He stepped closer to her and ran his fingertips along her arms. "All I'm asking for is what we have right here. Some time alone to work through this. I know it's not going to be easy, but if we just talk, we can figure it out. You have to know she meant nothing to me."

Skye pushed away in an instant, turning her back on him because she couldn't bear to look at him right now. "Well, that makes it so much better. You cheated on me with a woman who means nothing to you. What ever would I have done if she actually meant something?"

When he remained silent for some time, she turned back to face him, and saw the injured surprise in his expression. He sat back, wobbly on one of the kitchen island barstools, looking as if she had just slapped him. In the entire time she had known him, this was the first time she had ever seen him at a loss for words. "I'm sorry," she said. "That was below the belt."

"Are you ever going to be able to forgive me?" he asked, as though it was occurring to him for the first time that she might not.

Skye could feel the tears building in her eyes, but she willed them back. "Yes. As my friend, I can forgive you. I could forgive you almost anything. But I can't build a life with you Andrew—not after this. The trust I had for you as a life companion and lover is gone."

Skye then walked over to the hard-sided suitcase she had yet to unpack and drew out a small, velvet box. Returning to him, she placed it in his hand and then curled his large fingers around it so he wouldn't drop it. His face grimaced into a painful expression as he held it. "When I came in and saw you weren't wearing this, it was the first moment I realized I was truly scared of losing you. I thought if I gave you time you would . . ."

His thoughts seemed to drift for a moment before he gripped the box firmly in his fist and slipped it into his pocket. "I'm not sure what I thought."

"I'm sorry, Andrew. I'm not doing this to hurt you. I just know in my heart that if you truly loved me as you should . . . as it should be . . . then *she* would've never happened. Right now I have to trust that, but I would like us to still be friends . . . at the very least for my father's sake, since he adores you so. Do you think we could do that?"

Andrew looked at her, his expression completely blank as he surprised her with, "I don't know. Give me some time." *He was now asking her for time?* She hadn't thought far enough ahead to consider the possibility of losing him in her life altogether. "Ever since I was old enough to know any better, I've wanted you as my wife, Skye . . . not as a friend."

Skye squeezed her hands over his, but he pulled them away, almost as if she were causing him physical pain. "I can stay with you," he offered. "At least until your father gets here. I don't like the idea of you being alone after everything you've been through this week."

"I'm fine," she sighed. "It really wasn't a big deal. They were detaining me, but I was well taken care of."

Skye felt more than slightly guilty as she said that. She thought about that last moment, where Kane had her flat on her back on the bed, curling his body into hers and kissing her senseless. Not one of her finer moments, and slightly hypocritical. But Skye felt in her heart that breaking completely from Andrew was best for both of them. She could now move forward with her life, completely devoted to her assignments and free of her problems with Andrew and that distracting womanizer, Kane. *Thank God*, she wasn't involved with him. There would be no way that walking sex symbol would stay faithful to any woman.

About an hour later, Skye finally saw Andrew off. He had a friend who lived in Edmonton, a few hours away, so she didn't have to feel too guilty about sending him on his way instead of offering him a place to stay for the night. Given where they left things, however, she guessed he wouldn't have wanted to, anyway.

After his car disappeared into the distance, Skye walked back into the small, four-room wood cabin, where there was just enough space for a modest, open main room, a bathroom, and a decent-sized master suite with private bath. Her father had built it for her mother with his own hands before Skye was even born. In many ways, this place was like a second home, since she and her two older sisters had come here with their parents every summer for years and years. But that was before Star, daughter number four, was born and the Matthews family became too large for the quaint cabin in the woods. Though they all took turns using it every once in a while for a nice getaway, the cabin remained empty most of the time, which was a shame. Time may have brought on a few rough spots, but her father's wonderful wood craftsmanship and her mother's sense of homey touches still made the cabin feel cozy, even after all this time.

It had been no accident, though, that her father had chosen this particular place to locate the cabin. It was, conveniently, only about an hour away from the Lycan Dead Zone. Close enough so you could get to it quickly, but far enough away so you could sleep at night. She was going to need some sleep if she were to properly focus on her assignment again in the morning.

Skye stepped back inside and closed the solid pine door, letting her weight fall back against it for a moment as she inhaled a deep breath and closed her eyes. It had been a long day—a long couple of days—what with the drive here and the encounter with Andrew, so she looked forward to getting some much needed rest.

But when she opened her eyes, she inhaled sharply in disbelief as she saw the enormous black jaguar sitting calmly on the floor in front of her, his ears lifted expectantly.

"Bogart . . . ?"

CHAPTER FOURTEEN

"What're you doing here?" Skye screeched at the giant cat—as if it made perfectly logical sense for a jaguar to understand English—"... and better yet, how did you get here?"

For his part, Bogart simply plopped down on his belly, resting his head over his outstretched paws, appearing almost bored as Skye began to have what could only be described as an apoplectic fit in the middle of the small cabin kitchen. She paced back and forth several times in not that many steps, trying to decide if she was terrified or excited by the logical answer to that question. How did the big cat get here?

"There's only one way you could have done it," she said with quite a bit of panic, and then she bolted back out the door, scanning the single lane drive to the house as she ran, and then circled around the back, expecting to see some sign that Kane and The Brethren had found her. But, in a strange way, that didn't make any sense to her. Why, once she had left them all to a peaceful, drug-induced sleep, would they bother to track her all the way here? Surely, they had better things to do than track an unarmed woman back into Alberta. Didn't Kane mention something about some nasty warlocks they had to deal with?

Skye ran back inside and slammed the door behind her, falling back against it with her hand over her heart. "Are they here?" she asked Bogart with nothing but her breath driving her words. "Of, course they're here. They have to be here. Or they're close," she sighed.

Bogart tilted his head, looking at her as if he thought she was insane for speaking to him as if she expected him to answer . . . *which she was.* If she were smart, she would pack up the few things she had managed to get unpacked and be out the door in the next thirty seconds. Her father had told her to stay here until he arrived, but The Brethren had many resources.

They would know how to find her if they really wanted to, and she couldn't allow that to happen. She couldn't give them the answers they wanted, and she was running out of time to complete her assignment. She was tired of running. She was tired, period.

Then the most unexpected thing happened. Skye burst into a jittery sort of laugh and sank to her knees in an awkward heap right there on her mother's favorite shag carpet. She dropped her head into her hands and asked out loud to herself —since Bogart obviously wasn't going to answer, "Is he here?" Her voice this time was much shakier. "Because I don't know if can deal with seeing Kane right now."

Suddenly, feeling too exhausted to do much else, Skye reached for a pillow from the sofa and curled up there on the rug. A few tears fell from her eyes and over her cheeks—and she decided she just needed to let them come. She had just broken off her engagement to the man she had grown up with since she was a girl and the lover he had become for the past two years. In her heart she knew she had done the right thing. Something was just not right, even though she couldn't put her finger on one specific thing. The answer seemed to more lie in a whole lot of small things that added up to one big 'no'.

It was then she felt the weight of Bogart's big body press against her back. How on earth could she forget about an enormous jaguar? The heat of his coat seeped in to her almost immediately, along with the steady thunder of his heart. With one giant lick over her cheek he tried to remove her tears, followed by several smaller glides of his tongue that, in some weird way, felt more like little textured kisses. "I'll figure it all out tomorrow," she murmured with slowly blinking eyes. Within minutes, she was fast asleep.

✳✳✳

The next morning, Skye came awake upon feeling a sharp chill, then quickly curled back under the comfort and warmth of the thick wool blanket covering her. It was odd how she had been so tired the night before that she didn't even remember grabbing the blanket, or moving up from the floor to the much cozier living room sofa.

She did feel well rested and relaxed but decided it had been a bad idea to fall asleep the night before without something solid in her stomach, because her mind was playing tricks on her now. Her favorite breakfast scents—pancakes, eggs, bacon, fresh roasted coffee—all drifted over her like the perfect 5-star brunch. The scents were positively heavenly and a nice accompaniment to the warmth of the morning sun that was shining onto her cheeks as it beamed through the cabin's windows. That was when it occurred to her she would not only have to feed herself but Bogart, as well. Just what the heck did you feed a three-hundred-pound jaguar, anyway?

The chill she experienced as she awoke was because Bogart wasn't curled behind her anymore, which also left her feeling strangely bereft. Skye had felt comforted by the large cat's presence and had slept better than she could remember in a long while. Then the sizzling sound of something in a hot pan made Skye realize that the fresh smell of breakfast was not a figment of her imagination. She sat up with a start and stared over the backrest and toward the kitchen, rubbing her hands over her eyes to clear her vision . . . because she couldn't believe what—who—she was seeing.

"So, you're finally up," Kane said in a throaty, morning voice that sent an immediate warm shiver through her. "For a minute there I thought you might sleep all morning."

Skye rubbed her eyes again before she could fully focus upon Kane standing there in faded blue jeans, bare feet and a white-collared shirt that was open all the way down the front, making it impossible to ignore his wonderfully sculpted abs. *Mercy*, did the man ever know how to work a spatula as he flipped a couple of pancakes onto a plate already loaded with fried eggs and fragrant bacon . . . and a large glass of juice already poured.

"W—what? H—how did you . . . ?" was all Skye could manage to say as Kane smiled at her.

"Oh, I let myself in a couple of hours ago. I'm assuming the 'how' you muttered is how did I find you so quickly." He stared at her with the most innocent quirk to his lips. "Did I forget to mention my job for The Brethren is tracking? Or, should I say, my *assignment?*"

Skye shot him a scrunched little scowl. Yes, he had forgotten to mention that critical little piece of information. "Where's Bogart?" she nearly snapped, and it surprised her how quickly he affected her mood. But, then again, being outsmarted tended to do that to her.

He laughed quietly to himself in response. "Oh, he's around here somewhere. You seem to have taken quite a liking to him."

"He's a good companion," she said with an expectant lift to her brows. "He knows his manners and is much more entertaining than *some* people I know." The pointed insult was impossible to miss, yet it didn't seem to bother him in the slightest.

"I suppose that's true," he replied easily, squeezing on an ungodly amount of maple syrup over the buttered short-stack he'd just loaded onto the plate and carrying it toward her. The combination of the man and the maple syrup practically caused Skye to moan out loud. She loved extra butter and extra syrup on her pancakes, and her stomach took notice, rumbling with a loud '*yes, please*' in her belly as he approached.

"I assume you came with Bogart," she said, straightening up in her seat and wrapping the blanket around her, trying to shake the feeling that Kane's every motion, especially bringing her pancakes loaded with extra maple syrup felt so *familiar*. "I'm surprised you didn't just barge in last night."

Kane set the plate on the coffee table in front the sofa and then took a seat in a nearby chair. Morning light was especially kind to Kane—not that any light was unfriendly to him. But in the morning, the softer light shimmered through his naturally black waves of hair and brightened his already amazingly silver eyes to the point they sparkled. "You didn't really seem up for a visitor last night."

Skye jerked her head up at him, realizing that he had overheard her argument with Andrew. "That was a private conversation—and quite frankly, none of your business."

"You're right," he replied as he leaned further back into his chair. "That's why I waited until this morning.

There went her little jutted chin. "Well, this is my family's property. And as an uninvited guest, you are officially trespassing. So I have the right to kick you out—"

"But you won't," he answered, simply, then nodded toward the plate. "Have something. You haven't eaten in a while. I've given you enough choices here so something should be to your liking."

Actually, *all* of them were to her liking. Breakfast was her favorite meal—period. So much so that she often had it for lunch and/or dinner. She could do it three times a day, if she had to, and she decided long ago that it was at least as much because of the maple syrup. In her opinion, there were limitless options for what could be dripped in maple syrup—pancakes, French toast, crepes, bacon, potatoes . . . OK, so maybe she was the only one who put it on her potatoes, but it was delicious all the same.

Kane just continued to sit with ease in his chair as he watched her. He was so relaxed in this unfamiliar place that it triggered her curiosity on many levels. Just how was it that he acclimated to situations so easily? She wasn't sure she had ever known a man with Kane's unshakable confidence or the effortlessness with which he seemed to live his life. "I don't need all of this—just a little coffee."

Kane's expression turned to a doubtful frown. "Are you forgetting that I've seen your last few morning meals? The last thing you are is shy about eating—which I like, by the way."

Was this guy for real? She had drugged his juice and left him passed out without so much as a note, and now he was grinning at her from ear to ear and complimenting her healthy appetite? "Why are you here?"

Kane kicked his feet up on the coffee table and leaned his head back against his hands on until his fit body was displayed in the most delicious '*come and get me*' pose. "Well, I was a bit put-off at having my juice Mickey'd . . . and just when things were about to get interesting between us, I suspect."

Skye swallowed hard. She only wished she could have drugged herself so she didn't have to remember how close she had come to begging him to take her. "Nothing interesting was going to happen," she lied.

A huge grin came over his face. "Whatever . . . But I still need to solve this question of why the Wraith is here. And he seems to only be interested in chasing after you. So here I am, your knight in shining armor, working to keep you safe even if you refuse to give a damn about it yourself."

"I'm not in danger," she replied. "The Wraith is back up there. I'm down here. I just need to be left alone so I can . . ."

His brows lifted. "So you can . . . ?" And when it became obvious she was not going to offer any more, he added, "So we're back to this again, are we? Well, personally, I would've thought you'd be more sympathetic, considering your little specialty cocktail nearly did me in."

Skye's head shot up from her attention to her plate, and a sense of panic came over her as she tried to determine whether or not he was telling the truth.

"That's right. Gideon was a nervous wreck because he felt sure after that 'not so little' dosing I would kiss this world goodbye before night's end."

✳✳✳

The horrified look on Skye's face was exactly what she deserved. Kane at least had to make her suffer a little after the worry she caused him when she took off like that. Of course, he'd never admit that, especially since that had been exactly the plan before she'd outsmarted him.

When he arrived at the cabin yesterday and heard her breaking up with Mr. Wonderful, he supposed he should have felt bad for the guy. But he didn't. Not even the slightest bit. Honestly, it had been music to his ears because he still wanted this woman desperately.

Kane had wanted to come to her the night before in human form, but he re-thought that decision and stayed in shifted form after watching her crumble to her knees. She appeared so tired and fragile in that moment, it was somehow very important that she let him comfort her in some small way—which she never would have done if she'd known it was Kane. Seeing her like that, her teary face hidden in her small hands and her hair all spiky and unkempt, was equivalent to someone ripping his heart out of his chest. It shocked him how powerfully this woman affected him . . . and how quickly.

Once she'd fallen asleep, he shifted to his human form and curled up behind her, holding her, easing the restless dreaming she once again seemed to fall prey to. It was the only time in his life he had cuddled with a woman all night, and it was nice. Better than nice; it was comfortable, and he didn't have to sacrifice rule number two to do it—because there was no bed involved.

Slowly, he was able to assure himself she was all right by listening to her even breathing and by taking in the familiar scents along her body. From the subtle fragrance of her shampoo to that damn Frangipani flower that had become his own personal aphrodisiac, to the natural womanly scent that lurked beneath all the other fragrances and only sweetened his thoughts of the territory between her thighs, he was addicted to how this woman smelled. Period. He wanted her more than he could remember wanting *any* woman in his life. To the point, he felt certain he was fairly mad with want. But the good news was, there was a solution to his unending agony. He needed to seduce this woman—at least two or three times, he decided—so this desire for her would be swept from his system.

Damn, he couldn't wait to get back to the simple life he knew . . . of seducing willing beauties in The Oracle's kitchen . . . or in a random phone booth . . . or in one of The Oracle's training rooms. Those encounters were uncomplicated and much less troublesome. He wasn't chasing them around Canada like some sappy, romantic idiot!

"I'm sorry," she said miserably, snapping him from his current thoughts. "I never meant to hurt you. My father taught me how to measure dosage, but I think I was a little nervous, so I must have poured too much."

Well, how could he continue to make her feel bad after an apology like that? She simply warmed him like the sun.

Kane knew she hadn't meant to hurt him—which, of course, *she hadn't*, except for the rather large headache that followed and the giant bruise to his ego. He got up and moved to take the seat beside her on the sofa. Vulnerability continued to weaken her expression as her body sagged against his side like the perfect weight. A better man would have put her at ease right away.

Too bad he wasn't a better man.

"Well, there's nothing to be done now," he sighed. "I'm afraid I've lost some permanent hearing in my left ear, and also I have this annoying tick in my left eye,"—he demonstrated with a bunch of odd squinting of his lid—"that I can't seem to control." Her own eyes started to narrow questioningly as he continued. "I probably will never be able to say abracathabra again correctly. "

"You mean abracadabra?"

"Yes, of course! You see how it gets stuck on my tongue?"

"*You* are evil," she said, slapping him against his arm. "I truly believed I hurt you, and you're making fun of me." But before she could stop him, Kane pulled her up, over and onto his lap with the same powerful arm that was now cinched low across her back. He leaned so far back against the sofa that Skye had no choice but to fall flat against his chest with a rough exhale.

"You deserved it, darlin'," he said with a small grunt, "for that little stunt. All of my sweet memories of what happened in that bedroom before you knocked me out are gone." He then stared at her with a sincerity and intensity he knew he had never shown another woman in his life. "And I want them all back."

***

Oh, God, the warmth she found against his body. Every sharp line, every hard plane of his masculine form seemed to lie in wait of her softer curves. She never remembered feeling this way when she was pressed against Andrew, never remembered her blood heating up this fast or her pulse beating this quickly. Skye appreciated how Andrew had gone to such great lengths to kick-start her rather lifeless libido. She'd seen it as a sign of how much he cared for her. But in light of his unfaithfulness, and her body's seemingly instant attraction to Kane now, she questioned whether it was a sign that she had been more attracted to his kindness as a person rather than to him, physically, as a man.

For that reason alone, she knew she had done the right thing in giving him back his ring. It wasn't fair to either of them for her to continue pretending it could work between them when another man had taken over her fantasies. Not that she was going to do anything about her fantasies. She couldn't.

Even though she had chosen to let Andrew go—and despite her resentment that destiny had let her down so completely—she understood she had given herself to him and would always be tied to him as it was written. She just needed her body to get on board with that concept, which, at the moment, it wasn't.

Straddled over Kane's hips, Skye remained trapped against him as his scent, his strength, his presence, seemed to almost overwhelm her and melt her resistance. She was breathing more slowly now, and there was a familiar, impressive bulge pressed against her inner thigh as his heavy breathing warmed her temple. This man wanted her. There was no doubt about that. But basic sexual need was very different from his *needing* her on a level higher than just satisfying his current fantasy. Kane would never need a woman to share his life with, even in some small way. That was not how he worked. He didn't do commitment, and she didn't do casual. No matter how much she wanted him, casual went against everything that she was raised to believe about herself.

Given this reasoning, she pushed back from him, eliciting his groan as her hands pressed at his chest while she declared, "Kane, stop. Two days ago you respected that I belonged to another man . . . and I'm sure you'll give me the same level of respect regardless of the conversation you overheard last night. Because, despite how hard you try to convince people otherwise, you're actually a very decent human being."

She then scurried off his lap and hurried the few steps into the kitchen. Despite what she had just said about him being a decent human being—which she did truly believe—he was still very dangerous to be too close to.

After taking a couple of steadying breaths, she turned back to tell him he would have to leave, but she was caught off guard to find him right there on her heels. He had crossed the room without making a sound and in an instant had pinned her against the kitchen counter with just the intensity of his gaze.

"That doesn't sound like me, Skye," he said in that deep, throaty voice of his. "I know myself pretty well, and I can tell you, I'm not a decent man. You know why?"

Skye was shaking her head fiercely, praying that he would leave his next words unspoken.

"Because I don't feel one bit sorry for the poor schlep whose heart you broke last night. In fact, I love that you no longer belong to him. That means you're fair game, Miss Matthews. And it's a game I intend to win." He raked his fingers through her hair and curled his hand at the base of her skull, pulling her forward 'til his breath crashed against her cheek and his free hand caressed her hip. Somehow, she again found herself pulled tight against his body, feeling as if every inch of her was heating from the inside out. Had she ever met a sexual force like Kane? His words, his promises, were like a fierce storm that simply blew in and took you over.

"This is just a game to you," she replied.

"When it comes to what I want, Skye, I don't play games." He then proved his point by lavishing her skin with kisses that had her feeling weak in the knees. First her cheek, then her jaw, then the corner of her mouth, each one sinking her deeper into him as need began clawing its way to the surface. She was in trouble here.

"I . . . I . . ." she croaked, pushing him back. "I think it's a good idea for you to leave. I refuse to get caught up in this self-inflated ego trip you've got going on to best another man you don't even know—a good man."

"Are you talking about the schlep? Because I already said I don't give a damn about him."

"Listen carefully," she said with a bit a warning to her voice. "You and I cannot happen. It isn't supposed to happen. I know that might not make sense to you, but I can't explain it any better than that."

He just smiled at her with a truly knowing and sinful smile. "Do you really believe that, Skye? Because I think you can feel what *is* happening between us every bit as much as I can."

Incredible. She had just flat out refused the man, and still he played her like he had the upper hand, which, in her emotional confusion, it sort of felt like he did. Honestly, the man seemed to thrive on rejection.

"Tell me that you can't feel it," he challenged her, but in the absence of her response he leaned into her, stealing her lips and cutting off her breath for a few seconds. The hunger in his kiss seemed to kick-start her heartbeat faster than a thunderbolt could. He kissed like he dared anyone to break them apart at that moment. "You don't want me?" he whispered just over the seam of her lips. "Then tell me no."

Before Skye knew what was happening a strong arm encircled her back, holding her firm in place. Kane's panting breaths rushed past her ear and were echoed by her own as his hand tugged at the black leggings she was still wearing from the night before. It took almost no effort for him to pull the garment down her thighs to access the little silk panties she wore underneath, and then slip his hand inside. "I'll stop with just one word from you. One word . . ."

One word? Skye couldn't even muster one thought. She was turned on beyond belief as his fingers masterfully slid into the silky-hot warmth that he found waiting for him. She needed him, and he knew it. For a moment, just a moment, he held her like that, wanting, teasing—leaving her gasping for breath as she stared into those hungry silver eyes. Then, when it felt like she couldn't stand the emptiness anymore, he slowly curled his fingers into the warmth and began to stroke her, causing her to swallow a fierce gulp of air as her chin lifted higher and her head fell back.

Still she said nothing, just allowed herself to feel a cacophony of sensations.

Her blood suddenly surged like fire through her veins, her heart speeded up like the beats to a drum and her belly tightened. Then he pushed two fingers deep inside her soft flesh —and she nearly squealed in response.

There seemed to be no controlling the desire she felt at that point. She clenched at his upper arms with her fingers, trying to steady herself before her knees buckled beneath her sagging weight. *Oh, my god,* it felt so good! She wished she had the will to stop this, even as the guilt that she just broke up with Andrew last night swept through her . . . but she didn't.

Kane had been right. She wanted this. She wanted all of it, and it confused her. How did this man that she barely knew make her feel so . . . special? Her own breathy moan seemed to answer and her internal muscles gripped at his stroking fingers, squeezing them as if she had never experienced such pleasure in her life. *Had she?* The man was truly, unbelievably, gifted with just his fingers—like he had known how to please her body his entire life. One minute she was just standing next to a counter, and the next she was totally breathless, lifting onto her toes and digging her nails into his arms.

"Oh, you want me, Skye," he nearly purred. "There is no doubt about that. Feel how wet you are. Have you been wet for me since you woke to find me here this morning?"

She cried out and dropped her forehead into his chest. "No," she whispered, though they both knew she was lying. Worse yet, she was making no move to stop him, only pushing her pelvis harder against his hand.

Unresponsive, her ass! Her body was completely responding to this man. *This* was what it felt like to be wholly impassioned and swept up by a single moment. There was no gradual build-up here. *This* was a full-fledged assault that ripped through her body without care for how much it shook her on the way through. Kane was giving this to her, letting her relish in the confidence she felt as a beautiful, desirable woman more than she ever had in her life, and she could see the pleasure reflected in his own eyes. He was into this moment just as much she was, clawing at it, in fact. And *that* made her feel incredibly powerful, sexy and feminine.

His fingers swirled again and then returned to a faster stroking motion before curling back against the inside wall of her pubic bone. Once he began stroking there it felt like all hell was breaking loose. *My God, how did he know how to do this?* "Did you dream of me the last two nights you've been away from me, darlin'?"

Skye could only answer him with a sudden cry as her whole body heated to an unbearable level. Her hips leapt forward against his hand and her nails practically cut into his skin. "Yes," she panted weakly.

Admitting it made her feel *so* vulnerable, but she was completely incapable of denying it at that moment. Her body fell harder against him as she rose onto her toes. Then she heard Kane's deep, approving growl rumble against her throat. "I've got you," he rasped. "I'll get you there . . . Just relax, darlin'."

Relax? Was he kidding? Skye could feel every square inch of her skin flush as each stroke of his finger over that small area seemed only to swell her pleasure. She hadn't even been aware that such an area existed within her, but now that she was it was like trying to hold back the force of a freight train. *Impossible.*

Kane already had her practically lifted off her feet when he completed the deed and hauled her up onto the kitchen island, tugging the leggings he objected to earlier down below her knees and then pushing his fingers deeper inside her. Skye felt completely lost and dizzy. This had to end soon or she would implode!

"Look at me, Skye," he ordered.

Her glazed expression lifted to his. Their eyes locked and she felt completely trapped by him, unable to move if her life depended on it as he continued to work his magic fingers. "I want to watch that lost look in your eyes as you come for me. That's for me. Just for me."

Oh, he was arrogant, but she liked it. She liked it a lot. "Kane!" she squealed one final time as her head fell back and her body let go in waves. She felt completely lost in the next seconds. Her breath was trapped under a silent scream and her tenuous grip on this earth seemed to be slipping away.

"*God,* you're beautiful," he breathed against her mouth and then kissed her again as she was still gasping for breath. "So beautiful . . . So very beautiful."

Colors like fireworks sparked in front of her eyes. *What had this man just done to her?* Skye was lost inside the loud pounding of her own heart in her head when she heard some sort of strange cry rend the air in the distance. It didn't sound human, but more like a screeching animal. For a split second she questioned whether it had just been her own impassioned cry as she came, but it wasn't. This sound was haunting, angry.

Kane tensed against her, every muscle in his body trained to respond instinctively to danger. His fingers slid from her flesh and he righted her clothing as best he could before kissing her full on the lips one last time and said, "Stay here. Lock the door. Don't let anyone in until I return." As he let her go she slid from the counter, but when her feet touched the floor she continued to crumble until she was lying, spent, on the rough-hewn floor.

Then, in those few seconds, he was gone.

Skye was still trembling, trying to collect herself as the cold air from the opening and closing of the front door blew over her. Only then did it strike her that they were in an area that was almost completely isolated. There shouldn't be any strange screeching sounds nearby. Her fingers gripped the edge of the counter as she pulled herself up slowly to her feet. She didn't have a good feeling about this, and Kane just ran out there alone. As far as she could tell, no one else had come with him from The Trek, which she found strange. *Why hadn't Aiden at least backed him up?* She knew that as a member of The Brethren Kane would be well trained to handle himself against the supernatural world, but he was just one man.

Her heartbeat began to accelerate again as these fearful thoughts ran wild in her head. She needed to be sure nothing would happen to him. It was a primitive imperative she had no control over.

And without another thought, she pulled up her leggings, grabbed her boots and a long winter coat, and raced after him in the morning cold.

CHAPTER FIFTEEN

The sun that had warmed Skye's cheek when she woke earlier that morning was now gone and in its place was a cool morning mist that hung over the dense forest surrounding the cabin like a wet blanket, making it difficult to see which direction Kane had gone.

"Kane, where are you?" she muttered to herself in frustration. How could the man just disappear on her like that? She had practically followed him right out the door.

Skye found herself irritated at the fact he had just charged into danger without even giving her a chance to recover her wits—especially after he was the one who so thoroughly muddled them. She could help him. She knew she could. She knew this land, knew the mountainous terrain, and was confident in her ability to track down the direction of the sound . . . just as soon as she heard it again.

Right now, the forest around her was way too quiet, too still, as if every living creature within a mile radius had stopped moving, stopped breathing. There wasn't even the slightest breeze swaying through the trees. Something was definitely not right.

Then a loud, guttural howl broke through the air again, only this time it was much closer. The sound grated against her ears, sounding more like a Howler Monkey than a wolf or dog. *Good Lord, what were they doing out here?* All that was missing from this bad B-flick was a little darkness and a full moon.

Skye wasn't afraid for herself. In fact, she'd found herself in much more dangerous situations than this, but what about *Kane?* Sure, being with The Brethren, he was undoubtedly well trained, though, she fudged a little bit on how familiar she was with The Brethren and their supernatural dealings. She knew of them only from her father mentioning the very secretive group in passing. But Kane had been caught off guard by the sound—they both had—and had run outside unarmed and half dressed, chasing after a sound that had supernatural written all over it.

She pressed forward in the general direction of the creature's last howl, which had sounded as if it was echoing off rock, and that meant he must be near the small canyon she knew was a quarter-mile or so north of her. It was a dangerous area if one wasn't careful because there were several points where a steep drop-off started just as the forest thicket ended. As she made her way through the trees, the padding of her own feet against the ground was the only sound she heard until a low, curdled growl vibrated through the air behind her. This sound was definitely animal. Large and catlike, and it didn't sound happy *at all* to be sharing the same forest with her. She picked up her pace, praying it was Bogart running around out there and not some other large *creature* that wanted to make a meal of her.

Suddenly, the forest opened up, giving way to a grassy clearing about the length of a football field. She knew this particular spot was the best exit point because the edge of the canyon was still about forty yards ahead of her, but at that moment she couldn't see it because it was hidden by a thick morning mist rising from the river below, swirling around her knees as if it were a living, breathing thing trying to swallow her up. The cloud-like mass rolled over the flat ground at great speed, spinning from the edge of the canyon in front of her like a waterfall.

Skye moved along carefully but found herself having to suddenly throw her arms out to her side for balance when the earth started to shake violently under her feet. At first she thought she was in the middle of an earthquake, but the thunderous shaking seemed to be coming from her left and was rolling straight toward her. As the vibrations grew closer she heard several hard grunts and what sounded like a lot of weight hitting the ground. Skye couldn't even blink as she concentrated on trying to pierce the fog by staring right into it. She had a really, *really* bad feeling about the current spot where she was standing.

Then, without warning, the mist was shattered violently as a large, powerful brown mass charged straight toward her.

Eeek, correction . . . make that a grizzly bear!

There was no Discovery Channel special in the world that could have prepared her for how big this thing was as it bounced with hefty force along the ground. The bear was about thirty yards away but closing the gap between them at a speed much faster than she thought an animal of his size was capable of. He—because she simply could imagine a female bear being this large—was so enormous that she couldn't even see all of him because of the mist.

Digging her feet into the ground, she tried to remain calm, as she knew she should in this situation. All she needed to do was let the animal pass by her by, but that didn't make the image of being run over by a thousand-pound-plus grizzly any less terrifying. And as the bear got closer, the ground shuddered as if trying to throw her from her feet. But strangely, the animal appeared just as frightened as she was, like he was running away from something behind him rather than toward her.

Skye was preparing to move a few steps either direction when she heard a tremendous roar over her right shoulder. She turned to catch Bogart leaping from his hind feet and landing directly in front of her. "Bogart, no!" she cried. "He can't see me!"

Bogart was, by far, the largest feline Skye had ever seen. But even his well-muscled frame was still no match for a male grizzly. She had to do something, but before she could react, Bogart's body started to shake against the ground in front of her. His claws seemed to dig into the earth and she had to blink back her shock as she watched the giant cat's body fill out and change right before her very eyes. His sleek black, jaguar limbs grew to powerfully humped shoulders and a thick body covered with a coarse blond coat. Crowned with a large head and snapping snout, his feet became giant pads with long claws capable of cutting into flesh with little effort. Within seconds, Bogart 'the jaguar' had transformed into an even larger polar bear, his ear-shattering roar blasting into the air and announcing he was ready for a fight.

"A Natural Shifter!" she whispered to herself in utter astonishment.

Natural Shifters, beings who can shift into more than one form—unlike a Lycan who can only shift between that and their human form—were incredibly rare. Skye knew enough about the supernatural world to know that. And this whole time she had been sleeping next to one!

But there was no time to process any of this, as the two bears were practically on top of one another, each snarling and roaring at the other as Bogart braced to force the grizzly back from her. The brown bear seemed to stall for a moment, confused by what it had just witnessed, but it was only a moment. He enlarged himself by rising to his hind legs, extending himself to nearly ten feet, then launched toward Bogart with its powerful claws bared. Bogart matched the challenger at every step as they pounded against each other, wrestling like ancient beasts from a time long past. The sound of their battle was terrifying, and Skye felt useless as she just tried to get out of the way. Fur flew in a mix of both their coats as the two animals exchanged brutal blows. For Bogart, though, things appeared much worse because every time a strike drew blood the scarlet color stood out in sharp contrast to his blond coat.

Skye was trying to think of how to help when the ground began to vibrate even harder under her feet, a rumble that was coming from what seemed like all directions. This time, she knew they were dealing with a heck of a lot more coming at them than one grizzly bear. The noise and vibration were enough to make both fighting bears pause in their battle and look toward the edge of the forest behind them. At first, the mist hid what was coming, but the rumbling felt practically on top of them as the brown grizzly sent a final roar at Bogart and took off in another direction. Bogart turned and pinned Skye with his large grey eyes. *No, not grey—a brilliant silver—*and suddenly she was aware of a crucial detail with Bogart she had noticed but hadn't fully made the connection.

A single name was about to fall from her lips when the thundering became too loud to ignore.

The mist was now scattered and appeared blown to the edges, revealing instead a torn-up cloud of mud and dirt. Literally dozens upon dozens of animals, all shapes, sizes and species, were charging toward them as if they couldn't see either Skye or the giant polar bear in front of them. The chaos was so massive that the animals paid no attention to how close they pushed each other to the canyon's edge. As she watched, a deer was bucked over the edge by a much larger elk, and in that instant she realized . . . the herd was being driven by an enemy much more powerful than the basic food chain—fear!

Fear the likes of which she had never witnessed before.

There was nowhere to run because the animals came from everywhere. Skye tried to hold her balance while the turbulent ground continued to try to throw her off her feet. Bogart roared and then charged toward her, and she wondered if she was about to be accidently trampled by fourteen hundred pounds of bear. But then his enormous body stopped right in front of her, shielding her like a wall from the out-of-control herd that was practically on top of them. It wouldn't matter if none of the animals could see her. With that many charging all at once, something was bound to run her over, if only by accident. She tucked herself against Bogart's massive body, the only shelter she had. And she was ashamed that she couldn't stop a single muscle from shaking in the midst of all the chaos and noise around them.

The herd hit them, and the violence of it was terrifying. Skye clung to the bear's coat, afraid to move. Bogart was taking direct hits to his body, though the force of them never passed through to her. After what seemed like an unending onslaught, things finally began to calm down. Fewer and fewer animals raced passed until it was almost dead silent again and the only sound she could hear was her own terrified breathing.

A few seconds later, that familiar buzzing sound came through the trees, just as Skye peeked around Bogart's side. The Wraith was blowing straight toward them in a humongous, whirling blur. Bogart let out a warning growl that would have terrified an ornery rhino as he dug his claws into the earth, somehow finding the strength to continue defending both of them. Skye knew, however, there would be no escaping the

Wraith this time, and she refused to allow Bogart to be hurt or killed because of her.

Skye jumped to her feet and moved away from Bogart so the Wraith could clearly see her, but he was already well aware that she was there. The blistering swirl of motion instantly shifted directions, coming straight at her. Skye braced herself, but it wasn't enough. She was blown backwards off her feet as the force of air coming at her threw her at least twenty feet. She bounced once on her backside and then managed to wrap her arms around a nearby tree trunk and shield her head and face with the trunk just as she heard Bogart's enraged roar behind her. Suddenly, that strange cry that had drawn them out in the first place blasted right past her ear. Only now, somehow, the sound was more . . . more human. Like a man in pain.

Within that split second she peeked from behind the trunk and caught the outline of hands reaching toward her from deep within all that wild, windy chaos. Then everything stopped! Only a much gentler whoosh of air was left to blow over her. The chaos was gone as if it had never been there in the first place. And then it, too, subsided and was gone.

Skye hadn't realized how badly she was shaking until the absolute silence had settled in and her hard breathing and pounding heart seemed like the noisiest thing around her. She lifted her head from its instinctively defensive position against the tree trunk to find Bogart lying, collapsed, on the ground.

"Bogart!" she cried out as she pushed to her feet and raced toward him. In the time it took for her rise up and cover the short distance that separated them, Skye witnessed Bogart shift again in front of her. Except this time his form didn't return to the familiar jaguar, but to that of a very naked man . . . a familiar man—even though she could only see his back side.

And now she knew! She just knew.

"Kane!" she called as she dropped to her knees behind him. His skin was pale, much paler than normal, and cool to the touch. His every muscle in his body appeared stiff with tension, while his breathing sawed in and out against his back. Skye was absolutely terrified, and that awful feeling increased five-fold when she noticed the long, bleeding gash that ran along his side and hip. He had been slashed by the bear's claws, and she could also see the beginnings of some severe bruising that must have occurred when he had been mauled by the stampeding animals. "*Oh, God,* please say something," she murmured, so quietly it was barely audible. "Tell me how I can help."

After what seemed to her an endless silence, he replied in a croaky but calm voice, "I'm all right. Go back to the cabin—*straight* back to the cabin—and wait for me. I'll be behind you shortly."

Was he out of his mind? "I'm not leaving you here!" Skye said as she stubbornly continued to shake her head at him—even though he was refusing to even look at her. How could he not know that all she needed from him at that moment was to see his face—*to see* that he would be OK?

She shrugged out of her coat and tore the sleeves from her shirt, balling the fabric up and using it to create a sort of pressure bandage over the wound on his side. His whole body jerked at the contact, and he growled in response, "Skye, *damnit!* I said to get back to the cabin."

"No!" she replied, wondering if his anger about her refusal to leave or the fact she was pushing painfully against his cut? "I'm staying here with you, so just deal with it." She continued to press a hand against his wound while using the other to cover him with her coat. Not surprisingly, the garment was way too small for him, but at least it had some length and it could keep him from freezing to death on the spot.

"You are the most stubborn—"

"Look, don't get me started," she replied firmly. "Later, you and I are going to discuss why you didn't tell me the truth about being a Shifter. But right now we need to get you—"

"Woman!" he interjected right back at her. "I'm not in the mood for this. It's not safe out here for you, and you know it. That Wraith could come back at any second." He then turned to look at her for the first time, trying to show her how serious he was, but all she could see was the pain he was trying to keep concealed from her with a bland expression. "Trust me, I'm a fast healer. I'll be right behind you. Now will you please . . . just for once . . . do as I ask?"

"I'm. Not. Leaving. You," she repeated slowly, making sure each word sank into his thick head. *And oh,* that did it. Now he was mumbling fierce curses under his breath before pushing up onto his hands and knees. Skye didn't care if he was upset at her. Right now she needed him to get a little angry, find some strength. Because there was no way she would be able to get him back to the cabin without his help. He was too heavy. "So if you want me back at that cabin, then you have two choices; either you shift into something small enough for me to carry, like a rabbit, or you're going to have to march me there yourself."

For a moment, he looked like he wanted to throttle her until she had some sense knocked into her. Or he wanted to kiss her again . . . she wasn't quite sure which. "Shift into a rabbit . . . ? It doesn't work that way. I have to maintain a similar mass or project something larger. But it wouldn't matter right now. I don't have the energy to shift."

"Well, that's not helpful," Skye complained, knowing absolutely that she was pushing him.

He blinked at her. "Well, I'm sorry," he replied—with obvious sarcasm. "Shifting into three different forms and fighting off a grizzly bear somewhere there in the middle tends to take the energy right out of a person." He then started to get up slowly. *Thank God.*

"Here," she said, sliding her coat down over his hips. "Tie this around you. It will help keep pressure on the cut as well as . . ."—she cleared her throat—"keep you covered."

"Look your fill, darlin'," he said cracking a pained smile. "Nudity has not embarrassed me and it never will."

"Why does that not surprise me?" she sighed as she helped him to his feet.

Kane eventually took mercy on her and pulled the coat around his hips, for which she was grateful because she didn't want to keep trying to pretend that his amazing body was nothing more than she had seen before on a man. *Ha!* That was a lie. They might be in a crisis situation here, but she wasn't dead. Every part of her body hummed with the need to be closer to him. She just knew her nipples were erect and pushing against her shirt, but there was no way she was going to draw his attention to it by checking for herself.

She positioned herself slightly behind him and curled his arm around her neck for balance. At the contact, her skin broke out into shivery goose bumps that ran over her like an electric charge. He was, quite simply, delicious . . . and she couldn't feel any guiltier about the fact that he was probably in terrible pain while all *she* wanted to do was rip her coat from his hip and spend the next hour out here in the freezing cold examining him. *What on earth was wrong with her?* Whenever she was around this man she feared there was a sex addict lurking inside her somewhere.

The walk back was slow and arduous. Somewhere along the way she finally admitted that she had, *quite possibly,* strayed farther from the cabin than she had initially intended. Evidently, Kane agreed with that assessment. He couldn't stop grumbling about how stupid it had been for her to go out there alone after he had expressly told her to wait for him at the cabin. Men could be so silly sometimes about thinking a woman was completely helpless in a tough situation. But then again, there had been a moment there where she did feel a bit helpless.

Kane leaned into her 'til her knees were close to buckling under his weight. He must have realized it at some point, because he recovered and continue to push himself forward. For the most part, he had been doing a lot better the further they went. In fact, she believed the walking was good for him, keeping the blood pumping to his heart.

When they finally came to the last hundred yards or so from the cabin, she noted that his steps were even stronger, and she was greatly relieved that they had made it. She decided the first thing she would do when they got inside was get Kane situated on the sofa, where she could get a good look at his wound. Her father had taught her and her sisters some basic first aid, which had proven handy more than a few times. Once she stitched him up she would get him some hot food and some of his favorite juice, then start a warm fire to take the chill out of their bones. Yep, being able to help him, for a change, would definitely be nice.

Kane, however, had other plans. "Lock the door," he growled as soon as they stepped across the threshold. She did, and then proceeded to turn around just in time to see him collapse to the floor. Skye worked quickly for the next few minutes, turning on the kettle that was always on the stove, grabbing some blankets and covering him to keep him warm (and to hide that gorgeous body from her sight so she could stay focused), fetching some clean towels, and gathering the first aid essentials her father had stored away in a closet.

Kane had fallen forward onto his stomach, and as she tried to reposition him so she would have better access to his wound, he grumbled and used his hand to try and push her away before eventually falling silent again. One thing was clear. There was no way she was going to be able to stitch him up without causing him a lot of pain and probably putting him in a very foul mood.

Nope, regrettably, she was going to have to dose him again. And after the incident with the juice, she could only imagine what he would have to say about this. Oh, well, it was for his own good.

By early evening, Skye's worries began to ease as she gathered up and disposed of the last of the bloody towels and supplies. Looking back, Kane would undoubtedly be glad he was out of it while she cleaned and stitched his wound, because it had been painful for her just to watch her own work. The gash in his side had been long and deep, and despite the fact he was a quick healer, it needed to be cleaned and closed quickly so it wouldn't develop an infection . . . if Natural Shifters caught infections.

His long limbs were sprawled in exactly the same place on the floor, only now they were surrounded by an array of pillows and blankets to keep him comfortable and warm, as comfortable and warm as one could be on the floor.

He stirred a lot in his sleep. She knew, though, from the mild snoring sound he made that the muscle relaxer would be in effect for a while. Listening to his snore actually brought a smile to her lips, at least until she remembered how upset she was with him for not telling her he was a Shifter. Several times he must have had quite a laugh at her expense. She grimaced at remembering all the heartfelt things she had confessed in front of Bogart. Her fears and her desires—more specifically, her desire for him! What a fool she was.

Had she showered and changed in front of him? She couldn't remember. God, she was going to kill him. For three nights he had slept with her on that bed in his Bogart form, and she had welcomed it because he made her feel so safe. Still did. She was so stupid not to see it before now. *Hell,* she was the one who pointed out that the jaguar's eyes reminded her of Kane. And now that she thought more about it, she realized that lazy, sexy stalk of his—that always drew her attention—was the exact same stalk of the jaguar. Yes, they were one and the same.

She also recalled all the details of his body as he had lain there in the clearing. He was beautiful. Her cheeks flushed with more than just embarrassment. He may have kept the rather important *detail* he was a SHIFTER from her, but it didn't change the fact that she wanted him. This thing she felt for Kane wasn't just a fleeting thought or a passing infatuation. This was need, desire—passion, plain and simple—for a specific man that she couldn't seem to temper down. But she couldn't be with him, either, so what was the point of all this desire? What was she going to do?

Maybe pack her things tonight and leave, never looking back. That's what she could do. Shifters were exceptional healers, so he would no doubt be back on his feet by morning. Now that he was fixed up and she was fairly certain he would be OK, there would be absolutely nothing to feel guilty about. This was about self-preservation. This was about a small window of time during which she had to put some distance between her and this man who seem to draw her as quickly as maple syrup over a short stack. And she needed to do it now, before she lost her heart completely.

Yes, this was the plan.

It was a good plan.

After a shower and a change of clothes, her mind had been completely made up. She'd be gone within the hour. Quickly, she packed her things. Once, Kane stirred, uttering a small, growling sound. She gasped, fearing he had somehow heard her very thoughts. But no, that wasn't it.

"He's a restless sleeper," she murmured with a sigh. "Just like me."

CHAPTER SIXTEEN

Kane woke sometime during the night, a little cloudy on what had happened and where he was. As it came back to him, he slid his hand to his side, where the bear had clawed him, and could feel the even line of stitches.

It was good work. Someone had been holding out on him about her first aid skills. The wound was repairing itself quickly, which was good and just what he expected of his Shifter body. In fact, the wound was repairing itself so quickly he would need to remove the sutures soon before they were trapped beneath the rapidly healing top layers of his skin. Then he wondered how in the world she had stitched him up without waking him.

The heavy feeling in his head answered that question. She had drugged him again. He really was going to have to have a serious talk with her about this need to have him immobile and unconscious. Most women preferred him conscious.

He raised his head and couldn't help the troublesome sense of dread that ran through him as he searched for her in the dark room. He remembered she had made it back to the cabin uninjured and safe, but right now he just needed to see that for himself. The room was far too quiet. He was still lying on the floor, nearly swallowed by what must have been at least a dozen pillows and a scarily similar number of blankets, all but two of which he had pushed off himself at some point during the night. The woman had gone overboard trying to make him comfortable when he didn't really need it. He was used to sleeping on hard surfaces, especially in his shifted form. It was nice, though, that she wanted to make him comfortable.

He pushed up into a crouch but didn't see her. His heart seemed to beat a little faster with every additional second that went by. Had she run from him again? She'd better pray she hadn't, because when he found her—*and he would find her*— he would literally tie her . . .

He found her.

Rather, he found her scent. The second the floral bouquet had alerted him, he was led to her curled form on the sofa behind him. She made a tiny moaning sound as she turned in her sleep, and immediately let out a deep sigh. He couldn't remember ever being so relieved to see someone. He had about lost his mind when she stepped away from his protection and put herself directly in the Wraith's path—not that he hadn't already lost his mind from her being out there in the first place. One thing was absolutely clear, however. This Wraith wanted Skye Matthews very badly. For the life of him, he had no idea why. She was just your average, illogical, stubborn woman . . . who was also smart, beautiful, effervescent and feisty. And the thought of anyone hurting her was driving him crazy.

Pushing the remaining blankets off him, he smiled when he realized he still had no clothes on. He loved that she hadn't tried to dress him. Lord knows, he was most comfortable in nothing but his own skin. But a lot of people were uncomfortable around his almost constant nudity. He remembered how ridiculous he felt while walking back to the cabin with that small coat wrapped around his hips. But he hadn't missed the extra-cautious glances she stole to inspect his body. There was no way she was unaffected by him.

She had cleaned him from head to toe. Just the thought of her washing him, looking at him, touching every inch of his skin, excited him—and made him regret that he hadn't been conscious enough to enjoy it. He hoped she hadn't gotten her fill. Not even close. Because he certainly didn't intend for it to be the last time she saw him naked.

Kane almost recklessly cut out his sutures with a sharp knife from the kitchen area, showered, then threw on a pair of loose charcoal sweats from his bag. Returning to her still sleeping form there on the sofa, he admitted to himself that she was the most beautiful woman he'd ever seen in his life. She was so beguilingly innocent as she slept—with all that wispy, blond hair shooting all over the place and those pouty little lips murmuring something in her sleep. He had some wicked thoughts running through his head in that moment, but she needed to be awake for him to fulfill them. He wanted to snuggle right up next her and kiss every curve, every line of her sweet face until she awoke. But the sofa wouldn't be comfortable enough for the whole night. Oh, no. He wanted room for pleasure.

Tucking his arms underneath her slight frame and working hard not to wake her as he let her head rest against his shoulder, he carried her to the cabin's one bedroom. The decor was clean and simple—natural pine floors, soft, neutral-colored bed linens, and a single oversized lounging chair and ottoman in matching chocolate leather—a great spot to cozy up with his favorite person for hours, he thought. But right now he had other ideas, and they centered on the room's other feature, an antique cast-iron bed.

There was simply no way a man could have picked out the rather effeminate leafy motif and still call himself a man. But, at the same time, he couldn't see how any man would object to the sturdy steel hooks that were created within the intricate leafy design. Quite a nice surprise for this rather unassuming little cabin.

As he laid her down gently and carefully slid in beside her, he marveled at how this was *the fourth time* he had been with this woman in a bed—and he still hadn't slept with her. Even more surprising was that he wanted to be with her on a bed, holding her, protecting her, showering her with kisses everywhere he could. *Wasn't this against his rules?* Yup. Rule number two, in fact. A *big*, important rule, especially considering there were only two main ones. But with Skye, he just didn't seem to care. He wanted to spend all day and all night with her in his arms, and if they were going to lounge around like that in luxury, then the bed was the best place to do it. Besides, he assured himself that he was, technically, holding onto a shred of his rule—because it wasn't his own bed.

He pushed away a wisp of her golden hair that had fallen over her eye, tucking it to the side as he placed a soft, slow kiss on the beautiful cheek his gesture had uncovered. She murmured and stirred, turning her body into his quite naturally while her small but mouthwatering breasts rose to attention. The hard tips now pressed through the thin white fabric of her shirt and had his body on full alert beneath his sweats. Why had he even bothered putting on a pair of sweats after his shower?

Oh, that's right . . . He didn't want to scare the woman by having a hungry, hard, naked man hovering over her when she woke.

Kane reached for the blanket at the foot of the bed to cover them both as he snuggled in even further and pulled her even closer, unable to stop kissing her. She moaned again, in the most perfect, breathy little sounds he had ever heard, and then fluttered open her eyes. When she realized who it was next to her, Skye's eyes widened as if she wasn't sure what she should do—which, considering he was lying beside her hard and half naked, was a perfectly normal reaction for her to have. Kane slowly stroked his fingertips over her temple. "Don't be afraid," he murmured.

***

Afraid? If there was one thing Skye knew for sure at this moment, it was that this fluttery feeling invading her stomach was not because she was afraid, not in the least.

She *should* be afraid. She *should* have a few choice words for this gorgeous egomaniac about waking in a bed in his arms. But as he stared down at her with those smiling silver eyes, nestled against her side, Skye knew this man was most dangerous to her heart when he was being flirty and playful like this. He reminded her of a little boy who knew he was behaving badly but also knew his charming smile would let him get away with it.

And it would. Of course he would get away with it simply because she had to admit to herself there was no place she would rather be than right there in his arms. She knew that in the moment she decided not to leave him after suturing his wound. All packed and ready to go, her feet had just refused to let her walk out that door. "You seem to be feeling better," she noted with a smile and obviously referring to the hard erection she could feel pressing against her hip.

He snuggled playfully, placing several kisses along her jawline before nibbling at the corner of her mouth. "Yes, I'm feeling remarkably better. Would you like me to show you how much better?" She opened her mouth to answer, but before she could get a word out he set his thumb over her lips and his hand cupped her cheek. "Before you answer that, we should get a couple of things straight."

She could only blink at him, unsure about what else was appropriate, since he wouldn't remove his thumb.

"First, let me say thank you . . . for taking care of me last night. Even though I would've managed just fine on my own if you had left me out there as I had asked . . ."—he lifted her hand and tenderly kissed the ends of her fingertips—"I would always prefer to have these gentle hands taking care of me."

Skye smiled in reply. She couldn't help but smile.

"But darlin', if you ever put yourself in danger like that again, I'm going to bend you over my knee and paddle your ass 'til it's cherry red."

Her smile faded. "You're the one who needs to be paddled," she blurted before thinking better of it. In pure reflex, Kane lifted his brows as if he were contemplating that idea. "I didn't mean it like that." Then a wrinkle formed between her brows, and he could see she was being serious. "You deceived me. Why didn't you just tell me you were a Natural Shifter?"

He curled in closer—even as she stiffened in his arms. "Yes . . . well that *was* bad . . . especially since you've been so up front and open with me." His sarcasm was not lost on her. Skye opened her mouth, about to refute what he was saying, but then her momentum died off miserably. He was right. She had told him almost nothing about herself, so why should he trust telling her anything? "Besides, you made it quite clear you weren't about to let *me* into your room that first night. And that room was where I wanted to be. How else was I going to get all up in your business?"

She scowled at him, though there was no malice in it. "Is that all you think about?"

"Pretty much," he said with a waggle of his dark brows, "when I'm not trying to save your ass from this Wraith."

"You don't have to save—"

He covered her lips with his finger again. "And, may I add, it's a particularly fine ass."

Kane shifted above her, nudging her legs apart so he could nests his hips comfortably between her spread thighs, resting his weight on his elbows while kissing the tip of her nose. Their bodies aligned so naturally that it amazed her, considering how much larger he was. "So, I saw you had packed your things," he said, nipping gently at the end of said nose with his teeth, letting her know he didn't approve. "You had a convenient excuse to drug me again and were planning on running, weren't you?"

Her eyes slid away from him for a moment, and that was all the confirmation he needed. "I was going to leave . . . I should've left." When she returned her gaze to him she was surprised by the confusion she saw in his eyes. She wasn't quite sure what to make of it. "But you scared me," she continued. "You really scared me when I saw that cut in your side and how deep it was." She reached her hand to smooth it over the quickly healing skin. "I couldn't go until I knew for sure you would be all right."

His hand threaded through her hair, that intense gaze of his seeming to ignite, just like a sparkler. "You know, I'm not going to let you leave now, darlin'. Not until we finish what we've started here."

There was a long silence between them as she dropped her chin. He was right. She couldn't leave, despite knowing there would never be anything more—just one night. But she wanted that one night. She wanted the memory to carry with her, even if by doing so it went against everything she had been raised to believe.

Kane refused to be deterred, dropping his chin, as well, and finding her lips, stealing another kiss. One given with such slow deliberateness and yet such ease that she felt like she was going to combust right there against the blankets. He licked and nibbled at the corner of her lips, playing with them as if he had nothing else on the agenda for the entire evening. He was taking his time . . . as if he had all the time in the world.

A breathy little moan escaped her just before his tongue slipped inside her mouth and cut off every thought of protest, leaving only her hum of satisfaction. Kane's kisses were now different, a little harder and more possessive, and it only served to make her stomach flip faster. Skye was sure that a little devil was sitting on her shoulder, egging her on, as her hands slid under his sweats and caressed his bare, firm glutes. Then she slid her hands forward, and he groaned thickly in response, his head dropping into the V of her neck. "Damn," he whispered, his weight falling more fully against her as he took her wrists and pulled them above her head. "You touch me there, darlin' and this is going to go a whole lot faster than either of us wants it to."

"But I want to touch you."

"Oh, we'll be touching—as much as you want, sweetheart. But only after I've had my fill of touching you. My hands can be very demanding that way."

She pouted, but Kane covered that pout with another kiss. "That's not fair."

"You want to know what's not fair?" he growled in her ear. "That you have so many damn clothes on." His head dropped over her right breast and took it into his mouth along with her thin shirt. He sucked and played her with his tongue, like a musical instrument, until she inhaled sharply, arching her back upward and clear from the mattress. Kane's hands then tightened around her wrists to continue restraining her.

This definitely was not fair.

He chuckled low against her breast and then bit down on the small tip, causing her to squeal with both pleasure and a small bit of pain as her hips went flying up into his. "But you know," he murmured as he rolled slightly to his side and transferred both her wrists into one of his hands, freeing the other to work on tugging her shirt upward, "I'm really starting to like this little rebellious side to you. You're not a passive love-maker, are you, Skye?"

'Passive' certainly didn't seem to be her problem at the moment. Over-eagerness might be. "Maybe if you would stop talking you, would find out."

Kane smiled at that. "Yes, ma'am." He then pulled her shirt over her head, finally exposing her bare breast to his view. She was a smaller size, always had been. It just came with the territory of being a smaller woman. Andrew had not spent a lot of time on her breasts when they were together, making her sometimes question their desirability. But Kane didn't seem to mind. In fact, his delighted expression looked as if someone had just awarded him a grand prize for his efforts. It was rather cute. He also didn't seem to mind that she was not wearing a bra underneath. That was the upside of small breasts. You could get away with going bare a lot. "*Damn*, you're pretty. Do you know that, Skye? Do you know how sweet you are? How sweet you taste?"

Skye smiled and watched him, her excitement building as he pulled the long sleeves of her shirt down to her wrists. But instead of freeing her, he began to ring the shirt into a tight knot, trapping her wrists in the fabric as he stretched her arms above her head. She glanced up at them just as he looped her hands over one another and hooked the shirt firmly around one of the steel leaves that decorated the headboard. "What are you *doing?*" Her last word came out as a squeal because he had already fastened his mouth over her other breast, taking it confidently between his lips, kissing, sucking, administering a small bite here and there. His hands remained busy, too. One squeezed her free breast in his palm, while the other caressed the curving lines of her body, seeming to take every inch of her into his memory.

"Making sure you can't run away from me again."

Skye squealed several more times. She couldn't explain it, but her body just responded to this man. He made her feel so indescribably special and desirable. If she had only one night with him, she would enjoy it. And she would not regret it in the morning—not in the least. She was a grown woman who was discovering she had a very healthy desire to be touched—to be seduced. It was good to truly know what that felt like—at least once. "I'm not running anymore," she answered sincerely, and he stopped for a moment, his breathing hard even though he'd hardly exerted himself. "Not tonight." The silence that followed was a long, significant moment between them that was palpable; her words seemed to hang in the air. It was so crazy intimate, it nearly pitched her over into orgasm without his doing a damn thing except staring at her.

"Not tonight," he repeated as his hands slid beneath the band of her bottoms and began tugging them down on her hips while he returned his attention to her breasts. He tugged on the material of her pants just enough so he could slip his hand between her thighs and press two fingers inside her to test her readiness for him. Hot, wet flesh greeted him, and he growled, biting her nipple again while proceeding to coat his thumb with her juices. Skye was going crazy and she really needed her hands free so she could touch him, but once he began circling over that pea-sized nub she lost all rational thoughts about what she wanted and just allowed herself to feel.

Soon, it was happening again. Skye could feel her body tightening, her inner muscles clenching. She moaned and her back arched, preparing herself to fall away into the same wonderful bliss he had given her before, when suddenly he stopped. Skye let her eyes open, not sure what was happening, only to see his devilishly handsome smile staring down at her as he licked his lips. "Trust me, darling, we'll get there."

She moaned her compliance as his lips and tongue began to trace a warm, wet line down her body, his tongue lingering hotly over anything that seemed to interest him. She was going to kill him for making her wait like this! Did he not realize just how few orgasms she had experienced in her whole life? Make that *one*—the one he'd given her earlier . . . and she wanted another!

"Kane . . . ," she pleaded as he worked his way lower and lower, his hands pulling her bottoms down until they were drawn free of her ankles. Quickly, he pulled away, stood up, and shucked his own sweats. And there he was, standing beside the bed in all his naked glory in, like, two seconds. *Mercy!* Skye had seen Andrew naked before and enjoyed looking at him, had been intrigued by his body. But Kane was something else entirely. His body was cut perfectly. Broad at the shoulders, slim at the hips, toned and firm, but not overly muscled, with a smooth dusting of dark hair spread over his chest, and a narrow line that led from his stomach to a thicker patch at his groin.

Kane stood there with a smile on his lips, evidently pleased by her thorough inspection of him. He was completely unselfconscious, obviously comfortable—even insolently pleased with his body. His cock was a nice size, standing proudly erect, reaching for his navel. She wondered if her small body could take him inside comfortably. Meanwhile, he was looking at her as though the only thing he was questioning was how many times she *would* take him.

He crawled back onto the bed like the predator that he was and reached for a condom on the nightstand, setting it down by her hip. "You let me know if something I do doesn't feel good, or doesn't please you. All right?"

Skye nodded; that was really all her brain could think to do for a second, but then she said, "Not having my hands free doesn't please me. Let me touch you."

He chuckled low, kissed her gently on the lips, then brushed his mouth over her ear. "Soon. Just relax, darlin'." He moved lower once again, making his way down her body, but this time not in a straight line. He meandered to the left and then to the right, and Skye wanted to scream for him to hurry up, but she knew that if she did that, he'd probably only move slower. "*Damn*," he growled. "Your entire body smells of that damned flower. I don't think I'll ever get that scent out of my head."

Skye wasn't sure if she would ever get this night out of her head as Kane licked her inner thigh with his tongue and stared back up at her with a wicked glint to his eyes. *Oh, God*, just what was he going to do? "Kane, I don't think—"

Skye cried out as his head lowered and his warm tongue drew her sensitive flesh between his lips. Her hips wanted to spring from the bed, but he was holding her firmly in place. Every pleasurable sensation Skye had ever felt in her life had been nothing compared to the sensations swirling up inside her now. He was patient, and he was thorough, and it was about to drive her insane. She thought she would pass out, or at the very least embarrass herself by pulling a muscle as her thighs began to shake.

Andrew, the only other sexual experience she could draw on, had never made her feel like this. It was as though Kane knew instinctively how to touch her, how to please her, knew her body better than any other living soul on the planet. Never had Skye felt such a whirlwind of sensations. He had her panting and moaning, not giving a fig for how loud or how needy it sounded. He liked it, too, his fingers showing it as they kneaded almost desperately into her thighs.

His tongue then swirled over her clit once last time. That did it. Skye flew over the edge in one giant jolt of sensations. *My God,* she needed a few more of these! She fell back against the mattress, her mind numb as she let herself just embrace all of the wonderful sensations rolling through her body. It was a perfect moment, a perfect summer storm, a perfect way to fly— and she never wanted to come down.

She sensed that Kane was moving above her, but she was unable to register much more than that as she tried to catch her breath. He reached up for her wrists and freed them from the headboard, and then released her from the shirt twisted around them. As she had once done for him, he kissed the tender skin that had been pulling against the fabric, his gesture an implied promise to soothe them some more later. She then heard the tear in the condom wrapper and the next thing she knew he was cupping her head in his hands, his eyes filled with skyrocketing lust as he positioned himself between her legs. "I need you, Skye."

Kane's hands slid to the taut swells of her bottom and his fingers dug in, positioning her hips exactly as he wanted before he pushed forward with an almost desperate gasp of relief. For a moment, it was as if she couldn't breathe for all the pleasure she felt at his finally being inside her. She wanted to drown in the moment, commit it to memory in case she might have to live with this one night as the best sex of her life—for the rest of her life. Soon she felt full, and then really, really full as he continued to work himself inside her body. And just when Skye believed she could finally breathe again because she had taken all of him, his face tightened and his hips flexed. "We're gonna make this real sweet for you. But tell me if it's too much," he whispered in her ear.

Skye could only gasp her response, swearing she was feeling the full length of him swell even more inside her.

***

Kane was a bastard—and he knew it. Skye's small body could barely take him in, and yet in his lust-filled sexual daze he was continuing to swell inside her with no end in sight. He couldn't stop himself.

This was why women argued over him in kitchens. Why they flocked to be with him again after he'd given them pleasure. He was a Natural Shifter, and that meant he could reshape or enlarge just about any part of his body at will . . . and that included his private parts. He took pride in being able to stretch a woman to her limits in order to raise her to the greatest heights of pleasure. But in the past, if it was too much, he could ease it as well. The point was, it was in *his control,* with all the women he'd ever been with . . . until Skye.

Kane's mind and body were so drunk with the pleasure of being inside her, so lost in the delirium of how her flesh tightened around him like a firm fist, that he seemed to have lost all his control. It was the damndest thing.

One thing, however, was absolutely clear, he had to move. His hands lifted her hips as he stared down into her dilated eyes. She was just as lost in the pleasure as he was, and it made him feel like a God. He pulled back slowly, then thrust forward, dragging from her one of those breathy little sounds that he adored as she dug her nails into his back. Then he drew back and lunged forward again, this time with more force, just praying that he wasn't hurting her. He knew he wasn't being gentle, and he barely had control of his own sanity at that moment.

Just when he decided that the devil needed to surface and drag him down to hell, Skye sighed. The most beautiful, contented sigh he had ever heard from a woman. It made him want to roar with pride. He could live the rest of his life with the memory of that one sound to draw on whenever he wanted. It would sustain him in the worst of times.

It wasn't long before she tightened beneath him, her legs curling higher around his waist and her heels beginning to dig into his back. He groaned, loving how sex with this woman felt, because somehow he knew exactly how to please her, how to make her body sing for him like a finely tuned instrument. It was instinctual, it was ingrained. And it was absolutely imperative that he do it again!

Her fingers gripped his sides while he felt an orgasm building that would explode in what was sure to be one of the most profound sexual moments of his life—the first time with *her.* He was right there, at the raw edge of a monstrous release and using every bit of control he possessed not to fly over until she had come around him, come sweetly for him, just one more time.

"Kane!" she cried as her hips lifted and her nails dug even deeper into his skin. She screamed out her next release, and he couldn't wait a second more. He was stretched so tight inside her and came so hard into the condom that he feared it would blow apart. Gripping the steel headboard to the point he thought it might crumble, he tried to hold himself steady as his hips canted forward and another blast of semen shot from what felt like the back his spine. He was praying the condom would hold, and then all the energy seemed to leave his body at once and he collapsed against her.

Moments later, he was still panting into her shoulder as his brain again became able to function enough to remind him to shift his heavy weight from her. Once Kane regained his wits, he rolled onto his back, removing the condom and tossing it into the trash-can. He was sweating, even shaking a bit as he rolled back and wrapped his arms around her quiet, still form. She had already passed out from exhaustion, but she held on to him even in sleep.

He couldn't sleep. His mind was still trying to process what the hell had just happened. Usually, after sex he was tired, ready to say his polite goodbyes and head back to his room, where he could sleep somewhat better than if he had not found comfort in a woman.

This was very different. He wasn't just tired or relaxed—he was completely, utterly, wholly sated. Sexually speaking, this woman just rocked his world! Inhaling a deep breath, he nestled against her, the scent of her body combined with the scent of their sex creating a potent aphrodisiac for him. He was already looking forward to the next time he could have her, and he would be damned if he would share her with any other man while she was with him, and that included ex-fiancés.

He snorted, recognizing his own jealousy. That was something new. Just what the hell was he supposed to do with that?"

CHAPTER SEVENTEEN

Skye awoke in the midst of feeling the most decadent of sensations, the warmth of skin against her cheek, a gentle kiss on the top of her head, and a man's strong heartbeat thundering into her ear.

The memory of the day and night before was so perfect, she debated whether to lie there pretending to be asleep so she could just continue to re-live it in her mind.

"I can tell you're awake." It was Kane's morning voice, rough and crackling. "You're breathing differently."

Well, so much for pretending. Her eyes fluttered open and she raised her head to the man who was wrapped around her, one arm holding her against his chest while the other stroked over her hip. He had obviously just showered, which was completely unfair because he smelled entirely too yummy. The light brushing of the masculine hair on his legs and chest against her skin electrified her, making her so utterly aware of him as a man that she didn't want to think about what it would be like when he was gone. And he would leave. He had told her that.

One night with Kane had been so different from the last two years with Andrew. Andrew had been good and gentle, but Kane . . . He had changed her somehow. All of her responses to him came so naturally. She didn't feel self conscious about her flaws—like her small breasts, which he'd managed to make her forget in no time—or embarrassed by her complete loss of self-control when it came to her own orgasmic screams. In fact, the more she had begged and pleaded, the better he seemed to like it. He allowed her to be herself and not feel uncomfortable about her sexuality.

"For a minute, there, I thought you planned to sleep the morning away," his voice still filtering through that rough, morning-gravel that made her smile. She knew it meant that he had slept more deeply after their lovemaking than he had on the night before, when he was injured.

Skye glanced at the clock on the nightstand. "I've only been asleep for two hours since the last time you—"

Skye stopped herself short of saying '*made love to me*'. There was no point in ruining a perfectly nice night with words that were likely to make him bolt from the bed. It pleased her, though, when he squeezed her a little tighter and teased in her ear, "I know. You'd think you were going to make a man wait all morning to seduce you again."

"Seduce, huh," she said with a twitch to her lips. "Well, all right, then. Let's see what you've got this time, Shifter."

Kane laughed, a good, deep, strong laugh. "Not satisfied with the first few go-'rounds, eh, darlin'?"

"It's your own fault if I'm curious how you plan to top yourself this morning. You've set the bar awfully high, you know."

Kane slid down on the mattress till they were practically nose to nose, then buried his head into the fleshy part of her shoulder and inhaled deeply. "I liked being with you last night, Skye Matthews."

Her heart seemed to skip a beat because the moment felt incredibly personal for him as well as her. He was letting her in, something she certainly hadn't expected.

"I didn't hurt you, did I?" he asked, his brows pinched slightly with concern. "I mean, I could've been gentler . . . and I could've warned you . . ."

Evidently, an always confident Kane wasn't quite sure how to ask if it had somehow been a problem that his cock had swelled inside her till she was stretched to her very limits. Which, it wasn't . . . *after* her body had had a chance to adjust. "Yes, that was a bit surprising," she replied. "No, you didn't hurt me. I liked being with you, too. I'd like . . . ," she paused for a moment, not sure if it was wise to continue. " . . . I'd like to know more about you. Something . . ."

Skye couldn't believe she was hesitant to ask him such a simple question. She had told him almost nothing about herself, yet she wanted to know more about him so she would have something to hold on to in her memories.

Instead, he kissed her. Cupping his hands over her cheeks, he pulled her to him and planted one lengthy, toe-tingling kiss that had her heart skipping several beats. When he pulled back to stare into her eyes, he smiled, "My father was from the South. Montgomery, Alabama. He called my mother, darlin'—almost hourly, it seemed on some days. They both died when I was young . . . just turned five, I think. His pet name for her is one of the few clear memories I have of either of them."

Skye smiled, then pulled it back when she realized she shouldn't be smiling, since he had just told her his parents had died when he was so young. Kane had shared something about his family, something deeply personal to him. She wouldn't pretend it was in any way significant with regard to how he felt about her, just as his referring to her as *darlin'* wasn't. He probably used that endearment with a lot of the women he had been with, if nothing else, because he seemed to be a creature of habit. But it still meant a lot to her that he had shared where it had come from. It felt like some little part of him she could tuck in her pocket and keep for herself. "I'm sorry about your parents. It must've been painful to lose them both when you were so young."

"It was," he agreed. "After they died, a family friend moved me to live with one of my mother's friends in Vancouver, B.C. I liked the family—and I obviously didn't mind growing up in a houseful of women. But I never quite felt like I belonged." He shrugged. "That's why I dropped the last name. It just didn't seem to matter anymore. And eventually, I found a home at The Oracle."

"How did they die?" She couldn't stop herself from asking.

He paused for a moment as he thought back. "My father was a collector of rare artifacts. His favorites were Christian, Greek and Roman. He would travel the world to find them, and once he had enough pieces to open his own shop, he moved us to upstate New York." Kane's expression scrunched up into a frown, and Skye found herself holding her breath, knowing that the rest of the story wouldn't have a happy ending. "One night, near closing, some men robbed the store while my mother was with him. She'd asked me to stay in the car. The bastards shot them without any warning. They both died instantly."

Skye blinked several times. She hadn't expected to hear that they had both died so violently. "Kane," she began softly, "you don't have to—"

"It's all right," he said. "It happened a long time ago, and I have to admit my memories of them are pretty much gone now, though, I can never escape that feeling of uselessness I experienced just sitting in a car while my parents were both murdered twenty feet away."

"You were just a child. There wasn't anything you could have done to stop it. Death is just a part of life." Skye stroked his hand, not really sure why she needed to do it—but she did. His hands were so large and masculine, rough, but they appealed to her a great deal. They were hands of strength.

"My skin warms where you touch me," he said quietly. "Every time you touch me. But then, I think you know that, don't you?"

"What makes you say that?"

"Because I felt it when your sisters touched me as well."

She did know that; she could feel it with each contact. That was how it was supposed to be for her and all of her sisters, but she had to be careful not to use it too much. She tried to pull her hands back, but he stopped her. "No, don't. I like when you touch me."

She allowed a small smile, knowing there was no possible way to contain it. He just made her feel giddy with happiness when she was with him. "So, which one of them was a shifter? Your father or mother?"

With a coy smile, he asked, "How do you know they both weren't shifters?"

"Because I know Natural Shifters like you are very rare. Honestly, I thought I'd never meet one in this lifetime. It would make sense that only one of your parents was a Natural."

"Well, I'm sorry to disappoint you, darlin', but I don't have the answer to that. I don't remember seeing either of them being able to shift. And they both died in that robbery. If they'd had gifts, they should've been able to defend themselves."

"Maybe they intentionally kept it from you. Maybe they were giving you time to accept that part of who you are."

Kane's expression grimaced thoughtfully. "I suppose that's possible. I didn't actually start shifting into other forms until after I went to live with the Weitz family, but I kept it from them, as well."

"Really? Why? They must've had some idea that you were different."

He stroked his fingers through her hair, his gaze thoughtful. "I guess I was waiting to see other people who were like me. I knew I was different. I had questions . . . But there never was another person like me."

Skye's heart ached for him, imagining what it would be like to know you were different and having no one to talk to about it without revealing yourself. That would make it very hard to trust people—and all too easy to feel like an outcast—to feel alone. She then realized how much she was amazed by the person Kane had become. He didn't appear to be angry or vengeful about his circumstances, the way his parent's had been brutally taken from him when he was just a boy, being moved across the country to a strange family, or never meeting another shifter like himself. He was funny, intelligent, a loyal friend. He and Aiden were obviously very close. These were all things to be admired.

"Once I was old enough to drive I left Vancouver and my adopted family. It was becoming impossible to hide what I was from them. By the time I was eighteen, I was living in Calgary and met a sharp-tongued, pain-in-the-ass teenager named Lucas Rayner."

Skye gasped and her light touch over Kane's hand hardened into a full grip. "He was your friend that died at Brahm Hill, wasn't he?"

Kane nodded and was quiet for a long while. "Lucas said when he met me he knew that I was gifted. I was surprised. I hadn't revealed my abilities to him."

"Did you ever ask him how he knew?"

Kane nodded. "A few years later . . . He said I was too cocky for eighteen and alone in the world—that I owned life like I'd done it all before. He was right, in a way. No matter how alone I

felt, I always knew I had my gift. Somehow it was enough."
Kane paused as if he were recalling some private memories that
brought a touch of a smile to his face. "He eventually brought
me to The Oracle. There I was able to ask questions, learn
about my gifts so that I could understand them . . . control
them. Even though he's gone now, finding me is something I'll
always be grateful to him for."

Skye touched her hand to his cheek, her gaze meeting his
with so much feeling and sincerity in her heart she hoped he
could feel it. "I'm sorry you lost him. That you lost both of them
that night."

"Phin's still alive. I know he is. Maybe I couldn't save Lucas,
but I'll find Phin. I have to."

Skye swung her arms around his neck and hugged him close.
"You will. I know you will." She wanted to say thank you for
sharing a part of himself, but it sounded so corny in her own
head she decided against it.

"Yes . . . you see how that works. I share something with you,
and you . . ."

"Share something," Skye finished for him. "Yes, I see the
pattern." Skye glanced away from him, biting at her lower lip as
she tried to figure out what to say. She wasn't allowed to tell
Kane about her family. Not even a little. And then there was the
matter of all his questions regarding her father. There was so
much more at stake than just what she wanted; she had to
remember that. But it didn't stop her from wishing he was the
one person she could tell everything to. "Kane, I can't tell you
what you want to know about my father."

He frowned slightly at that, his left hand holding her face as
he stroked through her hair with his right. "I didn't ask about
your father. I asked about you. Tell me something about you."

She could feel her expression falling because she knew he
was going to be disappointed with her answer. "I can't tell you
that, either."

"Why?"

"Because I can't," she said, straightening herself up and
pulling the sheet with her until she was seated with her back
against the headboard.

His lips thinned in displeasure. "That's a child's answer, Skye."

"Well, it's all I have," she defended weakly. "So stop pushing me."

Those words caused her instant regret. Kane's expression changed so fast it was like a thunderbolt of anger hitting the room. He pushed from the bed to his feet, the lone towel around his waist threatening to slide to the floor. He looked as if he was about to say something but simply turned away from her and walked out of the room, shutting the door behind him.

She had hurt him.

She didn't want to hurt him, but there were rules meant to protect her and her family, to keep them safe from discovery, to allow them to do their jobs. She couldn't break them just because she was basking in the glow of a one-night stand.

Skye frowned at the path her thoughts were taking. To Kane, their night was probably just good sex, something he had more than likely experienced many times, whereas, to her it was really, *really* good sex—a connected-in-every-way kind of good sex. Even though she didn't have a lot to compare it with, she hoped he considered it more than just fucking.

Throwing back the covers, she headed toward the small in-suite bathroom. For several minutes, she stood there staring at her own reflection in the mirror until her bottom lip quivered, She bit down on it purposefully because she didn't quite trust herself to not start crying. Tossing her clothing to the floor in a heap, she stepped under a hot stream of water that fogged up the bathroom quickly while she sluiced the water from her face with a sigh. She had done the right thing by not revealing anything about her family. Her father would have expected no less.

So why did it *feel* wrong? Why did it hurt so much?

Eeek, she was a foolish, dramatic girl, filling her head with foolish, childish dreams. It was a wonder that she could get any of her assignments done.

Frustrated, she quickly rubbed a towel over her skin and grabbed Kane's tee shirt from the foot of the bed, not caring that she'd be running into the main room with damp hair, no makeup, and just a soft blue tee shirt covering her—his tee shirt. From the kitchen, Kane glanced up at her as she appeared and, at first, tried to show little interest, but soon his silver gaze began to positively smoke as it settled over her half-dressed form. His nostrils flared and his chest rose with a swift and deep intake of breath. Even from clear across the room he could smell every scent that had been in the bath products she just used. And he approved, outwardly shifting in his stance. Inwardly, however, he was still angry and had a point to make. So he tried to cover his growing desire—and, she guessed, the growing erection he must be experiencing under cover of the island counter—by scowling at her as though she'd just run into the room in a clown suit.

That tactic worked pretty well—because now she felt a little ridiculous. In her haste to confront him, she hadn't exactly made a plan, so she just stood there for a long moment while he cursed under his breath. "Are you just going to stand there and drip all over the floor?" he growled as he began shuffling through the cupboards for what she guessed was nothing in particular, making an excessive amount of noise as he pulled random items down to the counter.

He *had* managed to find some clothes, worn blue jeans and a collared shirt, though nothing was straightened or buttoned, rather as though she had interrupted before he could finish. The man was positively devastating to a woman's senses—and so worth the scolding she would undoubtedly receive from her father over this very moment at some point in the future. "I like breakfast foods for dinner," she blurted, all the while tugging at the hem of his tee shirt in a futile move toward modesty.

Kane continued to avoid her gaze, and she wondered if he had any idea how much it was hurting her, "Nice try," he replied, still without looking up, "but I already know that. I'm not sure there's a food invented that you wouldn't put maple syrup on."

Damn, that certainly was true enough, although, she couldn't imagine putting maple syrup on meat or fish. Salad maybe—with apples, nuts, and dried cranberries. *Yummy!*

"I have a terrifying fear of thunderstorms," she blurted quickly, as if to offer some sort of valid statement. "I know exactly what causes thunder—warm and cold air mixing over hot land. So it's an illogical fear, but they can just be so loud . . ."

Kane gave her a look that she couldn't quite decipher before pulling some butter and eggs from the fridge. Was it boredom?

OK, so this wasn't quite working the way she had planned. But then, what was she talking about? She hadn't planned any of this!

Her fingers tensed at her sides as if trying to hold onto a lifeline that was slipping away from her. He wanted more from her, and right now she couldn't think of anyone else in her life that she wanted to give more to. "I know what's it's like to lose a parent," she said in one long exhale. "I lost my mother two years ago. She died in her sleep."

That got his attention.

He set down the items in his hands and crossed the room, stopping just inches from her, reaching forward to stroke his fingers lightly along the backs of her arms. His expression was thoughtful, focused, and he remained silent while waiting for her to continue. "My mother's name was Merryn. I don't really ever talk about it . . . about her. So, I suppose I compensate a lot by talking about my father. Which is horribly unfair to her memory, isn't it?"

But Skye didn't wait for him to answer; she just wanted to throw up her hands in surrender, knowing she was now just babbling. "She was an amazing woman. I'd be lucky to be anything like her. I looked the most like her of all my sisters. Although my nose is a little more squished," she said, absently pressing the tip of her finger into her nose. "And her eyes were blue . . . a very pretty sea blue."

Kane erased the little distance left between them, his arms wrapping around her, oh, so gently, as he kissed her temple and dropped his forehead against hers. "Thank you," he said, so quietly she almost didn't hear him. They stayed like that for a long while, and he didn't ask her anything else, which was a relief. It was still difficult for her to discuss her mother, but Kane seemed to understand that.

His breathing was soft against her lips as he asked, "Would you like some breakfast?"

Skye smiled up at him. "Yeah, I would."

Kane took her hand and led her to the island counter. It wasn't long before they fell into easy conversation again. He talked of his days growing up as the only boy in a family of females. How his bad-boy ways started at an early age. He even confided that once he had hit puberty he would often shift into one of his sister's forms so he could watch their friends undress, unaware, in front of him.

"That's awful!" Skye declared. "How did they not see what a little devil you were?" He shrugged almost imperceptibly while she got busy picturing the precocious young boy discovering he had quite a gift. She still marveled at how difficult it must have been to hide who and what he was from his adopted family. He must have felt so alone at times. Even though she had lost her mother, one of her greatest confidants, she still had her sisters and her father, which had helped her get through some of the worst days. Kane had had no one after he lost his parents. She couldn't imagine how lonely that must have made him feel.

After breakfast, they ended up on the sofa. Kane sank into the cushions and pulled Skye down to sit straddled over his lap. The position felt natural with him, even though it was rather intimate for two people who had known each other for such a short time. "So, I've been thinking . . . ," he began as his hands cupped around her bottom and hauled her firmly against him. "If your father is sending you out on these *assignments*, there has to be a reason for it. He has to know what he's sending you to do. Which means . . . either *he* knows, or *someone else* is directing him."

Skye inhaled slowly. She must be cautious. She knew Kane was intuitive, but his perceptive interpretation caught her off guard. Clearly, he had a sharp mind to go with his rare good looks. She wanted him to know her better, but she wanted to do so without betraying her family. Had she just made a huge mistake telling him what little she had?

❋❋❋

Skye tried to push away from Kane, but he resisted. He curled his arms around her and pulled her back to him. "No, stay," he said. "I promise I won't betray you or your family."

She was resting her small hands on his chest, her shallow breathing puffing just over his lips. She was a nice weight against him, he thought, and he could feel the heat of his body reaching out for her through his clothing. *God*, how he wanted her—again. But it wasn't just her body he wanted, it was her trust. He could see the conflict in her eyes as she chewed at her lip. It was making him crazy that she was holding back from him, and he couldn't understand why. He never really cared before about what secrets a woman might be keeping.

"You know that's not a promise you can make. Doesn't your association with The Brethren demand loyalty—answers? Aren't you bound to confide anything—everything—I tell you that touches them or the supernatural world?"

That was certainly true enough. He had at least two messages on his cell phone right now from Alec, probably wondering why Skye was not already back at The Oracle for questioning. "I am sworn to my duty, but I care about you. I want to help you."

"I didn't say I needed any help."

He kissed her.

He had to kiss her. She had been staring at him, continuing to chew on her lower lip as if she wanted to believe him, but she was obviously weighing the consequences in her pretty little head. He needed her to just stop thinking and instead to trust him.

Kane gently caressed her lips with his, slowly tasting her, inhaling her flowering scent, until she relaxed and her body sagged against him like the perfect weight. He could feel her warmth, the heat between her thighs that was shooting signals through his body and exciting him to the point he felt weak. Because whether this woman knew it or not, she now had his complete attention. He would give her anything she wanted if she just would just keep touching him.

"Kane, I . . . ," she began, pulling back a little, her emerald eyes shimmering with uncertainty.

He hated seeing that! So he tipped his head forward until their foreheads met and whispered, "Trust me."

She was quiet for a long while, and he filled that silence with more reassuring kisses and some soft stroking along her back, skin-to-skin under her tee shirt. A small murmur escaped her as she pulled just off his lips, holding his scruffy morning face in her hands. She closed her eyes in a long blink, opened them, and said, "My father can see what's destined. It comes to him in his dreams. That's how he knows where to send us."

Kane continued to run his fingers up and down her back as he considered that for a moment. She was saying that Argus Matthews was a clairvoyant with precognition; he could see into the future and beyond. He wasn't sure he believed that any man or woman had those powers. Even in the supernatural world there was little evidence to support such a thing.

Kane had thought through this concept many times before. As simple as the idea sounded, and as much as humans loved to believe there were those among them with the ability to predict future events and outcomes, it was simply impossible, because the future was always shifting. Logic told him that by the very virtue of someone being able to see into the future, that future would be changed, its course would be altered.

It was clear, however, from the determined look in Skye's eyes, that she believed it and wanted him to believe her. Right now, that was enough for him. "OK," he responded, "let's agree that your father can see the future. Are you saying he sends you on these assignments because he wants you to change what he sees?"

She shook her head. "No. We are to make sure the future stays as he sees it. There's great pressure and responsibility on him to ensure that things happen as they are supposed to occur. Especially when the outcome is something he struggles with."

Kane steadily held her gaze, willing her to continue. "I worry for him," she said with a sad smile. "Recently, he's talked a lot about the consequences of trying to change what's destined. I've never told anyone this, but I think my father might have seen my mother's death coming. I worry that in an effort to save her he may have done something that has had a ripple effect on the supernatural world."

"I thought you said your mother died in her sleep?"

"She did. But I keep thinking that she was supposed to die another way and he changed that." Skye scrubbed her hands over her weary expression and began shaking her head. "Don't you see? He may have changed something important by what he did. *I* may have changed things now by telling you—an outsider."

Again she tried to squirm away, but Kane gently pulled her back to him. "It's all right," he soothed, whispering directly into her ear. "I won't say anything. I'll keep your secret. Just be here with me."

He continued to hold her, calming her with his words, all the while trying to understand how this could feel so right. She relaxed into him. The moment his lips met hers he felt the sincerity, the absolute goodness within himself that her kiss invoked. Somehow he was meant to be here with this woman. The heat of his own body seemed to flare up, rapidly rising beyond his control, and he gave in to the truth that her lips were the sweetest thing he'd ever tasted on this earth. All his mind could process was how he wanted to carry her back into the bedroom and spread her over that bed like the five-star Sunday brunch that she was. A bouquet meant to be sampled and savored until every bite of his hunger was satisfied.

Right now, though, his body wasn't cooperating with the plan to move. Arousal-wise, he was hard as concrete and, given the position they were settled in, pinched painfully within his jeans. "Skye, I need you again," he said roughly, "I need you." He started to caress his hands over her skin but she surprised him, her small hands encircling his wrists and bringing them back up to stretch along the back of the sofa.

Kane dropped his head back onto the backrest of the sofa and pinched his eyes closed, whispering her name like the sweetest prayer on his lips, while at the same time trying to calm his suddenly enflamed body. "Please don't tell me you're not in the mood, darlin', because I'm on fire here."

She merely responded by kissing him behind the ear, a particularly sensitive spot that she had discovered the night before. He groaned, feeling the animal inside him being called to the surface as she squeezed his wrist and ground the heat of her sex against him. *Had he ever felt anything this good or this right?* This woman was soft and sweet as honey, wet for him, and the evidence of it was currently notched over him under that damn tee shirt of his she wore.

"Remember when you tied yourself to my bed?" she asked him in a hoarse whisper.

Remember? It was marked on his mental calendar as a day to pay homage to every single year at this time.

"How you longed to be free from the ropes so you pulled until they tore at your wrists?" Her hands rubbed gently over his, as if she was trying to invoke the memory,

"Yes," he answered as she pushed his arms and hands over the back of the sofa until his chest and shoulders were stretched as tightly as they had been that day. "I remember."

"I really wanted you then. I fantasized about taking you inside me, holding you there while you struggled with your desire to move." *Good God*, his dick just went from concrete to the consistency of a diamond at the sound of those wicked words. Did she have any idea what she was doing to him? "I fantasized about having the control, taking you as *I* wanted."

His mouth was dry and he groaned so hard the sound seemed to scrape at the back of his throat. "Skye, you're killing me."

She stretched out her arms to reach his hands, squeezed over them as they gripped the back of the sofa, and then let her own hands return to the center of them and slide down the front of his chest to the bulge in his jeans, where his erection felt like it was about to pop the seams. "I won't deny you, Kane," she whispered as he released the top fastener of his jeans and began popping the botton-fly below, "but you must keep your arms right there on the sofa . . . ," she instructed, " . . . as if they were bound—like our first time. Let me have my fantasy."

Kane was panting. *Actually panting!* He had already begun to feel as though he was going to come right in his jeans—and that had been before she slipped her small hands inside them. For a moment he just sat there, growling, as she held him, then squeezed him slowly. "Skye!" he blurted out in a rough rasp, sweating as he watched her slide to her knees in front of him.

He cursed inwardly several times in response. If this woman put those sweet lips on him there was no way he was going to last. No way in hell! And there would be no way he'd keep his damn hands on the back of the sofa, so she'd better not expect it.

She tugged his jeans down his hips as he lifted his body a few inches to accommodate her, while her hot, emerald gaze watched him, literally welding him to his seat on the sofa as the muscles in his arms flexed violently. "Keep your arms there," she warned, "or I'll have to stop until you behave."

Well, that certainly changed things. There was no way he wanted her to stop, so he would just have to suffer in this state of sexual agony.

Skye's hand wrapped firmly around his base and stroked him a few times before she tucked him inside her mouth. At just that first contact, Kane felt like he was about to burst, implode, spontaneously combust—any adjective that described a man being shot into a pleasure so great that it bordered on searing pain. She sucked him slowly and worked her tongue back and forth over that sensitive seam underneath. His teeth ground against his jaw, and the muscles in his shoulders and arms flexed so tight he felt as though he would break the sofa in half.

Fuck, he couldn't ever remember a woman pleasing him to the point that he would beg—literally, beg her not to stop. He prided himself on his control, his ability to focus on the woman. Usually his sexual encounters were about the unique pleasure *he* could give *her.* How he could stretch to them, fit to them, so they could experience the sharpest release possible. The women, once lost in it, forgot about everything but that moment . . . including how they might please him in return. Kane never expected such intimacies from one-night stands, which, let's face it, made up the majority of his sexual encounters. Though he secretly longed for oral sex, he understood that a lot of women needed to be more comfortable with their partner before they would venture into that territory. So he just accepted the idea that he would receive his pleasure from their pleasure. The more a woman lost control, the more it turned him on. That was enough.

Until now . . .

This woman, his beautiful Skye, had him flying so high he feared he would never be able to come back down from it. And just how was a man supposed to handle a permanent erotic high like this without his head exploding? "Skye, please.

Please!" Yes, he was begging. "I'm so close, darlin'. I can't . . ." He groaned so hard this time his voice sounded as if it were grating against steel. "I want—I need to be inside you."

Those beautiful lips sucked him deep one last time before gripping him at the base and holding him tight. "Do you have protection on you?"

Had she just asked him a question? She rifled around in his jean pockets at his knees, while he sat there ridiculously, his gasping breaths noisily sawing in and out of his chest. He hissed as he felt the condom being rolled over his throbbing flesh, then she settled onto her knees above him. His mind could barely process anything, but, thankfully, she wasn't wearing any panties under that damn tee shirt so there was no delay to him feeling her sliding down onto him.

Damn, but he was lost. She was taking him slowly, her internal muscles working hard as they both gasped. He was a lot to take, especially since he seemed to have no control over his swelling inside her. As he thickened he cursed aloud, wondering how it was going to be possible for him to last more than ten seconds. She was hot. She was wet. And she was inciting him to the point he swore he had never been this hard, this thick—*this deep*—inside a woman before in his life.

She bit her bottom lip deliciously as she settled onto him, her body full—too full, really. "Kane!" she gasped.

And he wanted to roar with possessive pride, his hands feeling like they could rip away the upholstery on the back of the sofa with very little effort. Somewhere in the back of his sexually charged brain he remembered her saying she fantasized about wanting the control to move on him. *Damn,* but there was no way he could sit still. He wished he was a more patient man, but his patience was gone the second she settled fully on him.

Kane thrust his hips upward in one sharp motion. The startled moan that emerged from her throat, followed by her deep sigh of satisfaction, told him she would forgive him for needing to take control. "Again!" she murmured, gripping his shoulders as if she were holding on for dear life. He couldn't even speak. Only raspy, passion-filled sounds that were more like grunts roared out of him. His palms pushed inward against the back of the sofa for stability as his hips began to thrust in a repeated rhythm, lifting her, driving high into her body. Her beautiful, green eyes were staring at him with that unmistakable glazed, unfocused look of a woman who was entirely lost to the sensations. He had no idea how he had managed not to explode inside her already, other than the fact he just had to watch and feel her fly over the edge with him. And after several more thrusts, she did.

Skye howled, a long, ragged cry, as her hips locked and her nails clawed into his shoulders. In that moment, Kane accepted the fact he would need to hear that sweet sound from her at least a dozen more times before he could get this woman completely out of his system. His breath hitched under his own orgasm, a release that had all of the veins in his neck popping out against his throat. An electric convulsion now tore through him with a vengeance he had experienced only twice before in his life—just hours earlier, with her.

This woman was *it* for him. *It!* He was still thinking that thought as his body finished and Skye fell slack against him in exhaustion.

It was several minutes later when Kane was finally able to coordinate his muscles enough to release his grip on the sofa back and lovingly wrap his arms around her huddled form. He was still inside her, semi-hard but sated and at a complete loss as to what he was going to do next. He didn't do relationships. He didn't do commitment. But if he couldn't have this woman again, and again, he feared he would chase this feeling for the rest of his life, the splendor of it vanished from his memory bank forever.

He was unsure how much time had passed when she murmured sleepily against his shoulder, "Kane, take me to bed."

He kissed her reverently across her temple. "Yes, my darlin'."

My darlin'. It sounded good to him. Possessive, he supposed —but absolutely right.

CHAPTER EIGHTEEN

After a few hours of some of the most blissful sleep Kane had ever experienced, he and Skye spent the rest of the night slowly kissing and exploring each other's bodies until they couldn't stand it any longer and he took her all over again.

Kane had never imagined he would spend a day in bed with one woman and lie there wishing for it to never end, but that's what was happening. He stared at the ceiling, his body limp from exhaustion as the back of his finger stroked their way all over Skye's sleeping form, nude beside him.

He was brought back to reality as the obnoxious, vibrating sound of his phone on the bedside table shocked him to full consciousness. He remembered that the phone's buzzing had been going off at intervals all afternoon, maybe even at the exact same moment he was going off inside Skye. That would certainly have been no time to answer it. But he'd forgotten the buzzing noise more than once as they were swept into the next round, only to be reminded again the next time it would go off . . . at the exact same time he did.

He grabbed the phone and kissed Skye on her cheek before leaving the bed. She murmured something incoherent and rolled sleepily onto her other side. It made him ache to crawl right back into bed with her. The act of leaving her didn't put him in the best mood as he walked into the other room, but he laughed despite himself as he looked down his naked form and realized that he was hard again. The woman had cursed him somehow, but it was the sweetest curse he had ever known. "Yeah," he answered in a lazy drawl.

"Why the hell haven't you been picking up your phone?" Aiden barked at him in a most irritated way. "I thought you were in trouble."

Oh, he was in trouble, all right. "I've been a little busy."

"Shit," Aiden hissed. "I know that relaxed voice. You've fucked her, haven't you?" He then covered his hand over the phone. "Sorry, Gideon."

"You said that shit with Gideon right there? Thanks a lot, man. Now *he* can tell Alec, and I can get my ass chewed from both sides."

"Well, if you'd answer your damn phone you would know that Gideon and I are on our way to you. Argus Matthews showed up yesterday and was pissed to high heaven. As expected, he didn't give us any information, but he did give us an earful about what he would do to you when he found you. The man really can't stand you."

Kane could manage to offer only a careless snort.

"I think we were able to send him in the wrong direction, at least for a few hours, but he's eventually going to figure it out."

"Let 'em," Kane answered simply.

"Has our Wraith showed up down there? He seems to have disappeared."

"Almost on her tail. It's like he knew exactly where to track her. And then he just disappeared again. He *literally* moved to take her, then disappeared in front of my eyes. It's the damndest thing."

"Listen . . . Gideon has some answers for you."

"Well, it's about fucking time! Put him on the phone."

"Trust me. This is a conversation better had in person."

"I don't care. Put him on the phone."

Aiden ignored him. "We'll be there within the hour. And for God's sake, whatever you do, *do not* sleep with her again. Or, as Alec would say, *keep it in your pants.*"

"Fuck off," he growled, hanging up the phone and throwing it on the sofa. He wasn't sure how to pinpoint exactly what had soured his mood. There were so many things to choose from. He knew he hadn't pressed very hard to demand answers from Aiden and Gideon, and it was because he no longer wanted to know all of Skye's secrets. At least, not right away. He liked that she was beginning to trust him, slowly unveiling pieces of the woman underneath, in her own time. She was like solving a puzzle, and it drew him to her like a bee to honey.

When Aiden and Gideon arrived with answers, he knew that it might be the end of his time with her. Once he understood how to help her—and he would help her—there would be no reason to keep her tied to him any longer. He couldn't very well go around playing the '*you're my captive*' brute forever. He would have to let her go.

That had been the plan in the first place, hadn't it?

As he strolled back into the bedroom, Skye fluttered open those beautiful green eyes of hers and looked up at him with all the innocence of a child, even as she managed to eat up every inch of his nude body with her gaze. It devastated him and made him sexually hungrier than he had ever been, all at the same time. "Who was that?" she asked.

"Nothing for you to worry about," he said as he crawled back onto the bed with her.

She looked up at him. "You sounded upset."

He shook his head. "I'm good." He curled his hand around her soft thighs and pulled her beneath him. She opened her legs to him willingly as he positioned himself at her entrance. With a groan, he sank into the heat of her body about one second after he rolled the condom on—no preliminaries necessary. "Now," he said thickly, his face contorted with intense pleasure. "Where were we?"

✳✳✳

About forty minutes later Skye was panting, exhausted, against Kane's warm, solid chest when a smile spread over her lips. He had just made her come for the fifth time in one afternoon. Her body had never been this responsive, or this happy, and she wished somehow she could stay here with him forever. Let the rest of the world, the rest of her responsibilities, fall away.

"Why don't you treat yourself to a hot bath," he hummed into her ear in that heavy, sated timbre of his. "I assure you, you've earned it."

"Are you saying you don't want to join me?" Her heart beat faster in anticipation of his answer.

"Oh, darlin'," he rolled into a position above her and, with a lazy smile, stroked his thumb along the crest of her cheek.

"There's nothing I would rather do. But I'd only end up taking you again, and you've got to be a little sore by now."

Skye flushed. She was sore, but she just wanted to spend more time with him. She frowned inwardly, realizing she was letting her dream-world fantasies convince her that she actually belonged with him. Of course, that wasn't true. . Eventually, she would have to face reality. She understood that she must return to Andrew, even though the very idea of trying to feel something for him again after she had been with Kane seemed near impossible. It was, in her mind, her duty.

"Go," he said, smacking her lightly across her bottom. "Enjoy your bath. I'll make you something to eat. Perhaps there's even some maple syrup left."

Skye laughed, determined to hold onto the happiness of this moment for as long as she could before jumping out of bed, completely unselfconscious about prancing around nude in front of him. That seemed amazing to her. Before Kane, she had always been a little uncertain about her body in its bare form. She supposed it was just another way Kane had managed to change her way of thinking about herself as a sexual person. And she liked it. She liked it very much.

Skye had been soaking in her bubbly paradise for about twenty minutes when she thought she heard raised voices coming from the main area, several voices, uttering words that sounded like an argument. She got out of the bath, dressed quickly in some dark jeans and a soft, white cardigan to keep her warm, and headed into the main room. Seeing Aiden and Gideon standing there, she was stopped short. A sudden sense of dread hit her heart, and she knew she had been feeling that pang right from the moment she had laid eyes on Gideon. He had a gentle look on his face, one that said he had answers— and that he was sorry, all at the same time.

Kane turned to see her there and must have been able to see the sudden dread in her expression. "It's all right, darlin'," he said, coming to her immediately and pressing a kiss on her temple. He didn't try to hide the fact that things had become intimate with them. "I just need to talk to Gideon about a couple of things outside. Aiden's going to stay here with you."

"Kane . . . please," she whispered, but she wasn't even sure what she was pleading for.

"Hey," he replied in a quiet voice just meant for their ears. "I'll be right back. I promise."

"You knew they were coming? That was the phone call?"

He nodded at her quietly in return. Skye hated how the dread she felt was starting to take over every part of her. At that point it wasn't reasonable fear—it was instinct. She *knew* her time with Kane was coming to an end. "My father?" she asked, glancing past Kane's shoulder back to Aiden.

"He'll be here by nightfall, I imagine."

She nodded in acceptance, knowing that her world would soon be returning to the one she had always known. And for the first time she could remember, she didn't want it.

"He'll want you to leave with him, I'm sure," Aiden continued. Would you like some help with your things—?"

"She doesn't need her things packed!" Kane bit back angrily.

Gideon broke the strained silence that followed with one of his characteristic throat clearings. "Kane," he began gently, "perhaps we should talk before you decide the next best course of action."

Kane looked to be considering something deeply before pointing a warning finger at his friend meant to remind Aiden that he was not to touch Skye's things. "I'll be right back." He then took one last look at Skye and smiled softly before following Gideon out the door.

And Skye couldn't help but think it was out of her life, as well.

✱✱✱

"What do you know?" Kane began abruptly after he and Gideon had created enough distance from the house so they couldn't be overheard. Gideon had made sure of that, but Kane wasn't in the mood for any of it. He hadn't liked seeing that look on Skye's face. Her expression seemed a mixture of dread and resignation. His immediate instinct was to turn right back around and go to her, to ease whatever bad thoughts she had swirling around in her head.

"I'm afraid, Kane, as much as you and I would like the answers to be simple here, they're not."

"Gideon . . . ,"Kane replied in a frustrated voice, letting the man know he didn't want one of his typical long, drawn out explanations for things.

Thankfully, Gideon seemed to get the message. "Are you familiar with the term 'Muse'?"

Kane's brow scrunched. "What? Like the band?"

"No," Gideon smiled with amusement. "I mean as in Greek Mythology."

Kane rubbed his hands over his face before staring back at Gideon with a tired expression. "As in pre-Christian Greek Mythology? The stuff they teach in school? What the hell does that have to do with the supernatural world today?"

"Quite a lot, actually. There are Guides among The Brethren who believe the Greek and Roman stories of myth were actually influenced by early brushes of humans with the supernatural world. For centuries, it was assumed that the Greeks created their teachings of Gods and heroes to explain their own existence. But their stories may have come from fear —a fear of having already realized the existence of something much more powerful than themselves."

"What? Like the Greeks had a run in with a Lycan thousands of years ago?"

"Possibly. We know that Lycans have been around for thousands of years."

"And is this something you believe?" Kane asked him.

"I didn't have enough information on the subject to form an opinion either way . . . until today." Gideon finally stopped walking and turned to Kane, his expression even more serious than usual. "When it appeared to be of repeated significance that Skye was one of nine daughters, I was led back to roots of Greek Mythology. You see, the Muses were the nine daughters of Zeus and Mnemosyne. They were Goddesses who presided over the arts and sciences, studies the Greeks valued for their relationship to life and the earth. Again, back then it helped explain their existence. But today we think of Muses more as a literary term—a guiding spirit. We credit them for our creative inspirations, but they are not a person or force that is seen."

Kane sighed. "You are getting to the part where this is important, right?"

"Well, yes," he replied as if surprised by the question. "At first, it appeared I'd hit a dead end because I couldn't make any sort of connection to Muses in the supernatural world, but Yannis' insight into Greek and Roman mythology as it translates to the supernatural world was really quite remarkable."

"Yannis? The same Yannis you were waiting for information from?"

Gideon nodded.

"Of course," Kane sighed. "Go on."

"Yannis helped me realize that I needed to be looking in the supernatural text for references of females who are referred to as Expressives. And boom, there it was!" Gideon's eyes popped wide as if he had just made the greatest discovery in history, but it still didn't make sense to Kane, who fought the urge to slap the point right out of the man.

"There what was?"

"Expressives. You see, they are the supernatural equivalent to a Muse in human form. The more I researched, the more I found, throughout history, several references to nine sisters being led by a man named Argus. Even Yannis admitted it would be difficult at best to put the instances together unless you knew exactly what you were looking for. The daughters' names always changed to protect their identity."

"Well, good for Yannis," Kane said in a half-hearted cheer. "So are you suggesting that because Skye's in a family of nine daughters led by a man named Argus that she's one of these Muses—?"

"Expressives," Gideon corrected, " . . . if she's indeed connected with the supernatural world, which I'm almost certain she is. And no, I don't think it's merely because she's in a family of nine daughters led by a man named Argus— although it fits quite nicely. It has more to do with her use of the phrase '*assignments*'."

"OK, so . . . ?" Kane felt as though he was trying to squeeze a raisin from a grape here.

"In the supernatural world, Expressives are responsible for maintaining the balance between good and evil. It is seen as a supreme imperative to not let the scales be tipped too far in any one direction at any given time. These *assignments* she keeps referring to, I believe are acts by her and her sisters to maintain that fragile balance."

"I don't understand," Kane said with a furrowed brow. "Don't we want the world to be on the side of good?"

"*We do*—but those higher than us understand that goodness can't exist to the exclusion of evil. Looking at it philosophically, we know good cannot exist without evil. How would you identify a good deed without having seen a bad one?"

Kane massaged his chin between his thumb and forefinger, as he always did when he was given something considerable to think about. "OK . . . so let's say these Expressives run around keeping the world in balance. Aren't we, The Brethren, also affecting that balance everyday when we fight the demons?"

"Yes, but you have to think of it in terms of working on a different level—a level above us. By nurturing and inspiring, by leading good supernatural beings such as yourself on the path that will ultimately lift you to your greatest potential, the Expressives are leveling the playing field, so to speak. They are putting you at the best advantage to win before you even start, which is critical because evil, in its insidious nature, always has the advantage at the outset."

"A higher level? You're talking Gods. Come on, Gideon. Skye acts like a normal human woman! I mean, she likes maple syrup and hates thunderstorms, for Christ's sake."

"I know this is hard to process," he replied with no change in his facial expression. "But Skye is a higher being. Rather, she's the soul of a higher being born into human form for the duration of that lifetime. She will age and die, and then be reborn into another human form for the next lifetime. Their human form is what allows her and her sisters to interact with both the supernatural and human world without drawing attention. And, just like us, she will experience human emotion and heartbreak. She will have human weaknesses . . . like a fear of thunderstorms. But she is eternal in the truest sense of the word."

"This is crazy!" Kane cried. "What you're saying is crazy. Skye doesn't act like some all-powerful Goddess affecting the balance of the world. If she is, then she's on some sort of vacation here because she's . . ." *Normal.* That's what Kane wanted to say. She's normal and sweet and beautiful and . . . *his.* That's what he wanted to say.

"I believe that's rather the point," Gideon finally added. "She is here to affect our world, but not to be noticed by it."

"What about Argus?" Kane asked in a calmer voice. "Is he a higher being as well?"

"Not on the same level, no . . . The text only talks of the nine daughters as being higher. He and his wife, Merryn, may be part of the supernatural world, but it can't even be known for sure if they are the sisters' real parents. At least, not how we think of them biologically."

Kane had to snort at that. Argus certainly seemed to act like Skye's biological father, given the control he seemed to want to exert over her. It pissed him off.

"Think of him and Merryn more like foster parents," Gideon continued. "Their job is to teach the women to understand their role—their significance—lifetime after lifetime. The women are born knowing what they must do, but they must also develop. Merryn draws out the women's ability to nurture and inspire, and Argus has been given the gift of second sight. Once he sees the future, it's his job to direct the women, until such time as they are strong enough to feel their way for themselves."

"So there's a point where they no longer need them?" Kane asked, remembering about how much Skye seemed affected by her mother's recent death.

Gideon nodded. "Once Merryn and Argus have passed on, the cycle can begin again. The sisters will have learned how to rely on themselves and each other. And, similar to mythology, each sister is instinctually keyed to a specific aspect of the supernatural world—like nature, the sixth sense, and the spoken word."

"And Skye . . . ?" Kane asked.

"Skye mentioned she was the third daughter. That would make her the Daughter of Tragedy."

"Tragedy? You mean death?"

Gideon shook his head. "Not necessarily. You need to think of things in terms of maintaining a balance in the supernatural world. Tragedy can also imply struggle or change. For example, let's assume for a moment that Olivia Greyson had been one of Skye's assignments. Argus must have foreseen her struggle to stay on the side of good after Davin imprisoned her, so he sent Skye."

"So you're saying Skye was there that night at Brahm Hill to help Olivia?"

"Yes, I believe so," Gideon replied. "Olivia was near death and facing an important crossroads in her life, where Davin was forcing her to choose between the path of good or evil. Just by Skye's presence—'*the angel*', as Olivia put it—reminded her of what was most important, her love for her mate, Caleb. She could then choose life, choose to fight for him. In essence, Skye was influencing Olivia to the side of good, knowing how important The Charmer was to maintaining the overall balance."

Kane began to feel as if the whole world around him was changing, and he was confused as to why it mattered. He had always adapted to any change, to any situation, however complex or confounding. Adapting was part of his nature. But right now he wanted nothing more than to dig his feet into the earth and force it to stand still. "If this is true, then you're saying that Skye and her sisters have been wandering around in their human form doing these assignments for centuries?"

Gideon placed a reassuring hand on Kane's shoulder, but at the moment, Kane wasn't feeling very reassured—because if it was true, her cause, her responsibility, was much greater than a simple one-night roll in the hay with a shifter.

"Much longer than that, I'm afraid," said Gideon. "Expressives are meant to exist within the human and supernatural world, but they cannot interfere with the natural day-to-day order of things. They are only to affect things that pertain to a higher balance. She will live among us, and she will be seen in each lifetime only by her family and those whose world she's affecting with her assignments . . . until her assignments are complete."

Kane let out an odd sound of disbelief. "What are you saying, Gideon? That she's going to disappear? That the only reason the Lycans and the animals can't see her is because she not really here?"

"Animals?" Gideon questioned, but Kane was too stunned to stop at this point.

"She's really here! I know because I've just spent the last two days with her." *And one amazing night.*

"I'm saying that the only reason you can see her . . . that any of us can . . . is because her assignment is somehow affecting our lives. Once that assignment is complete and she no longer needs for us to see her,"—Gideon seemed to take an abnormally long pause—"she'll no longer be visible . . . to any of us."

Kane wasn't sure how he was still standing on two legs that felt cut off at the knees. Why didn't Gideon just whack him with a crowbar while he was at it? Kane always assumed his time with Skye would end, but he thought it would be on *his* terms. It would be because she, like all the other women he had been with, was just not meant for him. But Kane was suddenly furious that the power of choice was being taken away from him. That it was taken out of his hands, out of both of their hands. "This is crazy," was all Kane could manage to say for a second time.

"I'm afraid there's more," Gideon said quietly. "I don't like having to tell you this, but you need to hear it . . . since it's obvious in the short time you've known each other you've become rather attached to Miss Matthews."

Kane stared blankly at the man. He wasn't sure he wanted to hear anything more. The simple act of breathing now seemed nearly impossible.

"An Expressive's role in the supernatural world is critical. Just think about it for a moment. Much of our success—The Brethren's success—depends on them holding that balance. Though they are in human form, they cannot afford to be distracted by everyday human pursuits. They are not free to make commitments to things we all take for granted, such as planting roots or having children. All her life, she and her family move to where they are needed. And no matter how many lives she lives, Skye will never know what it's like to be a mother. She will have to rely almost solely on Argus and Merryn and her sisters for companionship and survival."

"That doesn't sound like much of a life," Kane muttered bitterly under his breath, his anger beginning to rise within him.

"She sacrifices for the greater good, yes. But it's not all sacrifice. For their efforts, each sister is granted eternal life and one human indulgence—an eternal soul mate. One that is reborn with them, lifetime after lifetime. A companion they are allowed to share their lives with, someone to confide in. But one who also understands and accepts the vital responsibilities she bears. He must share her for the greater good. And, in exchange, he will hold her heart in every lifetime."

Kane blinked. He couldn't explain it, couldn't even begin to justify it, but he was furious. He was not that man for her. It wasn't logical. It went against every cell in his nature to be committed to one woman. But there it was. *He wanted it!* He wanted her. It was possessive, it was controlling, to an extent he had never felt before. But it was also impossible! How much longer would she even be visible to him before she just vanished?

"The sisters are re-united with their soul mates in each life when they are very young. The boys grow up with them, each becoming aware of the woman they are meant to be with as they spend time together, and a bond is formed. Once the woman feels she is ready, she will give herself to her soul mate physically, so that their connection may be sealed. That connection will become critical for the woman to succeed in her role. And once it is made, the memories of the love that they have shared in every life will come to the surface. Until that point, they will have no clear recollection of it, just instances of the familiar—like déjà vu."

And the hits just kept on coming.

Kane seriously wanted to hit something in that moment. Unfortunately, aside from a few trees, Gideon was the only thing around. He thought he should say something, to at least make an effort to show that he was not completely struck dumb by this information, but he couldn't.

"I'm sorry Aiden was not more tactful when he expressed his concern that you'd been with Miss Matthews sexually," Gideon continued. "As your close friend, I think he was worried that you might be falling for her. And considering what I just told you . . ."

"If you're trying to find a subtle way of asking me if I had plans for anything more than enjoying a couple nights with her, English-man, *don't*. She told me before we left The Trek that she belonged to someone else. So, you see—we were just having a bit of fun . . . as I always do."

But Kane, right now, felt like a damn idiot, and he only had himself to blame. She had told him she could not be with him sexually, and instead of listening to her the challenge of conquering her had only spurred on his desire for her more. And now he actually cared for her . . . deeply.

What the hell was he supposed to do with that? *With any of this?*

Was he getting exactly what he deserved after so confidently deciding he only needed to be with her once to get her out of his system? Well, he'd now been lost inside her at least a half-dozen times and was nowhere near ready to give her up. He wanted more. He wanted to know if she was ticklish behind her knees, or if it was just the bottom of her feet. Would she dance naked for him in the sunlight, her body calling to his with soft sway of her hips? Could he make her come just by suckling those beautiful breasts alone? His tongue licked across his teeth at the decadent thought. He knew he could.

Grinding his teeth against his jaw, he thought selfishly about how, since his parents had died, he had never belonged to anyone. But suddenly there was someone he wanted to belong to, and once again the connection was being taken away from him as suddenly as his parents had been. He wanted to belong to Skye Matthews, and that realization was terrifying.

But wishing was fodder for fools. In light of everything Gideon had told him, there was little point to him trying to continue to help her. I mean, when you're in the realm of Muses and Goddesses you really don't need a simple shifter to fix things, do you?

As he and Gideon walked back toward the cabin in strained silence, Gideon finally bridged the void with a sympathetic observation. "I know this all must be a bit of a shock," he began, "but keep in mind, she's here for a reason. She denied it when I asked her, but I believe that reason has something to do with you. You may not be her soul mate, but I believe she cares for you a great deal. She would have to, if she would break her connection with him even temporarily"

"If she cared for me, Gideon," he began, somberly, "she would've found a way to tell me this herself."

"Would you have believed her?"

His answering smile was half-hearted. "I guess we'll never —"

Their conversation was interrupted by a loud, booming voice coming from inside the cabin. Then several female voices seemed to pipe in all at once, blending together so no one conversation was clear. But Kane recognized one of the high-pitched voices.

It was Lake Matthews.

Shit. Skye's sisters were here.

CHAPTER NINETEEN

Kane rushed through the squeaky screen door and discovered, to his surprise, that the small cabin overcrowded with people —more specifically, women.

"Oh, my," he heard Gideon murmur behind him as he pinned his gaze on Aiden, who appeared to be perplexed and surrounded by all eight of Skye's sisters. Each was bundled warmly in thermal pants and coats, but nearly all of them were dressed in white. Physically, they all looked very different from each other, but all were attractive in their own way.

Kane certainly couldn't argue the fact that the sisters were affecting his world right now—in a particularly loud way— which might explain why he and his companions could see all of them. Aiden met Kane's gaze and with wide eyes, pleading wordlessly for some assistance. It certainly wasn't as if you could hear him over all of the sisters talking at him at once, some even speaking in French.

"They were just here," Aiden practically yelled over them. "I didn't even hear a car."

Come to think of it, Kane and Gideon hadn't seen or heard a vehicle as they headed back to the cabin, either. *What? Did they all come across Canada by horseback?*

The women's gazes followed Aiden's voice across the room until eight striking pairs of eyes landed on Kane at exactly the same moment. Normally, this kind of cramped, enclosed space brimming with women of every variety of appeal from smoky-dark brunettes to slim, honeyed blonds, to curvy, vibrant redheads, was right up Kane's alley. A few charming words and a slightly crooked smile—and he'd expect to have them all swooning. It was just the way things had worked for him during his entire life. But now his heart wasn't in it, and there was only one woman he wanted to see. Gideon had dealt him a walloping blow with the truth about Skye and her family, one that he was still trying to process. He wanted to be angry at her for not finding a way to tell him the truth, for not trusting him . . . and yet how could she? She'd only known him for a few days, and how did you explain a story like that?

Gideon was right to ask, would he have believed her?

There was no way to stay with her, and he had to start accepting that, no matter how much his brain was screaming at him to challenge that acceptance. Her calling was much bigger than any *one* man, and the sacrifices she would have to make— was already making—would be more measurable than most. It would be selfish of him to think differently. But that didn't mean he couldn't be bitter about the whole mess.

"Kane!" Lake squealed happily, running up to him to plant a big kiss on his cheek. He couldn't help but smile at her. Her combination of flirtatious energy and enthusiastic innocence was contagious in just about any room. Lake Matthews was the precocious little sister who exuded love and life.

"Is this him?" a golden-eyed woman asked as she came up beside Lake. This one was not quite slim but still quite pretty, more an earthy beauty, distinguished by the combination of no makeup and a gentle softness to her that reminded him of Skye when she was feeling her most vulnerable with him.

"Yep, this is . . ."—Lake sighed, her attention dreamily fixed on him—"Kane . . . Doesn't that name just fit him?"

"That's quite enough, Lake," her sister replied with a reprimanding smile.

Lake managed to scowl back at her sister with almost complete innocence. "You guys never let me have any fun."

"And yet you still manage to find yourself in trouble on almost a daily basis." She extended her hand out to Kane. "Hello. My name is Star."

Kane immediately felt his skin warming under the contact with her hand and was reminded how his skin always warmed with Skye's touch, as well. The women's 'touch' was part of their gift, of how they influenced people. It was calming, reassuring, enabling the mind of the one being touched to focus completely on what the sister was saying. "I am Skye's younger sister—or fourth daughter, if you prefer to look at it that way. Lake here has told us much about you."

Kane's brow lifted at that. "I hope she told you your sister was never in any danger from me or the others while she stayed with us." For some reason, it was important to Kane that the sisters to know he would never hurt Skye.

Lake nearly snorted, almost slapping at his arm. "Well, of course I told them that."

Star smiled. "Yes. Lake rather boisterously explained that to us after father left Ontario. Unfortunately, father doesn't seem to share our opinion of you. He had some not so nice things to say about your kidnapping our sister. So Lake offered up the complete story . . ."

"The complete story, huh?" Kane questioned.

"For sure," Lake smiled.

Star then turned and introduced each of the women. "These are my sisters—Rain's at the far left there, then Aurora, Dawn, Misty and Storm. And, of course, you've already met Autumn and Lake."

Lake planted her hands on her hips as her mouth turned into a disapproving pout. "Papa's in the bedroom with Skye. He's in a bad mood."

"Yes," Star agreed. "I'm afraid he's been in a rather foul mood over this whole situation. That's why we sisters all decided to come here and lend Skye our support."

"So your father didn't know you were coming, then?"

Star shook her head.

"Well, if you don't mind me asking . . . How did you know Skye was here?"

Kane had been expected a much more divine or mystical answer, one fitting with a Goddess in human form. But it was surprisingly a simple one. "Skye called me," Star answered, "after you were injured. She was upset, and I think she was looking for someone to support her decision to stay with you until she knew you were out of danger. She realized, of course, that father wouldn't."

Kane was surprised. Skye had let her sisters know she was all right, and still she chose to stay with her 'detainer', for lack of a better word, to help him with his injury instead of returning to them, where he now knew she belonged. The idea warmed him to his soul as he looked thoughtfully around the room at the faces of each sister. They all had the most vivid eye coloring—from burnished gold, to crystal blue, to the smokiest gray. It seemed to him that their eyes were somehow brighter than everyone else's—enhanced. But other than that shared characteristic, the sisters appeared very different from one another. These women were soul sisters reborn, but the human forms they were born into were not necessarily related by familial physical characteristics in this life.

It was strange how, in this moment, Kane realized that the men who had loved these women, who were bound to them for eternity, were soul mates—in the purest sense of the word. The physical appearance of the women might change in each life. Yet what these men were drawn to was not physical form, it was a spiritual energy—something they recognized on the inside—that part of a woman that could not be duplicated by any other woman and told the man she belonged only to him. He was envious of them for having something so powerful at their disposal.

Kane would be losing Skye, but she wouldn't be leaving him unaffected . . . and he needed to see her one last time.

His gaze slid to the closed door to the bedroom. "Is she all right?" he asked Star, and he wasn't sure why, because he was going to damned well make sure for himself.

"You know," Star answered with a soft smile, "I think she is —for the first time in a long while."

Kane wasn't quite sure what Star was implying, but there wasn't time to sort it out. He felt everyone's gaze on him as he charged toward the room. The closer he got, the more he could hear Argus's stern voice on the other side of the door. Kane burst through, slamming it behind him in warning to the others not to interfere. Skye was standing beside the bed, on which the sheets and blankets were tossed wildly from their lovemaking. Her expression was tired; she looked like she wouldn't mind crawling back into bed and sleeping for hours. He wanted to go to her and wrap his arms around her until she relaxed against him, but he couldn't. There was a bigger, much more pressing obstacle to deal with in the form of a tall, grizzled man with a hard scowl plastered on his face.

Oh, Argus Matthews was angry, indeed. He might be Kane's senior by twenty-plus years, but Kane had little doubt the man wanted to knock him to the floor with a sound fist to his jaw. And surprisingly, he looked fully capable of doing it, as well. His face was weathered and rough, making Kane think that at one time he could have ruled the Russian mafia or something. He was a couple of inches taller than Kane and had silvered, buzz-cut hair, as well as eyes that were an almost eerie ice blue —an unusual ice blue that seemed strangely familiar.

"You," he said, raising a lethally-pointed finger.

"Father, don't," Skye pleaded as she stepped between them, but Argus would not budge.

"Don't defend him, Skye. I want to know what possible explanation this man has for kidnapping *my daughter,* holding her against her will, and then fleeing out of town like a coward before he had to face me."

Kane's body was tight, his every muscle ready to respond. He inhaled slow, breathing steadily, doing his best to keep the animal inside him under control. He was well trained to keep his emotions in check so that they could not be used against him in a fight, but with Skye placing herself in danger by standing between them—and her sweet scent taking over his senses with the smell of that damn exotic flower he loved— that task seemed nearly impossible.

Kane pulled Skye to his side before replying, "Let's get two things straight, shall we. One, I've never been afraid to face you. And two, you'd better get that finger out of my face before I break it off."

Argus just smiled at him smoothly, as if he didn't have the slightest reason to feel threatened by Kane. "I suppose you think you feel something for her."

"Father, he doesn't—"

"I do," Kane answered confidently, causing Skye to blink up at him.

Argus's smile only widened. "I've known men like you . . . too many to count. You're too arrogant to ever truly know how to love someone as special as my daughter."

Skye gasped. "Father . . ."

A smile curled the corner of Kane's lip. *This man should talk.* Argus Matthews, a seer, acted as if he had the power of a God—but Kane already knew that he had that power only because of these remarkable women. There was an irony to that, and Kane wondered if the man had lost sight of how to just love these women instead of *commanding* them. "You speak as though you know me. Have we met before?"

Argus didn't answer.

"No? Well then maybe all this blustering on your part is simply *you* coming to terms with the fact that, very soon, your daughters won't need you to order them around anymore. As a man who sees the future, I should think that would be very clear."

"You're right. I have seen the future. And I've seen that you will be alone, just as you've always been. Oh, you'll continue to bed the nearest beautiful woman on occasion, but it will be an empty gesture. It's always empty. And a more sweet justice I cannot imagine for such a skirt-chasing simpleton."

Ok, forget the training. Kane was going to pound this man's face into the carpet, father or not! Unfortunately, there was a blond ball of fire beside him who had other ideas. "That's enough, father," Skye snapped as she successfully wedged herself back in between the two men, her pert little rear pressing back against Kane as she pushed against her father. As if Kane needed any further distractions at the moment—God help him, he was thinking about sex with her at that very moment, even after what her father had just accused him of.

Maybe Argus was right: he was no more than a skirt-chasing simpleton.

Argus's ice-blue eyes were glowing with anger as he leaned forward over his daughter to give Kane a warning he intended to give only once. "You have two minutes to get out of my house. And you will *never* see my daughter again."

"No!" Skye cried, pushing back on him once again. "This is not your decision. It's mine. And you'll let me have a few minutes with Kane so that I can say goodbye—without any interference from you."

"Leave you alone with this . . . ?" He rolled his eyes as if he didn't even want to contemplate the answer. "You can forget that!"

Skye straightened her spine, and there went that jutted little chin of hers. Damn, but Kane was going to miss that. "You *will,* or Kane won't be the only one who leaves this house tonight."

Argus's finely controlled emotions twisted into something just short of fury. Kane's hand slid around Skye's waist, ready to draw her back out of harm's way, if necessary, though he doubted her father would actually ever hurt her. He seemed more like a man who held onto to all of his daughters much too tightly, perhaps out of some sort of misguided love. But right now, Argus Matthews appeared to be holding on by a very thin thread, and that was never a good sign.

"What is the matter with you?" he almost seethed at Skye. "I mean, look at this," he bellowed, drawing his hand through the air across the disheveled bedcovers. "How can you do this? I didn't raise a daughter who would betray the man she is promised to—like this."

Skye covered her shocked gasp with her hand, the visceral comment seeming to have the power to blow her off her feet. Kane held her steady, tightening his grasp, reminding her that he was there. "You're right, father. You didn't raise a daughter that would betray him," she said in a shaky voice. "Because *he* betrayed *me.*"

Argus blinked as if he'd just been told the earth was square. "That's impossible!"

"Believe me, I wish it were," Skye replied, now allowing her voice to reflect her bitterness. "Now, I'm going to ask you one more time to give me some time to say goodbye to Kane. And you're going to give it to me . . . or so help me, I will never do another assignment again."

Argus' hands tensed at his sides. "You don't mean that."

Skye said nothing, didn't even flinch, and Kane was pleased to see that her resistance startled the bluster right out of Argus Matthews. "Very well," he said in a calmer voice that hardened once more as he snarled at Kane. "I'll be waiting in the other room . . ." He turned his attention back to his daughter now, but the hardness remained as he said to her, " . . . with your sisters. So we can leave immediately."

"That won't be necessary," Kane shot back, hating the words that were about to come out of his mouth. "I'll be leaving after I speak with Skye. The Brethren won't be bothering you or your daughters again."

Skye's shoulders seemed to slump a little as he delivered these words, and he hated himself for hurting her even in any small measure. They both watched Argus leave the room, the same scowl marring his face he had worn when Kane had come in.

"Nice to meet you," Kane called, sarcastically, through the door just before Argus slammed it. He was then met with a stiff elbow to his stomach, which caused him to groan and tip forward. "*What?*"

Kane was smiling, albeit half-heartedly, when Skye finally turned around to face him, looking miserable. "I'm sorry," she sighed. "He doesn't usually behave so despicably."

"It's nice to know I've made such an impression on him." She gave him the smallest of smiles, and Kane ran his thumb over her bottom lip and then kissed her, wanting to ease her worry so they could focus on just themselves for these last few minutes they had together. He grasped her hand gently with both of his and led her deeper inside the room and then into the back bathroom, closing another door between them and the rest of the world.

"What're you doing?" she asked.

"Making sure we have some privacy."

The room was still scented by the bath products Skye had used earlier, and as he inhaled he swore he didn't know how he was going to live without those scents implanted in his brain on a daily basis. He relaxed back against the stone countertop and brought her with him until her head lay against his chest and his arms curled protectively around her. "You could have told me," he murmured.

"And what would I have said?" she asked in a sad voice. "That even though I was drawn to you from almost the moment I met you—that it was selfish and wrong."

He held her tighter, more fiercely now, against him. "What you and I feel for each other is not wrong. I'll never believe that."

"But it is selfish. I risk changing something that's not meant to be changed by what has already happened between us. There's too much at stake. That's why I'm allowed to talk about it with only my family and . . ."

She stopped herself, and he knew why. She was about to say 'my soul mate', a man who was not him—and he hated it! His fingers tucked into her short, wispy hair as he drew her head back and kissed her gently, his lips sipping at hers like some decadent treat as he inhaled all her scents one more time. He closed his eyes against the pain stabbing at his chest and dropped his forehead against hers. *Why was it so hard to let this woman go?* He had let many, many woman go in his lifetime. It was really rather a simple process.

"I don't want to say goodbye to you," Skye murmured weakly against his lips.

"Then don't. Don't leave me, Skye. Give us a chance to figure out what this is. It may not be something written lifetime after lifetime, but it is something." Kane took full possession of her mouth just then as he felt her hands fist into his shirt. If only there was a way to make this moment last forever.

When Skye finally broke their kiss she replied breathily, "It's not something that's in my control. It's not my choice."

He groaned, somewhere between anguish and anger, realizing it wasn't under the control of either of them. He pressed her until her mouth opened to him, and then slid his tongue inside, swirling it against hers. Her taste was heaven, pure heaven, and he couldn't believe how quickly his body was responding. It was like he was discovering the difference between sex and true passion for the very first time in his life. And he wanted it, he wanted all of it.

"Come here, Skye," he ordered in a raw whisper, drawing her tight against his body. He tore at her jeans, pushing them open and sliding one hand inside, cupping the soft V between her thighs and praying his fingers would find her ready to accept him because they didn't have a lot of time. *Ah, bingo!* Perfection. She was soft and wet, nearly melting against him as she lifted onto her toes and curled into his hand. He couldn't remember ever wanting something this badly in his life.

"Skye, I can't let you go," he said, shoving her jeans and panties down to her ankles in one efficient motion.

She drew back in surprise as he hauled her off her feet with a single arm bracing at her low back. "Kane!" she said in whispered panic as he fumbled to get his own jeans open. "My father's just in the other room. We can't—. . . *Ooohh . . . oh, God. . .*"

Skye didn't even get a chance to finish her sentence before he was taking her, right there against the bathroom counter. Or more accurately, she was taking him, slowly sliding down his incredibly long length like warm silk.

He was breathing hard, his body screaming at him to wrap her hips in his hands and thrust himself deeper inside this woman, to possess her completely, so completely that she would never, ever forget him.

He flipped their positions around until her bottom was firmly planted on the stone counter, then withdrew from her hot flesh amid her protest, but only long enough to shove his own pants further down and dig his fingers into the firm swell of her bottom, spreading her wide and then sinking back inside her in a single, hard thrust. Skye dropped her head into his neck and buried a harsh cry against his skin, trying to keep the sound muffled for fear they would be discovered at any moment. Right now he didn't give a damn who found them as he rocked into her body over and over again, pushing the pleasure in his brain into overload. *Damn*, she was making him crazy, sighing beneath him in those perfect, breathy little moans. He just couldn't get enough.

His hips continued thrusting, faster and faster, swelling inside her until she was stretched to her very limits. He loved that sensation! He could already feel her internal muscles tightening around him. She wanted release as much as he did— needed it as much as he did. In fact, she appeared desperate to contain her passion as her back arched and her skin flushed the most glorious shade of pink, her breasts rounding into small perfect swells under her tee shirt. He was about two seconds away from taking those swells into his mouth and savoring them properly, but there was no time.

Then, out of nowhere, four words popped into his brain. "Inveniam viam aut faciam," he spoke in a wild rush of breath. He had no idea where the words came from or what they meant. He just had to say them.

Skye gasped and froze in his arms, even though he was still pounding into her like a madman and she hadn't yet found her release. "Just relax, darlin'," he murmured over her ear. "Let go for me. Let me feel you come."

"Say it again. Please!"

Far be it from Kane to deny this woman anything she wanted. "Let me feel you come."

"No! The other words."

"Inveniam viam aut faciam." Kane pumped into her faster now and she moaned helplessly in response. "Inveniam viam aut faciam . . . Inveniam viam aut faciam . . ."

What the hell did they even mean?

No, he knew—he somehow knew! He'd heard the words before. They came so easily, he just wanted to say them again and again, like a critical promise, a solemn prayer.

Skye then moaned something beneath him that he didn't quite hear because he was so lost in the sensations that were building at the base of his spine. "Skye," he groaned, pulling her legs higher around him so he could get as deep as possible inside her. He wanted her to feel possessed by him—owned.

Somewhere in the distance he heard a door close, but the thought left him just as quickly. Right now he only wanted to concentrate on feeling every ripple of her release when she let go. Then he would announce this woman as *his* in front of her whole family. There was no way he was giving this woman up. *Higher beings be damned!* She was his. He could feel it in his muscles, in his limbs, and down his spine as he rocked into her. He felt it in the sharp teeth that were now pushing against his gums. She was drawing out the inner jaguar in him. Doing more than just sating the man's lust, she was reaching the animal inside the man.

Damn, but he was in love with this woman. When the hell did that happen?

As ridiculous as the notion seemed to him, he knew it was the truth. He wasn't leaving here without her. Argus Matthews could just choke on it. Kane would take her somewhere he could make love to her like this over and over again until she was too busy to complete her damn assignment. Then she couldn't disappear on him. Sure it was selfish, and he wanted to figure more out in his head but the release that had been working inside him was currently threatening to burst forward with the power of a sonic missile.

"Oh, God, Jairus!" Skye cried out beneath him, startling his thoughts to a complete halt. "I love you. I love you. I love you."

Kane was still trying to process what she had just said when her release literally exploded around him. For a split second, he had considered pulling from her body, but that was before her inner muscles had clamped down on him and sucked him so deep inside her that it was impossible to even think about leaving her. His hips jutted forward with his booming release— and he instantly realized his mistake.

He wasn't wearing a condom.

He hadn't even thought about wearing a condom. He'd wanted her so badly that for the first time in his life the thought of the woman's protection, protection for both of them, had completely left him.

Kane groaned so hard he felt like the veins in his neck would pop as he continued to come inside her with no end in sight. *Jairus? Fucking, Jairus?* He was giving her something he had never given another single woman in his entire life. He was coming inside her, and she was calling out another man's name.

Then it occurred to him it had to be *his* name, her ex-fiancés name. *He hated the man!* His brain tried to quickly recall if he'd heard it that day they were arguing, but he couldn't think, he couldn't focus. Once his body was finally spent inside her, Kane forced himself from her wet grip. He was breathing impossibly hard, but still managed to ask, "What did you just call me?"

He hated that he was unable to keep the injured surprise from his voice. Those beautiful emerald eyes blinked up at him. Clearly, she was trying to bring herself back into the moment, but Kane was already tucking himself back into his pants.

"No, Kane, wait!" She placed her hands at his cheeks and stared up at him with desperate pleading in her eyes. "Just give yourself a minute—"

He didn't even give her another second. He pulled away from her and straightened his clothes, leaving her there stunned and half dressed on the counter as he tore from the room.

"Kane, please! Wait!"

The door slammed behind him as he left the bathroom and nearly ran smack into Aiden. His friend looked about as uncomfortable as he had ever seen him. "I was supposed to be coming to get you," he explained, " . . . about five minutes ago. If you don't want to get shot where you stand, we better get out of here."

"I'm ready," Kane said, not waiting for him as he bolted into the other room, passing the sisters without saying so much as a goodbye.

"Kane, don't go!" he heard Lake cry.

"Lake! Do not interfere," Argus ordered the young girl.

"But Papa . . ."

Kane was out the door before he even heard the rest. When he, Gideon and Aiden reached the SUV he opened the back and started ripping the clothes from his body, throwing them inside.

"What're you doing?" Aiden asked, Gideon watching with concern over his shoulder.

"I'll meet you back at The Oracle," he answered quickly, causing both men to do a double take at each other. "I need to stretch my legs."

"Kane, just slow down," Aiden replied trying to calm him. "What the hell happened?"

Kane wasn't in a place where he could hear anything. He could feel the shift already happening inside him. Within seconds he was pitching forward onto his paws and moving in the other direction, the jaguar's long strides taking him away from this place that now caused him pain and into the familiar comfort of night . . . alone.

CHAPTER TWENTY

"Son of a bitch," Kane hissed as he pulled the blade back from his skin, watching several scarlet drops plop onto the rubber-matted floor at his feet before setting down a pair of curved combat knives and reaching for his tee shirt, which was hanging on some nearby equipment.

When had he gotten so sloppy in his fighting mechanics? Kane wrapped the shirt around his forearm and applied pressure while standing there, dressed in only in a pair of grey sweats, his body damp from the nearly three hours of non-stop physical exertion he had put himself through that morning.

He had to.

He couldn't sleep.

Raising his glance from the floor to the mirrored wall in front of him, he could see the image staring back at him; it was somber, indeed. Kane *looked* like a man who had barely slept the past few nights since he'd been back at The Oracle. And now he was having trouble concentrating on even simple execution drills. *Damn,* why didn't someone just give him the title of 'rank amateur' instead of 'Guardian' and call it a day?

Four days had passed since he'd left Skye half dressed and sitting on that bathroom countertop. That certainly hadn't made him much of a gentleman. And what was worse, he'd left her there within just a few minutes of having had the most powerful sex of his life. In fact, *powerful* didn't even begin to cover it. Neither did the word sex. His experience with Skye Matthews had been more than just sex. He had made love to her. Deep, soul-searing, mind-bending, passionate love to her . . . and it had been a quickie. What the hell would've happened if he'd actually had the time to have her as he wanted? Would there be any chance they'd still be together right now?

Nope. None. Not as long as she cried out another man's name when he was giving her every part of himself he had to give—every part he had ever *given* a woman.

Women screamed, moaned and breathed *his* name, not some other man's. That had never happened to him before, especially because he had just come inside her. No condom, no pulling out, and no rhythm method. Although honestly, why would any man want to abstain for days at a time when a perfectly good condom was available?

Of course, to be fair, there was no way for Skye to know what a monumentally big deal it was for Kane to come inside her. But he knew. It was rule number one. I mean, the whole reason it was rule number one was because it *was* a monumentally big deal! He was giving a part of himself he had never given any woman. Yet he couldn't ever remember anything feeling so right. Just the memory of it alone made him groan. His body tightened, his blood pumped, and his heart beat wildly—all for her. She had the power to do that to him, even four days later.

He'd spent hours that morning, as he did every morning, reminding himself why he had to leave her, praying that he hadn't made the biggest mistake of his life. But how could it be a mistake? By now she probably wasn't even visible to him anymore.

What the hell was wrong with him? He needed to get over this. If he resembled at all the womanizing stud he used to be, he would get over Skye Matthews with a snap of his fingers and sate his lust inside another equally fine beauty. After all, wasn't it his motto that there were plenty of fish in the sea? *Why, yes it was.*

Take the leggy and beautiful Astrid Falls, for example. The sexually confident Dhampir definitely enjoyed a good roll in the sack and made no apologies for what she wanted. He liked that about her. And after a particularly bendy evening in The Oracle's Game Room about two months ago, the strawberry blond had made it clear she'd wanted to play more games with him. *Ahh,* it could be so delicious. Why, she'd flirted with him just this morning after finding him here. But this morning he had been sulking over Skye and not in the mood. So he had lied and told Astrid he needed to get some training in. She stared at him in response, as if he'd just suddenly announced he was gay.

"You're *training?*" she questioned in complete bafflement. "In here?"

Kane hadn't been quite sure what all the mystery was about. It was a *training room,* for Pete's sake. Granted, in the past, he was usually finding other activities to do in here to occupy his time, but he did have to train, especially since he was getting older. He was staring down the barrel at thirty-five. Things were no longer as easy as they were when he was twenty-five, though his shifter blood helped keep him in peak physical condition.

But now, after adjusting his attitude a little, he was ready for some games with Astrid. He was over Skye Matthews! Completely, one hundred percent, over, over, over her.

Well . . . maybe more like sixty-forty.

What he needed to do to wipe out that sixty percent doubt was to find the sexy Astrid and bring her back here. Yes, he could picture it now. He would take her nice and slow in front of these mirrors where he could enter her from behind and watch her face light up in wonder as she cried out *his name* with her release.

Got that Skye Matthews—*his name! Kane!*

That would make him feel better! *Right?*

No, it wouldn't.

Training would.

He retrieved his curved blades and braced his stance, swiping them through the air with the skill of a man who, if even a tenth of a degree off, could sever a limb.

So what if Skye wasn't falling all over herself to be with him? Women had fallen over him his entire life. What was *one* woman?

Lunging forward, he completed his set with a sigh. Except this woman was the one woman he really wanted—a woman who was about to disappear on him. And it was *damned* inconvenient, and making him *damned* grumpy. So he trained himself into exhaustion during the day, just so he could try and forget her while he slept at night . . . but it wasn't working. He'd lie awake on his sheets with the constant hard on from hell, and imagine her breathy little sounds beneath him while his hand stroked himself to completion. The process would then repeat itself about an hour later. This was really a problem, because he needed sex . . . and he needed sleep. More specifically, he needed sex with her and then sleep. So much in fact, that last night he hadn't even bothered getting into his bed. What was the point?

Kane's thoughts were interrupted when a familiar man entered the training room. His name was Simon Kendrick; he was a male witch who had just transferred in a week earlier from The Hallow site in London. And though Kane found him to be a bit of a cocky son of a bitch he did *not* trust as far as he could throw him, the man seemed to be getting a lot of female attention around The Oracle. Not that he was worried for himself with the ladies. It was just that Simon reminded Kane of himself in his wilder, more self-centered days—which, unfortunately, was only about two weeks ago . . . or maybe two minutes ago, considering the direction of his thoughts.

An easy smile sprung to Simon's lips after spotting Kane, and his eyes scanned the room. "Sorry, man," he said in a hushed voice, as if he were afraid someone else was going to hear him. "I didn't mean to interrupt."

Kane frowned. "You're not inter—"

"Where is she?"

Kane tipped his head in confusion. "Where's who?"

Simon snorted as he approached and punched Kane in the arm playfully. *What the hell? They were not buds.* "Aw, I get it. I just missed her, didn't I? You dog."

"I would recommend," Kane began through his teeth, "in the future, *not* referring to a Shape-shifter jaguar as a dog."

Simon laughed, mistakenly believing he had some type of bromance going on with Kane, which couldn't be further from the truth. "Come on . . . You were obviously . . ."—he cleared his throat—"entertaining someone."

"Entertaining?" Kane echoed slowly. "I've been training, you moron. Don't you see the blood and sweat on me?" Kane shoved he's bleeding arm up as if to offer uncontroversial evidence. "This *is* a training room."

Simon appeared unaffected by Kane's grumpiness (either that or he really was a moron). Clicking his tongue, the younger man gave him a quick wink. "Good one."

Kane was at a complete loss for words and was about to set the idiot straight when Gideon walked into the room, which was good because he had probably just saved Simon's life. "There you are," he declared, fixing his gaze on him. "I've been looking for you all morning."

Kane swung his arms in display over his sweaty body. "Well I've been right here . . . *training*," he scowled at Simon.

"Yes, yes. I'm sure you have," Gideon said, almost dismissively, which had Kane wondering if he needed to just start this day all over again. Did no one believe he actually worked out in the training room? How the hell did they think he kept in shape? As much as he wished it, sex alone couldn't maintain this fine physique of his. He had tried!

"I was just finishing up the details of my report regarding the Wraith for Elder Lambert and was wondering if you had already given him yours."

Kane's brows shot up. "Um . . . not quite." Which was code for '*I never write reports; I wait for Alec to chew my ass out in his office, and then I give him a verbal report*'.

"Oh, good," Gideon said, as if he were incredibly relieved, and then pulled a one-inch stack of paperwork out of his bag. Anchoring his pencil behind his ear he added, "I was hoping we could compare notes of our account."

Kane rolled his eyes. "Are you kidding?"

Gideon stopped and stared up at him with a sincere expression. "No." There was a long, awkward pause before Gideon continued. "It's just that there are a couple of holes in my report. Mostly from that last night, when you were in the bedroom *discussing* things, shall we say, with Skye and Argus?"

"Right . . ."

"Some of that information could be most valuable. And as you know, Elder Lambert is quite anxious to have all the details since he's not pleased about your returning before you had answers for him regarding the Wraith."

Simon was, of course, watching all of this as he snacked on a bag of Doritos. The nacho cheese scent must have caught Gideon's attention. "Oh, may I have a crisp? Those are my favorite."

"They're chips, Gideon. Not *crisps*." Kane grumbled back at the Englishmen. "And Alec can just kiss my ass! My final conversation with Skye and her father was personal, none of his goddamn business. And it certainly doesn't need to go in some report somewhere."

Gideon looked disapprovingly at Kane and then over to Simon, who had become fully engrossed in their conversation.

Kane knew immediately he'd botched it again. No one was ever to show disrespect to their Brethren Elder in front of another member. And Simon certainly had not been with them long enough to understand the *complex* nature (at least that's how Kane saw it) of his and Alec's relationship. "Don't you have some class you should be attending, newbie," Kane snarled at Simon.

Simon looked at his watch. "Not for another hour or—"

"Go!" Kane ordered, in a voice that left no doubt the young man was not welcome at the moment.

After Simon wisely exited the room, Kane turned his attention back to Gideon, who was wearing a not unexpected frown of his own.

"What happened to your arm?" he asked, noticing the blood that had soaked through his shirt.

Kane removed it, since the bleeding had stopped, and tossed the bloody heap toward his bag. "I nicked myself with the knives. But it's already starting to heal."

"Oh," Gideon said with surprise, "so you really were training?"

Kane ground his teeth and continued, "As I was saying . . . My private conversations with Skye have no bearing to Alec's report."

"Yes, I can certainly respect that. But I was more interested in your conversation with Argus Matthews. You see, I find it fascinating that he took such an immediate dislike to you— especially since you had never met him. I wondered if he might have revealed anything to you in your conversations."

Kane snorted. "Well, I'm glad you find that so fascinating, but I don't really care. I never cared what that cranky bastard thought of me."

"Yes, you've always been rather self assured that way. Quite impressive."

Why did Kane feel like that was not a compliment?

"Normally, of course, I wouldn't ask," Gideon continued, "but it just strikes me as rather illogical for a man with his responsibilities to be so narrowly focused on someone of such inconsequence to him."

Kane grabbed a towel from a stack that was neatly folded and began to wipe the sweat from his face and chest. "I did practically kidnap his daughter. I tend to think that's what might have set him off."

"That is true, but Skye certainly never felt a prisoner. Lake confirmed as much to me when I spoke to her."

"Lake Matthews?" Kane sputtered in disbelief. "Gideon, you don't have normal conversations with regular women, let alone an overly-flirty teenage girl."

Gideon's face wrinkled into a confused expression and then began to blush. Kane knew the nerdy Englishmen would never think of a young girl like Lake Matthews in a sexual way, but it was fun to watch the man get flustered. "Oh, don't be ridiculous. It was nothing like that. She was simply telling me what Skye had said to her the night when you were injured and she called the house."

Gideon just stood there, staring at Kane as if there was nothing more of consequence to say on the subject.

Kane, on the other hand, waited for what he swore was at least thirty seconds (but was probably more like two), then threw his hands up. "And . . . ?"

"Oh. Well, I was just going to make the point that Lake— truly a special and lovely girl, by the way—said that her father acted as if he knew of you before he even left Ontario with Oliver."

Kane squeezed his fingers over the bridge of his nose, trying to thwart the massive headache he suspected would be coming on at any moment. *Wasn't the answer to that question quite obvious?* "The man can see the future, Gideon. He'd probably recognized me from some sort of vision or something."

Kane then paused, considering that for a moment. *Shouldn't Argus have seen Kane was going to detain his daughter and tried to stop him before it happened?*

Seemed like an important thing for a seer to miss.

Gideon smiled, his eyes alight. "That does seem logical. So I guess the question would be what *did* he see—but more importantly, *when* did he see it?"

Just like that, Gideon straightened his stack of papers, stuffed them back in his bag, and headed toward the doors. He turned back to Kane only briefly, his hand on the door handle. "Might I suggest, Kane, that it's time for you to start considering how *you* might know *him*."

✿✿✿

Kane entered his room on the ninth floor of The Oracle scratching his head. Gideon didn't make sense on most occasions, but today he seemed particularly vague. And that, '*I'm a nerdy genius, so try to keep up with me*' way about him, annoyed Kane more often than not. Today it definitely did, but then, maybe it was because of the subject matter. He certainly hadn't been himself since returning to The Oracle; things didn't seem to roll off of him as they normally did. And when it came to the subject of Skye or her father, he was particularly off kilter.

Inside his tiny bathroom, which was the only size they seemed to have at The Oracle, he examined his arm. There was barely enough room for him to stand between the pedestal sink, toilet and shower. Kane didn't mind, though. He was just grateful to have an in-room bathroom. The Oracle at one time had been a European-style hotel and had been remodeled and modified for The Brethren's use about twenty-five years ago.

There were a total of twelve floors, with the main living, dining and training areas on the first three floors and The Elder's suites, offices and conference areas on the top two floors. The rest of the building consisted of rooms for members and staff, with larger and more lavishly appointed rooms the higher you went. Based on his position, rank and years of service, Kane had been offered a mini suite on the ninth floor during the prior year. The term *suite* had to be taken lightly, however. The room was still small, but it offered the aforementioned bath quarters, (so he didn't have to share common ones like the other floors) a separate bedroom with a queen sized bed he liked to sprawl on, a main space large enough for a loveseat, chair and desk, and a nice view from a small, private balcony of the rather spectacular grounds.

What else could a man need?

Once he was satisfied his cut was clean, he bandaged it, then grabbed a quick shower. He couldn't afford to take long showers anymore because all they managed to do was remind him of what it would be like to shower with Skye. Sometimes he swore he could feel his hands smoothing over every small curve of her body, lavishing her in an exotic mix of the shampoos and soaps she loved so much. He would caress her, pinch her nipples between his fingers, and kiss her until she was breathless. Then he would start all over again, lovingly touching her until he couldn't stand the temptation any longer to take her. Pressing her up against the shower wall, he would thrust inside her in one stroke, making love to her until they both fell slack with their release under the warm water.

Sometimes the vision of it was so clear that it was almost as though it was happening at that moment. His muscles flexed as if responding to her every touch, every sensation. When they'd spent those two magical days together, they hadn't shared a shower. He was an idiot, for sure, for not adding it to the list, but they had spent so much of their time in that damned bed that he could barely stand up. Yet, sometimes his mind played tricks on him, as though he knew exactly what it felt like to be with her in that way. The image was just too clear. It was what he wanted, and the thought of her reminded him of how the rest of his life—his meaningless trysts with women—would mean nothing. It was all so pointless. Had he really not noticed how empty his life had been before Skye?

He tried to shake the thoughts from his head and fell back against the mattress. God, he just needed to sleep for a little while to clear his mind. Kane knew he should consider himself lucky he even had the chance to sleep and wasn't being hauled into Alec's office right now to try and explain the fiasco that had been the last two weeks. Suspiciously, Alec had left him alone after he managed to kidnap (though he still liked to think of it as detaining) what he believed, at the time, was a human woman, fall in love with her, enrage her father and probably the Russian Mafia, and lose track of the Wraith—all within a single week.

That was impressive even for him.

Alec, however, would not be amused. In fact, he was going to be one pissed-off Elder. The only thing that had saved Kane's ass up to now was the fact that Alec had not been at The Oracle when Kane had returned—that, plus the fact that Aiden volunteered to go back up north and keep tracking the Wraith.

He laughed out loud, but humorlessly. If tracking the Wraith was really what Aiden was doing, there was no doubt Kane would be with him, but he was sure the only person Aiden was watching was Skye . . . and he just couldn't do it. He couldn't be there to watch her disappear to him forever. It would just be too painful, even if she hadn't called him by another man's name.

Kane had actually been expecting a call from Aiden informing him that she had vanished. That would be the final blow.

Kane felt his eyes blinking more slowly now, staying closed for entire seconds rather than just for the length of a blink. The need for sleep surpassed everything. So he closed his eyes, deciding he would figure the rest all out later.

CHAPTER TWENTY-ONE

On a sunny but cold afternoon, Skye hiked back to the open clearing where Kane had saved her life from the stampeding herd.

She found a spot by a rock where she neatly set, but oddly didn't spread, the plaid blanket she had brought with her. Sitting down comfortably, she glanced around the peaceful setting that was now so different from that day. Skye hadn't intentionally picked a place that would remind her of Kane—at least she didn't think she did—but after walking around for a while, she decided this open field was the best place in which to finish her assignment. She would have room to work, which she needed, and there really wasn't a point to delaying it any longer. No matter how much it pained her, it was time to move on with her life . . . with her duty.

Four days had passed since Kane had left her irrevocably shaken and heartbroken on that bathroom countertop. Shaken because she knew he didn't only have sex with her, *he had made love with her.* He said it with his eyes, in the depth which those beautiful pools of silver held her in their warmth. He said it with how he moved within her, with total intimacy, as though he had known her body a lifetime. And he said it with those four words, with all the reverence and passion of the greatest lover.

Inveniam viam aut faciam.

They were the words of her heart. Words that—once spoken from his lips—had left her broken down to her very soul because she had realized—too late—that the man she had fallen in love with in two short days, Kane, was also her eternal soul mate, Jairus Marcus Antonius.

The memories had come flooding back to her in that moment like the rush of the wind. Memories of a man who meant more to her than her very own life, more than all the lives she had lived put together.

After he had left her there, she had straightened her clothes, garments that still carried the scent of their lovemaking, and prepared as best she could to face her family. She hadn't been sure she could even stand on her own numb feet after witnessing him run out on her like that. It felt as though he had stabbed her so deeply she couldn't breathe, and yet she understood and accepted why he had run.

He didn't remember her.

For the last four days, her pent up anger toward one man had left her wanting to scream to the heavens until her throat was raw. "*How could he betray her?*" she thought. Not Kane, but the one man she had trusted with her life, with her security, with her secrets. The one man who, she now realized, had violated her trust in a way she had never thought possible —her father.

Although Argus and Merryn were not their biological parents, all of their girls never considered them anything less than exactly that—parents. Skye was now feeling, firsthand, how when a bond like that is betrayed, broken, the pieces left are worth very little. Her father and her sisters were the only ones in this life who were allowed to truly know her, understand her, love her for who she was.

Except for her soul mate—the one gift she was promised by those above her for all her sacrifice. And now *he* might very well be lost to her, too.

Skye had not spoken to Argus since that day. It was not that he hadn't tried to communicate. It was simply that Skye refused to listen. For all of Argus's commanding and fierce blustering in the past, when one of his daughters was angry with him—the truly-not-speaking-to-him kind of angry—he would usually become a wreck until he could fix it. Skye and her sisters had sometimes found it amusing. Not this time. Skye didn't care if he was a wreck. She didn't care if he was in pain. He had hurt her to the point that she felt breathless and lifeless when she was in the same room with him.

The only thing that had saved Argus Matthews from hearing the full throat of his daughter's anger was the fact that Star and Lake were still at the cabin with them. They had been worried about her—all of her sisters had—once Kane ran out so suddenly. Skye hadn't told them anything, and they all had respected her wishes not to discuss it. How could she when her father was right at the center of it?

Besides, what must her sisters think when they believed she had betrayed Andrew? What had been going on in that cabin before they had arrived had been quite obvious to all of them. But none had any way of knowing that Kane was really her soul mate, not Andrew. Except maybe Lake. Lake had never really hit it off with Andrew, which had always been a bit of a puzzle to Skye. He had always gone out of his way to be nice to her. But now she understood why. Andrew wasn't her soul mate, and Lake could see it.

Why had her sister never said anything to her? How could Lake be around Skye for the last few miserable days and say nothing? Skye blamed herself this whole time for allowing herself to be drawn to another man, even though Andrew had already betrayed her with another woman. She lived for years in a quiet pain that was full of plastered-on smiles, half truths, and acquiescence, and it was all because of *one* man.

"You can't continue to shut me out, Apphia," Argus spoke from behind her, and she closed her eyes against the pain of hearing him call her by her true given name. He often said that he could see her as a woman of no other name, no matter how many lifetimes had gone by. "You know I love you. I've always loved you as if you were my own. Everything I have ever done has been out of that love for you and your sisters."

"Don't," she replied, her voice choking with emotion she couldn't control. "Don't tell me you love me after you've hurt me so deeply."

"Let me explain."

Skye swung on him, feeling as if she were drowning in both pain and anger. "Kane is my soul mate! And you had to have known, but you kept it from me. It wasn't Andrew. It was never Andrew!"

Skye knew that her voice sounded totally out of control, but she couldn't help it. All of her emotions, her anger, her hurt, seemed to flow out with every word. "Kane is the man I love, have always loved. The one who has been promised to me by those above us. But you led me to believe it was Andrew. Why?"

"Apphia, I'm sorry—"

"No! You don't get to apologize to me now! You don't get to tell me how you wish things were different, or that if you could go back and change it, you would. It's too late! Kane doesn't remember me, because somehow you separated him from me before we could make our connection."

Skye placed her hand on her stomach and tried to settle the urge she had to purge herself of every single miserable thought and emotion she had experienced the past four days. She just wanted it all gone! "Then you placed Andrew in Kane's place, like a little doll you could substitute for the good of your daughter."

Argus stood there speechless, staring at her as if he didn't know where to begin, and that only hurt Skye more. Tears filled her eyes and rolled down her cheeks unbidden. There was no way for her to stop them; she was in too much pain. "*God*, I not only hate you for this, I hate myself, because I knew in here,"—Skye patted her hand over her heart—"that something was not right. And I didn't trust my own instincts. Instead, I trusted you!"

Argus reached for her. "Apphia, just give yourself a minute to calm down. Let yourself think about this. Andrew has been very good to you—"

"Very good to me?" Skye blinked, pulling back from him. "Was that before or after he cheated on me?"

Argus's cheeks flattened and his eyes remained cold as ice. She hated it when he seemed so detached on the outside, even though she knew that he really wasn't; the color of his eyes just made it appear that way. "I didn't know he cheated on you! If I had, I would've castrated him myself."

"You're unbelievable! He cheated on me because he was never meant to be with me—because of the situation you forced upon him. And all this time I thought there was something wrong with me. That I wasn't pretty enough . . . wasn't communicating enough . . . that I wasn't *enough,* period."

"Stop it!" he hissed. "You know you are more than enough for any man."

"No! I am more than enough for *one* man. Kane! My Jairus! I remember him. I remember *every word, every touch, every life* I ever had with him. But now we are no longer connected, and it feels as if my heart has been ripped open." She curled her hand back over her stomach as her other hand came to her mouth. "*And oh, God, I* broke that connection when I gave myself to Andrew. *I* was the one who betrayed our bond."

Then, much to Argus's shock, Skye suddenly threw up her hands and started screaming at the sky, just trying to get all of her anger out. Argus was truly and utterly shocked at the display and appeared terrified. He reached for her from behind, wrapping his arms around her to try and hold her upright as she dropped to her knees against the ground. He went down with her and continued to hold her as her tears continued to fall.

"I waited and waited," she said miserably, "before giving myself completely to Andrew. And I didn't understand why. I thought I was some kind of terrified prude, and it made no sense after so many lifetimes." Her voice became very quiet in his arms as she continued to shake against him. "If only I had waited a little longer . . . just a little bit longer."

Argus held his daughter close. "I'm sorry. I'm so, so sorry." He whispered the words over and over into her ear, as if hoping one of his expressions of sorrow would penetrate the pain and allow her to forgive him.

Minutes passed; Skye began to calm down, more from exhaustion than as the result of any softening toward her father. "Why?" she asked painfully. "Why would you do this to me?"

Argus spoke gently, as if hoping not to upset her any further. "You said you remembered your past lives with him . . . our lives."

Skye nodded. "That last day he made love to me," she murmured, knowing her father didn't want to hear this—but she didn't care. It was time for everything to be out in the open. "He said the words he has promised me in many lifetimes, and it was as though someone had flipped a switch inside me. Suddenly, it was all there. My Jairus!" She pounded her open palm against her heart. "Mine!" I thought it would come to him too, but it didn't. He didn't remember me, and he ran out on me."

"Then he was never truly worthy of you in the first place." Argus turned her around in his arms to face him. "Don't you see? If you could disappear from his heart so easily, he was never worthy of you." Argus was shaking her slightly, as if the action would help his words sink in. "Do you remember that he tried to take you away from me? In our last life? He accused me of being too controlling—your own father. I've never wanted anything but what was best for you—you and your sisters."

She pulled out of his arms, blinking up into his agonized expression. "He didn't try to take me away from you. *I* was the one who wanted distance," she replied. "You know I love you, but you have never approved of Jairus. I just wanted some time to be with him, but I didn't want to hurt you . . ."

Argus looked at her as if she had just slapped him across the cheek. "I don't believe this. You're protecting him, just as you always have."

"No, it's the truth! I was a coward for not facing you myself. I admit I was wrong. But you had no right to do this. He's mine, promised to me. How dare you take that away! How dare you think you can just substitute someone in that *you* believe is more worthy."

"I was doing what I thought was best. You've always trusted my instincts."

"They are wrong on this! And don't pretend you did this because your instincts told you it was best for me. You did this because it is what *you* wanted. It would make things easier for you. But did you even think twice about what this will do to us —you and me? To our family?"

"You're my daughter. I refuse to lose you over this."

"You've already lost me!"

The terror that streaked across Argus's expression at her words assured Skye that he finally understood the significance of his actions. And though it made her feel a little bit better, she still was in so much pain that his interference had now cost her both of the most important men in her life. "How will I ever be able to trust you after this? I can't even look at you without remembering what you've taken from me. You've no idea how painful this is—to be with him again, to love him as I always have . . . and then have it all taken away. To know that I may not only have lost my connection to him in this life, but in the next life, as well."

"Apphia, please!" Argus grabbed hold of her arms. "In all this time, I've loved you as if you were my own daughter. I may have made a mistake here, but surely you can find it in your heart to forgive me."

"You don't get it!" Skye yelled. "This wasn't *a* mistake. How old was I when you took him away from me?"

"It's not impor—"

"How old?"

"You weren't born yet." At this, what little wind Skye had left whooshed out of her chest. "I'd innocently crossed paths with him at a grocery store, and I knew almost immediately he was Jairus, but it was confirmed when I dreamt of him that night."

"So every year of this life you've continued to lie to me. Every year you had a chance to come to your senses and tell me the truth . . . to bring him back into my life—but you didn't. This wasn't one little lie; it was an entire lifetime of lies."

Skye rubbed her hands over her face to clear off her tears, then nearly broke into laughter at her own stupidity. "And all this time I believed you had done something to change mother's future. I thought that was why you warned me constantly of the consequences of changing what is meant to be. But it wasn't *mother* you were talking about at all, was it? With one act, you'd changed *my* future. *My God,* did she know of this?"

"No!" Argus blurted, then calmed down as if re-thinking his answer. "Merryn suspected something was wrong. She confronted me about it shortly before she died. I denied it, of course, but I've been haunted by the notion that she knew the truth and just never said anything more to me—that her disappointment with me could have been partially responsible for her sudden death."

"I can't believe you did this," Skye said in a rasping whisper. "Look at how many lives you've affected with your selfishness. Mine, Kane's, Andrew's—and possibly mothers. And Lake knows, doesn't she?"

Argus's expression revealed that he really didn't want to be discussing this any further, but he realized he had little choice if he wanted any chance of her forgiving him. "She knows," he finally said. "She knew it the first day she met Kane—when she touched him."

"Why has she not said anything to me? Did you stop her?"

"She is young and naive. She believes you are already on the correct path, and that if she does not interfere, your path will correct itself—that it won't matter in the end."

Skye snorted at that. "Well, after watching him run out on me like I was the very devil, I can assure her that *the path* is sufficiently screwed up."

There was a long silence between them before Argus finally offered, "When I sent you on this assignment, I had no idea it would lead you back to Jairus. The higher ones kept me blind to the path you were on. Perhaps the joke's on me."

"I assure you, father, there's nothing funny about this. And you didn't see the look on his face when he left. I have lost him. But I'm going to finish this assignment—"

"Forget the damned assignment," he bit out. "It doesn't matter anymore."

Skye jerked her head at him. "Of course it matters. It will help him! It will help all of them . . . and it's one final way I can show him how much I love him. Even if he never remembers me, I will always know I gave him this."

Skye went and picked up the folded blanket she had brought out with her and turned quietly to leave.

Argus looked nearly helpless as he watched her begin to walk away. "Apphia, please. Don't leave. I need to hear you say you can forgive me."

"You want my forgiveness?"

"I don't expect your forgiveness now, but I need to know that we can work through this—that you won't continue to let this divide us."

Skye turned back to him slowly. "I don't know if I can forgive you. If you ask me right now I would tell you that I won't. But out of respect for mother I will give it time before I make any final decisions."

"Apphia . . ."

"Tomorrow I hope to finish my assignment. And then, the day after that, I will try to find a way to be happy with my life going forward so that I can continue to help those who need me."

"What about Andrew? You could find happiness with him if you would just give him a chance. He loves you. It may not be the same as Jairus, but you and he have been friends since you were children."

"That's all we've ever been—friends. Now that I know the truth, I won't betray Jairus anymore than I already have."

"You didn't betray, Jairus! And he certainly has not been faithful to you. In case you missed it, he has led a life of whoring with woman after woman. How could you even want to be with him after knowing that?"

Skye whipped a sharp finger back at her father. "Before you interfered, Jairus had never once betrayed me with another woman! And if he knew the truth of who he was in this life, I know he never would have. If he's lost, it's because you've stolen something from him he doesn't even realize is missing, and he searching for it. I *hate* that you've done that to him. Your meddling has doomed him to a life of emptiness, just as it has mine."

She strode back to within inches of her father's face, her hands balled into tight fists at her sides, revealing all the fury she could no longer contain. "Was it worth it, father? Is seeing both of us miserable and alone enough for you?"

"You know I never wanted you to be alone. I wanted you with someone worthy of you. *Andrew* is that man, not Jairus. Kane—the man he is today—will get over this and go on sating his lust in the body of any convenient woman."

Skye flinched at that remark as surely as if he had slapped her across the cheek. She couldn't even think about Kane being with another woman. It would break what little strength she was holding onto.

She swallowed hard and jutted her chin with as much pride as she could possibly muster. "Andrew's a good and decent man who, unbeknownst to him, has spent the better part of his life chasing after a woman who never really wanted him. All because he believed he was destined for me. If you want to do something useful, I would suggest you break all ties with him, because that is exactly what I'm going to do! The sooner we are out of his life and not affecting it, the sooner we will no longer be visible to him. Then maybe he can move on to find someone who will truly love him."

"Apphia, I refuse to see you live your life alone. You've too much love to give."

Skye snorted as she marched away from him—for good this time. "That thought really should've occurred to you before you stole my soul mate away from me."

CHAPTER TWENTY-TWO

When Kane's eyes slid open, his mind was in that blissful place between dreamless sleep and the quicker heartbeats of consciousness.

He blinked a few times at the realization that he had actually slept, then rolled his head to the side and saw the afternoon light still peeking through the window. It had only been a couple of hours—more of a nap, really—but it was a moral victory. It had been several *days* since his body felt relaxed enough to sleep—four, to be precise.

He had just inhaled a deep breath and closed his eyes again when an image popped into his mind with such startling clarity that it jarred him straight to his feet. "Holy shit!" he gasped. "It was him!"

Without another word, Kane tore out of the room, dressed only in a pair of worn jeans and his bare feet. There was no time to think about proprieties as he ran down the long corridor. Minutes later, he charged into Gideon's third floor office without knocking. The Guide was sitting at his desk and looked up, startled, from the book he had been reading to see Kane standing there, half dressed and staring back at him with a nearly murderous expression. "I need to know something," Kane said, without any preliminaries—then swallowed, hard.

Gideon said nothing and set his book down, leaning fully back in his chair, just waiting.

"You said that each of the nine daughters represented an important element of the supernatural world—Skye's being the 'Daughter of Tragedy'."

"That's right."

Kane slammed his hands down on Gideon's desk. "Lake—what does she represent?"

Gideon arched a brow. "Lake is . . . ?"

That pissed Kane off because he suspected Gideon knew damned well which Daughter Lake Matthews was. *What?*

Was the man just going for dramatic effect here? "She's the youngest," he ground through his teeth, "the last daughter."

Kane's heart beat in an almost exaggerated thump as he waited not so patiently for Gideon's answer.

Gideon smiled. "Love," Gideon replied, simply. "She's the 'Daughter of Love'."

Kane pitched forward, anchoring his hands to the edge of Gideon's desk. His whole expression twisted in misery as his chest heaved and he shook his head, biting back a vicious curse that he swore he had not used in some time. *He had been such an idiot!*

"Kane?" Gideon asked with clear worry in his tone, but he was too late; Kane had already spun around and was headed, full steam ahead, back out the door.

The next few minutes were a blur for Kane until he found himself facing several armed guards as he stepped off the elevator on the twelfth floor. Somewhere in the general blur there must have been a moment when he had been clear-headed enough to make a quick stop at his room to grab shoes and a tee shirt before going up to Alec's quarters on the executive floor. There would be no way the guards would let him on the floor to see Alec if he was only half dressed; that would be considered disrespectful—even though Kane was sometimes cut some slack because he was a shifter. Obviously, he doubted he would get any sympathy from Alec today. "Tell him I'm here to see him," Kane nearly barked.

"You know how this works, Kane," Alec's head guard Sampson replied. "And right now he's in a meeting."

"*Tell him . . .*" Kane said in a low voice, "it's me. Trust me; he'll want to see me. I'm quite sure he's wanted to chew my ass out ever since he got back."

Sampson just rolled his eyes. "What the hell did you do now?"

Kane gestured to the communications link that hung on his ear. "Just call him."

It took only about two minutes for Kane to find himself once again in Alec's office, sitting in a chair facing the Elder's desk as the big man paced the floor with an unbecoming scowl on his face. There was no denying that Alec was a handsome man—strong, intelligent—but these days, he was way too uptight, in Kane's opinion. The man needed to spend a few days just hanging out in jeans instead of those fancy Italian pants. He used to be more fun when he wore jeans.

"What the hell's this all about?" Alec demanded. "I don't respond well to people practically charging into my office—demanding to see me. Especially a person I sent on a mission and who returned without the woman I ordered brought in for questioning—and with no answers about this Wraith, either!"

Kane just knew that Alec would bring this stuff up. Some tiny little circumventing of the rules on Kane's part and the boss was ready to erupt.

"You're just lucky that Aiden's covering your ass up there," he continued, not even stopping for breath. "It's the only reason I can keep my sanity while I speak with you."

"Well, then you'll be happy to know, I'm leaving ASAP to join him."

Alec stopped and blinked back at Kane as if he had just said a most ridiculous thing. "No, you're not."

Kane's eyes popped. In the five minutes it had taken him to formulate his plan while he headed up here, he really hadn't considered that Alec might say no. "What do you mean, *no?* You need me there to help Aiden track down this Wraith. At this point, we're the two who know the most about him."

"Really? And what do we know about him, Kane? I'm still waiting for your report on what happened up there."

Kane bolted from his chair. "You know damned well there's no report coming."

Alec snorted. "Well, then, I guess you better get to writing one if you want my approval to go back up there."

Kane threw up his hands, stunned nearly dumb. "I don't . . ." He took a deep breath, but then started over so he wouldn't say something he would truly regret. "I'm taking some personal days—with or without your permission."

Unfortunately, the restated version didn't have any more positive effect than the first one would have had.

Alec's scowl grew deeper, and Kane sighed, finding himself slowed to a crawl by Alec's attitude. "Look," said Kane in a steady, almost patronizing tone, "I don't have time to stand here and argue with you about this." Kane acknowledged just then that he might possibly have pushed the Elder too far. As a rule, Alec never tolerated his authority being blatantly disregarded by one of his own men. He did sometimes go a bit easier on Kane because they both understood the inherent truth that there was never any actual malice behind Kane's defiance. In fact, in some weird way, it was almost a sign of respect.

Alec was a good leader; there was no questioning that in anyone's mind, even Kane's. But right now, Kane just needed a friend. Instead he got an order: "Well, you're going to take time to explain to me what the hell's going on, or you may find yourself banned from more than just the dining hall."

"Fuck this," Kane cursed as he threw up his hands and swung on his heels toward the door. "I'm taking some personal time. If you want to ban me from The Oracle when I return, so be it."

✱✱✱

An amused twitch worked its way into the corners of Alec's lips as he stared at the heavy door that still vibrated on its hinges from the force with which Kane had slammed it on his way out. He turned and walked to the southern window that overlooked the lot where The Oracle's fleet of SUVs were parked. After no more than a few seconds, he heard Gideon enter through the private access door to his right. Alec made no move to look in Gideon's direction, appearing to be lost in thought—but still smiling that inscrutable smile.

"Is he on his way?" Gideon asked.

"Oh, I would say that's a definite 'yes'—with his fully emblazed ego intact."

"Well, you're lucky," Gideon began, clearing his throat. "At least he managed to find a shirt before he came storming into your office."

Alec continued to stare at the vehicles. "Mmm, yes," he sounded. "The man does seem to detest clothing."

Gideon laughed quietly. "It's in his nature."

"Agreed."

"You do realize, though, that if I am right about this, we may lose him?"

Alec nodded into the silence as Gideon joined him at the window, both men now watching as Kane appeared below and climbed into one of the sleek, black vehicles, tossing ahead of him and onto the front passenger seat a small bag that had surely been packed in advance for just such an occasion. Kane frequently didn't know when he would have to shift on the fly, which meant he always had to be prepared.

Alec had to laugh inwardly. Kane never considered for even a moment that he might be denied one of the vehicles for his personal use. He wouldn't be, of course. Alec had already cleared it, knowing after some finely placed suggestions from Gideon that the Shifter would get going in the right direction.

His brows lifted as he turned to Gideon. "So, are you right about this, old man?"

Gideon smiled, taking no offense to the Elder's reference to him as 'old man'. They had known each other too long for such pettiness. Gideon had watched Alec grow from a small boy to Guardian, and eventually Elder. With all of the difficulties Alec had been through in his life—the death of his father and the betrayal by his Uncle Reese as just two examples, Gideon was quite proud of the man Alec had become. "I believe I am. It's the only thing that makes logical sense."

Alec shoved his hands into his pockets. "Then we need to let things play themselves out. If Skye Matthews and her sisters have taught us anything, it's that we can't interfere with what's being designed above us."

"You would think that, of all people, Argus Matthews would recognize and honor that. Perhaps somewhere along the way he forgot his true purpose," Gideon offered by means of explanation, then turned to face Alec directly, a look of concern having spread across his countenance. "I am curious, though. Why did you fight Kane so hard about letting him go? Wasn't it your intention for him to do exactly that?"

Alec inhaled deeply, his face taking on a more serious expression. "For the first time in his life, Kane has to fight for something he really wants. For *someone* he really wants." The amused twitch then returned to his lips. "Far be it from me to make anything easy for him."

Gideon returned his gaze to the now moving vehicle that was accelerating quickly down the drive. "You two really do have a rather odd friendship."

"Yes, but I know this: somewhere above us, Phin and Lucas are laughing their asses off."

"Mmm. So you disagree with Kane that Phin is still alive?"

"I believe, at the very least, his soul is gone. And that's the only part of a man that really counts, isn't it?"

❈❈❈

Aiden cursed under his breath for, like, the fifth time as he tried to conceal his entire six-foot-six frame behind a rather small boulder. It was the only decent sized cover he had anywhere along the edges of the open field where Skye stood, about forty yards away from him. He certainly didn't want her to discover that he was there, watching her, but his long and rather inflexible limbs just didn't want to co-operate. On top of that, he couldn't for the life of him figure out what Skye was doing out here, only miles from the Lycan Dead Zone and wearing nothing for warmth but a light sweater and thin topcoat to protect her from the frigid temperatures.

Kane would have an apoplectic fit if he could see this.

Aiden could see, though, that Skye was beginning to realize her mistake as she rubbed her hands over her arms. Perhaps she hadn't expected to be out here this long. She did have a blanket with her, which would obviously help, but she wasn't using it. It was just lying nearby, neatly folded, almost as if she'd forgotten about it. He'd been following her since he had returned from The Oracle, and the entire time she had been carrying that same damned blanket but never actually using it. It made no sense.

"Yep," he thought. "Kane certainly knew how to pick 'em." This woman was a rare combination of irresistible charm and unique oddity, all at the same time. Of course, if Kane ever pressed him on the matter, he would just say she was charming and *mysterious.* That sounded better than odd. Then he smiled.

His best friend had fallen completely, head over heels, for this woman, and Aiden very much approved, which made learning that she would eventually disappear on them a definite problem. Kane deserved happiness after being alone for much of his life, though Kane would be the first to disagree that he was alone. He would say that he always had plenty of people around him, but that wasn't really the same as belonging to someone, was it? "Maybe," he thought, "that's the difference between aloneness and loneliness." It was in more unguarded and private moments that Kane would admit his desire to have someone for himself. With his sharp sense of humor and his leisurely approach to life, Kane was an easy person to get along with. But the long line of beauties he bedded for a night here or a weekend there certainly didn't qualify as 'belonging'.

It was different with Skye, though. Kane belonged with her. Aiden had no idea why the fates had conspired to keep them apart, but until she was gone completely, he would sit out here in the middle of nowhere for his friend, guarding this special woman, who appeared as if she had nothing better to do than scan the grass for a four-leaf clover. It was his way of repaying Kane for all he had done for him.

Ever since joining Kane on this little adventure and getting some much needed distance from The Oracle, which only served to remind him of the terrible mistakes he had made, he had felt more like himself than he had in a long while. He was laughing again and more in control of the anger that had taken him over after the transfusions. More importantly, his body felt desire again, something he had been numb to with all the drugs they had pumped into his system for the last year in an effort to try and control his anger.

Aiden couldn't remember ever being so grateful for a *feeling*, and he distinctly remembered the first moment it had hit him like a ninety-mile-per-hour fastball. It was just over a month ago, the night he first laid eyes on Lily Abbott. Aiden had been knocked unconscious, and she was there, her soft voice and light, citrusy scent practically knocking him on his ass when she leaned in to check on him. That was the moment his body had seemed to stand up and announce '*Hello, I'm back, and I want this woman*—and it terrified him.

He had been attuned to her every move for the next three weeks, and sometimes he swore that the sound of her voice carried to him on the breeze, even from far across The Oracle's property. On that last day he was there before leaving on this trip, at the moment he had seen her scramble out of the phone booth with Kane, he began to hurt, both emotionally and physically, and that's when he realized he had a big problem; he needed to get as far away from Lily Abbott as he could. Aiden could never have Lily as he wanted because he could never trust himself not to hurt any woman, especially one who could make his heart pump so fiercely.

Aiden had watched how the transfusions had changed good men, most of them his friends, from everyday heroes to violent, uncontrolled zombies. As weeks had passed they had grown more despondent, eventually becoming no longer able to control the anger that was caused by the tainted blood pumping through their veins. Unfortunately, they inevitably would act out their anger on whatever woman stirred their blood the most. It was as if they could no longer separate their strong, positive desire from the negative, hot-blooded anger that was slowly driving them mad . . . and they blamed the women for it.

For Aiden and the only other remaining survivor of the transfusions, Guardian Zane Merrick, it was probably just a matter of time before the same symptoms would begin to affect them, as well. In fact, Aiden suspected that Zane was already having trouble dealing with things, though he worked hard not to show it, just as Aiden did. Secrecy was a natural reaction to being watched, poked and tested nearly all day every day for the prior year.

His cell phone vibrated in his pocket, drawing him back from his thoughts. *Well, speak of the devil.* "So . . ." he whispered, "have you come to your senses yet?" He checked to be sure that Skye could not hear his whisper.

"Dude, tell me you've got an eye on her right now."

Aiden smiled broadly. "I've got two, actually. And she looks awfully fetching today in her sweet little white sweater and her fur-line—"

"Are you trying to piss me off?" Kane interrupted with a growl. "If you so much as look at her ass, I'm going to kick yours."

Aiden chuckled and then playfully hissed, "Too late . . ."

"Aiden!"

"I'm teasing you, man. The only ass-watching I'm doing is to make sure hers stays safe . . . until such time as you finally come to your senses and take over the ass-watching duties yourself." Aiden was then quiet for a moment, his tone much more serious as he spoke, "I know none of this is fair, Kane, but you at least need to say goodbye to her."

"I'm on my way now—should be there in an hour."

Aiden smiled. "So, you have come to your senses, then?"

"Let's just say I've been reminded of something I should have remembered a long time ago. And she needs to know that I remember. But first I need to speak with her father."

"Well, you're in luck. Star and Lake left this morning, so I'm out here in the middle of an open field watching Skye . . . stand around. Which means, Argus is at the cabin by himself."

"*She's where?*" Kane growled. "Not the meadow by the canyon? The Wraith attacked her there once already! What the hell's she doing there without protection?"

"I'm not chopped liver, here!"

"That doesn't count," he snapped back quickly. "She doesn't know you're there!"

"True, but do you remember the part where she's a higher being? She can probably handle herself. Besides, she's been out here for awhile and there's been no sign of our Wraith."

"I don't care!" Kane cried in a higher voice. "I'm still going to paddle her ass when I see her."

"Personally, I think you're just looking for reasons to paddle her ass," Aiden laughed. "By the way, does Alec know you're back up here?"

There was an unnatural pause at the other end of the line, and Aiden groaned. "*Shit*, what did you do now?"

"Nothing that a little groveling won't fix," Kane insisted. "But if he calls in the meantime, I wouldn't pick it up, if I were you."

"Fine. I'll ignore my phone and you deal with her father. I gotta go. She's moving."

"Don't you dare lose her, man."

✳✳✳

Kane pulled up at the cabin a little over an hour later. There was really no point in concealing his approach. A Seer, for all intensive purposes, should know he was coming. Wrapping his knuckles against the door just once, Kane charged right in, fully prepared to find Argus Matthews in a strongly defensive position. But instead, he was stunned silent by what he saw. The older man was quietly sitting on the couch with a full glass of Scotch—if Kane smelled correctly—just staring at the wall in front of him. Kane wasn't aware that higher beings liked Scotch.

"Have a seat," Argus said, calmly and with no ire behind it. "I've been expecting you."

Kane felt his hands tensing at his sides as he moved deeper into the space. He would have much preferred to find an angry Argus Matthews so he'd have an excuse to break the man's jaw. "I think I'll stand," Kane replied in a low, controlled voice. "So . . . you already saw this little encounter coming?"

Argus's accessing fixed on Kane with absolutely no warmth, but also—strangely—with no anger. It was as though all the fight had been drained out of him—a complete contrast to the over-protective parent he had appeared to be with Skye only days before. Actually, the man looked tired. Not that Kane gave a damn. "I am a Seer," he replied. "What do *you* think?"

Kane leaned closer, his voice vibrating with warning. "Then you must've foreseen me putting you on notice. You've lost here. I know who I am now, you son of a bitch! And I *know* I belong with Skye. *Only* Skye."

Argus slid his gaze toward him slowly, and Kane could see the question in his eyes, the same icy-blue eyes that had been so familiar to him. "You remember, then?"

Kane snorted with disgust. "That you were the family *friend* who took me to Vancouver after my parents died? Yeah, I remember. You looked thirty years younger and a lot less grey, but it should have come to me sooner. It's the eyes." Kane then shook his head, trying to wipe the pain from his expression. He didn't want to give this man the satisfaction of seeing how much pain he had inflicted. "Did you even know my parents?"

"Come now, Jairus. If you truly remember, then you know how this works. They were not your real parents. They merely provided a host for your soul. Surely, you must've questioned why they weren't Shape-Shifters like yourself."

Kane didn't want to admit that he hadn't questioned it, but now a lot more made sense. Why they were not able to defend themselves during that robbery. Why he never remembered either of them being able to shift. "Did *you* know them?" Kane snapped.

"No," Argus replied simply. "This was never about them."

"No. It was about *you* kidnapping a five-year-old boy and bringing him all the way to the other side of Canada to ensure I would never meet your daughter."

Argus smiled humorlessly. "Yes, it was."

Kane blinked, amazed at how he would admit the truth so easily.

"You tried to take my own daughter away from me," he said bitterly. "Oh, she's defending you now—saying it was her idea. But I know the truth. And I wasn't about to let it happen in this life."

"You're right. I did think you tried to control her too much . . . still do. When I saw what it was doing to her, I had no issue about being the one to come to you and tell you to back off."

"You had no right—"

"I had every right! I'm the man who's sworn to love her in every life. To put her needs above my own. And I do it gladly because I love her more in each life. Were you really so threatened by me you would steal that away from her before she was even born?"

Argus came to his feet and threw his Scotch glass against the wall, where it shattered into hundreds of pieces, then he beat his hand furiously against his chest. "I wanted you to know what it felt like to lose her. To have her taken from you— just as you took her from me. Everything I did, I did because I love that girl just as if she were my very own flesh and blood. *You* don't really know the meaning of the word! Are you going to stand there and tell me you've been pining away for her while you've been screwing every woman you could manage to drag under the sheets? My daughter deserves better than a man who has single-handedly managed to spread his seed throughout Canada and the lower forty-eight."

Kane could feel his face flaming. None of those women would ever have happened if Argus hadn't fucked with their lives, broken their connection. But there would be no way he could change the fact that he had betrayed his soul mate over and over again with each woman he took beneath him, and he hated it, hated himself for it. He was just left to hope that, in time, Skye would somehow forgive him.

"*I* found her better," Argus continued to spout like a madman. "Andrew *is* better. He would make her happy."

The man was obviously delusional if he thought that Kane would ever allow himself to be replaced in Skye's heart by another man now that he remembered the truth. Kane stalked forward until his eyes were just inches from the Seer's face. "He's never going to get the chance," he growled in warning. "She's mine! She's always been mine. And I won't lose her—ever! So, you'll just have to deal with it, Pops."

Argus was fuming now, appearing as though he could very well erupt. Mount Vesuvius would have nothing on this guy. But then his whole expression seemed to blank, as if he had somehow folded into himself. Then he dropped back onto the sofa. "I won't, actually."

"You won't what?" Kane was about to pop the man for his arrogance, but it was hard to pop someone who was sitting there looking so utterly defeated.

"Have to deal with it," he sighed. "My desire to make sure you could never take Apphia from me has cost me what I wanted most . . . to remain with them, all of them."

Kane was shaking his head. "You're not making any sense, old man."

"The Higher Ones disapproved of my interference. So I—and Merryn, by virtue of being my soul mate—will not be the girls' guardians in our next life."

Kane blinked. Surely he hadn't heard the man right. Now that he remembered everything, he knew Argus and Merryn had been the girl's guardians for thousands of years. He may have hated what Argus had done, but he knew the girls couldn't have loved them any more if they had been their biological parents.

"I saw it in my visions last night. We will be reassigned and replaced by others."

Kane was stunned silent for the longest time. "Damn you!" he finally said. "Damn you for your own arrogance. This will break her heart. It will break all of their hearts."

Kane would have thought he'd be relieved knowing that Argus would not be able to separate him from Skye ever again, but he wasn't. He knew the pain Skye would feel from this, no matter how angry she was with him right now. He also understood the guilt she would carry. She would believe that if she hadn't tried to get some space from her father in the first place, none of this would have happened.

Kane wouldn't allow that. It would become his number one priority to assure her that none of this was her fault. Argus had made his own choices, and he had to accept the consequences for those choices. "Have you told her?"

Argus shook his head. "No, and I'm not going to . . . at least not yet. I have some time still to earn her forgiveness. I don't want it out of guilt."

"So why are you telling me this now?"

Argus met his gaze sincerely. "Because if I fail to win her forgiveness before I pass on—I want you to prepare her and the sisters for what will happen in the next life."

Kane stared at the man with an incredulous glare. "After everything you've done, you expect me to be your confessor?"

"Whatever differences you and I may have, you know she loves me like a father. You know they love Merryn. That should come first—*they* should come first. I'm merely asking you to do what you already know is right."

"It's not right! They need to hear it from you before you're gone. Or they will take that pain with them into the next life. They aren't even going to get a chance to say goodbye to Merryn."

Argus suddenly rose to his feet again, energized once more by his very sadness. "You think because we are more than human that we don't know loss? Everyone experiences loss in some form. *Everyone.* It's what reminds us that we are alive. Higher beings are not above that."

Kane turned away from him with his hands on his hips and sighed. His first instinct was to take Skye away from all this, to somehow shelter her from all the pain, but he knew that would not be possible. Skye would need her sisters once she learned the truth. Argus was right in the fact that the sisters needed to come first. "I'll make you no promises today. But as long as you stop your interference between Skye and me I'll give you some space to make things right with her. So you can tell her the truth yourself. You owe her that much."

Argus gave a quick nod. "I accept that."

Kane moved to the window and ran his hands over his face. He wanted to see her, needed to see that beautiful smile on her face. He was tired; so tired.

"Apphia is a strong woman, Kane. She will learn to accept this in time. Just as they all will."

"I know," Kane said quietly, more to assure himself than Argus, but it still didn't ease his worry for Skye.

"Perhaps I haven't given her enough credit for that. I saw it in how fiercely she challenged my actions once she remembered the truth."

"She remembers me, then? That I am hers."

"She does." There was a long pause before Argus added, "I think somehow she knew that on the very first day you made contact with her again, but she fought it, out of fear she would be doing something wrong." Argus then exhaled, a long, heavy sigh from a man who had little left to fight for. "I regret doing nothing to ease her mind in that regard. You may not believe this, but I would take it all back if it would give me one more lifetime with her—with all of them."

Kane fisted his hands at his sides, his blood coursing powerfully though his veins, reminding him that *he did* have more lifetime with her. He had many more lives with her, and he couldn't believe he'd almost been stupid enough to walk away from her. "I need to see her," he said, more to himself—and with more emotion than he intended.

Argus nodded. "I know."

CHAPTER TWENTY-THREE

Kane burst through the cabin door and straight into the biting afternoon chill, headed for the meadow to find the woman he had not been able to get out of his thoughts for a single moment in the last five days.

There was no force between heaven and hell that would stop him because, finally, *finally,* after fighting it for all this time, he could allow himself to accept that she was *his* woman, *his* soul mate, *his* for lifetime after lifetime, and no one, *no one,* could keep her from him a single moment longer. For the first time in his life he was running *toward* something—*to* someone who was his—someone who was permanent. She was his family—always had been. And damn, it felt good!

His heart pounded in his chest and blood raced through his body at just the thought of seeing her beautiful face again. Had it really been less than a week since he had last seen her? It felt as though he had been denied an entire lifetime, and—in a way —he had. Now he understood why he moved so quickly from woman to woman. Why he couldn't bring them to his bed. And why his heart could so easily detach. Somehow his mind, *his soul,* was trying to tell him that he belonged somewhere else— to someone else. He just hadn't understood.

How he was such a lucky bastard he would never know.

Skye made him want to roar from the gut, claw at the ground, and pound his chest in pride. He had to run, and urgency dictated that he go faster than his two human legs could carry him. Clothing flew off in several directions as his bare feet connected rhythmically with the rough terrain. His jacket, shirt, and then his pants were gone as his hands launched out in front of him, propelling him forward at the same moment the familiar shift happened within his body. A deep, prideful growl vibrated in his own ears as giant paws reached for the earth ahead of him in a flat out sprint. At that pace, he reached the clearing within minutes. And when the view opened ahead of him he spotted Skye kneeling against the sunlit ground at the far end of the field.

What the heck was she doing? She didn't appear injured or stressed; rather, she was sitting still with her hands politely resting in her lap, as if she was waiting for something.

He didn't like it one bit.

Elongating his strides, he was about to roar out his disapproval when a low humming sound welled in the distance, growing louder and sharper until it pervaded the atmosphere with the subtlety of a blare horn. Skye's head snapped around as she reached inside the blanket at her hip, pulling out a long dagger that had been hidden in its folds. She separated the sharp blade from its sheath and held it high. The short sword looked to be of solid steel, with a heavy triangular blade built to slice through anything in its path. Ruby insets circled the hilt in an ornate pattern that sparkled as she held it against the light.

Wait a minute . . . no, not rubies, thought Kane. He somehow recognized this dagger. They were not rubies, they were very rare red diamonds that gleamed at him across the remaining distance like a wink meant to remind him of its familiarity. An image from the night at Brahm Hill suddenly flashed through his mind—a horrible image of Alec's uncle, Reese Lambert, sinking that very blade into Guardian Lucas Rayner's chest. Lucas had gasped his last breath as the diamond-studded dagger entered his chest and he stared at his killer with a look of utter disbelief that their former leader could betray them all like that.

Kane now felt the tension gripping every muscle in his jaguar body as he closed the distance between him and Skye. What was she doing with that dagger?

Skye looked up and saw him at the very moment that a loud pop rent the air, followed by the appearance of a sharp band of light suspended above the field not far from her. Kane roared louder this time, a roar of warning across the entire field as a massive, whirling funnel of fury spilled from the light onto the open landscape, headed straight for Skye.

The Wraith was back, and he once again had his sights set on Skye.

Skye was focused on Kane, almost as if she were stunned, ignoring the specter that was racing toward her. *Damnit,* he was still too far away!

The thunderous wind of the approaching Wraith grew louder, snapping Skye into action. She gripped the hilt of the dagger between her two small hands and drove it into the ground with all the strength she had in her slim shoulders, then she held on as if she expected it to save her against the force of the air that was coming directly for her. *It was completely insane!* Kane had never felt such panic in his life. She may be a higher being and all, but her oh-so-human body could get her butt blown across the landscape as easy as the next person. He couldn't lose her now, not after he just found her again.

Unable to reach her before the Wraith blew over her like a tornado, Kane was just about to curse in the form of angry growls when he saw Aiden break through the tree line and race at inhuman speed toward Skye. He wrapped one long arm around her, pulling her to him and taking them both toward the ground. His hand went over her head, trying to shield her from the storm now coming at them. Kane could see the tremendous force Aiden was using to try and keep him and Skye from being blown back. The muscles in his shoulders flexed against the force of the wind as he tried to find a way to dig his feet into the ground, but he couldn't hold it. The funnelling chaos around them was too much.

Every action to that point had happened quickly, but suddenly time seemed to slow down and become a single, unnaturally protracted moment. Kane's animal heartbeat pounded in his ears as he watched Skye and Aiden get blown into the air like a leaf in a wind storm, their arms failing wildly from their sides before they both crashed back to the ground. Skye had travelled about ten feet farther than Aiden when the leading edge force of the cyclone hit them. For a moment, Kane was sure his lungs had stopped taking in critical air as he pushed his elongated stride to the brink—to as fast as he could get his jaguar form to go. He watched Aiden roll to his feet against the force of the air still coming at him and push toward

Skye, whose head had just smacked hard against the ground, leaving her dazed—or maybe unconscious.

Damnit! The animal in him roared with such fury that he thought he would explode, that his body couldn't contain the wrath he felt. He cut across the landscape, certain of only one thing: this Wraith was going to be extinct by the time he was done with him. Kane launched forward from his powerful paws with a sheer determination he knew he had never before felt— ever! His only purpose in life now was to save Skye and to pit his rage-filled body against the power of the oncoming storm. He had absolute confidence in his shifted, jaguar form, the form he felt most powerful in. The strength in his brute muscles, the sharp focus of his mind became one as he concentrated on one future point—where the two colliding forces would meet.

Kane! No! Don't hurt him!"

Skye was calling out to him but he couldn't even let that distract him. There was no stopping him now. His timing would have to be split-second perfect in order to hit the Wraith instead of allowing the speeding force to blow right by him completely. But he had it. He knew he had it. His huge, razor-sharp foreclaws extended to the ready and his jaw opened, exposing a pair of deadly canines, ready to sink into whatever flesh he was now facing. But in the split second before he and the murderous storm came together, Kane looked into the heart of the whirling funnel and saw something that made him hesitate, something that made him pull back just enough.

The Wraith and the jaguar collided in mid air with an ear-shattering roar, and the impact drove him to the ground, pinning him down in place just long enough for his sharp eyes to see the true face of the enemy that was trying to hurt Skye . . . and he couldn't believe what he saw!

What the hell?

❋❋❋

He was here! Kane was here! To Skye, it didn't even matter if he wasn't there for her. She was just amazed to see him when she believed she never would again. Her heart was positively racing when she saw him in his jaguar form coming across that field with powerful, purposeful strides. All she wanted to do was go to him and throw her arms around him so tightly that the poor animal would fear he was being squeezed to death. But at least he would feel how much she had missed him.

"Kane!" she called out with what little voice she had left inside her.

She then tried to free herself from Aiden's protective grip, which, at the moment felt more like iron rings than human arms wrapped around her. "Stay here," Aiden warned. "It's too dangerous." There was just no way this man was merely human. He was *too* strong. His long body covered her with the fortitude of a wall, prepared to fight an entire army if need be to keep her safe. But he didn't understand that she *had* to get to Kane. She had to know that he was all right.

The jaguar, leaping high into the air, had clashed so violently against the Wraith that she feared he might be seriously injured. Her breath felt trapped inside her chest for what seemed like an eternity as she watched the swirling dust rise, then begin to settle. When the jaguar finally cleared the dust and debris, his completely naked human form lifted slowly to its feet above the other naked human form lying motionless on the ground. Thankfully, Kane appeared uninjured but breathing hard and seemingly in shock as he slowly took a step backward, away from the unmoving body.

"What the fuck . . . ?" Aiden said in a fading voice right above her ear.

Sensing Kane's and Aiden's shock, and feeling Aiden's response to it, seemed to snap Skye back into the moment, reminding her that she still had a job to do and very much needed to focus so she could help the one person she really wanted to help—Kane.

But first she had to put to an end to the now crushing grip that Aiden was applying to her upper body.

"Aiden," Skye said—as calmly as she could. When his gaze swung back to her from its lock on the body a few yards away she had to bite back a harsh cry of pain because her arms were surely going to break off at any moment.

Instantly, his eyes widened in true horror as he realized how much he was hurting her. "I'm sorry," he whispered, releasing her as if he had been hugging fire. The poor man was now somewhere in between shock and alarm.

"It's all right, Aiden. It's all right," she tried to assure him as she moved away from him and ran toward Kane, who was now crouched on bended knee in front of the man on the ground, his eyes blinking slowly as if he were still trying to process what he was seeing.

The Wraith rolled to his side with a hard moan, then stiffly pushed to his knees. There was no mistaking that their Wraith, though pale and a little dirty as he scratched his hand through his hair, was a very fit human man. He didn't appear to have any injuries but was definitely shaken by what had just happened.

Kane reached a hesitant hand out to the man, his expression cautious—as if he didn't entirely know what to expect once he made contact with his opponent's shoulder. But when he did, the Wraith disappeared like a puff of smoke right in front of him and Kane blinked in utter astonishment.

"No!" Skye cried out. *She couldn't lose the Wraith again!* She swung on her heels to find the dagger, which was still embedded in the ground where she had left it. Racing back for it, she could barely manage enough strength to pull it free from its sheath in the earth. And no sooner had she freed it than she lifted the diamond-encrusted weapon high over her head once again and drove the blade back into the soil with all the force she could muster.

As if on command, the hum in the air returned almost immediately, and another pop sparked right in front of her. Skye could feel a tremendous wave of heat that came over her, as if someone had just opened the door to a hot oven. She stretched her hand out to the open air, her other hand still firmly gripping the dagger's hilt as the Wraith re-appeared right in front of her. "Hold on to me!" she ordered.

The Wraith reached for the lifeline offered, curling his fingers fiercely over hers. Skye held on for dear life and pulled his hand over the hilt of the dagger then closed her other hand on top of his, trying not to get blown back off her feet again. As the wind around them calmed back down, the man's head bent forward. He inhaled several times, rough breaths, his body shaking violently.

"Give yourself a minute." Skye felt the warmth transferring through her hands as she held his very cold ones. "It's going to be all right. Just focus on the words I'm saying to you. Focus on staying right here. You're home now. I need you to keep hold of the dagger and slow down your breathing."

He seemed to understand what she was trying to tell him, nodding as his hand tightened on the hilt. "That's it. Nice and slow. This is where you're supposed to be, Lucas. Fight for it. Fight!"

Lucas Rayner, the Brethren Guardian they all believed they had lost that night at Brahm Hill, stared back at her with a vulnerability that was difficult to reconcile with the fierce fighter she knew, as a member of The Brethren, he would be. She could tell just by looking at him that he'd been spin-dried through quite an ordeal since the night of Brahm Hill. Skye empathized deeply with this man and what he'd been through because she felt as though she knew him, mostly as a force of will or a power of positive memories that became evident through Kane's mourning of his lost friend. Lucas was important to Kane, so he was important to her.

"Skye! Skye!" Kane called as he dropped to his knees beside her and pulled her into his arms. For a moment he was practically smothering her against his body—a body, of course, that had no clothes on—as he searched for any cuts or broken bones. She was overwhelmed. And once he was satisfied that nothing was mortally wrong with her, he pulled her into a steady embrace. He held her as though no time had passed since the last time they lay lovingly in bed.

"Are you hurt?"

When Skye didn't answer him right away because of her fear that if she spoke, the moment would disappear, Kane turned her around to face him more fully. Those amazing silver eyes of his gazed upon her with a warmth that seemed to surround her like a giant, invisible hug as his hand pressed against her cheek. The love she had felt for him over and over again, lifetime after lifetime literally squeezed over her heart. She accepted the pain—breathed it in—because it was based on something real, even if only for a little while. "You're scaring me here, darlin'. Are you all right?"

She nodded mutely and then backed it up, finally, by saying, "I'm fine . . . well, aside from the bump on the back of my head."

Kane dropped his forehead gently against hers, his fingers searching the back of her head until he located the bump and ran his fingertips over it gently. He then kissed her forehead and inhaled a long, quiet breath of relief. The moment was so perfect, just as tender and sweet as any moment they had shared in bed together during those two perfect days, and she felt lost in it.

"You were there that night," Lucas interrupted, looking to Skye, and she was reminded that she still had a job to do. "Brahm Hill . . ."

"You remember?" she asked him.

He shook his head. "Not really. I only remember your voice telling me not to be afraid. You've been here every time I've crossed back. Do you know what's happening to me?"

Skye glanced first at Kane, who still seemed to be partially suspended in disbelief as he continued to hold her firmly in his arms. Then she turned back to Lucas with a sympathetic smile. "It's going to be OK. I've been sent here to help you."

"Lucas . . . ?" she heard Aiden questioned behind her in a hollow voice. Though still clearly stunned, he at least had enough presence of mind to grab the blanket Skye had brought out with her to the meadow. Kane finally released his hold on Skye and reached for the blanket, wrapping it around Lucas's shoulders. He rubbed his hands quickly back and forth along his friend's arms for warmth, even though he could probably use the warmth just as much as himself.

"It's good to fucking see you, man," Lucas said to Kane with a dazed expression, as if he didn't truly believe that this was all real. And then, to Aiden he said, "Both of you."

"Lucas, how is this possible?" Kane asked in amazement. "We all saw you die that night."

Lucas shook his head as he closed his eyes. "I don't know. I don't remember anything. Just suddenly being pulled between here and a place that looks like this one—but wasn't the same."

Kane and Aiden glanced at each other, both men clearly surprised. "What place?" Kane asked.

Lucas nodded as if to acknowledge that he understood their confusion. "I know. *Shit*, it sounds fucking crazy . . . but it's real. It's another world, much like this one . . . only the colors are brighter. The sky is bluer. It even smells different . . . I can't explain it. And the people . . . They're people I know, but, they're not."

"It's not crazy," Skye reassured him. "You've been going back and forth between this world and an alternate one—another plane of existence. The timeline is similar . . . events . . . people . . . but the events that brought them and you to that point are different."

Kane frowned in confusion. "Between worlds? Just how the hell can he do that?"

"It's the dagger . . . ," she replied, then paused as if to search for the right words. "It's mystical and very powerful. That night at Brahm Hill, once the blade penetrated his heart, it began transforming him."

"To what? An immortal?" Aiden blinked.

Lucas scowled at him. "I'm not a goddamn vampire or anything."

Looking at Aiden, Skye shook her head and replied, "No, not a vampire. I was sent to Brahm Hill to help Lucas with his transition. My father foresaw that he would be taken down by Reese that night." Turning her attention to Lucas, she went on. "We knew you wouldn't understand what was happening to you, so I stayed with you when you were being transported back by Alec's guards. But after you woke and before I had a chance to explain what was happening, you experienced your first slide."

"Slide? Are you saying he just pops over from one plane to another? That's crazy. Besides, Alec would have said something if Lucas's body had gone missing. Hell, we all thought we buried him."

Skye touched Kane's arm, her warmth trying to reassure him. "Alec didn't say anything because he felt responsible when the guards had returned to The Oracle that night and they told him that Lucas's body was missing. He knew you were all grieving Lucas's loss enough as it was. He couldn't face the idea that after everything was over, they had lost the body to mourn. *He* needed a body to mourn. It's why he's not been the same since that night. He needed to bury his friend."

Kane rubbed his hand across the back of his head, his expression tight as he watched Lucas absorb the news about how Alec was handling his supposed death. The two of them were closer than brothers. Lucas would never want Alec to suffer in the way he had. "That explains a lot about the mood he's been in," Kane mused.

"The dagger . . . ," Lucas growled, his emotions on the subject a little too close to the surface even in his shaken state. "What is it? Why is it doing this to me?"

Skye gave him a sympathetic smile. "I'm afraid I don't have all the answers for you."

"But you're a higher being!" Kane exclaimed. And though he hadn't meant it to come out as critical, it caught her off guard. "Shouldn't you be the one who knows of these things?"

"Higher being?" Lucas questioned, but Aiden shook his head in a quick movement, as if to signal 'not the right time'.

Skye glanced away from both men and took in a steadying breath, then felt Kane's hand touch her elbow. The contact was reassuring and brought her attention back to him.

Recognizing his glance as something of an apology, she continued, "There are many forces at work in the supernatural world. "Some of them are dark forces. My father believes a dark force is responsible for the dagger's creation, but even he does not know who created it or why." She glanced back to Lucas. "Reese must have discovered something of the dagger's origins and the power it possessed when he set out to retrieved it. He had a purpose for it—that is clear."

"That purpose was not meant for me," Lucas stated plainly. "It was meant for Alec."

The three men all exchanged meaningful looks. They had all believed Alec was Reese's intended target the night of Brahm Hill. Lucas had just gotten in the way.

For a few moments the conversation died; each person involved was going deeply into individual thoughts. Finally,

Lucas broke the silence. "I'm going to kill that fucker the next time I see him. I don't care if he's Alec's uncle."

"Too late," Kane muttered. "The Lycan's already made a meal of him."

Lucas blew out a hard snort, his body still shaking harder now from the cold. "Couldn't have happened to a nicer asshole."

Kane snorted his agreement. "Have you been jumping between worlds this whole time?"

"Whole time? It's only been a couple of days."

"It hasn't," Skye said, her head shaking a firm 'no'. "Time is always moving when you are sliding between dimensions. Sort of like a rock skipping over water. For you, the experience will not have seemed that long."

"How long has it been?"

"You've been gone a month," Kane replied.

"A month? You're kidding!"

Kane was shaking his head. "I wish. This is all so hard to believe." Then he looked to Skye. "Why were you after Skye?"

"I wasn't," Lucas replied. "It felt more like she was pulling *me* to *her*. Every time I came back to this side, she was there. After a while it just made sense that she was the one I needed to get answers from. Since then I've been trying to reach her, but I don't seem to have any control over the slides. They pull me where they want me to go."

"You can get control of them with this," Skye said, returning her hand to the dagger. "It wasn't me drawing you—it was this. I just was the one in possession of it."

"That's what you were hiding in your suitcase?" Aiden questioned.

She nodded. "I needed it to succeed in bringing him back to this side. So much time had passed . . ."

"Because I was keeping you from your assignment," Kane said, a somber note creeping into his voice. "Why didn't you just tell me it was Lucas? I would've helped you any way I could."

"We all would've," Aiden chimed in.

"I didn't know who . . ." Seeing the confusion on Kane's face, she didn't finish. He must be wondering why she had not said anything about Lucas being alive when he had clearly been mourning his friend. "If I had known it was *you*, I would have told you." Skye feared that answer might confuse Kane, not knowing if he remembered he was *her* Jairus, her soul mate, and thus she would be allowed to tell him anything.

But Kane seemed to accept that answer and nodded his head ever so slightly.

"Now that you're here," Skye said to Lucas, "the dagger will help hold you to this side—slow time down to a more normal pace. You can then learn how to control the slides better."

"Control them?" Lucas scowled. "Fuck, I can't even control what direction I'm going or the fact that I'm naked most of the time now . . . because, evidently, clothes don't like to slide to other planes of existence. I'm going to be fucking worse than Kane."

An amused smile tugged at the corners of Kane's mouth. "You'll get used to it."

"So what's up with the whole dust-ball express thing you've got going on?" Aiden asked Lucas while handing Kane his coat, adding, "I've learned to travel in layers with you, my friend."

Kane snatched the coat with a sarcastic frown and threw it on.

"It's weird," Lucas began. "It actually feels like everything around me is moving fast while I'm moving slow."

"We can assure you," Skye replied, "quite the opposite is true. What you're feeling is the force you're creating when returning onto this plane."

Aiden snorted. "The physics of that would have Gideon rambling on for hours."

"He would," Kane agreed with a half-hearted smile that soon thinned into concern when he saw Lucas continuing to shake from the cold. "We need to get you inside. Aiden, can you—?"

Lucas stopped Kane with a bracing arm, still keeping one hand on the dagger. "There's something you need to know." His expression looked as if he would rather be scratching his own eyes out than revealing to Kane whatever he was about to say. "The first time I slid back to from the other side I didn't understand what was happening . . . but something else did. Some creature attached on to me right before the slide."

"Creature?" Aiden echoed.

Lucas confirmed with a nod. "Whatever it was, it didn't look human—more like some type of reptile."

Kane cursed under his breath. "That's what's been killing all of the Lycans. And I have a bad feeling it's headed straight for The Lycan Dead Zone."

"The same Dead Zone where Phin may be," Aiden added quietly.

"Phin?" Lucas blinked back. "What are you talking about?"

Kane raised a hand to his friend's shoulder and squeezed reassuringly. "We'll catch you up on everything, but first we need to get you inside and out of the cold."

Lucas closed his eyes for a moment. "I caused this, Kane. I brought this thing over into this world. I need to fix it."

"You aren't going to do that alone," Kane replied. "We'll help you."

There was much said with just those few words. Lucas didn't smile, but his eyes indicated that he wanted to, and it warmed Skye's heart. Kane was reunited with his friend, the brother he thought he lost, and now he could begin to heal. That was what Skye wanted most for him, to give him peace. She turned her head away, not trusting that she could control the conflicting emotions building in her. Her heart over the last few days felt like it had been physically damaged, and she had no idea how to make the emotional pain stop. How was she going to be able to accept living this life without her Jairus? Or the next?

"Let's get you back to the cabin before you freeze to death," she heard Kane say to Lucas. Then he added, "If that's all right with you, Skye."

Damn. Sure, it was her family's cabin, but he had asked her that intentionally, demanding her direct attention. Now she was going to have to turn around and look at him. There was no way she could trust herself to look into those beautiful silver eyes and not risk all her emotions spilling out. "Of course," she replied, keeping her gaze averted, but she couldn't hide the slight crack in her voice.

"Some clothes and some food would be nice," Lucas replied. "And maybe some sleep. It feels like forever since I fuckin' slept."

Lucas released his grip from the dagger's hilt. "No!" Skye cried, throwing her hands back over his. "Don't let go of it. At least not until you have a better hold on this side."

"She's right," Kane agreed. "Keep that damn thing glued to your hip until we figure out what we're dealing with. We'll have to come up with a plan."

Lucas didn't argue, gripping the dagger as if his life depended on it.

"Aiden," Kane began, while scanning the darkening skies. "Take Lucas back to the cabin. We'll plan on leaving for The Oracle in the morning."

As she watched Aiden and Lucas leave in the direction of the cabin, the last of Skye's hope dropped with a giant thud inside her stomach. Kane would be leaving her again in just a matter of hours, and she wasn't sure her heart could bear it. She thought she could survive anything as long as she didn't have to watch him run out on her again as he had the last time they'd been together. But now she realized he could simply *walk* away —and it was still going to destroy her.

How could she let him do it? Simple—because she loved him. She loved him enough to let him go. She loved him endlessly and wanted him to be happy, even if that meant never learning the truth of who he was and giving him the freedom to return to the life he'd built without her.

But Kane surprised her by returning his head to rest against hers. He inhaled a slow, steady breath, a breath that seemed to ease through him as his shoulders relaxed. "Are you sure you're all right?" he asked in a soothing voice.

"I'm fine," she replied, touching the fingers of one hand to his exposed thigh. His skin was ice cold, but he wasn't shaking. "You're the one we need to worry about. You're freezing."

She tried to pull him to his feet, but he wouldn't allow it. Instead, he held her close in his arms, his eyes piercing into and through her with such feeling it caused her to shiver under the intensity. She knew that look. It was one he had given her lifetime after lifetime. Maybe it was too much to hope it was love, but for a moment, perhaps, she could allow herself to believe that everything was going to be OK. He stroked her cheek. His fingers were just as cold as the rest of him as he moved them up and threaded them through her hair, but Skye didn't mind. On the contrary, she was positively bursting with heat. There wasn't one single thing she would change about this moment, except that she wished it could last longer, even forever.

"I remember, Apphia," he said, the rough timbre of his voice humming through her. "I remember everything—every lifetime with you."

She gasped, her expression breaking before she dropped her head to his shoulder, literally feeling the relief sag through to him. "I'm sorry," she murmured while shaking her head. "I'm so sorry I didn't wait for you . . . that I broke our bond."

He pulled her tighter against him. "Darlin', you've nothing to be sorry for. Your father did this to us—not you."

She stared up at him as the warm tears she had been trying to hold back finally slid down her frigid cheeks. His frosty thumbs wiped them away, but they kept coming. "But I should've known. I should have remembered that first time I saw you again. Now we've lost so much."

"We have," he agreed, his hand lifting her chin to him. He obviously wanted to say something more but Skye stopped him.

"Please . . ." she replied, unable to absorb the pain of the guilt that now attacked her spirit with a vengeance. Kane was her eternal soul mate, her gift from those above her. As a higher being it was her responsibility to honor that gift, to be worthy of it, and let no other man touch her but him. Instead, she hadn't trusted her instincts, and for a long time had been slowly destroying their bond as each day she had allowed herself to stay with a man that she knew, deep in her heart, was not right for her.

The single shiver brought on by the cold turned into a steady shaking within Kane's arms as she processed her emotions. "Hey," he voiced with clear concern. "You're shaking. Come on—we need to get you back."

She didn't object, and the trek back to the cabin was a blur. She remembered talking a little—but she remembered not a single word she had said.

"There you are," Aiden called as they reached the cabin. "Lucas had something to eat and he's taking a shower." He turned to Skye. "I hope you don't mind. There was no one here to ask."

Skye blinked at him. "My father's not here?"

Aiden shook his head. "There was this." Aiden handed her a small envelope, which she tore open quickly.

My Dearest Apphia,

The past two days have afforded me something a man never wants too much of . . . time to reflect upon his mistakes. In doing so, I find I am a man filled with regret for having caused such pain to you, a woman who embodies nothing but patience, beauty and grace. Every time I see the pain in your eyes I will be reminded of how selfish my actions have been. I know it won't be easy for you to forgive me, but I promise you I will earn it. Let me know where you'll be so we may talk.

Love Always,

Dad

CHAPTER TWENTY-FOUR

Kane was glaring at the cabin's master bedroom door.

Glaring! In fact, he felt pretty confident he could burn a hole through it with the heat of his glare alone. Skye Matthews was on the other side . . . hiding. She actually thought he was going to leave in the morning without her. *What?* Was she expecting they would just be polite and go their separate ways on a handshake?

Not going to happen.

He had sensed her hesitation when they were walking back to the cabin and wanted to put a stop to any notion right then and there, but she just kept talking, almost as if she were in a daze—or as though she was talking to herself. She rambled on about how she wanted to save Lucas from Reese's blade but that her father warned her she was not to interfere with what was destined (fine time for Argus to be all high and mighty about keeping his nose out of things). She talked about how she wished she could've told him that Lucas was alive sooner, but it was forbidden to discuss such things outside of her family . . . and, of course, how at that time she didn't know who he really was.

She was hurting inside, and it was killing him.

He was about to put a stop to it, but Aiden was there—the turd. Along with superhuman strength, speed, and hearing, his friend seemed to have developed a notoriously bad sense of timing. He suspected that had nothing to do with vampire blood transfusions.

The four of them had all relaxed at dinner, quietly listening to Lucas explain some of what he experienced in the other dimension. It was a total trip. Evidently, Kane was like some sort of bad-ass super soldier, obsessed with the cause and living with two women: Lily Abbott—which really didn't go over well at all with Aiden—and some mess of a woman named Poppy Honeywell. The 'mess' part was Lucas's word.

Apparently the woman, though sweetly easy on the eyes, was always causing trouble and always tripping over herself.

"Honeywell?" Kane said with amusement, trying to lighten the mood for the evening while tapping a finger over his chin. "Yeah, a woman with the word 'honey' in her name sounds about right." Kane had only been teasing, but it had been a thoughtless thing to say. Skye had been quiet all evening but grew even more so after his comment. His alternate world with the Lemon and Honey (which he had to admit sounded like a delicious combination) meant that Argus's interference had broken his connection to Skye in that world, as well—at least temporarily. He watched a quiet and somber Skye closely through dinner, realizing she must have come to the same conclusion he had. And he couldn't help but wonder if their path would get corrected on that side, or if he would remain lost to her. That didn't sound like a world he wanted to be in, but he didn't get a chance to express that thought aloud. Skye excused herself from the group early and suddenly, giving the excuse that it would be a long day traveling home tomorrow, so she wanted to get some rest.

Traveling? She was going to be traveling, but not home. And not anywhere without him!

Hence, the current stare-down with the bedroom door for the last hour, as if he had the power to blow it down by mere thought.

"Have you burned a hole through it yet?" Aiden asked in a gravelly, relaxed voice as he lay back on the sofa. It had been a long day for all of them. Lucas had been completely exhausted, as if his body had not experienced any significant rest in the month he'd been gone. He fell fast asleep on the floor, the dagger strapped to his hip and covered with nothing more than a thin blanket, resting his head on a sofa pillow.

"Do you get the impression she thinks I'm leaving here tomorrow without her?" Kane questioned with a sincere frown.

Aiden's brows lifted. "Figured that out, have ya? You're all over it tonight, buddy."

"Oh, shut up, smart-ass," Kane shot back, accompanying his retort with a full-fledged scowl. "If this were Lemon we were talking about, you'd be panicked by now."

"Don't bring Lem—. . . Lily into this. And, by the way, I don't care what you do in that other dimension," Aiden began, pointing his finger in warning, "but in this one, you won't be touching Lily again."

There it finally was. And it brought a grin to Kane's face. His friend was smitten, completely and utterly smitten—had to be. He had never let his feelings about any woman out for public consumption before. It was like some unwritten rule with the guy. Unfortunately, it made it hard for the woman of the moment to tell he had feelings for her, which was also probably true in Lily's case.

Realizing he had just let his jealousy get the better of him, Aiden quickly changed the subject back to focus on Kane's dilemma. "Just what exactly are you going to do to straighten this out, dumbass?"

Kane's lips scrunched up and his brow furrowed with great concentration as he turned back to the door. "I'm working on it."

Aiden snorted. "Well you better work faster, or you, my friend, are going to find yourself sleeping on the floor tonight, because I'm claiming this rather comfortable sofa."

Kane smiled. "It is comfortable. We had—"

"Don't say it!" Aiden cut in, throwing his hand up as if to block the terrifying words. "I don't want to know what you two did here."

"I was going to say . . . breakfast," Kane finished, flashing a devilish grin in Aiden's direction.

"Right," Aiden replied, then stood up and stretched out his exceedingly long arms. "I think I might go for a walk before bed. A long walk," he added. "Somewhere far, far away, where my sensitive hearing won't pick up a thing."

Kane stood, as well, and clapped his compatriot on the shoulder. "You do that, buddy—because I have no intention of sleeping on that floor tonight."

A few minutes later, Kane quietly opened the door to what he now considered to be his and Skye's room. The brightness of a full moon poured through the large window and bathed the space in a soft, grayish light. The bed was tossed and she lay there looking like an angel who had just had a pillow fight and had lost to exhaustion. Blond wisps of hair fell in her eyes, and her bare leg and shoulder were exposed in a tangle of bed covers. It was obvious she had been tossing and turning since the moment she'd hit the bed.

He listened to her quiet breathing as he began removing his own clothes and made a closer inspection of her. She shifted under the sheets, flashing her bare hip at him as the blankets coiled like a snake around her, successfully concealing the fact that she had not a stitch on underneath them. Irrationally, he found himself cursing the blanket manufacturer in his head for ever making such a concealing garment in the first place.

Fully unclothed, Kane walked to the other side of the bed and lifted the covers to slip in behind her. Her skin was silky-soft, warm, her quiet moans indicating that she was in the middle of some rather gentle dreams. This was his favorite way to be with her, just cuddled up next to her as she slept. At the feel of his hands on her skin, she moaned lightly once more and turned toward him with a tiny smile on her face, as if to say her dreams were making her happy at that moment. She looked beautiful. There was no way he would ever let this woman go again.

His hands coursed over her skin from shoulders to hip while his warm breath heated her cheek. Her eyes flittered open like giant green jewels. "Kane?"

"Were you expecting someone else?" he growled playfully.

"No!" she blinked back. "I—I mean, I just didn't think you'd."

Kane's fingers drew circles over her hip before he pulled her thigh over his, letting her feel just how excited he was to be lying next to her again. "You're naked under here, darlin'."

"I have gotten sort of used to sleeping that way in this bed."

He leaned over her, needing to be even closer. "My kind of woman," he purred. "That sounds like someone made just for me." He took possession of her mouth in a deep, exploratory kiss—definitely slow—because, unlike their sizzling encounter on the bathroom countertop nearly a week ago, he planned to take his time with her tonight . . . because they had all the time in the world.

She kissed him in return, but he could feel her tense up ever so slightly beneath him. He pulled back with a questioning stare, and her eyes appeared even greener in the smoky moonlight. "Kane . . . ," she began nervously. "You . . . I mean we . . . we . . ."

"I know who I am now, Skye," he murmured softly, wanting to reassure her. "I know where I belong—with you. It's always been with you. You will never again be with any other man . . . because you belong to me. You're my, Skye. Mine. I remember every lifetime with you. I remember every laugh, every smile, every time I made love to you. And I intend to spend the rest of this lifetime doing it all over again."

She smiled up at him and the smile expanded into a face full of grin. "You've come back to me, Jairus?"

"Oh darlin', I never left. Not really. You had me tied to you right here," he said, taking her hand and pressing it to his chest, just above his heart. I may have been lost, but my heart knew you were out there somewhere."

He was expecting her at that point to return his kiss, since the moment had been so unabashedly romantic, but instead a little crease appeared between her brows. That certainly wasn't what he expected. "I feared I had broken our connection forever . . . because of Andrew."

Kane placed a thumb over her lips to stop her words as he cupped her face in his hand. "Andrew never had the power to break what we have. No man does."

Skye inched even closer to him. "And my father?"

"I think we've proven that he doesn't, either."

She kissed him gently, just a slight brush of her lips against his, but he could feel all the love she had for him in that slight touch. "I'm sorry for what he did to you . . . to us," she whispered. "I don't know if it's possible for me to ever forgive him."

"You will . . . eventually. He's your father." Kane then nestled in closer, his hands no longer apologetic as they continued to explore her body underneath the blanket. "I'll tell you what.

How about we both work on forgiving him together? It may take some time, but if we do it together, anything is possible."

She smiled again, and this time it lit up the entire room. "I love you, Jairus Marcus Antonius."

Kane touched his nose to hers and placed a single, gentle kiss on her lips as he stroked her temple with his index finger. "I love you, my beautiful Apphia. I want to be with you, always. Say you'll come back to The Oracle with me tomorrow, so we can start this life together?"

As he asked, he felt suddenly struck with an uncertainty that caught him off guard for a moment. He wasn't a man who normally had any doubts about persuading a woman to do anything, but this was different. This was something he wanted more than anything else in the world—to live with her, to be faithful to just her. But what if she didn't want to live at The Oracle, where he had made a home for himself? What if she wanted to live closer to her family, to her father? He wasn't sure he could forgive Argus that fast. But he would do it if it was what she wanted. He would give her anything. Suddenly, he heard himself saying, "We don't have to live at The Oracle. I can find us a house nearby—hell, I can build one if I need to! Something small—like this, maybe—with a yard and a view of the lake. We can help each other . . . help other people, I mean. Then maybe I won't have to worry about this fine ass of yours so much," he said, smiling broadly as he gave a gentle squeeze to one of the rounded cheeks in question.

Tears started to shimmer in her eyes and he knew what her answer would be, which made him feel warm all over. "Besides, you're about to disappear on everyone, and I don't want to be caught at The Oracle humping a mattress."

She laughed, truly laughed. "I won't disappear on you," she promised. "Never on you."

In one smooth motion, Kane rolled her beneath him with a playful growl and nestled himself between her soft thighs, wrapping her legs snugly around his waist. "You better not, darlin'," he said as he delivered another slow, sensual kiss. And when he finished and released her lips she gave him one of those beautiful, breathy little sighs that he loved so much. Then added a few little nibbles and licks until she sighed again. Then he started the whole process over.

Kane wanted no doubt left in this woman's mind about how much he loved her, needed her. So he savored, he sampled, he enjoyed, giving every part of her body careful and thorough attention, especially her breasts. He loved paying attention to those small, perfect breasts. Soon, her first gasping orgasm burst forth beneath him, and it was a thing of pure beauty because he had accomplished it with nothing more than his lips and tongue . . . well . . . maybe a little teeth too. He'd always known he could make her orgasm from just cherishing her sensitive breasts.

Sliding down her body, he anchored his head between her thighs, his tongue reaching for her warm, heated flesh. He was pretty sure he could spend all night just tasting her this way. He held her hips still, drowning her in sinful little licks until she choked back a harsh cry and yanked a pillow over her face to cover the scream. She shook throughout her second orgasm.

When he then rose up above her, he positioned himself at her entrance and pushed forward slowly, relishing the escalating pleasure as her inner muscles tightened over him. He began to thrust within her in a steady rhythm, finding himself wishing it were daytime so he could see that perfect pink flush that happened all over her skin just before she was about to splinter. Just the image of it in his head had him swelling inside of her, filling her until she was stretched to the brink, all the way to that fine line between pleasure and pain.

He continued thrusting now with smooth, even strokes. The liquidity of their coupling as they moved together in perfect rhythm created within him the most splendid combination of sensations he had ever known. Pressure built at the base of his spine as he tried to hold back the storm that was brewing. He wanted this to last, but he could feel the totem animal inside him starting to prowl to the surface. Sliding his tongue over his teeth, he noticed that they definitely felt a little sharper. He held her hips tight to him as he picked up the pace of his thrusts. His eyes could now see clearly in the darkness as his lusty growls cut through the air around them. The animal was right there with him. God, she was perfect for him. He stroked faster, harder, every muscle in his arms and shoulders flexing with resistance.

"Oh God, Jairus!" she cried as her spine arched, her hips lifted, and her nails dug into his back, leaving crescent-shaped little moons in his skin. She exploded beneath him a third time; her inner muscles working over him as he pulled back and then plunged to her deepest place one final time. There it was—the trifecta of lovemaking. And he intended to do it over, and over, and over again with this woman for the rest of their lives together.

Kane shuddered then and came inside her until he thought he would pass out from the flawless euphoria of it. He would never wear a condom with her ever again. Being completely in that moment with her, feeling every part of her as her inner muscles milked him, knowing that from now on she would be the only one he would ever give that part of himself to, was simply the best part. In fact, the blasted condom had probably kept him from seeing—no, feeling—what was right in front of him in the first place.

Forget rule number one! Out with rule number two! The only rule he had now was respecting the life and home he would build with her, a place where he could make love to her any way he wanted—in a bed or on the kitchen counter.

Minutes later, Skye still lay beneath him, their limbs a tangled heap beneath the sheets. Kane rolled slightly to his side to remove his weight but brought her with him so he could remain inside her. He had no intention of pulling apart from her anytime soon.

Skye let a soft hum slip through her lips as she stared up at him. "I thought I'd lost you forever . . . in this life and the next."

Kane covered her with the heat of his body and pulled her close. "I promise you, my love—that will never happen. And I will make you the same promise in every life—'Inveniam viam aut faciam'."

"I shall find a way or I shall make one," he said.

EPILOGUE

In the morning, Kane woke just after sunrise.

Honestly, he could have remained in bed with Skye all day long, but he was anxious to head out so they could begin their new life together. He didn't have the heart to wake his sleeping beauty, who was still lying there, all soft and warm beside him. He brushed back a renegade strand of blond hair from her eyes and kissed her temple before slipping from the bed to shower and then to pack his things.

It was still early when he entered the main room of the cabin and heard voices just outside. Aiden and Lucas were standing by the SUV, scowling at each other as if they were having some kind of disagreement.

As Kane approached, Lucas's expressions evened but Aiden's turned into a sincere smile. "Did you sleep well?"

Kane tossed his bag into the back of the SUV. "Best night's sleep I've had in years, actually." He smiled broadly. He couldn't help it. "She's coming back to The Oracle with us today."

"Yes, we assumed that when you weren't camped out on the living room floor," Aiden smirked. "Congratulations, buddy, you're officially in a relationship."

"It's more than that. I'm committed to her and I'll marry her as soon as she'll let me . . . the way it's supposed to be." He clapped a hand loudly over Lucas's shoulder. "So consider me off the market, boys . . . which leaves all of those fine looking Dhampirs for the two of you."

Aiden snorted. "Alec's going to choke on his morning coffee over this one."

"Hey, if it saves me from another one of his lectures, it's already worth it."

"Don't count on that," Lucas said with a humorless smile. "He enjoys those lectures far more than he would ever let on."

"I suspected as much," Kane replied. "So are you two going to tell me what I walked in on out here?"

The men gave each other a look that Kane could already tell was not good. "I was telling Aiden that I'm not going back with you today," Lucas answered in a rather unconcerned voice.

Kane blinked at him in disbelief. "*What?* Of course you are. Lucas, you're going to need help to control what's happening to you. You know The Oracle has the staff and facilities to do that, not to mention that Alec needs to know that you're *fucking* alive. You heard what Skye said. Your death has devastated him."

"That's exactly what I told him," Aiden grumbled.

Lucas shoved his hands into both pockets and appeared to be considering something, then raised his head to both men. "Look," he said with difficulty. "I felt it last night. I felt the other side still trying to pull me to it. For a moment there I didn't think I was going to be able to stop it."

"And Alec would want to know!" Kane answered angrily. "He would want to help you."

"You're not hearing what I'm saying. I'm saying it's a fucking miracle that I'm standing here right now. I don't want any of this but any second I could be snatched back to that other side, and if it happens, I don't know if I can make it back. The pull is too strong."

"Lucas," Aiden said with concern, "why didn't you tell us last night?"

"Because it was nice to pretend that everything was back to normal for a few hours," he said in a quiet voice, "but I know it's not." Lucas turned away from them, appearing to keep a fragile hold on the emotions pulling at him. "Shit! He's my best friend —a brother. Of course I want him to know I'm OK—to be at his side protecting him—just as I always have." He turned back to them and looked tired, evidence that he had already been fighting this inner battle with himself for too long. "I can't protect *him* right now because I can't even help *myself.*"

"He wouldn't expect that of you," Kane said, roughly. "Not while you're dealing with this—and you know it. This isn't about your loyalty to him or your duty as a Guardian. This is about your best friend being in pain. You have the power to take that pain away."

"I *will* tell him," Lucas snapped, "once I have more control over the slides and know I can stay on this side. But I won't let him know I'm alive and then disappear on him two seconds later. He would spend his time and resources trying to find me instead of focusing on being the leader that all those people at The Oracle are counting on him to be."

"I don't agree with this!" Kane roared now, angry—because he knew Lucas had a point. Alec's duties as Elder came before all else. The cause and the people beneath him counted on that. Alec wasn't free to let his personal wants go ahead of the duties or the people he'd sworn to lead. "Alec should know."

"Just give me some time—enough to gain control of the slides and find some answers about why this has happened. Then I'll tell him."

"Skye said that the dagger was responsible for the slides. We should start there."

Lucas pulled the knife from its sheath, its red diamonds gleaming in the morning sunlight. "Until we know what the story is with . . ."

Lucas's words faded to the background while Kane remained focused on the dagger. The way Lucas held it, high against the rising sun, the way the red diamonds sparkled in the light, triggered a memory like a flashcard in Kane's mind.

" . . . control the slides," Lucas finished.

Kane drew his hand to his forehead and both men quieted, staring at Kane with concern. "What is it?"

"I . . . I just had a flash . . . a vision of the past." Kane touched the hilt of the dagger in Lucas's hand. "It's a memory of my father holding this sword in his hand. He showed it to me when I was a boy. I remember him asking me if I'd ever seen anything so beautiful."

"It's certainly possible," Aiden said carefully. "Didn't you tell me once that your father was a collector of rare artifacts?"

Kane nodded. "He scoured the world for them. He had this dagger in his possession before he died. I'm sure of it. That's why I recognized it at Brahm Hill."

Lucas continued to hold up the knife, his mind, silently turning over the information he'd just received, as he stared at it carefully. "It seems there are many questions that need to be answered about this dagger. Not the least of which is why Reese Lambert went to the trouble of hunting it down and then went after Alec with it."

"We've got work to do," Aiden said, a fierce tone reflecting in his voice.

"Yes," Kane murmured, also internally processing the situation. "We need to stay with Lucas—get him set up with a place to stay, some food, clothing, cash. But even more, if we're going to keep this from Alec, we need to have a plan. He'll get suspicious if we are both gone from The Oracle for any length of time."

"Alec offered me some monitored time away if I wanted it," Aiden announced. "It was a while ago, and he might wonder why I've decided to accept it now, but I'll just tell him this time away from The Oracle has been good for me—that I feel like I need more."

"What do you mean by 'monitored'?" Lucas asked.

"I'd have to check in regularly with Dr Li. But they'll give me the time. And I wouldn't mind some additional time."

"That sounds like our best option," Kane finally said. "In the meantime, I'll keep Alec distracted from asking too many questions. I'm pretty good at that," he smiled.

After sorting out a few more critical details, the three men collectively nodded in agreement. "We've got a plan, boys."

ACKNOWLEDGMENTS

There are so many people I wish to thank for their efforts and contributions to this book. From the time I put that first sentence on the page it has been a long process from start to finish—but so worth the time in the end.

First, I would like to thank my parents, who have done an amazing job of supporting me and helping me juggle everything involved in the complex world of writing and publishing. Without their help I would have surely been stretched too thin a long time ago.

I would also like to send a special shout-out to my cover designer, Whitney. I gave her the difficult task of creating a series of five related covers that stood on their own merit but also coordinated with my first trilogy, *The Charmed,* since the two story lines are connected. I couldn't be happier with the results. The covers are moody, sexy and real, and they wonderfully represent my vision for the world of The Brethren. Thank you!

To my editor, Paul. As always, you did such a phenomenal job of being my second voice and challenging me along the way. Also, I would like to thank Denise, who is new to our editing team, but whose insight into the story and characters was vastly appreciated.

And lastly, I want to thank my best friend, Rachel. As a writer, I am sometimes too close to my own material and characters to see things clearly. In those moments, I'm reminded how lucky I am to have you to pull me back and view things from a wider perspective.

ABOUT THE AUTHOR

Christine is a graduate of Washington State University, where she received a BA in Interior Design. And true to form of using mostly her *'right brain'*, she splits her time between her commercial design career and her imaginary world of writing.

She lives in the scenic Pacific Northwest where she enjoys hiking, camping and photographing many of the wonderful places that served as inspiration for her three-volume *Charmed Trilogy*.

Her biggest reward in life comes on any given day when one of her books connects with a reader because she herself is such a lover of reading.

Some of her favorite authors include Lisa Kleypas, Julia Quinn, and Kimberly Derting.

www.ingramcontent.com/pod-product-compliance
Lightning Source LLC
Chambersburg PA
CBHW061939170626
46813CB00006B/2467